Dedication

Freedom Ships is a novel but readers will see that it is firmly grounded on the facts of freed slaves who sailed to Africa in ships arranged by the American Colonization Society with the cooperation of the United States Government. This book is dedicated to those brave black pioneers, and to their white friends in the Society who raised funds and supported the pioneers in their efforts to establish a colony, stamp out the slave trade on their newly found shores, and create the first black republic in Africa.

This book is also dedicated to those indigenous Africans who joined the pioneers in their fight against the slave trade and in the building of a nation. The Bassa coastal chief who first joined in this effort called the settlers' ship "kwi woh, dyeapo"--freedom ship--and hoped that more would come to help stop the tragic trade that had engulfed them all. He risked his life to help make that happen.

The authors both served in Liberia as educators and have great respect for the heroes and heroines of that courageous struggle to fashion a unique nation despite tremendous hardships and sometimes a violent clash of cultures.

Part of the profits of this book will go to programs of reconciliation and rebuilding of war-torn Liberia and Sierra Leone. Currently, these funds will go to the "Operation Classroom" program. *Every book you buy will help--buy some as gifts for your friends or your organization. Write to us for quantity discounts.*

R.D.C. and J.H.F

Acknowledgements

An historical novel blends factual research with creative imagination to make history come alive for modern readers. The authors combed through hundreds of emigrant and Society letters, diaries, newspaper and journal accounts in major university libraries and the Library of Congress, and official documents in Navy and Congressional archives.

We have been helped by many people, including Debra L. Newman of the Library of Congress; Dr. Mabel S. Haith of Washington, D.C.; Dr. Elwood Dunn of the University of the South, Sewanee, Tennessee; John Innis and Nancy Nah of Liberia; Edward Whittlesey of Miami, Florida; Wilma Carrick of Topeka, Kansas, and Dr. Kendra Gaines from Tucson, Arizona.

We are indebited to our spouses who have encouraged and helped us in hours of thinking and planning this novel. Melody Ruffalo Furbay contributed her artistic skills to the cover art, and LaDonna Clemings Carey lent her many remembrances of people and places in Liberia.

R.D.C. and J. H. F.

Prologue

The plight of freed black American slaves in the early part of the 19th century was desperate. Most of them had been manumitted, or had worked to pay back their owners; a few had won their freedom by fighting in the War of 1812. When the war ended, these returned home with the hope of building new lives as free men. They quickly found that free or slave, they were still black, and the great northern cities where many blacks tried to settle rejected them. Jobs went to white immigrants, and without work black freedmen--like Elijah Johnson, his wife Mary, and their three small children--were forced to contend with near starvation and brutal winters in flimsy shacks.

By 1816, their numbers had grown to such a degree that Robert Finley, a New Jersey minister, decided to take action to relieve their suffering. Going to Washington, D.C., he sought the help of his brother-in-law, Elias Caldwell, who was Clerk of the Supreme Court, and Francis Scott Key, a noted Georgetown lawyer. Both had given legal help to freed slaves in danger of being returned to slavery in the South. Finley proposed the formation of a society for the colonization of free Negroes in Africa. There, he said, freed slaves could be truly free, reap the rewards of their own labor and eventually function as full citizens of their own country. Giving freed slaves a place to go would provide an incentive to slaveholders to free their slaves voluntarily. This would ease the threatening conflict between northern abolitionists and southern slaveholders. Finley won Caldwell and Key over, and they began to plan for the society.

On New Year's day, 1817, they succeeded in launching it. Fifty prominent men, including Bushrod Washington, the President's nephew, joined their signatures to the constitution of the American Colonization Society and then elected officers. Caldwell was made Secretary and Key put on the Board of Managers. Finley rushed to Philadelphia to meet with a group of Negro leaders who had wasted no time in accusing the Society of wanting to deport freedman as a "dangerous and useless element." Within days of founding the American Colonization Society, the controversy over its motivation had begun. Blacks took strong positions on both sides of the colonization issue.

To men like Elijah Johnson, however, this argument was foolish in the face of such an opportunity. They wanted to go to Africa, the land of their ancestors, where they could be really free, make a good living and have a say-so about government--and the Colonization Society promised to make it possible! By January of 1820 the Society had collected enough money to send a ship, the *Elizabeth*, to the west coast of Africa. Hundreds were on the waiting list, but Elijah had made sure he and his family would be on board this first ship.

Contents

Prologue

Part I -- Finding a Home

Map of Colony and Picture of Cape

Part II -- Birthing a Nation

Names of Freedom Ships and Passenger List

Part I

Finding a Home

July 13, 1818*
"...We love this country and its liberties, if we could
share in them; but our freedom is partial, and we
have no hope that it will ever be otherwise here;
therefore we had rather be gone, though we suffer
hunger and nakedness for years..."

Abraham Camp, a black man
living on the Wabash, in a
letter to Elias Caldwell, the
Secretary of the American
Colonization Society

*American Colonization Society Papers, Library of Congress

1   First Ship

New York
January 31, 1820

Elias Caldwell pulled up the collar of his greatcoat against the cold, feeling elated yet uneasy as he watched the crowd grow. Already several thousand New Yorkers had shown up to see the brig *Elizabeth* depart for Africa. People were bundled to their ears with scarves, muffs and fur hats; some of the poorer ones had wrapped themselves in blankets.

Newspapers had headlined the story, saying the *Elizabeth* was a 'Black Mayflower' taking pioneers to the 'new world' of Africa just like the Pilgrims had left Europe two hundred years ago for America. But the National Intelligencer in Washington had come out with its own twist before Caldwell left the capital--something dire about 'These brave pioneers will be facing deadly tropical fevers in Africa.' It had embarrassed and angered him--as if the Society hadn't taken precautions! Dr. Samuel Crozer had been selected to go with the emigrants as the Society's agent, but Caldwell realized he had forgotten to mention it to the editor.

Caldwell sighed, thinking of the remarks he'd have to fend off today about the Society's poor planning. As he pushed through the lively mob somebody tapped his shoulder.

"Hold on, Elias. What's the hurry?"

He turned to see a jubilant Francis Scott Key.

"We've done it, old friend!" Key slapped Elias' shoulder, and Elias gave in to his mood for a moment, smiling briefly.

"With plenty of help from others," he reminded Key. "Francis, can you round up the Society members? They should be arriving soon."

"How many d'you expect?" Key, taller than Caldwell, turned to sweep the bobbing heads of the crowd with his eyes.

"It's a momentous occasion for the Society--I hope a lot of them turn out! I have to dun them for more money."

"Again?" Key frowned. "I thought the Auxiliaries in New York and Philadelphia came through with their collections."

Caldwell couldn't reply because of shouts from the crowd. They both turned to listen.

1

"Block ice from the Hudson!" "Ice comin' down--goin' choke up the river docks!" "Captain better get that ship on its way soon!"

They were being separated by the surging crowd as people moved to see the ship better. Caldwell cupped his gloved hands and shouted to Key.

"This expedition's going to cost more than we'd planned--tell you about it later!" Then, spotting a low hill nearby, he pointed to it. "If you find any members send them over to me--I'll be on that hill over there!"

Halfway up the little hill Caldwell slipped and felt a twinge of pain in his right foot. Damn the gout! He knew he shouldn't be out on a day like this. He rested a moment, turning to look out across the crowd to the black emigrants standing on the wharf, being checked for boarding. There were eighty-eight freed Negroes in all--the first to go! *They are the brave ones*, he thought proudly.

"Hey there, Caldwell! We're coming up!"

It was Key with several Society members in tow at the foot of the hill. Caldwell smiled, beckoned them up with his arm, and then looked over the crowd for others. He'd better get busy raising some contributions to pay for those supplies being put on board the *Elizabeth*. Again his eyes caught the line of black emigrants down on the concourse.

"Charlie! Lewis! Get back over here with your Ma! We don't want you wanderin' off in this crowd, nohow!" Elijah Johnson gripped a hand of both his boys, pulling them firmly back in the line of emigrants waiting to be checked by the Society's white agents.

Mary, holding two-year old Lizzie in her arms, was full of questions.

"One of 'em is black, Lije," she said, nodding toward the head of the line. "Is he one of them agents, too?"

Elijah followed the direction of her nod, and laughed.

"Black? He's lighter'n you are! He's really high yaller! You call him black?"

"You know what I mean! Who's he?"

"That's Reverend Daniel Coker--that preacher they almost elected a bishop a coupl'a years ago. Ceptin' some said he was too light to be leadin' a new black church, so he backed off and then they 'lected Allen. I told you about it."

2

"I disremembers. Anyway, what's he doin' here?"

"He's goin' to be like a leader for us--all the blacks goin' on the ship. Cause he's got a education, I guess."

Mary shifted Lizzie to her right hip with a groan.

"You hold her for awhiles, Lije. My back's gettin' tired."

"Don't be afraid of this crowd, Mary. Put'er down once in awhile."

"Nope! Not in this crowd, I doesn't!"

Elijah let go of the boys' hands so he could take over Lizzie. Just as he reached for her they heard a woman's scream above the noise of the crowd.

"Who's that? What's goin' on?" Mary asked, pulling away from Elijah and tightening her arms around Lizzie.

"I don't know--I can't see," he said, craning his neck.

They heard it again, clearly. It was the screeching rage of an angry black woman, and the line of emigrants spread as others turned out to look back, too. Elijah, anticipating the confusion that might come if they broke ranks, raised his hands and lifted his voice in warning.

"Eva'body stay in line, so's we don't get mixed up with the crowd! I'll go see what's the big commotion."

Most of the emigrants nearby seemed to respect the sound of authority in his voice, and he walked back through the narrow space between the line and the crowd toward the screaming woman. She's sure mad at somebody, he thought. Pretty desperate, too, from the sound of her.

####

The woman's loud shriek didn't reach the place where Caldwell was shaking hands with Colonization Society members. More were finding their way to the small rise overlooking the teeming concourse. They were as excited as the crowd below.

"Amazing turnout!" "Causing quite a stir, isn't it?" "Makes you feel like all the effort was worth it."

Caldwell listened with quiet amusement to some of their self-congratulatory remarks, but was glad they took pride in this first expedition. Gabriel Disosway, a corpulent merchant still puffing from the climb, thrust a pudgy hand at Caldwell.

"All these people to see the first ship go!" he wheezed. "I'll wager our critics never thought we could do it. Hope they take

3

notice of this--will it be in the newspapers?"

Caldwell shook hands, but his smile soured.

"You can be sure of that, Gabriel! Some papers will praise us, I suppose, but most will snipe as usual."

"Well, by God, they'd better recognize all the hard work it took!"

"We didn't do all this by ourselves, you know," Caldwell explained. "President Monroe supplied some government help at the last minute."

Disosway looked surprised.

"I thought Congress refused to help!"

"They did. But last year when they passed the Slave Trade Act, they appropriated some money to send back to Africa any slaves captured by the Navy. And President Monroe then decided to ..."

"But slaves taken on the high seas are different from the freedmen we're trying to help!"

"Yes, I know," Caldwell said patiently, "but Monroe decided it was a chance for the Society and the Government to cooperate a bit."

"*He* decided?"

"Well, we sent a committee to suggest cooperation to the President, and he agreed. But some of his cabinet said the Act didn't authorize a colony, which would be unconstitutional. So Key suggested a way to conform with both the Act and the Constitution."

Disosway looked over to where Key was talking with some other Society members.

"Ahh--I heard that Key is getting to be a famous constitutional lawyer! So what did Monroe do?"

"He got the Cabinet to agree and then announced in his annual message that he was sending some agents and workers to Africa to set up a station for the relocation of rescued Africans."

Disosway's face looked puzzled, then his eyes lighted up.

"Sooo! This first ship is ...those black 'emigrants' are really the workers going out to..."

"That's right. And after they get the Government's station built, they'll stay and be the first settlers of a colony under the Society's auspices. We're sending an agent, too, and he'll buy the land for the colony because the U.S. can't legally found colonies itself."

Disosway eyed Caldwell shrewdly. "So you got some funds from the government!"

Caldwell winced, shifting his stance in the snow to favor his bad foot, and tried to concentrate on getting another contribution from Disosway.

"Not exactly--it's complicated to explain. The government's sending supplies and equipment to build the station. But we have to buy the land and supply the colony afterward, and we haven't raised enough funds to do that yet."

Caldwell looked Disosway squarely in the eye with his best money-raising stare. But Disosway turned to watch the crowd below and pointed at a swirling movement as people rushed to the end of the line of emigrants.

"Look there! Looks like somebody's trying to pull a man out of the line of passengers."

Caldwell suspected Disosway was distracting him from asking for money, but he saw the movement, too, and his heart jumped.

"Someone's pulling and shoving--people moving in closer to see it," he said.

Disosay squinted his eyes, studying the situation.

"This is dangerous, Caldwell! There must be four thousand blacks and whites mixed up together down there. If that fuss gets out of hand this place could explode! Wouldn't be any sailing at all! Shouldn't you do something? You're our Executive Secretary."

Caldwell decided not to be side-tracked.

"Samuel Bacon and John Bankson are down there--they're the government's agents. And our agent Samuel Crozer is there, too. They can handle it--see them at the head of the line?"

"But that's not where they need to be! The trouble is at the back end!"

Elijah Johnson had come down the line, trying to keep the emigrants in place with friendly warnings. But a short, cocky, ginger-colored man called Peter Small had other ideas.

"You can't tell me where I goes or what I does! I's free and I goes wheresomever I wants from now on! That's why we leavin' this place, don't you know that?"

"Yes, I know it. I'm just tryin' to be sure we all get on the ship. We gotta stay clear of the crowd, or we ..."

5

But the man was already ahead of him, going toward the screaming woman. Elijah sighed and followed him, still cautioning people about mixing with the crowd. One or two gettin' out of line to see what was going on wouldn't hurt, he thought, but this young fella struttin' ahead of him was a born trouble-maker.

"Young bloods is always hot-headed fools!" he muttered, remembering his own quick anger at that age.

But there was another young man, whom Elijah knew as John Bannon, already at the end of the line, light brown and slim, who stood with a hand on the shoulders of a coffee-haired girl, consoling her. She was crying and wringing her hands, watching the screaming woman fight off two policemen pulling at what must be the woman's husband. Elijah saw that the husband, struck dumb with fear, had planted his feet firmly and was leaning backwards, trying desperately to hold his place in the line.

"He's free! He's free! You takin' the wrong man! He's free I tells ya!"

The woman screamed it over and over, her hysterical voice now shrill and weak. She was throwing herself across the arms of the police, trying to break their hold on her man. They heaved her off each time, but she came back again and again, using her body as a weapon, shrieking her frantic claim. It had worked so far, but one of the police was now lifting his night stick to strike the woman on the head. Elijah rushed forward to stay his hand.

"Hold on!" he said. "She just protectin' her man! What you takin' him away for?"

Elijah, his brawny black arm still holding the policeman's wrist up high, glowered down at the short white man in uniform.

"Get out'a the way, nigger! You can't stop the Law from doin' its duty!" shouted the policeman.

Elijah knew he was in deep trouble, but he eased the policeman's arm down slowly and stepped in front of the woman.

"Wasn't aimin' to. Just wanted to know why you takin' one a' our emigrants away. We's just about to get on board."

"I don't have to tell you nothin', you big black buck! You goin' get yourself arrested so's you can't go, neither! Stand aside, you hear me!"

Elijah looked at the faces of the crowd, both black and white, pressing close around. The woman had stopped her screaming and he could feel the tension as the crowd fell silent, waiting to see what he would do. He forced a smile and stood back, watching the man's arm and stick closely. Then he spoke carefully, making every word clear.

"We got some white men up front would want to know what you doin' here with one a' their emigrants."

Elijah turned to the ginger-colored young man.

"Peter, you want to go tell them white men up front a' the line about this and ask'em to come back here quick?"

This time there was no cockiness. The shocked look on Peter's face showed he knew now how vulnerable all the emigrants were and he nodded assent, turning to move quickly through the ring of spectators toward the head of the line.

The shorter policeman turned to speak to his partner, raising his voice for everyone to hear.

"That's all right! We'll be dealin' with the proper authorities, not no uppity niggers. Goin' to get this over with for sure now. You got that there slave owner's handbill?"

His partner, holding the woman's husband, dropped one hand to feel the inner pocket of his police uniform.

"Yeah. It's right here!"

Caldwell, giving up on Disosway, turned to greet other Society members. A tall, rawboned man dressed like a country squire stepped up to him immediately.

"I'm James Harte from Virginia. This is a great day, Caldwell! The Society has done well. Congratulations!"

They shook hands and Caldwell looked closely at Harte's rough-hewn face. It had the weathered look of a real farmer, not at all like the aristocratic plantation owner he'd expected.

"General Harte! Your last letter said you'd be coming north on business--I'm glad you got here in time to see our first ship sail. We appreciate your help."

Caldwell remembered Harte's embossed vellum letters, often with generous contributions. He had become one of the Society's best supporters in Virgina--and here he was in person!

"Have you gotten your business taken care of already, General?"

"Yes. I made arrangements for importing new animal and plant stock from Europe. Finished it up quickly so I could get here to see this." He motioned toward the *Elizabeth*.

7

"Good," Caldwell said. "Are you ready to send any of your slaves over yet, General?"

Harte's eyes showed his surprise.

"Not hardly! My slaves won't be ready for a long time--can't count, can't figure, can't write. Best I've been able to do is get them started learning the trades."

Caldwell smiled.

"Oh, they don't need an education, General. We're sending the agents to help them get settled."

"What!" Harte stared in disbelief. "You can't be serious, Caldwell. Raw field hands can't even think for themselves--the overseers have seen to that." He sighed and looked away guiltily. "Its been a bad system. But they'll need to know a lot to start their own country. And I won't send any of mine until they're fully prepared!"

Caldwell murmured assent and then excused himself to move to where Key was talking to Mercer, the Congressman who'd written the Slave Trade Act and was an active member of the Society.

"What an irony!" Mercer was saying. "Everybody is talking about the Mayflower, saying it was the same size as our ship, and that our expedition will be like the voyage that brought the Pilgrims to our shores. The freedom ships! If they only knew." He shook his head sadly.

"What?" Key said, mystified. "What are you talking about? I thought that was a good comparison."

"Well, that part of it is alright. But the cargo the Mayflower carried on a later trip is the irony. Didn't you know? She went back to England, and later was chartered to West Africa and brought a cargo of slaves to Jamestown."

"My God! Are you sure?" Key asked.

"It's been in Ships Registry ever since."

"What an infernal irony! Why, it's Satanic! No wonder people don't talk about it."

Caldwell, shocked too, pondered it a bit.

"But it shows the twisted evil we've been up against all along, doesn't it? Ships for hire--a cargo to freedom or one to bondage. Whoever pays determines the purpose. Thank God ours is the noble one."

Caldwell felt inspired--he'd just made a brilliant opening for fund raising.

"Gentlemen, the *Elizabeth's* cargo isn't paid for yet. We've credited some supplies for the colony that are being loaded right now down there."

But Key interrupted.

"What's going on down there? The agents have stopped checking the emigrants. They're rushing to the end of the line."

The white agents, Bacon, Bankson, and Crozer, with the Reverend Coker bringing up the rear, broke through the crowd and reached the spot where Elijah faced the policeman.

"What's the trouble, Officer?" Bacon asked. "I know this man and woman, and their daughter here--the Reeves family. They're all free. We're getting ready to board them now."

"I'm 'fraid not, sir!" the policeman countered. "This man ain't free. See this--he's the runaway slave in this here handbill. Been missin' for years, but some bounty hunters flushed him out last week when the list of emigrants was posted."

Bacon took the handbill and read it carefully.

"How can you be sure? This is just a description ..."

"He fits it--every mark on his body, right down to the missin' finger! It's all legal, sir. His owner sent two men after'im yestiday. We has'ta take him in to the station."

Bacon's face blanched as he realized the cruel fate dealt the man by posting his name on the emigrant list.

"Good God, officer! Have you no heart? He could be aboard with his family in an hour and you could say you never saw ..."

He stopped short, aware that he was about to incriminate himself.

"Sorry, sir," the policeman said. "The Law's the law. But his woman, she's free--been freed a long time ago. And so's her daughter. No question about them. But he's a fugitive slave and we gotta take him to the police station now."

Bacon turned quickly to Elijah.

"Mr. Johnson, I'd appreciate it if you'd go with Dr. Crozer and the two of you'd find out what Mrs. Reeves and her daughter plan to do--stay here with the husband or go to Africa. Come right back when they've decided. We'll be finishing the check-in."

####

Elijah could feel the impatience of the crowd--or was it his own? He'd gotten back to Mary and the children and told them

9

about Mrs. Reeves' daughter, Carrie, being sent on to Africa, if the Johnson family would care for her. Mary had agreed, saying Carrie would be good help for her with the children. Now Elijah had reported back to Bacon.

"The checking-in is almost over," Bacon said. "It's time to get on board. We could use your help, Mr. Johnson, in starting the emigrants to the ship quietly--a few at a time--so the crowd won't notice. We'll get up on that balcony over there and Reverend Coker will lead a few songs and we'll have some words to say--a kind of goodbye program. When it's over you'll already have all the emigrants on board so the crowd won't crush in on'em at the last."

Elijah nodded, and waited to guide the emigrants to the gang plank until the agents got up on the balcony and began their program. Coker led into a hymn both blacks and whites knew, and row after row added their voices until it swelled through the great crowd. They sang another one, and then he switched to a Negro spiritual. The blacks responded to his lines about the 'coming of the Savior' on that 'great gittin-up morning' with a chorus of 'fare you wells' until the whole area rang. Whites stood in wonder as Coker's deep voice sang out the story of the promise--on that morning the righteous would 'go home to glory and live with God forever!' He ended with a mighty affirmation, arms lifted heavenward, his powerful bass voice booming out,

"My Lord, what a morning! My Lord, *what a morning!*"

It was a promise that many of the former slaves had long counted on. Now, as freedmen living in misery in northern cities, still denied the true freedom they sought, it meant even more to them. Africa, the motherland, would surely be the place to find real freedom and to go home to God. Many in the crowd had teary eyes.

In the hushed silence that followed, Bacon gave a formal statement from the Society and thanked everyone for coming to say goodby to the first emigrants. Coker offered a long, heart-felt prayer and then dismissed the crowd with a benediction. Coker and the agents went on board the *Elizabeth* to wait in their cabin for the wind to come up. Elijah joined his family on deck, feeling good that he'd done his part, getting the long line of emigrants on board with no hitches.

Caldwell was reluctant to start his journey back to Washington without knowing that the ship was really underway, and he stood on the dock long after the crowd had drifted away.

There was still the ice floe in the North River to be reckoned with--
if the wind didn't come soon it might be weeks before the ship could
break through a solid freeze-up. He watched sailors in the rigging
while his foot burned angrily, and he knew it was madness to stay
any longer in the cold. But the ship's bosun finally called out to
men on the yardarms, and he watched them scramble to set the
sails. Maybe there was enough breeze now to move the Elizabeth
out of her berth!

"Caldwell?" a deep voice inquired from behind him.

Startled, he turned to face a stranger with keen, piercing
eyes and a friendly smile who began shaking his hand vigorously.

"I'm Whittlesey--Elisha Whittlesey, state congressman from
Ohio, just passing through New York and saw a notice in the
papers about the expedition. Came down to see for myself. I saw
you on the hill with your group and figured you were in charge.
Right?"

Caldwell was taken aback. He could almost feel the man's
intense scrutiny.

"Uhh--yes, I'm Caldwell. The people up there were members
of the Colonization Society. And I'm the Executive Secretary."

"It's a funny thing, Caldwell! I was right there at the end of
the line of your emigrants when those policemen came to take one
away. Did you see the commotion from up on your hill?"

"Uhh--yes, we saw something. The agents took care of it,
'though."

"Not really. One of your black pioneers had it in hand and
sent for the agents. I know that man, too!"

"You do?"

"I was on General Harrison's staff at Fort Meigs during the
War of 1812. We went up to Lake Erie to plan with Commodore
Perry for a combined land and water attack on the British and
Indian forces. I saw your man when we parleyed on Perry's ship. I
swear it--he was a jack-tar swabbing the decks! They called him
'Johnson.' You've got a good man going with your pioneers,
Caldwell. I hope you know that."

Whittlesey was shaking his hand again.

"I've got to be off, Caldwell. Thanks for the good work!"

"You're welcome. I hope you'll ..."

"I'll write when I get back to Ohio. Maybe folks there will
help the cause. Goodbye!"

Caldwell watched Whittlesey stride off. Again he'd gotten

11

no money! He sighed--a bad day for raising funds. But Whittlesey might be important to the Society if they could expand the auxiliaries to Ohio and other new states. And so could Disosway and Harte and the others. It would take a great deal of money and many ships to help all the freedmen who'd signed up to go. He turned to head back to the inn--the stage coach for Washington would leave early in the morning, but he'd give his foot a good night's rest first.

2   Storm at Sea

Mid-Atlantic
February 10, 1820

     Elijah Johnson stood at the starboard rail watching the ship knife gracefully through short, steep waves. A light breeze and billowing expanse of canvas over his head pushed the *Elizabeth* along at what he guessed would be 5 to 7 knots. But towering black clouds in the distance seemed to spread wider on the seas as the ship rode steadily towards them. His wife was talking to Carrie Reeves as they sat nearby the cargo hatch, watching the children playing on the deck. Mary stood up and walked to the rail unsteadily.

     "Oooh--it looks like a big black goose-down quilt 'bout to smother the whole ocean," she said, awed by the sky.

     Elijah, deep in thought, didn't reply. The *Elizabeth* was only four days out of New York, with Mary just beginning to get over her seasickness. Now their first real storm was coming on--it would be just their luck to have somebody swept overboard by a storm! The Smith family had already lost one child from the measles during the six days they were blocked in the ice on the North River. If it hadn't been for that young Cornelius Vanderbilt and his boat crew prying a way open with timbers, they'd still be stuck in the ice floe. Then they were becalmed in the lee of the lighthouse in New York harbor, losing the *U.S.S. Cyane*, their convoy ship for Africa, in the fog. And losing Carrie's folks on the dock because of those damned slave catchers! Everything was going wrong! Would they ever get to Africa?

     The chief mate began to move around the deck telling the emigrants to go below. Elijah turned and called to the children.

     "Time to go below, now! Storm comin' up soon. Lizzie, Charlie, Lewis--come on!"

     He saw Carrie sitting on the hatch, and knew she'd heard him. Let her take her own time, he figured. She needed a rest from the children--been good help with'em. He'd tried to keep his family up on deck and as active as possible. The damp air and smell of vomit in the hold was enough to make anybody sick. Charlie and Lizzie were laid up only two days, but Lewis, trying to be like his pa, would't admit he'd had it at all. Carrie'd had it light, too.

The Johnsons waited their turn at the main hatchway, Lizzie beginning to whimper and Charlie tight-lipped and silent. Lewis, the oldest, tried to comfort his baby sister. Elijah scooped up Lizzie in his right arm and snapped "Move!" to the boys.

They knew he meant business and climbed down the hatchway ladder. Elijah helped Mary get down and they made their way to their place in the hold. The ship's carpenters had divided it into stalls with posts and rails and planking for the walls, with an aisle down the middle. Ship's lanterns hung on gimbals from deck beams overhead. Everybody had hung sheets or blankets at stall doorways to have some privacy. Mary stretched out on her pallet with a sigh, eyeing the children settling on theirs.

Elijah heard the chief mate order the hatch to be slid into place. It slammed home with a rumble and a loud bang--shutting off the light from the sky abruptly. This was the first time it had been closed, and everyone looked up, startled. Only the dim light from the grating illuminated their dark world of splintered bulkheads, moldy deck beams, and rough plank walls. There was a sudden stillness.

Sounds of trampling feet and creaking pulleys came through the deck above. Those in the hold stopped to listen, hearing the mate calling orders. The wind started to whistle in the rigging, and the ship began pitching and rolling violently. Elijah could tell when the gale hit because the *Elizabeth* suddenly heeled over on one side. Screams split the air, things tumbled out, and some of the people slid toward the ship's down side, scrambling to hold on to their belongings.

The ship righted itself as the gale slackened, then rolled over on its other side, and the slipping and sliding reversed, everyone hollering more. Now the gale hurled its fury at the sails again and the ship seemed to lay over almost on it beam ends.

"Lord 'ave mercy--we's goin' to turn over!" someone shouted, and the screaming increased.

Elijah, sensing that their fright could turn to panic, stood in the aisle and called out.

"Hold on! They'll fix the sails so she can ride out the storm. Be just a few minutes. Hold on, now--don't go crazy--it'll be all right."

Elijah knew the sailors were in the rigging struggling to

14

furl the sails. Gale-force winds could break off spars or even snap a mast if the sails weren't taken in fast. He could understand the terror of his people, locked up in the hold like this. He'd ridden out a few gales on Lake Erie, but nothing this bad. He decided to keep telling them what was going on, to calm them down.

"They're lettin' the sails down now!" he shouted over the storm's roar. "Have to get'em closed up so's the wind won't blow the ship over!"

Elijah was sure the captain would give the order to turn the ship into the wind, and he felt his body sway slightly as the ship responded to a sharp right rudder. But now a pounding noise began in the hold as the brig headed into the heavy seas straight on. The force of the pounding increased and the *Elizabeth's* hull seemed to shudder at each blow.

"That's the waves beatin' against the bow! Sounds like a big sledge hammer in here. It's all right--nothin' to worry about."

The battle with the storm was just beginning, and Elijah kept up his talk, explaining how sailors handled a ship in bad weather. Once, when the gale slackened and the whine of the rigging let up, the people heard the sailors singing out to each other on the ropes as they trimmed the smaller sails and tied them to reefpoints on the yardarms.

"What's that funny sound--going shhuummp!" someone asked. "You hear that? Every time the boat's nose goes down. Hear it ... shhuummp! What is it?"

Elijah laughed.

"That's about a ton of water flyin' over the bow and landin' on the deck. Those poor sailors up there'll get washed into the scuppers if they're not careful! We're livin' in heaven down here, compared to them."

People seemed calmer, and Elijah stood in silence for awhile, tired of talking. When no one else said anything, he turned into his own stall and sat down beside his children. Mary was sick again, wretching over the pan Carrie held for her. When she lay back, Carrie wiped Mary's sweating forehead with a damp cloth wrung out from a pot of water.

In the flickering light of the lantern swinging overhead, Elijah watched Carrie, grateful for the caring way she helped his wife. With a start, he realized that she wasn't a child like he'd thought. Her budding breasts pressed against her simple cotton dress as she wrung the cloth again. Mary had been right when she'd told him he'd better watch Peter Small and John Bannon making eyes at Carrie.

He turned and saw Lizzie and Charlie lying on their pallets, misery in their faces as the ship pitched and yawed. Lewis sat against the wall, still unwilling to give way to any show of sickness. Elijah reached over and cuffed his eldest son with pride. They smiled at each other.

The gale blew fitfully hour after hour, the ship pitching so steeply as it plowed into the waves that no one dared to move around in the hold. They tried to wedge themselves and their belongings in tighter, and many gave way to moaning and wretching again. The smell of vomit and stink of bilge water swished around by the storm was almost too much even for Elijah.

About five o'clock in the afternoon the wind slackened briefly. Above deck, Bacon and Reverend Coker opened the cabin door slightly to get a look at any damage. Coker, never on a ship before, was awed by the heaving, mountainous waves. He looked up at the towering masts which, stripped of their sails, seemed to him to reach to the very heavens. They swung in a violent lashing arc as the ship climbed up a huge wave, quickly plunging downward into its trough.

Bacon, a former marine officer, made a wry comment, half in jest.

"We won't go to the bottom--not yet anyway."

Coker shot him a horrified look.

"Don't talk like that, Mr. Bacon! God will protect us!"

A blast of spray drenched their faces. They shut the cabin door hastily and returned to their bunks, Bacon to read his Bible, Coker to write in his journal. Dipping his quill pen and stoppering the ink bottle each time before putting pen to paper made it slow going, and he gave up after blotching it a fourth time. Coker glanced up and saw Bacon looking into space, as if thinking. But Bacon's lips moved and he realized that Bacon was praying.

Crozer and Bankson, gray-faced and queasy, had been seasick since the voyage began, even when the ship was becalmed. In the violence of the storm they took to their bunks permanently. Nothing could move them, not even the supper hour. Bacon and Coker skipped the meal, too, not bothering to go to the galley because they couldn't see how the cook could struggle with pots and pans in the storm.

To ease his own fears, Coker began humming a spiritual his

people often sang in his church in Baltimore. He lay back in his bunk, finding great comfort in the old songs and humming one after another. Outside, the gale continued to blow on into the night, the seas running higher and higher. The captain decided to hold course in the teeth of the wind. He gave orders to lash the helm down and went to bed, leaving the ship to the mate and the hands on watch.

February 11, 1820

By dawn the wind had abated and the crew had put on sail, but to the passengers in the cabin it still sounded stormy and wet. Bacon called across to Coker as they awoke.

"And how is your faith this morning, Brother Coker?"

"It is not moved, Mr. Bacon!" Coker replied, stretching and sitting up.

"I'll say amen to that," Dr. Crozer added.

They all looked at Bankson.

Bacon said, "You're awfully quiet, Bankson."

"There's no way we can fail, sir!" the youthful Bankson replied, smiling in spite of his queasiness. "There are thousands praying for the success of this expedition."

"Sail ho!" came a muffled cry from the forward lookout. From the quarterdeck above they heard the mate ask for position. "Starboard bow, sir! It's dead in the water!"

Bacon jumped out of his bunk and moved quickly to the starboard porthole.

"It's a wreck!" he exclaimed. "Sails are torn, a spar gone--and floundering like it's rudderless!"

They heard Captain Sebor order the helmsman to change course and steer for the wreck. Coker and the agents joined the sailors gathered in the bow, all staring silently at the derelict. A cry went up when the name of the vessel could be seen on its bow.

"It says the *Elizabeth* from Boston!" "Fancy that, two of the old dames." "Damn me! The *Elizabeth* from New York meetin' the *Elizabeth* from Boston way out here." "Wonder if there's anybody alive on her?"

The two vessels closed and the longboat was put over the side. The seamen rowed the short distance, trying to hold the boat steady while the mate looked through portholes. On the crest of the waves, he glanced at the deck. They were all speechless, waiting to hear the mate's call that he'd found someone alive. The ship made an eerie sight, aimlessly pitching and rolling, deathly silent except for the slap of waves against her hull and a piece of sail flapping in the wind. The longboat circled her completely while the mate inspected the ravaged deck and tangled rigging, but he made no move to board her.

When the longboat returned and was winched up, the mate reported to the captain from the deck, so all hands could hear.

"She's been broken by heavy seas, Sir--very recent! No life aboard. Crew must have been swept away by the same storm we weathered, God rest'em."

They watched the captain pace the quarterdeck, trying to decide what to do. He turned.

"Aye, God rest'em! They must have put up a bloody good fight. Get underway, Mr. Wilson. Put it in the log--I'll give you the latitude when I can get a reading from the sun."

He leaned over the rail of the quarterdeck, looking at the agents below.

"Mr. Bacon, seeing that Sunday is day after tomorrow, I hope you'll take the fate of those brave men into account in your divine services."

"That we will, Captain, that we will," Bacon assured him.

Captain Sebor gave a friendly salute and went back to his cabin. The agents and Coker returned to theirs, but they were barely inside when Coker burst out with a question.

"Why were we spared, gentlemen? Why weren't we the ones swept away by the storm?"

They looked at him, wondering the same thing.

"Don't you see? It's because this expedition is in the hands of God!"

He closed his eyes and began to pray.

"Thank you, Lord, for sparing us from the storm! Lead us on across this awful sea, and make us strong as we face that great dark continent of Africa ... "

They linked their arms with his as he continued, and then said amen together.

February 16, 1820

By the following Wednesday afternoon most of the emigrants had recovered from the storm and were on deck, walking about and enjoying the pale sun's warmth. It's a powerful relief to get out of that dark, smelly hold, Mary kept thinking. Sitting on the edge of the hatch cover, she watched Lizzie and Charlie play jackstraws, and tried to keep Lewis in sight at the rail. She was half-listening to Sally Fisher, a woman beside her who had a baby boy in her lap.

"I been dreamin' about Africa since I was borned," Sally said. "Slavery days was mighty hard, but we's been free for two years now. Me and my husband, we couldn't live together 'til he bought us free. John is a carpenter and his master let'im work extra to pay for hisself, and then he worked to pay my master. Took'im five years."

"I always been free," Mary replied, "but my husband wasn't 'til he fought in the War of 1812. He got his freedom papers for fightin' in the Navy."

"He's plenty smart 'bout ships."

"Yes, he's that," Mary sighed, "but Elijah doesn't have a trade like your John. He jus' works on the docks when the Irish not takin' those jobs. But he's been gettin' some schoolin' at night and hopes to do a little preachin' someday." She yawned. "Don't know what he'll do in Africa after the recepshun center is built, but he wants us to stay on after."

"Oh, I wants to, too! So does my John. He says carpenters is needed anywheres, specially in buildin' a whole new place like a colony. So we's stayin'--Yessuh!"

Sally shifted her baby on her lap. Mary hoped that was all the talk, she was too tired to keep it up.

"I bet you is proud of your husband," Sally went on. "I can't read--John can't neither. Didn't 'low us niggers to do that on the plantations where we was. They said if they found a nigger who was readin' and writin' they'd cut off his arm at the elbow."

Mary felt like telling her not to say nigger. It wasn't dignified, specially now they were going to have their own country. But Sally rambled on.

"We had a nigger who married us, he's what we called a two-headed nigger--could read and write both. That's what me and John is goin' to do in Africa. We're goin' to help get a school started so's we and our chilluns can learn readin' and writin'."

She lifted her baby and squeezed him.

"That's what freedom is for! Nobody goin' stop my little Johnny from readin' and writin'--and cipherin' too!"

19

####

Elijah joined a small group of men at the bow idly watching the ship cut through the waves and listening to the pop and creak of the rigging. Splitting the long gentle swells, the *Elizabeth's* prow flung twin arcs of green water falling into swirls of foam at her sides, the hull sweeping through and leaving it behind to spread like a widening road sparkling brightly in the sunlight.

Elijah took in a deep breath of fresh air and turned to Fred James. "Best day we've had yet," he said. "Feels like we really goin' to Africa now."

"Yep. We's movin'direckly for it, that's what the mate said. Been throwed off course by the storm, but we's back on it now."

Fred put his arm on the shoulder of an old man next to him.

"This here's Terra Hall, Elijah. He signed up as a laborer to build the reception center, but his real trade is somethin' else. Tell Elijah what it is, Terra."

The lean, wiry old man laughed as he rubbed his frizzly white hair.

"Well, I was sayin' I been a hatter in Philadelphia for twelve years and now I'm goin' to Africa where they prob'ly don't wear nothin' like that! Not sure how I'll make my livin' in the colony, but I made up my mind I was goin' back if the chance ever come."

"Seems like you had a good job, you didn't need to come," someone said in a disgruntled voice.

Elijah turned and saw Peter Small with a frown on his face.

"Most of us never could get any real jobs like that," Peter said, jealously. "That's why I'm leavin'--couldn't support a family. But you--you had no need to go back!"

Elijah could see the anger and frustration in Peter's glare, but the old man stiffened up and glared back.

"Well, there's needs and there's needs. Which one you goin' hark to? A man's got to decide that for hisself! I was born in Africa--I al'us knowed I had to get back home someday."

Elijah jumped like he'd been struck and moved quickly to Terra Hall's other side.

"Born in Africa? What part you come from, Terra? How long you been in America?"

"Don' know how long, Elijah. Last time they sold me they said I was forty and three. I been free for twelve years working in

20

the hat-makin' business--and they said I was fourteen when I come." He squinted his eyes, trying to work it out, and then shook his head. "You figger it out!"

"That's forty-one you been in America," Elijah said. "So where'd you come from--in Africa, I mean!"

Terra grinned sheepishly. "Don' know that either! Ev'ry time I was sold I went to some diff'rent strangers. Only frien' I had of my own people was a man from my village, and he died on the slave boat comin' over. They wouldn't let me talk my language, an' I forgits it after a piece." He shook his head. "So now, no names, no places--nuthin' left!"

Terra's eyes misted and he blinked. Fred James put his arm on Terra's shoulder again.

"How'd you get the job makin' hats?" he asked softly.

"Well, I been sold three times, 'cause I run away ever time they treats me bad. Didn't never stand for that! They didn't cut me up much or let the dogs tear me 'cause I works too good. 'Stead, they sold me off ..."

He was silent, remembering. They waited, seeing the pain in the old man's eyes.

"Last time I runs away I knows more how to do it 'cause some white man come secret-like to our church meetin' in the woods. After I cross't the Ohio River, there was people to help and I gits all the way to Canada. But I come back--too cold up there! When I come to Philadelphia this Quaker man heard 'bout me bein' a good worker and he said I should work for him. He taught me the hattin' business and I got good at it."

Terra stopped and looked at Peter Small.

"But I never married 'cause I wasn't goin' to stay this side forever. It taken a long time, but I's goin' home now!"

Elijah saw the anger in Peter's eyes fade, and his ginger-colored face blushed. But Peter offered no apology to Terra, so Elijah consoled the old man.

"We're goin' to set up our colony near some place called Sherbro Island on the African coast. Maybe you'll find your people after we get settled."

Elijah paused, and looked off in the distance where he supposed Africa was.

"I wish I knew where my people come from," he said. "Only my ma ever talked about Africa--and she heard 'bout it from her pa and gran'pa. It's 'cause of her stories I knew I should come

21

back--but to where?" He threw up his hands helplessly.

"Well, I don't care where I come from," said Peter. "I just care where I'm goin'. I wants me some land. I'm goin' have me a big, two-story house settin' on it, and after I gets wealthy I'm goin' have plenty of field hands and a big farm. The smokehouse will al'us be full of bacon sides and cure' hams and sausage. There'll be plenty of syrup and sugar, and a whole barrel of whiskey." His voice was soft now. "I'll 'low my chillun lots of playin' time and no hard labor, and my wife will have all the fine clothes she wants."

He looked back along the starboard rail where he'd seen Carrie, but she was talking to John Bannon. The men at the bow followed Peter's eyes, and could see Carrie laughing happily. Peter turned back to the men, the anger in his eyes again.

"And there'll be no white man tellin' me what to do!"

"You make it sound like easy street, Peter, but it ain't likely," warned Elijah. "We're goin' out like pioneers and we han't got much to start with--jus' what the Society could raise for us. We'll get to keep all we make, sure 'nough, but I figure it's goin' to be a hard life for quite a spell."

"Yeah," Fred James said. "Don't forget, we've got to build the reception center first. That's what we's hired for."

"You do your figurin' and I'll do mine!" Peter snapped. "We're suppose' to have some land and a house, that's what the Society promised. Soon's the reception center is finished, I'm goin' take what the Society has for me and go into the tradin' business. That's the way to make money--tradin'! Then I'll buy all the land I want. Have me a whole damn plantation someday!"

February 19th, Saturday

A week after their first big storm the *Elizabeth* was nearing tropical waters, and calm seas had brought everyone out of the hold. The sun was so bright it hurt their eyes. Women were drying clothes, the captain having given his permission for some ratline to be strung temporarily between the cargo winches, with the warning that the owners of the clothes would have to come at once if the mate called to clear the deck. An exciting festive air took hold as the emigrants walked about, talking and laughing, proud of having gotten their "sea legs."

But the agents were in their cabin, working on a plan of the first town the colony would build, and the reception center for repatriated slaves nearby. Bacon was showing the rough sketch to Coker at the table, and Crozer and Bankson sat on the edge of their bunks watching.

"I'd like to see a church or two somewhere there," Coker said, his face close to the map .

"Good! Pick a place!" Bacon said, smiling and pointing to some spots. But then he stopped, his smile disappearing.

"But really, we can't do much more than this simple layout of the streets and lots. We don't even know where the town will be located."

Coker looked up at him, surprise in his eyes.

"I thought we were headed for Sherbro Island, south of Freetown."

Bacon shrugged.

"We are. But Mills and Burgess didn't describe Sherbro very well in their report to the Society. Our orders are simply to go there and negotiate with the chiefs for a place to settle. Exactly where we don't know!"

"Well, it would be wherever the ships land on the island, wouldn't it?" Bankson asked. "We'd have to build near a wharf for supplies coming by sea."

"How about water for the town?" Crozer asked. "Are there any springs, or some hills for fresh water runoff? We'll have to have good water."

Bacon pulled his chin, trying to remember.

"They said there was high ground on part of the island. I suppose they meant hills. The report recommended high ground to avoid the African fever."

Crozer was excited now. The health of the colony was his responsibility. He leaned over and hunted for a book in his foot locker.

"Here it is! I've just been reading Dr. Linn about the African climate--how unhealthy it is during the rainy season. So fever seems related to season as well as low, swampy ground."

He held out the book to Bacon, but Bacon waved it away.

"High ground, low ground, ships, drinking water--how can we plan for all that until we see the place?"

"Can we choose the place on the island?" Coker asked.

"That depends on the chiefs, I suppose. And we'd have to get the approval of the British colonial authorities."

"Would that be hard to get--the British approval?"

Bacon went to look out of the porthole, then turned back to the table. They saw the worried look in his eyes.

"I don't know! The Society sent Mills and Burgess to England first and they were treated royally. But when they got to Sierra Leone the Governor hinted that the merchants there wouldn't want another colony located too near--might interfere with their business prospects."

"So why do we have to go to the British at all? Why don't we just go straight to the chiefs?" Bankson asked.

Bacon frowned at his naive young assistant.

"We can't risk bad relationships between governments! We'll have to let the Governor know that our expedition is a follow-up of Mills and Burgess' visit, and that the United States' role in this is completely non-political."

"Non-political!" Coker almost shouted. "What do you mean?'

"I mean the United States isn't founding this colony--it's the Society, as a private organization, that's doing it."

"But isn't this ship chartered by government? Isn't the *USS Cyane* a Navy ship that's supposed to convoy us?" Coker waved his hands, bewildered.

"Remember," Bacon said patiently, "this is a group of workers hired by the United States to go out and build a reception center for slaves captured by the Navy. So it's natural that the government pays for the voyage and protects the ship. But after that, the workers all have chosen to become settlers in the Society's colony." He pointed at Crozer. "That's why Crozer is here as the Society's agent."

Coker looked at Crozer.

"What happens when the center is finished?"

"The land, the operation of the colony, and the well-being of the people in it will be the responsibility of the Society," Crozer said. "It will regulate the affairs of the colonists until they're able to assume their own governance."

"My Lord!" Coker's face turned ashen and he sat down heavily on the edge of his bunk. They watched him thinking it over, and finally he sighed.

"Well, I'm glad to get it straight--never heard it said that clear before. It ... it sounds alright to me--an organized government with somebody in charge until we learn to do it ourselves ... but ... "

24

Finally he pointed to the door. "Do you gentlemen realize what some of my people out there on the deck think?"

No one spoke, waiting for him to say it.

"They believe they're going to Africa to make their own homes, to live free, and to have the same opportunities the white man has in America. Some simply think they'll be free!"

Coker shook his head and looked squarely at Crozer.

"I don't believe many of them have any idea of the regulations and government you're planning to put in place over them. I hope you explain it to them soon, so they'll understand before they get to Africa."

Crozer turned to Bacon.

"They're under your orders until the center is built. Maybe you'd better talk to them."

"I've been thinking about it," Bacon said with a sigh, "but I've been putting it off. All the recent rumors about fighting and disorderliness in the hold have me worried. Maybe some won't submit to proper regulations in a colony if they can't even do it on the ship."

"It's pretty crowded down there," Coker said. "They're getting on each other's nerves and I've had to settle a few misunderstandings. But they're having a good day on deck now. That will help."

Bacon's face brightened and he snapped his fingers.

"That's it! I'd like to try something, Brother Coker. The people have let you settle some of their differences because you're like their pastor. But I'll appoint you as Justice of the Peace with the authority to decide on real cases of conflict down there. Let's see how they respect official authority. I'll delay giving them the directives of the Government and the Society for awhile."

February 23, Tuesday

The Elizabeth had entered the doldrums and lay becalmed for the third day. Captain Sebor ordered repairs for the hull where the storm had worked open the seams. A tarry smell invaded the hold as the crew hunted with lanterns to find leaks and caulk them. The damaged spar was replaced with all hands heaving on a boom rigged for lifting up the spare one. Split sails were loosed and lowered to the deck, and new ones from the sail locker sent aloft and bent on one by one. Fresh hemp rope, reaved through pulleys and lashed to stays and braces, allowed the rigging to be set taut, the yards nicely squared once more.

But the breathless air and tropical heat made life miserable for the emigrants, forced to stay in the hold when the captain ordered them out of the way of repairs. Tension increased as they realized the ship was going nowhere. Peter Small and John Bannon got into a fist fight and had to be separated. Carrie's name wasn't mentioned, but everyone knew what their fuss was all about.

Peter Small's dog was an irritant to many in the stuffy air and dim light below deck. Edward Wigfall tripped over it in the aisle between the two rows of stalls.

"Damn you, you stinkin' little mutt!"

Wigfall swung his foot hard, and the dog's yelp was heard in every stall. Peter came running down the aisle, shouting.

"Wigfall! What d'ya do that for? Pepe's only a little bitty thing."

"Well, do somethin' with'im! Tie'im up in your own place 'til you take'im walkin' on the deck. He shouldn't be runnin' around loose down here."

"I was doin' that, but the Captain stopped it when he saw dog crap somewhere on the deck. Says it was from my dog! But he's got one, too--only he walks it at night when we're gon'ta bed. Probably was his own dog's crap! Says he don't want'a see me bring my dog up again."

Wigfall turned and began to walk off, shaking his head.

"Well, man, it's your own makin'. I never would've brung no animal on a ship."

####

Bacon, Crozer, and Coker were in shirts open at the neck, sleeves rolled up, wiping a constant film of sweat from their faces and necks as they worked at the desk in the cabin. A lantern on the desk and one hanging from a gimbal added to the oppressive heat. The day's sun had made the room too hot for work, and Bacon had waited for early evening, hoping for a breeze that didn't come.

Now he wanted them to finish devising specific rules for the distribution of land and the system of government before they went out on deck for an evening stroll. Bankson had already asked to be let off, knowing that his clerical skills as Bacon's assistant wouldn't be needed until the final draft was to be copied for sending back to America.

"... a town lot and ten acres for a farm outside of town--that's what the Society suggested to me," Crozer was saying.

"What about those who want more farm land?" Bacon asked. "Shouldn't we encourage the ones who want to be full time farmers by making more acreage available to them?"

"Does all that have to be decided now?" Crozer protested. "The advisory council can work out some of those details later. Let's get to some regulations for behavior."

"That's right," Coker said. "We're having more trouble and I've been trying to settle arguments and fights without any rules to back me up. What do we do when they keep it up?"

Crozer sighed, opened a leather-bound case, and fished a paper out of it.

"All we've got to go on is this rather skimpy letter of instructions the Society approved and handed to me before I left."

He placed it on the desk and they all tried to read it in the quivering lantern light. A drop of sweat fell on the sheet. Bacon mopped his chin, and carefully touched his handkerchief to the widening blotch on the paper.

"It's really just some general suggestions about getting the land from the Africans," he said in a disappointed voice. "Not much help at all--we've got to make some rules about public order right away. I think the ..."

They heard quick, loud footsteps and the cabin door was flung open by Bankson.

"Mr. Bacon, come quick! The Captain's calling for you on deck by the forecastle! He's threatened to shoot Peter Small!"

"Oh, my God!"

Bacon breathed it out softly, scarcely believing it possible. But he pushed his chair back and sprang for the door.

"Quick, gentlemen! This might take all of us!"

He was out the door and running across to the starboard side before Crozer and Coker were fully standing. They followed him, pounding alongside the starboard rail, dodging rigging fixed to the bulwarks and skirting a pile of rope. They reached the open deck space at the bow just as the captain reached his boiling point.

"That's enough of your scurvy talk! No landlubber talks to

the Master of the ship like that!" They heard the angry shaking of his voice. "Mr. Wilson! Get me my pistols at once!"

The mate saw the agents arrive and he moved quickly astern. Their eyes grew accustomed to the evening shadow, and they could see Peter Small and Captain Sebor, each pulling angrily against a leash, restraining their growling dogs. Bacon spoke calmly.

"Captain ... Bacon here. Can I help?"

The quiet, matter-of-fact sound of his voice in the semi-darkness so contrasted with the two men's enraged shouting a moment before that it seemed to bring sanity to their minds. Coker went over to Peter Small and put his hand on the younger man's shoulder.

"Steady, Peter. Don't say anything. We can work this out."

Bacon approached the captain cautiously, waiting for him to speak. The captain exhaled slowly and took in several more deep breaths before he spoke. His voice was low and strained.

"Mr. Bacon, I have never encountered such insubordination in thirty years of seafaring! I will shoot this man's dog if it shows on this deck again. I hope you make it clear to that--that--to him!" He motioned toward Peter, and turned back to his cabin.

Bacon and Coker, relieved that the Captain's intention was not the rumor that Bankson had picked up, took a quiet but seething Peter Small down to his stall in the hold. But the rumor had already swept around the deck, and emigrants rushed below to get out of the captain's way, worried about the effect of Peter's action on the expedition.

3 Who's in Charge?

March 1, 1820

The wind had not been fair for days, the ship moving so slowly that people had given up on a possible early landfall. Bacon came into the mess room after a morning walk around the deck, aware that a strange resignation had taken hold of many of the emigrants.

"Have you heard the remarks from our people?" Bacon said as the agents and Coker sat down to breakfast.

"About what?" Crozer asked, stabbing his first slab of salt beef from the platter.

"I hear them saying 'It's all for the best' or 'We're in God's hands'--things like that. What's come over them? Last week they could hardly wait to get to Africa."

"I think they don't want to get their hopes up again and be disappointed," Coker chimed in. He reached for the plate of hard ship's biscuits and swept three onto his own plate with a clatter.

Bankson had his own idea.

"They're just getting so used to ship life that it's nothing to get worked up about whether we have a few more days of it or not."

Bacon was thoughtful.

"You know, this might be a good time to test our people--while everything's calm," he said.

"What do you mean, 'test'?" Coker asked.

"Test their loyalty as colonists by presenting the Society's directives about land   distribution and governance. They haven't objected to the rules for public order we made, have they?"

"Not so far. Some petty stealing has been the only serious case. All I did was tell them the law and warn them about the fine if they did it again."

"Good. That's a start."

"I don't know," Coker objected, "I thinks it's different than what you'll be doing when you present the Society's instructions."

"How so?" Crozer asked.

"Well ... it's been between colored people, my being Justice of the Peace and settling their difficulties. But this other is the Society--white people--telling them about what land they can or can't have and who's going to govern them. Some of them won't be expecting that."

"Now you've got me worried," Crozer said. "I have to be the Society's agent until the colony becomes self-governing. I don't want to fight with them about who's in charge."

"What about me?" Bacon said. "I take charge first, while the reception center is being built. Are they going to accept that without a lot of trouble?"

"I honestly don't know," Coker replied. "I guess that's why you're going to test them, isn't it? Remember, they don't know much about governing themselves--they just want to do it. You'll have to help them."

Bacon drained his coffee mug.

"You, too. We couldn't have gotten this far without you. Will you help them talk about the directives after I present them?"

Coker nodded his head. "Certainly."

"Alright then--today's the day!" Bacon stood up. "Let's meet by the forecastle after lunch with all the men. I'll read what I've got from the Secretary of the Navy about the reception center, and Crozer can read the instructions from the Society. Then ..."

"No," Crozer interrupted. "I'll give it to you. You read them both."

"Good. I'll add the little code of laws we've devised for now. Then we'll leave the deck to Coker, and he can lead a discussion with the men. We want them to give us their ideas of how the govenment should be. Is that agreeable?"

They nodded, getting up from the mess table and stretching.

####

Elijah, standing at the rail with several men, had to listen carefully to hear Bacon's voice above the gentle splash of waves against the barely moving ship. Other men were sitting about the forecastle, on coils of rope, the sail locker, and anchor winches. He felt a rising excitement inside himself as Bacon talked.

"... We should reach Freetown in about a week," Bacon said. "It's the major port of the British Colony of Sierra Leone, set up for freedmen just like the one we're going to build nearby on Sherbro Island. We'll notify the Sierra Leone authorities ..."

He went on explaining but Elijah was only half listening. He felt a strange glow--something was reaching for him, quickening

30

the marrow of his bones. Was he just feeling it ... hearing it ... or ... smelling it? He sniffed the air. Was that the smell of land on the breeze that just sprang up? Africa was only a week away--was it calling to him somehow?

"... we'll go on to Sherbro Island to negotiate with the chiefs for buying land for the colony and the reception center ..."

This is what his ma wanted, and her pa, and his pa before that--to go back to Africa--and now he himself would be the one to make all those dreams come true! He could almost hear the drums welcoming him back, a son of Africa returning, and there would be a great feast, and the people would dance.

"... most of you have said you would stay on after the facilities are built and become the first settlers of the colony. You should be informed now of the directives the Society has given about the colony ..."

Mary would see what he had told her so often, the forest and rivers, the green land bursting with food growing all around just waiting for picking. The warm days, no more ice or snow, just rain and sun to ripen the grain and fruit in an age-old rhythm of planting and harvest.

"... you will be under the direction of me and my assistant, Mr. Bankson, as agents of the United States Government, until the reception center is built. Thereafter you will be directed by Dr. Crozer as agent of the American Colonization Society ..."

Elijah heard someone mutter an oath, and looking around he saw Peter Small whispering to Adams and Wigfall and--he craned his neck to see--Fred James. What were they talking about?

"... each colonist will be given a plot of land upon which to build his house, and ten acres of farmland outside the settlement. The United States Government will provide food and supplies for everyone of you and your family during your brief stay at the center and six months after you move to your allotted land. You will need to plant your acreage as soon as possible so you will have ... "

Elijah was imagining the farm, a short walk from the settlement, where he and his boys would raise corn so tall--and big sweet watermelons--and some pigs and chickens. And Mary would put down preserves and he'd smoke hams. Peter Small and those three were not listening to Bacon. Their whispering was getting too loud--didn't they know any better?

" ... a plan has been laid out for assigning the lots in the town, but it depends on the actual site that can be purchased from the chiefs at Sherbro. Mr. Crozer will be in charge of the development of the settlement and the colony, until such time as the settlers--you and others who arrive after you--are able to ... "

Elijah saw Peter turn from his little group and point to Crozer, and heard his frenzied whispering, now almost outright talking.

"You see! You see! I told ya so! He's the one!"

Elijah's strange glow was gone, destroyed by the noise of Peter Small and his group. Elijah could see that Bacon was having difficulty making himself heard.

"... I repeat, during the first stage while we are establishing the center, I will be responsible for governance. I've already appointed Rev. Daniel Coker as Justice of the Peace, and I will appoint other officials and committees to assist me. This first system of government should be worked out before we arrive at Freetown. I'll leave you now to talk over among yourselves what that system might be. Brother Coker can act as chairman of your discussion."

Bacon left the bow quickly, passing through the men and heading for the cabin. But before he disappeared around the corner of the forecastle, a shout broke out.

"We didn't come all the way to Africa to be under no white man's government!"

Peter Small stood up and strode to the bow rail where Coker was standing. He turned and faced the men, his eyes burning with anger.

"We been deceived by the Society! They never told us nothin' like this! I say freedom and liberty means we governs ourselves! We can't be free with white men ..."

Elijah leaned on the rail, watching Peter shouting and shaking his fist at Bacon's back. He wasn't too surprised--he'd known from the fuss on the dock in New York that Peter would be a trouble-maker. In a way, Peter is right, Elijah thought. But there has to be good officers to make something big like a colony work--he knew that from the Navy. Officers have to know what to do, and the rank and file have to be good at what they do, too. Peter couldn't be a leader--he'd only been a laborer in New York, just like me.

"... we should decide about the colony, not them!" Peter was shouting. "We should buy the land we pleases and do what we want with it!"

Jonathon Adams, one of Peter's group, stood up.

"Yeah! And the goods belongs to us, too! All that stored there in the hold--it's for us--the Gov'ment gives it to us. We can use it like we wants; even trade it, and buy what we like. Every man should decide for hisself what he'll do with his part!" Adams paused. "I already knows what I'll do with mine," he gloated.

Nathaniel Peck was disgusted. He waved Adams down with his long, thin arm, not getting up from his seat on the anchor winch.

"We can't start with everybody goin' his own way! Some people'll waste their goods and land right away."

He glared at Adams.

"Then they'd want the rest of us to help them out of their mess! I believe in sharin' and helpin' each other, but not that. There has to be some regulation of it. Those supplies have to last a whole year--some's Government and some's Society goods."

"It isn't only the food and supplies," Elijah broke in. "It's the know-how and the what-for. None of us knows what to do to run a town or a colony just now."

"But we can learn it, just like white men!" Peter shouted again. "We should be free to do it like we thinks it should be. If we make mistakes, it's all right. It's our colony. And some day it might be a whole big nation!"

They clapped for that, and some whooped it up a little.

Joseph Blake got up from the starboard winch, but said nothing, just waiting for them to stop clapping. They saw he wanted quiet so they stopped their banter.

"You makin' sport of somethin' important," he said in a low, accusing voice.

They sobered and strained to catch his words. He was a tailor--a serious man.

"This ain't funnin' stuff we's talkin'. Peter says freedom and liberty. Freedom to do as we please. I think if everyone does like that we'll be arguin' 'til no one's free to do anything."

He pointed his two right fingers like a scissors at Peter's group and emphasized his words with it.

"Freedom has to be cut so ever'one is satisfied some. Maybe not all each one wants, but some. Give an' take here and there so ever'one feels it's a fair fit for'em. And liberty--that's what we all dreamt about when we was slaves. But I got a feelin' we don't hardly know what it is yet, an' we won't find it just gettin' away from the white man or gettin' to a new place. When we gets there we have to make it--makin' laws we all want to live by and then havin' room to do what we want inside o' that. That ain't goin' to be easy for us 'cause some of us is so quick to throw off white man's law we goin' lose the good part in it."

Blake sat down. There was clapping, but no laughing, and Elijah sensed how important the talk was getting.

Edward Wigfall, another of Peter's group, strode up to the bow rail, planted his feet, and raised his voice defiantly.

"A'course we need some rules! But we have to make'em! That's what we're sayin'. Liberty means we are goin' to make the rules, not no Society. And these agents from the Society is supposed to be here to help us, not rule us. That's not the way to be free!"

He walked back and sat down like he'd said it all. Elijah knew Wigfall had come to the real thing that was sticking in the craw of Peter's angry bunch.

Old man Hall, crippled a little from the damp sea air, straightened up slowly from where he sat on a coil of rope. He rubbed his back and then smiled.

"I likes the argufyin' we is havin'," he said. "But it's no simple thing we's talkin' about. We have a sayin' that you never try to catch a black cat in the night."

Someone called out, "What does it mean, Terra?"

"It means you got to understan' good before you go to do somethin' important. You can't hardly see a black cat in the dark--how you goin' to catch him? If we is goin' to Africa to start somethin' that will someday be a nation, that's a mighty big thing. And if we's goin' to build it on real liberty, we better see it extry clear. We's startin' now with a colony, and the Society's goin' to help us 'til we knows what we wants. They said when we is able to, then we can govern ourselves."

Hall rubbed his back some more, but stayed on his feet. No one moved, and Elijah noticed how everyone waited quietly, as if they knew the old man's wisdom might give them the best thing they would likely hear today on the matter.

"I been dreamin' since I was brought to America as a slave about when I would go back. It took a long time an' I seen a lot in travelin' around--'specially when I was a free man workin' in Philadelphia. I seen merchants, lawyers, doctors, courts, hospitals--it's goin' to take a long time before we have those."

He paused, and they waited as he took several breaths.

"What is we now? A hatter, shoemaker, some farmers, carpenters, a blacksmith, a tailor, some laborers ... I think we's goin' to need a powerful lot of help!"

He eased himself down slowly on the coil of rope and they sat there quietly thinking on it. Finally Fred James, the last of Peter Small's group, stood up.

"Terra Hall thinks we ain't fit to run a colony," he began thoughtfully. "But what about the agents--what makes them fit? I know Mr. Bacon is a Reverend. Does that make him fit to do it? What about his assistant, and Mr. Crozer, the Society's agent. Are they fit?"

"I can answer that," Coker said, straightening up from where he'd been leaning on the bow rail. "I've seen their papers."

He stepped to the bow and cleared his throat.

"Mr. Bacon graduated from Harvard, went into law, and practiced until the War of 1812. He served as a Marine Corps captain in that war. Afterwards he studied for the ministry and was ordained in the Protestant Episcopal Church. Then President Monroe commissioned him as the Government Agent for this expedition."

Elijah noticed that Coker had everyone's attention, the first time they'd heard from him since the talk began.

"Mr. Bankson is the Government's Vice Agent. He has a college education and is a candidate for holy orders of the Episcopal Church. I've watched him work hard at keeping the expedition's records. Doctor Crozer, commissioned as Agent of the Society, is the expedition's physician, but he knows machinery and construction, too. He's a strong Methodist layman."

The wind was springing up and Elijah felt it on his face. Coker raised his voice to ride over the noise of the rigging as the ship picked up the breeze and increased its speed.

"I've watched all three of these men everyday in the cabin as they prayed and planned for our welfare. They've left friends and family and the comforts of America to go with us, to share their skills and experience, but also the hardships and dangers we will go through."

Coker looked at Fred James still standing beside him.

"Does that help, Mr. James?"

Fred nodded his head and sat down. Coker turned to the men on the deck again.

"I propose that all of us who have confidence in the judgment and sincere friendship of the agents and are willing to abide by the regulations they make, should sign our names to a resolution put on paper. Those who don't feel that way can refuse. That way we can put a fair end to our discussion."

Most of the men nodded in agreement, but Peter Small and his band called out in a loud chorus, "No! No! No!"

Coker said he would go and bring paper and pen for the resolution and those who wished could sign it. He returned in a few minutes, and Nace Butler held the ink bottle. Elijah held the paper down on the sail locker while Coker dipped and penned the resolution. Then they began to sign their names.

Peter Small and his supporters stood watching the men sign, believing some would join in refusing to do it. When all but themselves had signed the resolution, they became alarmed and insisted that their names be added. Elijah saw the shocked look on Peter Small's face as he took the quill pen, dipped it, and wrote his name at the very bottom.

Elijah walked over to Fred James.

"Fred, seems like Peter and you all were so busy whisperin' you didn't hear the last part of Mr. Bacon's talk. He as't for our ideas for gov'ment of the center."

Fred's eyebrows went up.

"Bacon as't for what?"

"He as't for our ideas 'bout committees and officials for the plan of gov'ment."

"Lord a'mighty! We didn't hear that! Peter was makin' so much fuss, I guess. Wait--let me go tell him."

Elijah watched as Fred went over and gave Peter the news. He saw Peter's grim face relax. Right away Peter gathered his group about him, and Elijah smiled as he watched them talking excitedly. It must have taken the sting out of their losing, he thought. Now they'd be working on a plan of government instead of making a rebellion. But Peter would be scheming to turn it to his own way, and there'd be more trouble ahead, no doubt about it.

4   To Sherbro Island

March 9, 1820

"There it is! I see somethin'! Is that it?" Lewis shouted as he jumped up and down at the railing and pointed.

"Where! Lemme see! Where?" Charlie asked. "Awww--I don't see nothin' but that ol' fog!"

Elijah trembled, straining to see through the morning mist that rose from the sea in the distance. A low, dark cloud seemed to hang far off ... was it a cloud? Could it be Africa? Not sure, he said nothing, and looked along the portside rail at the other emigrants who had been on deck for what now seemed hours. All were eager for their first glimpse of Africa.

Yesterday Captain Sebor had said he reckoned landfall would be sometime this morning; and last night Elijah had been as excited as his boys. They'd slept fitfully; then were up, rushing on deck before dawn, leaving Mary and Lizzie to come when they could.

Only now was the sky lighting up in the east. There had been plenty of time for Mary to get Lizzie dressed and, with Carrie's help, to climb up the steep hatchway ladder. Elijah lifted Charlie in his arms, and stood back from the rail to make room for the women.

"Seen anythin' yet?" Mary asked.

"Nope. Too foggy to see any ..."

Elijah broke off, staring at a crimson spot on the horizon that began to spread outwards along the gray, misty line between sea and sky. Its glowing light took shape, the edge of a fire-red disk swelling up slowly.

"Look Lizzie! See the Af 'can sun!" Charlie called to his baby sister, still snuggled sleepily in Mary's arms.

They watched as the sun came languidly up to a full red-orange ball and the mist began to sink lazily into the sea. Lewis, still intent on the low, dark cloud in the distance, groaned when the sun freed itself from the earth's vapors and turned a hot yellow-orange, burning down on the dark cloud.

"It's meltin' away!" he cried out. "Nothin' but a cloud."

Elijah, as disappointed as his son, saw the cloud take on a

brief, golden yellow hue before it was burned away by the sun. But in its place a mountain ridge stood, green foliage sparkling fresh and lovely in the sunlight. At its base a thin yellow line of beach winked on and off, in turn hidden by high waves rushing shoreward, then bared as the great blue-green rollers spent themselves on the sand. Elijah's heart stopped. A bright green land--this has to be it! He sucked in air, and shouted.

"It's Africa!"

A cry went up from every throat.

"There she is!" "I see it, I see it!" "Praise God!" "Look'a there, Ma!" "That's our new home, son." "Lordy--it's so green!" "Africa! We's almost there!"

They began to laugh and cry--it was so beautiful! Some went down on their knees to thank God. Then Coker's powerful bass voice lifted them to their feet with the words of an old slave song about the Promised Land. They joined in, but he changed the words and sang them out two lines at a time so they could follow. They caught his rhythm and began to clap and sway as they sang the new song. It was about their ship on the stormy sea and how the Lord delivered Daniel from the lion's den and the Hebrew chillun from the fiery furnace and Jonah from the whale. And the Lord would deliver them--*right up to Afric's shore!*

It gave a new meaning to the Promised Land--not just a place in heaven where slaves would be free of endless toil and tribulation, but a new land that was here now, where they would be truly free! A jubilation feeling began to grip them, and some in deep ecstasy began to shout, "Lord, take us to that shore!" "Jus' a little bit more to go! Help us!" "Jesus! Come down and walk on the water!" "Show us the way!"

But as Coker led the people in song, Peter Small sat on the sail locker watching the crowd celebrate, a sour look on his face.

"That preacher got a whole storehouse of them songs to keep the people stirred up. Look at'em! Wastin' their time with all that ruckus."

Wigfall, sitting next to him, was shocked.

"You're not glad we's almost there? After all that long trip and storms and such?"

"I'll wait 'til I get there before I gets excited. 'Sides, I got more important things to think about."

"Like what?"

Peter stood up and walked to the other side of the ship,

away from the singing and clapping. Wigfall followed, curious now.

"You got somethin' up your sleeve, don't ya! I can tell."

"No, I don't. I'm just wonderin' when them agents are goin' to start this new government we're supposed to have."

"Bacon said it'd be soon as we got settled at Sherbro--you know that."

Wigfall looked closely at Small's face, and the truth dawned on him.

"Aaa-hah! You're mad 'cause you aren't on any of them committees, aren't ya!"

Peter turned away and looked out to sea, leaning on the starboard rail.

"It wasn't no committee. Bacon called it a council."

"Yeah, but there's both. The council is to advise him and his vice-agent. And then there's somethin' he called a committee of trade, didn't you hear that?"

"'Course I did--just forgot about it s'all. I wanted to be on the council so bad I ... didn't he have some other officials, too?"

Wigfall smiled and clapped Peter on the shoulder.

"You sure must'a been stuck on that council thing. He appointed Nathaniel Brander as colonial secretary and me as register of public ... public acts, I think that's what its called."

"That's why I didn't remember'em. They ain't really important. It's the council that's goin' to have the power."

Peter hit the rail hard with his right hand.

"We didn't get nothin' out of it! 'Spite of all the ideas we gave'em. Damn those agents!"

"You're wrong, Peter. I heard Bacon read Fred James' name for the committee of trade. Didn't you say you was goin' into tradin' right off when we finishes building the center?"

Peter's eyes lit up. He hit his right fist into the palm of his other hand.

"Yeah, you're right! Alright--Fred's on our side and he can see we get a tradin' license, can't he. That's not too bad ... get rich first in tradin' and then buy all the votes we wants. That's the way the whites do it."

He pounded his fist into his palm again, turning to look back at the noisy crowd.

"Yeah!" he said, his eyes almost closed, pounding and pounding. "Yeah! Yeah! Yeah!"

Wigfall watched in fascination. Each time Peter pounded,

his arm muscles bunched and he pushed hard, like he was grinding something or somebody in the palm of his hand. Then he noticed that Peter was looking at the forecastle where somebody stood.

####

John Bannon, taller than most in the happy crowd at the rail, had stopped his clapping and singing when he'd caught sight of Carrie standing alone, leaning against the forecastle. He'd eased out of the swaying circle of singers and made his way to her side.

"Aren't you happy?" he shouted above the noise of the singing. "We're almost there."

Carrie managed something between a smile and a grimace, and shook her head. She started to speak, but the words seemed to strangle her throat.

"I wish my ... my ma and pa ..."

John, not hearing it, put his ear down near her mouth. He heard her sob instead, and jerked his face around to see tears starting from her eyes. Instinctively, he knew what was bothering her, and turned to lean against the forecastle by her side, putting his arm across her shoulders.

"Yeah, I know," he said in her ear, patting her awkwardly. "You missin' your folks."

There wasn't much use of trying to say anything with the singing and clapping still going on, so he just stayed by her. When he saw she didn't have anything to cry into, he pulled his red bandana from his back pocket and gave it to her.

He watched her sobbing, his heart aching for her loneliness, because he missed his own parents, too. But he'd left them willingly, going off to Africa where he could be a man and make his fortune without any whites to take what he earned. That made his loneliness different--it was his own choice. Carrie was robbed of her parents at the last minute, there on the dock in New York. It was her mother who'd decided to send Carrie on to Africa and freedom.

He wished he knew how she felt about Africa. Would she stay? He looked at her beautiful light brown skin and coffee-colored hair, braided and coiled around her head, fastened with two big hair pins. He'd seen her hair combed out only once, the first day they had all come out on deck in the bright sun. They'd aired their things, washed clothes and hung them on lines, and women had washed their hair, drying it in the sun and fresh sea breeze. He'd walked around the corner of the forecastle and seen Carrie with her hair undone, and the beauty of her long tresses with their soft dark curls had tripped his heart.

He started to touch it now as her sobbing stopped and she dried her eyes, but she looked up at him and he pulled his hand back, arrested by her large, brimming eyes. The lustre of her laughing brown eyes was the most beautiful part of her, but now they were bloodshot and sad. He wanted to take her in his arms and comfort her, but she had never let him get that close.

"Th-thanks, John," she said, stifling the sobs and giving him back his bandana. "I ... I can't ever sing and be happy 'til my ma and pa come--my heart won't 'low it."

March 20, Monday

Sailing into the harbor at Freetown on March 9th had been just one of the high times of their trip, Elijah thought. Another one had been the day before that when Bacon had read the new 'Plan of Government' to them. They'd been discussing it for a week and had made their suggestions to the agents through Coker. So they'd arrived feeling proud about their helping to make a government for the colony, and they were eager to try it out when they got some land.

But everything after that seemed to be a letdown until today. Eleven days after touching Africa's shore they were finally reaching Sherbro! He and Mary stood with their children and the other families on the deck of the schooner *Augusta*, looking at the passing shoreline of Sherbro Island--the place that might be their new home. Eleven days of delays and disappointments! Elijah shook his head as he remembered.

It had taken three days for the agents just to get an audience with the Governor of the Sierra Leone colony, and the emigrants couldn't get off the ship until then. Cooped up in the ship in Freetown's harbor, they learned for the first time what tropical heat was really like. Tempers flared, especially Peter Small's. He complained to anyone who would listen, and encouraged jealousy of Coker and the agents, who went on shore twice and were invited to dine at the Governor's place. Coker told Elijah afterward that the Governor didn't discuss the expedition's

41

purpose nor offer any help, so the whole time seemed wasted.

It took another four days for Bacon to try to persuade Captain Sebor to sail the *Elizabeth* on south to the shallow coastal waters where Sherbro Island lay. A raging argument between them ended when the captain stomped off furiously to his cabin.

"Blast it! I won't put my ship in danger of running aground and rotting forever in those stinking shallows! That's final, Mr. Bacon!"

Elijah saw the desperate look in Bacon's eyes the next day when he went ashore to search for a shallow boat to accompany the ship, the only way Captain Sebor would consent to go at all. But Bacon succeeded in buying for $3,000 a small schooner--it had been a slaver taken by a British warship patrolling the coast to stamp out the slave trade. Bacon renamed the schooner the *Augusta*, telling the emigrants that it would be dedicated now to the cause of freedom, not slavery.

They spent three more days on their way from Freetown to Sherbro Island in the *Elizabeth* and the *Augusta*. African ship pilots who knew the shallow waters guided each vessel, but the nervous Captain Sebor fumed all the way, regretting every hour that he allowed his ship to court danger and run aground. He ordered the chief mate to close haul the sails as the ships felt their way through treacherous shoals, sounding for depth of water at fifteen minute intervals. The *Augusta*, running closer to shore, was grounded once, but managed to work itself free. The second time it happened, Captain Sebor bellowed out angrily.

"Belay there, Mr. Wilson! Drop anchor! We'll be lying-to right here--I've seen enough of these foul waters!"

They were still about thirty miles from Sherbro. As soon as the *Augusta* got free of the sandy shoal, Bacon ordered the married men, their families, and some of their personal goods off-loaded from the *Elizabeth* to the schooner, and the *Augusta* continued on.

Today they were about to set foot on Sherbro Island. Elijah looked at Mary and the others crowding the portside rail. Their eagerness had been dampened by all the delays, but the sight of land so close was stirring them. Briefed earlier by Bacon, Elijah knew what they were approaching.

"Look way over there!" he pointed. "That high ground on the mainland is the Bagroo country. It's the place the agents hope to get for the colony."

Everyone stared at the far-off green hills rising from lush

grasslands and low bushes nearer the shore. A steamy mid-day haze hung over the land, and at the base of the hills the trees, dwarfed by the distance, quivered strangely in the shimmering heat waves.

"Is that where we's goin'?" Lewis asked his father.

"Not now, son. We'll be stayin' on this island right in front of us. It's Sherbro Island."

"When do we go to the place you pointin' to?"

Elijah turned and looked quizzically at Coker standing behind them. Coker spoke up so everyone could hear him.

"We'll stay on Sherbro in some small houses built by Mr. Kizell's people. He's the one that met Mills and Burgess when they came out to explore this area for the Society. He wants to help us because he was a slave himself in South Carolina. The British rescued him during the Revolution, and somehow he ended up here. He's the president of the Friendly Society in Freetown," Coker added. "These houses are just temporary, for the rainy season."

"You don't mean we's goin' live in some native houses?" Fred James asked, holding one of his children up to see the island.

"Well ... " Coker hesitated. "Whatever they use here on Sherbro to make them. We should be glad that Kizell had them put up for us. We have to wait 'til the agents negotiate land for the colony before we can build our own houses, you know."

A murmur of complaint moved through the crowd.

"We should be seeing Mr. Kizell on shore soon," Coker said. "He sent word he'd keep watch for us."

They all began to look intently at the shore as the schooner moved in closer. They passed several small villages of eight or ten round thatched huts apiece, a scattering of people at each one sitting on the beach watching the schooner. Charlie, jabbering about everything he saw to his sister Lizzie, suddenly turned to his parents.

"Look, Ma, they're all naked! And look at the queer round houses they've got!"

Elijah quickly put his hand over Charlie's mouth.

"They're not naked! That's the way they dress--don't need no clothes on top like we're used to. And those houses are made just right for Africa--s'posed to be cool 'cause of the grass thatch on'em. Just look and be quiet!" he said.

Mary laughed softly at Elijah and he questioned her with

43

his eyes. She moved closer to share it privately, smiling at him.

"Our chilluns and a lot'a our people ain't so proud of bein' African like you is, and they're goin' to make fun of the things they sees. You don't need to go 'round defendin' everything like you made it yourself."

Elijah, knowing she had him figured dead on, smiled ruefully and then bent to kiss her for helping him once again see life straight. They broke off the delight of their kiss suddenly when they heard the African pilot shout to Coker.

"That's the place! Right there on the beach with all the old fire coals and burnt sticks. See that black spot? That's where they burned her alive--I saw it myself."

"What! Burned her alive?" Coker seemed skeptical, but the emigrants at the rail crowded around Coker and the pilot, bursting with questions.

"What for?" "What'd she do?" "Must'a done real bad!"

"Witchcraft!" Elijah heard the word jump from mouth to mouth quickly and saw shocked looks in the crowd. He moved to Fred James' side.

"What's they sayin', Fred?"

"The woman was burn't alive 'cause she done witchcraft!"

Elijah stepped closer and heard the pilot telling how the woman was accused of making witchcraft on someone, and her village chief and elders held a palaver about it.

"How did they decide if she was guilty?" Coker asked.

"They still use the red water ordeal around Sherbro to find the guilty one," the pilot said.

"What's that?" Elijah asked.

"That's sassywood poison. They boil sticks of it in water--makes it red. Then all the accused have to swallow some. The one's who're innocent vomit it up, but the guilty one can't.'

Elijah didn't want to dispute an African about ways to settle a life-and-death case, but he couldn't quite believe it.

"You mean the people don't decide? They leaves it up to a poison in the water?"

"Right! It works everytime." The pilot smiled and turned back to Coker.

Elijah watched the African in disbelief. The man talks like he's educated, Elijah mused, but he still believes this tribal nonsense! Elijah rubbed his chin. There must be more to it than that--Africans would have good reasons for what they did.

44

Someone was asking the pilot about the schooner they were on--did he think it a good ship for the colony to own? Elijah strained to hear his words.

"It's fast--built for slipping into coves to pick up slaves. It'll be good for the coastal trade of your colony."

Then he paused, as if reluctant to reveal more, but went on anyway.

"It was probably made for places like Galenas islands where it's a little deeper. More slave trade there, too."

"So the slave trade is all around these parts?" Elijah asked.

"Plenty of it. Last year a Spanish slaver dumped his load just south of here when a British cruiser chased him."

"You mean a load of slaves? Did they swim to shore?"

"Only six made it. The rest were dead. The Spaniard put poison in their food when he saw the jig was up. Had his crew heave them overboard before he was finally run down."

"My God!" Elijah said.

The crowd at the rail stood speechless; people looked at each other with horror in their eyes. Elijah tried to speak, but his voice caught. He tried again.

"H-H-How many did he have?"

"They don't know. But the story told along the coast is four hundred."

"Four hundred! Four hundred! ... hundred ... hundred ..."

It was whispered through the crowd on ashen lips, faces turning gray with shock. Elijah felt a chill as the picture of it took shape in his mind. He could see the crew lifting mute black bodies with poisoned bellies and pain-twisted faces, heaving them over the side like dead animals--the bodies splashing as they drop into cold green waves--to disappear forever! The monstrous evil of the Spanish slaver turned his chill to white-hot anger.

"There'll be no slavin' around our colony!" he shouted. "Any slavers comes near the place, we'll drive'em out! Blast them off the sea with our cannon! We know what it's like bein' sent over to a miserable life of slavery! We'll ... "

His arm was yanked, and he turned to see Coker firmly pulling him away from the pilot.

"Mr. Johnson! Can I speak with you over here please?"

Coker guided him toward the stern, out of earshot of the pilot and crowd.

"I wasn't through talking, Reverend," Elijah said. "Why'd

you pull me away like that?"

"I wanted to warn you about revealing too soon the colony's aim to fight the slave trade."

"Too soon? What d'ya mean?"

"The agents were told in Freetown by a friendly advisor that we'll be opposed by everyone connected with the slave trade if they know we are against it."

Elijah's anger came back with a rush.

"We'll fight anyone conneck't with it!"

"Of course! But what if you don't know who that is? People we might not even suspect may be involved and work against us behind our backs. They might even be able to prevent us from establishing the colony."

Elijah was silent a moment.

"You mean ... people like the pilot? Why, he's a black man! You heard him talkin' against slavin'."

"Who do you think brings the slaves to the slavers?" Coker said, his voice low and sorrowful.

"You mean the pilot works for slavers, too?"

"We were told in Freetown that some of the chiefs are up to their necks in it, too."

"Against their own people?"

Coker nodded.

"That's why we have to be careful. The man in Freetown was very strong about it--told the agents we should keep our eyes and ears open, but our mouths closed. We won't get any land if the chiefs know we intend to stop the slave trade."

Coker stood quietly, waiting for Elijah to take it all in. Then he motioned for them to go back to the crowd at the rail. But Elijah wasn't ready.

"Africans ... against their own people?" He shook his head.

They heard someone shouting about Mr. Kizell.

"There he is--that must be him! See over there?"

Elijah and Coker went back to the rail where everyone was watching the short, dark man standing on the beach, waving to them.

March 30, 1820

It was high noon and too hot to work--the Africans were right about that! Elijah thought they were lazy when he first saw

46

them stop working for a couple of hours in the middle of the day, but now here he was resting under the shade of some mangrove trees himself. He was bone-tired, off-loading cargo from the *Elizabeth* into the *Augusta* and then unloading it again here at Campelar, the village that Kizell's people had built. Elijah sighed wearily and leaned back against the spindly roots of a mangrove tree, recalling the fuss that Peter Small had stirred up

"We's supposed to be put down on Africa'self--not out here in the ocean!" Peter had protested. "It's too many miles to Sherbro. I ain't gon' tote this stuff all that far. 'Sides, I was a carpenter's helper, not no dock worker!"

He refused to unload the cargo, persuading several others to join him. Bacon expected all the emigrant males to help unload, but when Peter and his group refused, he assigned them to building storehouses at Campelar. Because Elijah was an old hand at stevedoring on the New York docks, Bacon put him in charge of cargo handling. It went slowly until the *USS Cyane* finally appeared in Freetown and sent a barge down to Sherbro to locate the emigrants.

The Navy convoy ship had lost sight of the *Elizabeth* in New York harbor's fog, and never regained contact until now. Elijah felt relieved when the barge's officer put a small crew on board the *Augusta* to operate it until they could complete the unloading of the colony's cargo. But they were still not done after ten days and Captain Sebor was raging at Bacon to hurry it up ...

The snap of a twig startled Elijah and he waked from his reverie under the mangrove tree to see Coker standing there.

"Sorry to disturb your noon rest, Elijah, but I wanted to talk to you before you go back to unloading cargo. It's taking a long time to get a palaver with the chiefs about the land. I thought you ought to know--to tell the men you're working with."

"I don't exactly know what a palaver is," Elijah said, "but I hope they hurry it up. Kizell said he sent a message to the kings and chiefs 'bout ten days ago."

"We've met several smaller chiefs who keep putting us off, but yesterday Mr. Kizell and I finally saw King Sherbro himself."

"What'd he say?"

Coker sighed and looked at the ground, avoiding Elijah's eyes.

"He's not the big one after all--just in name only. He's old and has no power. But we also met his son, the one they call Prince

Couber. He was very friendly."

"Friendly! Is that all?" Elijah said disgustedly.

"Well, he didn't give us a direct answer about getting any land, but he said he would in a few days."

"Is he the one who'll call the chiefs for the palaver?"

"Yes--he has great power, it seems. And he assured me that we shouldn't worry about getting a place, as he says, to 'sit down on.' Bacon and Crozer aren't back from Freetown yet, so I guess it will all work out in good time."

"Good time!" Elijah stood up to face Coker, his voice harsh. "It just keeps goin' on and on! Crozer said hisself we shouldn't spend the rainy season on low land like this. I don't want my wife and chilluns comin' down with fever! Besides, makin' a crop in this ground looks pretty chancy to me. And the women can't get any good tastin' water. We have got to move to higher ground, Reverend!"

Coker raised his hands in a calming gesture.

"We're all working on it, Elijah. Your men are getting the supplies landed and stored. Crozer is getting advice and medicine for treating the fever, and Bacon is getting the trade goods we were advised to buy to please the chiefs at the palaver. They'll want payment for the land in goods, Kizell says."

Elijah felt better.

"What kind of goods?" he asked.

"Let's see ... the list had things like tobacco, cloth, iron pots, guns and gun powder, spoons--things they need. Oh, and beads and trinkets for the women and children, too."

"There'll have to be plenty of rum, from what I hear."

"I'm afraid so," Coker shook his head sadly. "Kizell says the slavers have given the chiefs so much rum all these years in their wicked deals that now the chiefs won't make any agreements without it--and we'll have to include it, too."

Coker straightened up.

"Elijah, there's something else ..."

But Coker stood silent and Elijah knew it was something Coker didn't want to bring up. A thought leaped into Elijah's mind like a cat jumping out of nowhere--Nathanial Peck had let their secret out someway! He waited, and Coker cleared his throat, looking straight into Elijah's eyes.

"I've heard that some of the men have cooked up a scheme to attack a slave pen over at Shebar. Are you in on that?"

Elijah tried not to flinch.

"Yes, I am. How'd you find out?"

"I ... I can't say, Elijah. What do you plan to do?"

"We'll use the boat from the colony's supplies and the muskets the government supplied. I saw'em in the cargo."

"Don't you see this could hurt our chances of getting land? Shebar is near King Sherbro's place, and I think some of these chiefs are involved in the trade. They may be waiting to see what we do about it."

"Well, we all was slaves, or our parents was. We can't sit by and see the Africans sent across to slavery, or maybe die in the ship goin' over. They're our brothers, Reverend!"

"But you may get captured, too! You could be sent back as a slave yourself!"

"We won' get ... we've got guns and ... "

Elijah's words died in his mouth. The Spaniard who'd poisoned his cargo of slaves flashed through his mind--he could die like that. But the outrage and anger at the monstrous cruelty of it came back.

"We're goin' to stop the slave trade, Reverend! Anywhere we see it, we're goin' to drive it out! You don't have to join us--just stay out of our way!"

Coker looked at his feet.

"Elijah, I know I'm thinking only about the need for the colony to get land soon."

Then he was silent, kicking at a stone. Finally he looked up and began talking in a low, penitent voice.

"This morning Kizell and I came back from King Sherbro's place. Prince Couber sent us in his big canoe with eight men rowing it, so we were moving fast. When we passed the mouth of one cove hidden in the mangrove trees, Kizell caught my eye and pointed quietly into the narrow opening. I got just a glance as we passed, but I saw newly captured slaves standing with irons on their wrists and ankles--all joined by chains--in a long line, waiting to be marched on board a schooner anchored at a little bamboo dock. They looked so beaten and helpless!"

Coker shut his eyes and shook his head, trying to shrug off the sight. Elijah saw the agony brimming in his eyes when he opened them.

"I'll never-never forget that ghastly sight! Elijah ... I won't stop you from what you feel bound to do. But I feel bound, too--to help the agents negotiate for land as quickly as we can, and to let nothing get in the way of that."

Elijah swallowed hard, and cleared his throat.

"Alright, Reverend. We didn't tell you 'cause we figured you and the agents would probably try and stop us, bein's you have to worry about official gov'ment business. But we're goin' to attack the next ship, if this'n got away."

Elijah shook Coker's hand, feeling they had come to an understanding and a deeper respect for each other. Then he turned to go back to the *Augusta* for more cargo.

5 African Fever

Campelar
Sherbro Island
April 18, 1820

"Mr. Johnson--you're on your feet again. Thank God! Can you take on a special duty?"

Bacon had sent for him, and Elijah stood there watching the thin, emaciated agent as he bent over a patient in the mat-and-thatch shelter they'd built for a hospital when the fever first struck.

"I guess so," Elijah said. "Still a little shaky, but my fever's gone. My wife Mary pulled me through."

"Is she all right?"

"She's plenty tired. Got us all through it but my littlest boy, Charlie. But I believe he's goin' to make it now. She's been usin' that cinchona bark mixed with wine, and makin' us all drink plenty of broth, like Dr. Crozer said."

"Good. If everybody would just do that! Some of them refuse to take any medicine or even take care of themselves."

Bacon shook his head wearily.

"Practically the whole colony is down with it and I've run out of helpers, except for that Sierra Leone young man I sent after you this morning."

"You by yourself?" Elijah was shocked. "Where's the other agents and Coker?"

He looked out into Sherbro bay for the *Augusta* where the agents had been staying, then saw that it was beached near shore. It leaned crazily to one side, the sails sloppily furled, ropes dangling forlornly. There was no stirring on the deck, but the ship's small boat was tethered beside her--proof someone was aboard her, he thought.

Bacon was slow to reply, bending over another patient to feel the man's forehead.

"I tried to send them to Freetown last week," he said, straightening up. "Crozer, Bankson, the barge officer and his crew--they all took the fever hard and I thought the doctors in Freetown could help them. I was going to send Coker along to see they got the proper attention. He was just coming down with it, too."

"But they didn't go? They're still here?"

"You and Blake and James were sick, and none of the other emigrants would help to sail it to Freetown."

"They wouldn't?" Elijah couldn't believe it. "Why not?"

"Peter Small, Wigfall, Adams--that lot. They said they wanted a say in what was going on, and wouldn't let the *Augusta* leave until we got the land from the chiefs. So the schooner couldn't be sent off."

"What did Coker say?"

"He told them they needed the agents and crew to get well, so they could get the land and then move to it. But the people were all stirred up about their rights, and wouldn't listen to him. They said they could do it themselves."

"Damn that Peter Small!" Elijah raged. "Where is he? I've had enough'a his trouble makin'!"

"They're all sick now. It's too late, Mr. Johnson. A big storm broke the schooner's anchor cable and blew it in to shore."

"So the agents and Coker are out there on the *Augusta*, stuck on a sand bar?"

"All except Crozer and Townsend, the barge officer." Bacon's voice turned husky. "They're dead."

Bacon silently pointed to the west and Elijah saw it--two mounds marked by wooden crosses, just above the high-water mark on the beach. Elijah sucked in his breath.

"My God! When?"

"Three days ago ..." Bacon's voice broke and tears welled in his eyes. Elijah waited, shocked but understanding the other man's grief. The agent wiped his eyes with his handkerchief, and tried again, straining for control, his voice high and rasping.

"The young man I hired to look after them on the boat came rowing in to tell me and I went out there--Crozer was in his bunk and couldn't speak. I lifted him up to get some wine and bark down him, but he grasped my hand, put a paper in it, and then died in my arms and I ..." Bacon's grief choked off the words and he looked away. Again Elijah waited. Bacon finally took a deep breath and wiped his eyes dry.

"When's it goin' to stop?" Elijah asked softly.

"Fifty people have it, by my last count in the houses, and a few more get it every day. I've only brought the worst ones here. Nelly Binks says she's a nurse, and she's been helping some of the families in their houses. But this morning she took to her bed."

52

"So now you're the only one treatin' people?"

"On shore, yes. The young Sierra Leone man is treating Coker and Bankson and the sailors on the schooner."

"And you don't have any fever yourself?"

Bacon stood up straighter.

"I think God has spared me for a purpose. This is what I came for--to help your people find a place here in Africa. But first we have to get through the fever."

Elijah shook his head, wondering if Bacon was surviving just on willpower.

"So what's this special job you want me to do?" he asked.

"Somebody left the tap open on a keg of wine and let half of it waste on the ground. We've got to have the wine to extract the medicine from the cinchona bark--so we can't afford to lose another drop of it. There are only two more kegs of it in the storehouse."

Bacon motioned to Elijah and they went outside the shelter. Bacon stopped abruptly when he looked at a crate with a pan of water on it, then threw up his hands in disgust.

"Every time I turn my back some soap or washcloths disappear! This petty stealing is bad enough, but people are getting wasteful with food and other supplies. I can't understand it!"

He was almost shouting and Elijah could see creases in his forehead and around his eyes.

"Don't they realize they're stealing from themselves--wasting their own food and medicine? It won't last that way! Why can't they see that!"

Bacon kicked an empty crate out of the way, his face red with anger. But he stopped immediately, breathed deeply, and turned away to look at the sea. When he turned back to Elijah, shame-faced but in control of himself, he spoke calmly.

"Mr. Johnson, I want you to mount a guard at the two storehouses every night. If you can find another man you trust to help, that will be fine. But we have to protect the supplies. I'm going to start rationing the food tomorrow."

"Alright," Elijah said, "Fred James got over the fever this morning, too. Can I use him?"

"Good--you can be on duty alternate nights. And on the days we give out the rations, you both should be there."

"Do y'think there'll be trouble?" Elijah asked. "You could start the council and have it help you."

Bacon considered it a moment, then shook his head.

"If Coker were well, I would consult with him. That paper Dr. Crozer gave me on his death bed was his signed statement turning over all the property and records of the Society to Coker. So Coker is now the acting agent."

"Coker--the Society's agent! A black man?"

Elijah was surprised, and wondered if Peter Small's crowd would follow Coker. But Coker had already shown he could lead.

"Well, he'll do his very best, I know that," Elijah said. "I think most of us'll be proud of how he does."

"So, you see ...," Bacon pondered it. "We don't need to begin that council until we get a place to start a colony. We'll be in the Bagroo high country soon ..."

Elijah watched Bacon turn and look over to the mainland at the hills in the distance. They both gazed at the dark green humps lying mute along the horizon, veiled in the tropical haze. It was a long moment before Bacon spoke again, but there was a new urgency in his voice.

"Mr. Johnson, I've had enough of Kizell and his devious chiefs. We've got to get out of this place and over there on the highlands immediately! They don't need any more time to think about that palaver. Will you and Mr. James go with me to see Prince Couber without Kizell tagging along? I'm going to demand a meeting with all the chiefs right away."

"Let me see how Mary's doing with Charlie. If she says she can spare me, I'll go. And I'll ask Fred James." Elijah's heart stirred as he left Bacon. Now maybe something can happen!

####

Elijah sat watching Mary turning restlessly on the crude bed he'd made for her. She'd come down with the fever after he'd gotten back from the trip with Fred and Bacon. For three days now he'd nursed her himself, telling Bacon he couldn't keep the night watch on the storehouses until she got well. Her attacks of chills were so bad that she was tired just from the shaking. Now she needed her sleep, so he sat quietly, thinking about the trip to see Prince Couber.

Bacon had hired a canoe from some Kroo boatmen, who rowed to the eastern tip of Sherbro Island, bringing them right up to the beach by Prince Couber's town. They went directly to the

54

prince's house and asked to see him. He came out after awhile and showed them to a meeting house next to his that was little more than a thatch roof held up by poles. In place of walls it had a low mud-and-stick bench built around the edges of the circular mud floor. Prince Couber said this was a 'palaver house' where the chiefs and elders met to decide important matters.

Bacon pressed the prince for a definite answer about the highlands for the colony, and Couber invited them to stay overnight, promising to hold the palaver the next morning. When they met in the morning in the palaver hall, Prince Couber listened patiently to about twenty head men and chiefs, finally announcing to Bacon about noon that all had agreed to make land available to the colony.

Elijah wanted to jump up and shout at the good news. But before he could even rise from his place on the bench Couber went on to say he would send for King Torra, who owned the highlands the colony wanted, and they would then have the grand palaver. Elijah could hardly hold in his anger at this, but waited while Bacon thanked the prince. They got in the canoe and returned to Campelar without further talk about the visit, not wanting the Kroo paddlers to hear their remarks.

"Well, we made some progress," Bacon said as they walked up the beach to Kizell's mat-and-thatch houses.

"Yeah, I hope that King Torra's goin' to come soon," Fred James replied.

But Elijah snorted in disgust.

"That's just more of their shifty ways! They'll just delay and delay. Grand palaver--humph!"

Bacon stopped to look closely at Elijah.

"How can you be so sure about that, Mr. Johnson? If this is the African way of doing things, we'll get our land sooner if we do what they say--wait while they have their meetings."

"I believed that first," Elijah said, "but not no more. Anybody slippin' around tradin' with the slavers behind our backs can't be trusted, nohow. Besides, there could be people in Freetown in on it , too."

"What d'ya mean?" Fred asked.

"Some of the British merchants prob'ly sells trade goods to the slavers, who takes it to the chiefs, who captures the slaves--somethin' like that."

Bacon shook his head.

"I understand the slavers bring their own trade goods as outward cargo from Europe or America. But you may be on to something."

"How's that?" Elijah said.

"The Freetown merchants might be conniving with the chiefs to keep us away because they don't want competition in regular trade when we get established."

"So what do we do?"

"Have our own meeting with King Torra when he gets here and tell him the advantages we can bring," Bacon said, getting warmed up to the idea. "You know, like legitimate trade and schooling and medical treatment for his people. But we have to keep Kizell out of it."

Fred James looked shocked.

"He's the one who's been helpin' us most!"

"I'm not so sure about him," Bacon said. "It seems like he has changed, and wants to delay us. Maybe he's tied up with the Freetown people someway."

They'd said goodnight and gone home to their own houses, knowing they had no real choice but to wait for King Torra to come. Elijah ended his reverie about the trip and bent toward his wife.

"Mary," he called softly. "Mary ... can you hear me, honey?"

She opened her eyes, and he watched her take in the room, the thatch roof above her, mat walls to the sides, and poles and sticks that held it together. He wasn't sure she knew where she was. Then her eyes focused on his face, and she smiled faintly.

"I...I hear you...Lije." Her eyelids wavered and closed again.

That seemed to be all she could say. She must be dead tired, he thought. He'd have to get some more medicine down her. He decided to mimic her own talk when she was taking care of him and the children, making a joke of it.

"You have to take your medicine now. And some soup. Every time you sweat the fever out you have to replace the water you lost. That's what Dr. Crozer said, remember?"

She'd said it over and over to them, until even Charlie could say most of it from memory. Elijah waited, and then started again.

"You have to take your ..."

She nodded slowly, so he slipped his arm beneath her shoulders and lifted her up.

"Here you go."

He pressed the cup to her lips and she sipped at it.

"Little bit more," he urged.

She sipped again, then turned her face away with a grimace. He remembered the bitterness of the bark and wine as he gently laid her back down. He kissed her, feeling that her lips and face seemed back to normal, the high fever gone.

"Such nasty stuff," she said, slurring the words. "How could I'ave given it to the chilluns?"

Elijah chuckled.

"An' me too! But it kep' us alive. I'll be back with the broth right away, honey."

He went out the back way to the kitchen--a thatch roof on poles they shared with their neighbors--and lifted the small iron pot of meat broth Mrs. Camaran had put on the fire. She was sitting on a wooden crate, cutting up yams for both families' supper. He thanked her as he poured a small bowl of broth and headed back to Mary's bedside.

"You take good care of her, Elijah," Ann Camaran called after him. "She nurs't so many of us, we figured she was never gon' get it herself. Guess she finally wore out."

He fed Mary the broth, spooning it into her mouth slowly, because she swallowed with difficulty. He coaxed her to take another and another, until finally she turned her head away.

"No more," she mumbled.

But she smiled to show her thanks. He put the spoon down and, kneeling on the floor awhile longer, held her close. Had he given her enough broth this time? She'd dry up from the fever attacks if he didn't get a'plenty down her.

Elijah helped Mary slide back down into the blankets, kissed her again, and held her hand while she lapsed into sleep. This was the fourth day of the attack--an endless cycle of chills, fever, sweating--each one leaving her still weaker. His own attack had been light. Lizzie and Lewis had been down two weeks, but Charlie had lingered on for another week after that. Now he remembered something out of the haze of his own fever, when she had been tending him night and day.

"Let me help, Mrs. Johnson, you're too tired," Carrie had pleaded.

But Mary had waved her off, and gone to the window sill for the big bowl of broth cooling there. She'd staggered and put her hand out quickly for support on the window frame.

"No, Carrie, there's others needs you. Matsy Crook's down now, so there's no one to take care of her lil' Maria. Take part of this over and feed it to them both--just keep spoonin' it in--then come back for some bark and wine."

Now tears rolled down Elijah's cheeks as he realized what Mary's stagger had meant--the sacrifice she'd made for them by giving up Carrie's help, letting no one but herself look after her own family. She'd forced herself to keep going until the danger to her family was over, and then collapsed, having given every last bit of strength in her body. And *he* was the one who'd gotten them into this--not *her*! She had followed him to Africa because he thought they would have a better life here for themselves and the chillun. He reached for her hand again, as if his touch would send a message that he loved her and would nurse her and bring her through, like she had done for them.

But her hand felt cool, and he slid his own to her wrist to feel her pulse. It was racing, and he realized that the dreaded fever cycle was starting again. He felt her hand grow colder, then her arms, and he knew her feet and legs would be cold soon. She began to shiver, the chill spreading through her body. Her quivering grew more violent, and he wanted to smother her body with more blankets, or build a fire, or lie down beside her and warm her body with his--but he knew he was powerless to stop it. Her body shook and her teeth chattered; she bent double as if to curl into a ball for warmth, and then straightened with a jerk as each muscle demanded its own freedom to shake furiously at full length. He knelt on the floor and bent over the bed, holding her down gently to keep her from falling off.

"Mary ... Mary ... Mary ..."

He kept repeating her name softly, lovingly, hoping she could hear him and know he was near. But the shaking went on and on, this time lasting longer than before, sapping her energy.

When the shaking finally subsided, Elijah knew only too well what would come next. With a low moan Mary groped for her forehead and pressed the palms of both her hands on her temples. He remembered the blinding headache that began the second stage. Then the waves of intense heat would come. He waited, afraid to look, but wanting to help her at the right moment, if he could. He put his hand on her forehead and felt it warming gradually. She was too weak to throw off the blankets, but she tried once as the fever built up. So he reached beneath the blankets, and when the could feel her body burning, he laid them aside, hoping to give her a little comfort.

Wracked by fever now, Mary rolled over slowly to cool one side and then the other of her body. Elijah saw the sweat pop out in droplets on her forehead as the fever in her brain rose higher. She became delirious and made strange sounds that frightened him. She perspired from all the pores of her body and he brought a towel to soak up some of it. But the sweat continued to flow, as if flushing out poisons from every pore. He realized finally that the moisture was helping to cool her burning body, so he stopped mopping it off her. Her bed became drenched and he could see she was losing far more water than he'd been able to replace with the broth he had fed her. He resolved to try harder to get her to take more water as soon as this cycle was over and she was rested.

Then he noticed she was quiet. He remembered the total exhaustion that followed each round of chills and fever, and moved to arrange the blankets and make her comfortable for a good long sleep. But he couldn't hear her breathing, and the silence in the room was an instant alarm.

"Mary ... Wake up!"

He slapped her face with quick little slaps. She didn't respond. Fear tore at his heart. Don't go! he thought. Don't ...

"Mary! ... Mary-e-e-e-e-e!"

His voice echoed in his brain in one long howl of anquish and he knew she was gone forever. He flung himself across her body and cried out in great wracking sobs that wrenched his heart in two.

6   Retreat to Freetown

Yonie
Sherbro Island
August 12, 1820

The night was awash in bright moonlight glistening off leaves of bushes and trees, and Elijah got up to walk around the storehouse once again. It was his night to guard the colony's supplies, and as he walked around the south end of the mat-and-thatch storehouse the breeze struck him. He lifted his arms and took a deep breath, enjoying cool caresses of soft wind blowing across the tip of the island from the Atlantic. What a difference, he thought, to be on a higher part of Sherbro Island!

It had been a good thing to move to Yonie, even if it was just a few miles from Campelar, and only fifteen or twenty feet higher. It got them away from the swamp and the stifling mangrove trees, and the bitter brackish water. This was the first action Coker had taken after all the agents died. Before he succumbed to the fever, Bacon had turned over the government supplies to Coker's care, so he was now the acting agent for both the Society and the U.S. Government. Elijah was proud of Coker's decision to go to Chief Sherbro for help.

Now they were the guests of King Sherbro, and Coker had arranged to pay rent for the houses in his village. Most of the emigrants still alive were getting well. They had gotten permission from the chief to build a storehouse, and brought all the food and medicine with them. Coker had asked Elijah and Fred James about which supplies to leave at Campelar and which to take to Yonie. Elijah felt good to have had his opinions respected on such matters.

Elijah stood awhile in the breeze and then continued his walk around the storehouse to sit once more on the empty wooden cask by the door. The deadly attack of fever the colony had just survived cost them dearly, he thought. Twenty emigrants, including Mary, dead, besides the agents and the sailors from the *Cyane's* barge. That made twenty blacks and nine whites killed by African fever and bad water at Campelar. Why had Kizell built his houses in such a low, sickly place? Elijah remembered how angry Kizell had been when Coker insisted on moving up to Yonie. Had

Kizell thought that since he had provided houses at Campelar for the emigrants when they arrived he should have been the head of the colony after the agents died? No wonder he fought the move out of Campelar.

Elijah heard a noise and jerked to attention, but the loud thump was one he'd heard before--probably just a big heavy breadfruit falling from the tree behind the storehouse. The tree was huge, maybe seventy feet tall, and the fruit--big as a cannonball--fell like a round from a British cannon. There's that noise again--another thump! He listened carefully. Couldn't be two breadfruits drop so close together, could it? What else thumped like that when it fell? A small barrel of cornmeal or a wooden box of salt dropped on the ground would! He was up and running silently on the balls of his feet.

Elijah sped around the corner, spied two small barrels on the ground, and looked up to see a man crawling out of a hole where the roof thatch had been pushed aside. The man saw him and leaped over his head, landing on the run. Elijah took after him, but the dark figure was lean and wiry, pulling ahead. They pounded down the hill toward some bushes and Elijah knew the man could get away in them. In desperation he dove for the man's heel, slapping it sideways so the robber tripped and fell headlong. Elijah was up and on him before he recovered.

"Got'cha, you stinkin' thief!"

Elijah grabbed the man's arm and twisted it around behind his back, pushing it up into a hammerlock until the man groaned. Then Elijah rolled him sideways to see his face in the moonlight. The dark blue mark on the sweating black forehead was a giveaway.

"You're a Kroo man aren't ya! What's your name?"

Elijah shoved the man's arm up until he moaned.

"What be your name! Tell me name or I break your arm off!"

"Not me! I do it for Mista' Wigfall! Not fo' me!"

"Wigfall? You say you do it for Wigfall?"

"He the one! Boss man, don' hurt me. I do it for him."

Elijah twisted again.

"What for you do it?"

"Fo' small, small part. Wigfall say he give me my part of ever'ting I fetch fo' him." Putting his knee on the man's arm, Elijah swung the other arm behind too, pulled off his own belt, and

61

strapped both the man's hands together in a double hammerlock. Holding the belt tight, he swung off the man and pulled him to his feet.

"C'mon, I'm goin' tie you up good with rope and take you to Coker in the mornin'!"

####

Coker had called them all together for a meeting under the shade of the big breadfruit tree in back of the storehouse. But Elijah saw that there were more than just the emigrants assembling--some natives from the village were showing up. He expected some, because he'd reported to Coker that he'd bring the Kroo man who'd stolen supplies for Wigfall. All the Kroo people in the village would want to support their own. But Elijah also saw at least a half dozen of the Sherbro headmen in the crowd--and Kizell was there, too! Had Coker invited them, or had Wigfall secretly sent for them? Something was up, and Elijah's nerves were getting edgy. Coker waited until everyone had settled themselves, and then he stood up to address them.

"I asked all the people from the *Elizabeth* to meet here to hear about something that is threatening our colony. We haven't completed negotiations for the highlands yet because we're still waiting for King Torra and the grand palaver. We hope he ... "

"They're not goin' to make any deal with you, Coker!" someone shouted. "They only want to deal with a real black man."

Coker's light-skinned cheeks blushed, and he looked for the heckler, but then went on.

"We hope he'll get here soon. Prince Couber says that King Torra owns the Bagroo highlands the agents spoke for, so the king must bring his headmen to talk the palaver. Until that time, we will stay here in Yonie. We'll ration the supplies carefully, so that each one gets his fair share ... "

"We don't need no ration business--there's plenty in the storehouse for all of us!"

Coker turned to look for the heckler again, and spoke directly at the place in the crowd where the voice seemed to come from.

"I hope the person who's talking there is man enough to stand up and make himself known. Then we can discuss his points in a reasonable way."

Wigfall stood up.

"That's right, we're ready to stand up!"

He motioned to others near him and they stood up, too.

"This here is a seven-man committee, Mr. Acting Agent, and some of us are officials of the gov'ment that Bacon appointed on the ship but never started."

Elijah could see Coker's face reddening, but he went on explaining to them patiently.

"Mr. Bacon made it very clear that the plan of government would start when we had land on which to build the center and start the colony. I'm afraid I can't recognize any government until we get the land."

There was a murmuring in the crowd and Elijah knew things were coming to a head. He strained to see the members in this new group, but Fred James and Terra Hall were all he saw besides Wigfall that Bacon had appointed. Peter Small and John Adams were there, and two others, but they hadn't been chosen as officials for the new government.

"We demands to have a say-so in what goes on here!" Wigfall shouted. "Specially on the food. We know you're holding back on us, and we won't stand for that!"

Everyone could see now that Coker's light mulatto complexion was red with anger, but again his voice seemed calm.

"You're forgetting that part of those supplies are from the U.S. Government and must be used when the Navy captures slaves and frees them. The Navy will bring them to the center we're supposed to build, and the food will be shared with them, too. Don't forget that."

"You're just makin' that up! The building stuff is for the Navy, not the food. The food is ours and you better give each of us a proper share."

The crowd took it up, and began to call out.

"That's right, Reverend!" "You can't hold back our food--it wouldn't be right." "We want a gov'ment right away to decide these things!"

Coker held up his hands and waved the crowd to silence.

"We'll see about that. But I called you here today to see what someone had done to the supplies in that storehouse. See that hole in the roof? Last night an attempt was made to steal some food, but the person was caught."

Coker paused, looking at Wigfall, and Elijah wondered if

Coker dared accuse him now that the crowd seemed to be on Wigfall's side. But Coker continued.

"The man who broke in was caught by the guard, Mr.Elijah Johnson, and reported to me. He is a Kroo man and I'd like you all to hear what this man says, so you can judge for yourself."

Coker turned to Elijah and waved him to come out in front of the people with the culprit. Elijah turned to the Kroo man sitting next to him, his arms now trussed tightly with rope.

"Alright, you got to stand up with me and tell the people what you said. Come on."

He helped the Kroo man to his feet and began to walk him toward Coker.

A great shout rose from the headmen, and a small band of warriors exploded from the bushes to the west of the breadfruit tree. Loud war cries and hooting blasts from an antelope's horn startled the emigrants. Rushing toward Elijah, the warriors wildly brandished their deadly-looking spears and broad knives curved like murderous Arab scimitars. Fear struck Elijah's heart as sunlight glinted from sharpened edges of knives cutting the air in wide arcs. He knew he had no defense against them and he thought he should run, but his feet wouldn't move.

Howling with savage blood lust, they rushed upon him. He saw their wild-eyed, menacing faces marked with blue war paint. The glistening black bodies were naked except for loin cloths girded with green palm leaves. As they reached him he instinctively tightened his grip on the Kroo man. A slashing war blade whistled down past his ear and narrowly missed cutting off his arm at the shoulder. He shut his eyes, rigid with fear, and heard other blades swish viciously around him.

The Kroo man was jerked from his grasp, but Elijah knew that if he reached out the slashing knives would cut off his hand. Holding his arms tightly around his chest, eyes clamped shut, Elijah cringed from the whistling blades. But nothing was touching him and he suddenly understood that the ferocity of the attack was a sham--the wicked accuracy of the warriors purposely avoiding his body. He opened his eyes to see the Kroo man being swept away in the center of the whooping band, the noise and shouting fading as it disappeared into the bush.

The crowd under the breadfruit tree sat in stunned silence. Elijah stood where he was, feeling his heart beating rapidly, too dazed to do anything but look at Coker, whose face was grim, and then at the broadly smiling Wigfall.

Coker's eyes sparked with anger and he stepped toward Wigfall, pointing his finger and shouting.

"You're trying to divide us, Wigfall! I'm following what the agents were doing because we must make the food last!"

"We'll decide that, not you, Coker!"

"No! I've been made responsible for both the Government's and the Society's supplies. I am the official Agent for both! I'll have no more of this mutinizing of the people, Mr. Wigfall! We must stand together as one people, do you hear?"

Without stopping, he swung to the headmen, pointing his finger at them, his face purple with outrage.

"And you! You imposters and blood suckers, always after rum and trinkets for palavers and more palavers! No more! We want land on honest terms, without your endless delay and hypocrisy!"

He was not done, and turning to Kizell, he bore down with an accusing finger pointed directly in the little man's face.

"You don't deceive me anymore, Mr. Kizell! I'm on to your tricks! You've connived with the chiefs and the traders in Freetown to delay the grand palaver, and now you're encouraging discord in our people. We'll not have you negotiate for us any longer!"

With a wild look at Elijah, Coker turned and stomped off toward his house.

"I've got to go to Freetown to consult with Governor McCarthy," Coker said. "I've suggested we all should go. Yonie isn't much improvement over Campelar and we're running out of supplies."

Coker paced nervously back and forth behind Elijah's house, hungrily sniffing the vapors from a soup pot. After Mary and Ann Camaran died, Elijah had become the family cook, and often invited Coker over.

"I wish we'd hear from the Society or the Government," Coker fretted. "If the Navy landed some recaptives here we couldn't take care of them. I need some advice, and soon!"

Elijah listened as he stirred the soup simmering on the open fire. He checked it off in his mind: okra, onions, tomatoes, yams, goat meat, and--he'd forgotten the peppers! Reaching in a basket, he threw in three small green peppers, and added another stick of wood to the fire.

"The people are split, Reverend," Elijah said. "Some of 'em talk of goin' to Freetown with you. I want to go, too--got to think of my chilluns. But some of the people won't do anythin' you say. They're the ones intending on stayin' here."

"I know, I know," Coker said, pacing again, but passing by to smell the soup's aroma. "Since I blew up that day, they don't want to hear anything more I say. I can't seem to make any decision or judgment they'll respect."

He threw up his hands in frustration.

"Maybe I should resign as Agent!"

Elijah put the ladle to his lips, taking a small sip, then swallowing it all.

"M-m-m-m--that African pepper is better'n our 'Merican ones. No, don't resign, Reverend. We haven't got anybody as good as you."

He took the ladle and filled six bowls setting on a board nailed across the top of an empty flour barrel. Then he put a spoon in each bowl.

"Carrie!" he called. "Soup's ready!"

She came out of the house silently with Elijah's children and lined them up. She was still grieving for Mary and the little Maria Crook she'd tried to nurse, Elijah noticed. After the children took their bowls of soup, Carrie picked up hers and led them off to the shade of a tree. Elijah sighed, thinking of Mary, too, and then turned to Coker.

"Maybe if you took part of us to Freetown and left the other part here where's they could be free as they pleases, you could get some rest. You need that."

Coker looked doubtful.

"What would happen to those that stay here? They argue with each other and refuse to be governed by any agent or regulations of the Society. And last Sunday they even wanted to be paid to attend service!"

"Maybe they need to be left to their selves," Elijah said. "Might learn something"

He offered a bowl of soup to Coker and then started on his own. Coker spooned in the food hungrily, but stopped to worry the matter again.

"Yes, but the Africans are watching. If we leave and the

others keep arguing and fighting, the Africans might pit some of our people against each other and steal all the supplies left."

Elijah laughed.

"If the food runs out, I bet our people will find a way to get to Freetown right away!"

Coker's face looked stricken.

"There's one other thing, Elijah. I don't want to go to Freetown if people think their threats are making me do it. That would make me seem like a coward."

"You're not a coward, Reverend. I saw you cuss out ever' one the other day. They had it comin', too. Made some of us respect you for standin' up to 'em."

"No, I mean the Africans. Yesterday one headman shouted at me that I should be cut up in pound pieces."

"Pound pieces?"

"That's right. It was so ridiculous I just ignored him."

Elijah put his bowl down with a clatter.

"Wait a minute, Reverend! You sure about that? Pound pieces?"

"Why, yes. Exactly those words. Why?"

"That's cannibal talk, Reverend! Don't you know that?"

Coker laughed.

"You're crazy. They don't have cannibals around here."

"Well, maybe not. But you saw those warriors the other day, didn't you? They cut people up with those big knives when the chiefs send them out to fight!"

"You mean, I should take that headman seriously?"

"Yes-sir! I'm goin' take it serious. We can't proteck you in this place--the muskets and powder is still stored in Campelar!"

"But that would be running scared ..."

"Don't make any difference! You're the commandin' officer of this expedition, and we don't want anything to happen to you! You better make plans to leave right away for Freetown!"

7   A Time of Testing

Georgetown, D.C.
December, 1820

Elias Caldwell's horse and carriage raced along the cobblestone paving of Bridge Street, puffs of the horse's breath streaming past its flanks in the freezing afternoon air. Elias' eyes nervously swept the west side of the street for several blocks. When he saw Francis Key's residence, he jerked the reins abruptly.

"Whoa, girl, whoa!" he shouted above the noise of the mare's clattering hooves, pulling hard on the reins.

He slowed for a more dignified approach to the entrance, not wanting to show his rising panic over the tragic news he'd received just an hour ago. Despite his efforts to calm himself, his hands shook while he tied the horse to the iron hitching post. Brushing aside the green and red holiday wreath hanging on the door, he swung the heavy brass knocker rapidly. Instantly he regretted the loud banging noises resounding on the other side of the heavy wooden door.

Steady now, he thought. Talk with Key before you alarm everyone. The door opened and a bald, white-fringed old negro manservant took his hat and coat, disappeared for a moment, and returned to usher him into Key's study. Key got up from a table cluttered with law books and papers, took off his spectacles, and came forward to shake Elias' hand.

"Elias! You look like you've seen a ghost. What's happened?"

"D-Do I look that bad?"

"Yes, you do. Come sit down."

Key motioned to a chaise lounge and Elias sank into it with a sigh. Key sat down beside him, looking closely at his face.

"What is it? I've never seen you so pale."

"Some dispatches just came from the Secretary of the Navy, Francis. I ... I can't believe it ... so many dead! It's a disaster!"

Key's mouth dropped open, the ruddy color draining from his face.

"Dead?" he whispered. "Who? You don't mean the ..."

"Yes. The colonists that went out on the Elizabeth."

"My God! Our first ship ... the pioneers ... how?"

Elias pulled a packet of letters and Navy dispatches out of his waistcoat pocket, his hands still shaking.

"Fever! All of them were attacked by it--nobody escaped!"

Key shook his head in disbelief. "All of them? What went wrong?"''

"The 'deadly African fever'--that's what the Washington newspaper warned about when the ship sailed--remember?" Elias almost shouted. "But we sent Dr. Crozer and thought that would take care of it!"

Elias held his head in both hands, his face twisted with despair. He rocked back and forth.

"Calm down, Elias," Key said. "Let's read those letters and get the facts first."

Key's voice of reason was just what Elias needed. He opened the packet and they read a long report from the Rev. Daniel Coker about the colonists' troubles and suffering. Then they started on the two Navy captain's investigative reports.

"Look! Here it is!" Key almost shouted. "Right here at the beginning of Captain Trenchard's report--an official list of all the deaths."

Elias shuddered. "I'm not sure I want to hear their names. I knew quite a few"

"Alright--I'll just count them up," Key said, running his finger down the list. "Let's see ... twenty colonists ... and all three of the agents ... and the midshipman ... and his six crewmen. My God! That's thirty dead!"

Key walked over to his study table and grimly wrote the deathtoll figures down. Then he looked up.

"Now what about the rest of the sad story Coker wrote about? Maybe that's more important than the deaths. The Board of Managers will have to hear about that, too."

"You mean the rebellion of the colonists? That couldn't be worse than the deaths!"

"It might. It could reflect on the competence of the freedmen to govern themselves."

Elias stood up and strode across to Key at his desk.

"Then we'd better leave that part out! Give them a chance--we've got a second ship about ready to go. The newcomers will help the survivors from the first ship. If we report everything now the Board might stop the whole experiment. It'll be bad enough just reporting on the deaths."

"I'm on that Board, too, remember. I don't want us to have to make any decisions without all the facts."

"But it will shock everyone, Francis! The Board members will lose faith in the whole colonization plan!"

Key rose and took Elias' arm, walking him back to the chaise lounge.

"You've got to have a little faith in the Board. Now let's have another look at those dispatches."

They sat again, each one taking a report, finishing it and exchanging with the other. Then they tackled the reports from junior officers. Finally Elias broke the silence, his eyes wide with new insight.

"So ... Dix believes the negotiations for land failed because slave traders at Gallinas influenced the chiefs not to sell our people any land."

Key nodded. "Where is Gallinas?"

"Not far from Sherbro Island, I think," Elias said, trying to recall. "Mills and Burgess said it's a vast river delta ... mmm, yes ... they said it has so many streams and heavily forested islands that slave traders hide their ships in it easily ... and it's rumored to be one of the largest slave depots on the coast."

Key slapped the lieutenant's report down on the coffee table.

"That isn't all! Mervine says the British wanted the negotiations to fail, too--to protect their own colony's trade from competition. And even Kizell wanted them to fail, so our people would have to stay on his property and pay him rent!"

They sat still, reflecting on it. Key shook his head in grim astonishment.

"What devilish intrigue to delude our people. No wonder the expedition failed."

"While the emigrants died of fever, bad water, and God knows what else," Elias moaned.

Key looked at Elias with sympathy.

"You're going to have a difficult time reporting it all to the Board of Managers, aren't you."

Elias sank back on the chaise lounge and covered his eyes.

"I suppose I have to. But it may be the end of the Society."

####

For Elias it was a long, sad meeting. With the members of the Board of Managers listening in hushed, incredulous attention, Elias stood for nearly an hour, reporting the shocking news from the dispatches. Other letters had come back from Africa, and he added their tragic details. When it was over he was drained, scarcely able to participate in the discussion that followed.

To his amazement, Elias heard the members approve of the second ship. The *Nautilus* was to sail immediately with supplies for the remnant of colonists and for thirty-three new immigrants. The meeting went on and on, and Elias was dimly aware that the Board was discussing a directive about new land to be negotiated for by new agents. This time there were to be two agents for the Society, and, with two new ones from the Government, this would assure a better outcome.

But a deep depression settled over Elias as he realized that the Board members weren't discussing the real problem. He wanted to interrupt and shout at them that there wouldn't be a second sailing if supporters learned that the first one had failed! The Society's work would collapse completely when the tragic deaths were revealed and contributors refused to send any more money for a lost cause. But Elias was numbed with fatigue and couldn't clarify his points enough to speak out, and the meeting droned on. When it was over he looked for Key, but he had left. Elias needed someone to talk to. He didn't want to go home alone and see the faces of the dead in his sleep--the ones who'd been sent to 'freedom' by the Society--only to die of fever.

"It's a critical time, isn't it?" a voice said.

"Critical. Yes, very," Elias mumbled.

He turned to see a visitor who had watched the Board meeting from the audience. It was Whittlesey, the Congressman from Ohio, and Elias invited him to stay over for bed and breakfast. They sat by the fireside in Elias' house that evening, sipping hot tea before bed, but Elias' brooding eyes focused only on the fire. Whittlesey, finally realizing why he'd been invited, tried to help.

"Don't mourn the dead, my friend. They've gone to their reward. You have to think of the living now. The Board said you must share the tragic news with all the auxiliaries and supporters and ..."

"I know!" Elijah burst out. "But it will destroy people's confidence in the Society!"

"Nonsense--the Society has a noble purpose and thousands

of freedmen who need help. And there are auxiliaries and churches and people from all over the nation who've joined it."

Whittlesey's voice was strong and vibrant now.

"Elias, send out your report to everyone. Don't just peddle the sad news--light a fire under them! Inspire them to persevere! You can say it better than anyone else."

Elias straightened up. Slowly a new thought took shape in his mind.

"Yes ... it's like a time of testing, isn't it? We didn't say we would succeed without troubles ... or that God would smooth the way. We ... we only said we believed this must be done to right a wrong ... that we thought it was God's will."

"That's it! That's the message we need--it will inspire us all. I heard the Board request you to get the report ready for a meeting next week. That'll be just in time for my return to Ohio. I'll take some copies back with me. Might even start an auxiliary there, too."

Whittlesey did take copies with him, Elias remembered a few months after the *Nautilus* was sent off. And the Society had collected enough money to make it possible, although not without getting deeper into debt for the larger cargo of supplies. The *Nautilus* landed in Freetown, the new agents conferred with Reverend Daniel Coker, and they decided to look for land farther away from the British colony. Two of the agents sailed down the coast and negotiated with a King Ben, chief of the Bassa people, at the mouth of a large river.

But when a copy of the treaty with the Bassa chief was sent back to the Society in Washington, the Board refused to ratify the treaty because King Ben had insisted on a clause that the colony could not interfere with his slave trade. Outraged that the agents would even consider such a treaty, the Board relieved them from their duties, and approved an agreement with President Monroe to replace all the agents with one man, a Navy surgeon. Dr. Ayres would serve both as the Government's agent and the Society's. But before the Board adjourned, they considered the matter of more carefully selecting freedman for colonization. Elias informed them of General Harte in Virginia and his plan to train his slaves for freedom and with skills for building the colony in Africa.

8   Training for Freedom?

Ronda Plantation, Virginia
August 13, 1821

"Goodnight, Cissie. Goodnight, Leslie."

Laura began backing out of the girls' bedroom, looking fondly at James Harte's two youngest daughters.

"Goodnight, Mama Laura," they both murmured, already snuggled in their canopied white bed.

Laura looked at Anna, who sat in front of a dressing table brushing her long dark hair and counting the strokes to herself.

"Goodnight, Anna."

The counting stopped, but Anna continued to stare into the mirror.

"Goodnight," she said, stiffly formal.

Laura closed the door softly, then went down the hall to check on the boys. She knew that Anna, old enough to remember her real mother clearly, could never warm up to a stepmother as the younger girls had. Laura sighed--it was the same with the boys. She repeated the goodnight ritual in their room and got a warm reply from little Jamie, but a barely audible one from Richard, Harte's oldest child.

She decided she would sit in the sewing room parlour a few minutes. It was her private preserve, where she could look down over the vast front lawn with its formal garden, and the gently curving driveway wending its way down the hill.

Laura was still not used to this beautiful mansion, built by the General for his first wife, Jeanne. She wondered what Jeanne would have done with the parlour if she had lived long enough to enjoy it. Did she sew? But she probably had been too busy, bearing the children and seeing them safely through their early years. Now it was up to Laura to rear them, and they were growing so fast!

Walking toward the parlour, she looked with admiration at the white bannisters and dark handrails on the sweeping staircase descending to the first floor.

"Everything built to perfection, with the best craftsmen coming all the way from Richmond," the General had proudly said.

She knew he was proud also of the tall white columns and the Greek architecture which he and Thomas Jefferson had designed into the mansion's facade. They both had studied at William and Mary College, and now as distant neighbors they still worked together on public projects like the University of Virginia's buildings.

Laura passed the master bedroom and saw Hattie turning down the bed covers for the night. She remembered from her last visit to the sick ones on slave row that Hattie had two children of her own that needed bedding down for the night.

"Hattie, I'm sorry you're having to stay late this evening, but the General's not back yet."

"Yas'm, Missy--I'se here."

Laura heard the tired resignation and watched Hattie's drooping shoulders and slow shuffle as she prepared the washbowl, towels, and pitcher of water. Hattie comes at six every morning like the other house slaves, she thought, yet the General expects Hattie to serve his meal tonight no matter how late he comes home. Conscience-stricken, Laura turned to retreat to her sewing parlour, a pain twitching at the back of her neck.

They both heard the swish of carriage wheels and chumping of hooves on the gravel driveway. Laura shifted her thoughts immediately to the General's needs. After his trip to Charlottesville, he would be tired and hungry.

"That's him now, Hattie! Go tell Sukey the General's home. Help her get his supper served and then you go home to your children. I'll be down in a minute."

She went in and sat at her dressing table to fix her hair, wanting to look her best for her new husband. What she saw pleased her. The lustrous brown hair, luminous blue eyes, flawless skin, and almost perfect lips were all gifts from her beautiful mother. Laura's slim body defied her age and she rejoiced in its comeliness now, fighting off the reminder of her childless first marriage. She felt a rising excitement as she patted an errant lock of her hair and dabbed perfume in the hollow of her neck.

She started down the staircase just as Harte came in the front door. He spied her as he gave George, the doorman, his coat and his tired face brightened. Walking quickly to the bottom step, he waited with a spreading smile on his face. Laura tripped down the steps to him, laughing with delight when he caught her in his arms and lifted her off the last step in passionate embrace.

74

Their kiss set their bodies astir, and they realized how much they missed each other after just three days apart. Emotions that had been banked for years of widowhood had come alive for both of them, and Harte's absences only made them more eager for their new love. Laura decided she wasn't going to begrudge him the days that he gave to his business and benevolent causes if he came back so amorous each time.

Suddenly seeing George at the door, Laura blushed and withdrew from Harte's arms. Harte followed her eyes, turning to the doorman, and then laughed heartily.

"Don't worry about George. He's part of the family!"

He turned her toward the dining room. "I'm hungry! What's Sukey got for a starving man?"

Harte sat at his accustomed place at the head of the table, but Laura said she'd eaten earlier with the children, and sat next to him to talk. Hattie served the food and then left. Alone, they eagerly shared what had happened in the last few days, still strangers enough to be constantly discovering new facets in each other as they chatted.

Harte asked about the children and Laura recounted their escapades and her strugggle to keep them at their studies each morning.

"I can't really be of much help to Richard and Anna--nor to Leslie--they're getting so advanced in their subjects." She laughed. "But Jamie and Cissie are still at my level!"

She got up to serve him some more pork loin and gravy from the covered china bowls Hattie left on the sideboard.

"I hope you hear from your Northern friend about another school teacher soon. James, do you really think you can set up a school for the children here?"

"Certainly. We'll have the best academy between Charlottesville and Richmond right here at Ronda. I've advertised in the *Richmond Enquirer* for pupils--not more than twenty. It won't be like when I was a boy. I didn't have any schooling until I was eleven years old."

"Why was that?" she asked.

"Ronda was an isolated backwoods area then. Except for my sisters, I didn't have anyone to play with other than the negro boys. But I learned a lot about the woods and streams that way-- we used to fish and trap animals."

Harte put down his fork, wiped his mouth with the damask

napkin, and sat back.

"It was some of the best learning I ever did. Got to know every inch of the place. Knew everyone on slave row, even some of the river men."

Laura smiled, understanding now the roots of his love for the land and people of Ronda. That was what she'd admired about him the first time he showed her the plantation. She went again to the sideboard to prepare for serving the coffee and dessert.

"Where's Hattie?" Harte asked.

"I let her go. You were so late, and she has her own children to see to at night."

"They take care of the small children, Laura! Mammy Liza feeds and watches them while the people work."

She saw his irritation, but knew her action was right.

"Not at night, James. The children go to their own mother's cabins. I've seen Hattie's two children--they're wonderful, bright little tykes. They could learn to read and write just like the rest of us. Must be others like them."

"Well, you've got your hands full now. Don't take on slave row."

"I'm just visiting the sick. You and your overseer don't have time for that. And that field driver you have--he's a vicious, cruel man, James."

Harte jerked around to her as she drew coffee from the big urn for a small china pot.

"Laura, stay out of the field hands' place! If you want to look after the house slaves, that's enough! It takes discipline to make the field hands do their work. I'll hear if there's any cruelty going on. Leave that to me!"

"Alright, James," she soothed. "Have your coffee and cake and tell me about your trip."

"Let's take it to the library. You're having some, too?"

"Yes. The fire's laid--you go light it and I'll bring the tray."

When they had settled by the fireplace, she cut thin slices of yellow pound cake and poured the coffee, its robust fragrance steaming up from the Dresden cups. She felt his eyes on her as she added the very small amount of cream and sugar he liked. When she handed it to him, Laura's heart skipped a beat as she saw the desire in his smiling eyes. But it was too soon.

"Tell me about the trip," she said. "You had two meetings?"

"Yesterday was about the university. Jefferson, Cabell, and

I have worked four years to get it started. Jefferson and I are in charge of construction--I've sent some of Ronda's best carpenters and masons over there sometimes. But ... "

He sighed, sipped his coffee, and started on the cake.

"Why the 'but'? Is something wrong?"

"Jefferson wants a great show of architecture, spending too much on the buildings' beauty. I thought we ought to keep the buildings simple so fees would be within the means of sons of small farmers, too."

"But Jefferson is the one who talks about how a democracy needs educated citizens!" Laura burst out. "How can that be done if it's too expensive for most people?"

"Exactly!" Harte looked surprised. "You've cut right to the heart of the matter."

He finished his coffee, asked for more, and continued.

"But Jefferson says the buildings should be the best example of the world's great architecture we can create--built to stand forever, I suppose. Very impressive, I'll admit, but not very business-like. And it means we have to raise more money."

"How?" Laura asked.

"Donations. I've renewed my pledge, like most of the others, but I still think we're putting too much into buildings."

Harte gave her a wry grin.

"Well, you don't want to hear all that."

He put his cup down, moved closer to her on the settee, and took her hand. She squeezed it, but removed hers to pour more coffee for herself.

"Yes I do! I like to hear about the things you do. What was the meeting today?"

"Now, that meeting went better."

He sat back, looking a bit smug.

"It was business men and planters who know the realities. We've started a James River Improvement Association to build some locks and a canal to make it more navigable. Most of us ship our crops and supplies on the river, so it's a sound investment. I bought some stock in the canal company and became a director."

Laura wasn't much interested, but he seemed so proud about it. "What's so important about the river improvements?" she asked.

"Everything! It's part of the economic change Virginia needs so badly. We have to restore the lands, stop depending just

77

on tobacco, diversify into grains and other crops--and animals, too--and bring in business and industry."

He stood up excitedly, but grasped the tongs and lifted a burning stick back on the fire.

"We can't do *any* of that without better transportation on the river!" He emphasized it with the tongs. "And when the country develops, I think slavery will die out. It can't ... "

"Slavery will die out!" Laura interrupted. She couldn't believe her ears. "Is that what you said, James?" She put down her cup and stared at Harte.

"Yes."

"Oh, James ... if it only will! It pains me every day to have any part of this system that calls people property! It's the only thing at Ronda that destroys my happiness. God must be punishing me through all the anxiety I have about our injustice to them. I've even prayed He'd show me what my duty is."

Suddenly she realized what she was saying. She gasped and put her hands over her mouth. She'd blurted out the thing that had lain secretly on her heart all the days since coming to Ronda! What would James think? She didn't mean to condemn him--he wasn't the mean, inhuman kind of slave holder. But he did own many slaves. She was confused, more miserable than ever, and burst into tears. Harte moved quickly to take her in his arms, patting her back gently.

"Laura, I inherited my slaves years ago. And I decided not to turn them out unless they're ready for freedom and there's a place for them to go. Now there is, and I've begun to get them ready."

She stopped crying, still too troubled to do anything but listen.

"There will soon be a place in Africa where freed slaves can go to build their own colony. An expedition has been sent out to begin it--I saw it leave New York myself."

Laura sat up, drying her eyes with her handkerchief. It was almost unbelievable--a special place for the slaves to go and make it their own country. "Oh, James! Can they really do it?"

"I'm sure they can. They'll need to learn a trade and be able to read, write and cipher. And they must have good character, or they won't be able to survive the hardships in a new land."

She was beginning to get excited. "Are any of your people ready yet?"

He explained about the slaves who had been taught by the white carpenters, masons, and others who came to build the mansion.

"So that's how the mansion was built! That makes it even more beautiful to me, James." She kissed him joyfully. "So you're ready to begin teaching them to read, write, and cipher! But can character be taught?"

Harte thought a moment.

"If they can read Scriptures they'll soon learn the virtues they need."

"What kind of virtues are you talking about?" she pressed.

"Well ... thrift, self reliance, temperance, loyalty to their colony and each other."

She smiled happily and burst out with what she'd dreamed about since coming to Rondo. "So we need a school and chapel for the slaves!"

Harte laughed. "Whoa! Slow down! If we set up a school for slaves everyone in the South will turn against us. Even in the North there aren't any regular schools for freedmen."

"But what we do on our own plantation is no one else's business! Besides, if our people go to Africa, they won't be a threat to the South and its so-called property."

"There isn't a person in the entire South who'll teach a slave," Harte objected. "We won't be able to hire anyone. They'll be afraid of public reaction."

Harte's face showed his apprehension, but Laura pressed on. "Then why not get a teacher from the North, just like you're going to do for the children and the academy?"

"Well ... if there were a chapel for slaves, there could be some tutoring in it weeknights. We might even use the same teacher for the academy and the slaves, if she wanted to do it."

It wasn't a real school for the slaves, Laura thought. Just some teaching at night in a chapel. But maybe that's all to ask for now--a real school might come later.

"But don't get so excited you tell it all over the countryside, Laura. We would have to be very quiet about it."

"I'll be very quiet about it--I won't talk to anyone. Oh, James, you've had this plan to free your slaves all this time. I'm so proud of you! I love you!"

She kissed him fervently, ready for him now. His eyes flamed with desire as she let him take her up the winding staircase.

9   High Stakes Game

Cape Mesurado
December 14, 1821

Elijah was standing on the *Augusta's* deck as the sun rose, admiring the dark green cape still shrouded in mist. A high, heavily forested peninsula jutting into the sea, it helped form a shallow bay in which they'd anchored for three days. He smiled as he thought of their building the colony on top of the Cape. They would clear a place up there and the breeze would blow across it from the sea at night and from the land in the daytime. After the low, muggy swampland at Sherbro, it was like a miracle. There would be no fever, and it would probably save the lives of those new immigrants from the *Nautilus* still waiting in Freetown.

Today the negotiating party would go on shore to see King Peter again. Dr. Ayres, the new agent, had told Elijah to be ready, and they would join Lieutenant Stockton and two of his officers at eight bells. The *USS Alligator* was anchored a few leagues farther out in the bay, and each morning Stockton and a small crew had rowed by in the longboat to pick them up and go in for an audience with the King.

"One more day will do it! We'll make 'book' tomorrow, for sure!" Stockton had said yesterday as they came back to the ships a third time.

But it was an old story to Elijah--King Peter promising to see his headmen and to meet again tomorrow, accepting the rum and tobaccco gift with a greedy gleam in his eyes. Elijah remembered the shifty chief at Sherbro Island the first time they tried to buy land; and then the trip to Grand Bassa with new agents, where King Ben had done the same thing. And now Ayres and Stockton were so sure they'd get a treaty for this Cape Mesurado in two or three palavers! But Elijah knew from experience that African chiefs were too crafty to make a deal that quick. After the colony gets started, he thought, we'll have to learn how to deal with the Africans ourselves. He ought to watch both sides in their negotiations today--it would be his own apprenticeship for the future.

####

"The King promised to meet us here this morning--where is he?" Stockton asked, looking around. "Where is anyone?"

They stared in disbelief at the empty hall on the beach at Krootown where the other palavers had been held. There were no headmen around as on previous meetings, so Ayres went over to an old man lounging in a nearby shed.

"Where is everybody?" he asked.

"The king go back to his home. He say he not comin' today."

"But he told us to meet him for palaver right here--this morning!" Stockton burst out.

Elijah had not seen Stockton this upset before. The negotiating party waited for the old man to answer Stockton, but he refused, looking off in another direction.

"Why?" Ayres asked calmly. "Why isn't he coming today?"

The old man turned to look at Ayres, as if checking to see if he was angry, too.

"He say he won't let you have land."

"What! He told us he'd make "book" today!" Stockton shouted.

The old man shrugged his shoulders.

"That's all he say--no land for you."

Ayres and Stockton walked off a ways to talk privately, and Elijah and the two junior officers waited. Ayres and Stockton seemed to agree on something and returned quickly.

"We're not giving up now," Stockton said. "We've come too close. We'll beard the king in his own den." He turned to one of the officers. "McKean, find a guide in Kroo town who can lead us to the king's place."

A Kroo man came back with the officer in half an hour, carrying a long machete knife in his right hand. He was barefoot and stripped to a loin cloth, his sinewy muscles rippling under oiled black skin. The distance was far, he said, and after haggling over a fee, he motioned the party to follow and set off briskly. The path narrowed quickly, the guide slashing at dense thickets of bushes, clearing the way. Marshy ground appeared and soon they waded into slimy mud and warm, fetid water. It sucked at their feet and bubbled around their knees, giving off foul-smelling swamp gas. Rotting grass and reeds beneath the green scum dragged at their legs, slowing everyone in the party, but finally they reached solid ground. They stopped a moment to slough off the mud and look for leeches on their legs, then moved into tall trees.

No one in the party spoke a word as they entered the silent rain forest. A high canopy of branches and tangled vines shut out the sunlight and in the semi-darkness the forest seemed alien and menacing to Elijah. He felt trapped in the humid, sticky mass of jungle growth pressing all around the narrow path. The Kroo man hacked viciously at a rotted branch fallen across the path, the chopping sounds announcing the invading party's presence. Startled birds took flight screaming, and monkeys erupted in screeching chatter, swinging along above their heads.

The Kroo man seemed fearful of the forest.

"Come along, come along--the debil catch us," he urged when any of the party seemed to slow the pace.

Slashing at dangling branches and overhanging vines, the sweating guide moved through the forest's undergrowth, driven by his fears. In about three hours and as many shallow rivers forded, they broke through to grassland. The bright, open sky caused them all to squint until their eyes adjusted, and before them lay King Peter's village set on a small rise. A high mud wall circled the entire settlement, and the opening was narrow and low, forcing everyone to bend down when passing through.

Their guide was kept outside the wall, and one of the headmen from previous palavers at the beach conducted the party in to a mat-and-thatch reception hall spread with floor mats arranged in a circle, as if they were expected. They sat down where the headman indicated.

"Look at the masks up there!" Elijah exclaimed in awe.

"No look up!" a headman cautioned, waving his hands between Elijah's face and the masks hung in dark recesses of the pole rafters above them. "Not good to see! That be secret Poro business!"

What was 'Poro business'? Elijah wondered, as they waited for King Peter to appear. The hall began to fill up noisily with villagers and headmen, and he saw two men bring in a large chair which they placed across the circle from the visitors. Finally the king came in, dressed in his blue and white homespun robe. He sat down in the chair, his headmen standing behind him.

"What you want that land for?" the king's voice boomed out in the hall.

The abrupt, angry tone of it startled both Stockton and Ayres. The king stared fiercely at them, and finally Ayres began to repeat what he'd said at the previous meetings.

"We want the land for the American black people to have a place to build their houses, make farms, and raise their families. If they can make their settlement on your land they will make fine trade with you ..."

"These people not telling the truth!" someone shouted, cutting Ayres off. "King Ben give his son to them for learn book and they killed him! If we give'em land they cut our throats and bury us like they do to his boy in Freetown!" The crowd burst into outrage at this.

"No, that's not true!" Ayres shouted, trying to be heard above the roar of the crowd. "That boy died at school in Freetown and we've brought a witness on our ship. We'll be taking him down to King Ben's to explain first hand and make satisfaction according to your custom."

Some of the people were translating Ayres' version of the story to their neighbors, and the shouting began to die down. King Peter raised his hand and the silence was immediate. He motioned for Ayres to continue.

"You can send to the ship and see the boy who saw King Ben's son die of fever," Ayres said. "After we finish the palaver here we are going to Bassa and ..."

A man stepped into the center of the circle, pointing at Ayres and Stockton accusingly.

"I saw the black people on the ship yestiday. They' the ones who quarrel too much at Sherbro Island--they fight and make bad palaver last year. They not good people!"

The crowd responded with more angry cries and everyone stood again to hurl accusations. Another man stepped in and pointed directly at Stockton, shouting to be heard.

"He the one who stopped the Frenchman's ship for King Peter's slaves! He stopping King Peter's trade with slavers!"

It infuriated them and Elijah thought a riot would break out. But Stockton got up slowly, turned, took Ayres by the arm, and walked across the circle to seat Ayres on one side of King Peter. He seated himself on the other side. The shouting rose to a deafening clamor and some in the crowd began to brandish spears and knives. Again Stockton stood to his feet, and in full view of everyone he carefully unbuttoned his Navy frock coat, easing a small derringer pistol from his waistcoat pocket and handing it to Ayres. He slipped another out and, lifting it high for the crowd to see, calmly held the muzzle to King Peter's head. The angry crowd stopped instantly, shocked into silence.

Stockton told them coldly that he captured the French ship because it fired on him when he tried to board it to check its papers.

"They fired at me, so I fought them and took their ship! I will not allow the French or anyone else to make a fool of me. But now King Peter wants to make me a fool!"

Stockton cocked the pistol, looking down at the nervous king sitting in the throne chair. The king's courtiers cowered in horror. Elijah saw Stockton's eyes flash with anger, but his voice was controlled, hard as iron.

"For three days King Peter tells me he will make book for land. Three days he drinks up my rum and takes my tobacco. Now King Peter says we can't have land. This is fooling with me!"

Stockton tensed his arm, holding the muzzle tight to the king's head, and the crowd gasped. Then, with slow deliberation Stockton uncocked the pistol, put it back in his pocket, and turned to the crowd. His voice was softer, but Elijah heard his exasperated tone.

"We come in peace, not as enemies. We want land for our American black people--they're your brothers! There will be plenty of fine trade when they get settled. It will be good for both sides."

He stopped, looked expectantly at King Peter, and waited.

The crowd of headmen and villagers stood respectfully while the king thought on it. Elijah breathed a prayer that Stockton would give the king enough time. This was a crisis in the negotiations, and the king would need room to save his dignity.

King Peter consulted briefly in tribal language with his courtiers, and then one of them faced Stockton.

"King Peter say he talk to more kings, and see you at beach to make book tomorrow."

"What time?" Stockton asked.

"Same time as before."

"We will be there--on time." Stockton nodded stiffly, turned, and signalled McKean to lead the way. The silent crowd stood aside as the little negotiating party took its leave.

Elijah reflected on what he'd seen as they made the long trip back to the beach. Was it the ugly rumors that had caused the king to break off the talks on the beach and come back to his own village? If so, Ayres and Stockton had cleared up the rumors. But the old king had a cunning mind, and maybe he had set a trap for

Stockton by baiting him with false promises and then deliberately retreating to his tribal seat.

"Come along, boss mens! The debil catch us! Come along!" the Kroo guide urged the party. They followed him through the forest.

Stockton had got out of the trap by his pretense to be unarmed, surprising the king with his two little 'pea shooters' and a well-timed threat, Elijah mused. Maybe King Peter did give in to Stockton's threat. Maybe. More likely, he was thinking of the Navy ship sitting off Cape Mesurado. That's probably why the shrewd old king had known it was time to get down to some serious land palaver again. Stockton wasn't just a man with two guns in his pocket--he was the captain of a warship, and King Peter probably wasn't sure just what that power might do to his coastal kingdom. His kingdom depended on trade--both slave trade and goods.

"Blast the slimy, stinking place! Why don't they make a foot bridge here?" Stockton fretted.

They'd come out of the forest and faced the swamp again. Elijah entered the slimy water with the rest of the party, intent on his own thoughts.

They would be back on the beach soon, the longboat waiting to take them out to the ships. One more day of palaver finished--but tomorrow would be the real showdown. Who held the strongest hand--the captain with power on the sea or the king with power on the land? Tired as he was, Elijah was excited. The colony would have to do its own negotiations some day, and watching these two men bargain was a good way to learn how to do it.

But there was still something nagging in the back of Elijah's mind. The Sherbro people and these people lived far away from each other, but somehow these knew about the quarrels and confusion at Campelar and brought it up here in front of King Peter. How had the news gotten here? Was there a secret link? Maybe it was the secret society he'd heard about on Sherbro--the Poro. They have the Poro here, too--he'd seen the masks hidden away in the dark, smoky pole rafters of King Peter's palaver hall. He'd have to study this Poro thing out.

10 Treaty for the Cape

Krootown
Cape Mesurado
December 15, 1821

Elijah winced quietly and shifted his position, rubbing his legs as much as he could without losing his dignity. They'd sat in a circle on the mats in the palaver hall all morning and his muscles were cramped. This palaver had lasted four hours, beginning with the usual tobacco and rum gifts and verbal sparring between Stockton and King Peter. Finally King Peter had reluctantly asked Stockton and Ayres what land they wanted and the entire assembly of chiefs, princes, and headmen had gotten down to the business of agreeing on the land that was to be deeded. After that had come the making of the long list of items to be paid for it. All of it had laboriously been written down and then rewritten again and again until all were satisfied.

Elijah wanted to get up and stretch, but he dared not move because the mulatto scribe, John Mill, was giving the treaty its final reading and everyone in the palaver hall was listening closely. They hung on his words as he read the treaty slowly, loud enough for all in the circle to hear.

"KNOW ALL MEN, That this Contract, made on the fifteenth day of December, in the year of one thousand eight hundred twenty-one, between King Peter, King George, King ..."

It had to be translated into the languages of the two tribes, whom John Mill called the Dey and Mamba peoples. He stopped at the end of every sentence, waiting for the two translators, each in turn, to interpret it to their people. The reading was going so slowly that Elijah's mind wandered as he rubbed his aching legs. He remembered how simple the matter had seemed last night.

Stockton had come over to the *Augusta* after the evening meal to talk with Elijah and the other colonists about the land they would ask for. Stockton and Ayres suggested the cape with its long peninsula and the island in the Mesurado river mouth, because together they gave control of the shallow bay. It was a perfect spot for the colony and the station for recaptives, as well as a good watering place for the Navy's ships on coastal duty. Elijah pointed out that the tip of the cape would be a good place to have a few cannon to protect the bay and the island. James Blake said he'd heard this was the best spot for trade on the whole coast. All seven of the colonists agreed with Stockton and Ayres' suggestion, and then they'd asked Elijah to say a prayer for the negotiations. It was the first time he'd ever been asked to say one. He felt good afterward, because he still wanted to become a preacher some day.

"...WITNESSETH, That whereas certain persons, Citizens of the United States of America, are desirous to establish themselves on the Western Coast of Africa ..."

It sounded just like a proper lawyer had written it, but neither Stockton or Ayres, nor any of the colonists had such training. They had all been surprised this morning to learn that the mulatto scribe could do that, until it came out that John Mill had been sent to England by his father, an English trader, when Mill was just a boy. Mill was beginning to study law, but cut his education short and returned to Africa after his father died and left no money to continue it. Stockton and Ayres were impressed with John Mill and his trading establishment on the little island in the middle of the Mesurado River. But Elijah was suspicious because of the slaves he'd seen on the island earlier when he'd gone down the coast to Grand Bassa with Andrus.

"...and have invested Captain Robert F. Stockton and Eli Ayres with full powers to treat with and purchase from us the said Kings, Princes, and Headmen, certain Lands, viz: ..."

Now the treaty was coming to the important part, the description of land. Elijah had watched Stockton become completely frustrated earlier when he'd tried to tell the kings what land was wanted by the colonists. The Africans didn't use miles for distance nor degrees for points of the compass and the palaver council had broken down in confusion as everyone tried to talk at once. Stockton's impatience flared and King Peter stopped the palaver by raising his hand. In the sudden silence he fixed Stockton with his angry eyes, brows frowning sternly beneath his wooly white cap of hair.

"We no sabby white man talk! We talk country fashion. Bye m' bye we tell you!"

His rebuke was plain, and Stockton's face turned pink.

"Be patient, Captain," Mill said quietly. "It must be talked our African way--and that is how it will be in the treaty."

Stockton sat quietly, a chastened look on his face, as King Peter asked every chief or headman around the circle to speak in his turn.

When everyone was finished, King Peter considered, then turned to the scribe and instructed him briefly. John Mill wrote on the treaty paper while they all sat silently, listening to the scratch of his quill pen, watching him dip into the ink bottle three times. He finished, looked up at them, and laid the pen down on the little pan before him. There were broad smiles around the circle, and then the palaver had gone on.

"...Dozoa Island, and also all that portion of Land bounded north and west by the Atlantic Ocean, and on the south and east by a line drawn in a south-east direction from the north of the Mesurado river ... "

Elijah had been dumbfounded on the first reading of the treaty to hear the vague way the Africans described what Stockton attempted to explain so exactly. Who would be able to say specifically what the chiefs meant? But that was the way it must be.

"We, the said Kings, Princes, and Headmen, being fully convinced of the Pacific and Just views of the said Citizens of America, and being desirous to reciprocate the friendship and affection expressed for us and our people, DO HEREBY, in consideration of so much paid in hand, viz: ..."

Elijah remembered how the council had determined the price for the land. King Peter allowed every chief or headman in the circle to say what articles he wanted in payment for the land, and John Mill called out the items in English. Elijah had learned quickly what goods the Africans considered important and valuable.

"... Six muskets, one box Beads, two hogsheads Tobacco, one

cask Gunpowder, six bars Iron, ten iron Pots, one dozen Knives and Forks, one dozen Spoons, six pieces blue Baft, four Hats, three Coats, three pair Shoes, one box Kerchiefs, three pieces Calico, three Canes, four Umbrellas, one box Soap, one barrel Rum ..."

After the list had been finished, King Peter suddenly remembered something and he burst out in alarm.

"We no sell the Cape! That be devil bush--big, big palaver come on my head for that one! My people kill me, then my women cry plenty-o!"

King Peter switched to an African language and Elijah couldn't understand the rest of it, but he saw real fear in the old king's eyes. Elijah's heart tripped and his chest tightened at the thought that they were going to lose it all right here. He glanced at Stockton, thinking he'd be furious, but Stockton's face was controlled, waiting it out, so Elijah covered his anxiety as best he could. King Long Peter, a nephew, said something to the old king, and then engaged two other kings, Zoda and George, in a long conversation. They both turned and spoke to King Peter, and finally he nodded and gave instructions to their scribe.

"The price has just gone up, Captain," John Mill said quietly. "Part of the Cape has been a sacred place for the devil man--what you whites call a witch doctor. Many people will have to be paid off to move such a place. Maybe it can't even be done."

Again King Peter queried the chiefs and headmen, and each one in turn named more goods in payment of this new thing. All items were carefully recorded by Mill.

"... And to be paid, the following: three casks of Tobacco, one box Pipes, three barrels Rum, twelve pieces Cloth, six bars Iron, one box Beads, fifty knives, twenty Looking glasses, ten iron Pots different sizes, twelve Guns, three barrels Gunpowder, one dozen Plates, one dozen Knives and Forks, twenty hats, five casks Beef, five barrels Pork, ten barrels Biscuit, twelve Decanters, twelve glass Tumblers, and fifty Shoes, ..."

With the details of payment finally settled, Stockton had raised the matter of guarantees, and King Peter had become angry.

"Why you say that?" he burst out, forgetting his interpreters and drawing himself up with offended dignity. "I be big past all kings of this part of country!"

His arm swung in a quick sweep of the circle.

"See my people--they tell you! What I say is so!"

"No, no! I don't mean that!" Stockton hastened to say. "You are the big king! A mighty king! But is this treaty strong? How permanent--how long will it last? You must say something about that in the paper."

Elijah saw the anger in King Peter's face change to a quizzical look, and the old king turned to the scribe with a question. John Mill seemed to know what was needed and spoke to the patriarch in his own tongue. But another king in the palaver circle felt the offense and took it up. Elijah could see outrage in King George's eyes as he erupted with a long tirade, shaking his fist toward Stockton.

But again King Long Peter conversed with the young Zoda, and then turned to his uncle, who heard them out and instructed John Mill briefly. Elijah understood how the old king's nephew, Long Peter, served as his advisor and go-between, but the really strange matter was why the youthful Zoda's opinion seemed to carry more weight than the gray-bearded King George's. Elijah wished he knew their language, but more important, why Zoda was deferred to sometimes.

"... FOREVER CEDE AND RELINQUISH the above described Lands ... and WE, the said Kings, and Princes, and Headmen do pledge ourselves that we are the lawful owners of the above described Land, without manner of condition, limitation, or other matter ..."

King Peter had seemed annoyed that Stockton's demand for a guarantee was so easily accepted by his own chiefs, and he countered with a demand of his own.

"S'pose we give this land to you! Then you must make promise to we!" He struck his chest hard. "You no make war on we--on our trade!"

Elijah's heart jumped and he sucked in air, suspending his breathing, knowing they had finally come to the problem on which the whole treaty might founder. What did the king mean by 'trade'? Did he include slave trade, or was he just talking about goods trade? Stockton, as a captain of the Navy's African Squadron, was sworn to stamp out the slave trade. How could he answer the king now, and still get the land?

90

"My Government respects all lawful trade ..." Stockton said.
Elijah released some of the air in his lungs tentatively.

"... and our people come in peace and friendship, not war. They won't disturb your people if you don't disturb them ..."

Was it enough? Elijah wondered. He looked at King Peter's face warily. But Stockton had more.

"We can pledge this in good faith on behalf of our people."

King Peter sat silent for a long time, his eyes on the fly switch in his hand as he laid its long bristles out straight before him on the mat. But finally he looked up and nodded to John Mill. The scribe had obviously formulated it in his own mind already, and he began his scratching with the quill pen again.

"...The contracting Parties pledge themselves to live in peace and friendship forever; and do further contract not to make war, or otherwise molest or disturb each other ..."

Ayres had jumped in then with a final request--would the king's people be willing to build six large houses for the colonists to live in when they came? Ayres promised to pay the king for the labor and materials, saying the houses could be located anywhere he chose on the land contracted for. Elijah thought it was bad to make an open contract like that, but he saw the smiles on the faces of the kings and headmen and realized that this was a sweetener on the deal that would make them all happy and a little more wealthy. King Peter smiled briefly, then instructed Mill to write it down and finish the paper.

"... IN WITNESS whereof, the said Kings, Princes, and Headmen, of the one part; and Captain Robert Stockton and Eli Ayres, of the other part; do set their hands to this Covenant, on the day and year above written."

The final reading of the treaty was finished and Elijah started to get up to stretch his aching muscles. But King Peter solemnly lifted his fly switch up high, holding it still until everyone was silent. Elijah dared not move. The king waved his fly switch around the circle, and then laid it down with a ceremonial flourish, the handle pointing toward the center of the circle.

"Palaver set!" he said.

"Palaver set!" his councilmen echoed in unison.

Elijah watched as the chiefs began signing the treaty. John Mill set the little table in the center of the palaver circle and King Peter went to it first. With great solemnity he took the quill pen from John Mill and made a mark at the bottom of the paper.

"King Peter, his mark," announced Mill, writing the words beside the old man's large cross mark.

King George was second. Elijah smiled to see King George ranking next in line to the old patriarch--probably because he had spoken the longest and loudest in the palaver. Now, who would be third, Elijah wondered--Long Peter, the old king's nephew, or Zoda? It was Zoda who came up to the little table, took the quill pen from the hand of the scribe, and made his mark.

"King Zoda, his mark," intoned Mill, dipping and writing again.

Zoda had scrawled his mark with a flourish, leaving no doubt that he had part of the power that made this deed for land official. His pride showed in the lordly way he wore his blue and white chief's robe and carried his rare elephant tail fly switch. As Zoda returned to his place in the circle, Elijah pondered again why such a young man had this much authority in a council of old, powerful chiefs.

A thought struck Elijah--did his name mean he was a *zo*, or had inherited that title and would some day become a leader in the Poro? If what Elijah had learned on Sherbro Island was true, the Poro was a powerful secret society that provided a link between tribes when a great danger threatened them all. Maybe that was what he was beginning to see happening now--and Zoda might be part of it. Elijah decided to remember that for the future.

Now it was Stockton and Ayres' turn and they added their signatures with the same ceremonial flair as the others, John Mill confirming them solemnly.

"Captain Robert F. Stockton, his signature."

"Dr. Eli Ayres, his signature."

The treaty signed, everyone stood up and began shaking hands the African way, snapping fingers as they withdrew their hands, and repeating the magic words, smiling with great satisfaction.

"Palaver set!" "Palaver set!"

Elijah stood, grateful at last to unbend, and joined in, milling around the palaver hall reciting the ritual phrase to each person he met. "Palaver set!" He felt himself grinning like a cat as

92

the joy of it lifted his spirits. "Palaver set!" Yes, it was set! Done! Finished! A contract for the colony! His mind soared. After almost two years of voyages and deaths and palavers and trickery and deceit! And he'd seen it all! "Palaver set!"

Suddenly he was facing Stockton. They stuck out their right arms to each other and grasped hands firmly, squeezing hard.

"Mr. Johnson," Stockton said as a smile broke across his stern face. "It looks like your people might have a home at last."

"I sure hope so." Tears welled in Elijah eyes as he swallowed hard. "Thanks for not givin' up too soon, Captain!"

11 A Remnant

Freetown
Sierra Leone
January 1, 1822

"That Lott Carey sure is homely. Hard to listen to a preacher with a face like his," John Bannon said.

He wanted to start a conversation with Carrie Reeves as they lagged behind the others on the path back to the Le Fevre Plantation. Just south of Freetown, the plantation was their temporary headquarters until an expedition by the new agent, a few colonists, and a Navy captain could find land for the colony.

"You hadn't ought to say a thing like that!" Carrie protested. "He's a good man--comin' out here to be a missionary to Africans."

John reached for her hand, sure that none of the other colonists walking back from Sunday morning service would look behind to see them. But Carrie frowned and jerked her hand away.

"You need to hear a lot more of his good Baptist preachin'. Might make you behave!"

John smiled, teasing her.

"You going to take up with Baptists now? Elijah won't like that! He's a Methodist, like Reverend Coker. Besides, I never heard of a black missionary."

"Well, Daniel Coker's a missionary, too!" Carrie retorted.

"Never heard him say so. But I guess he does like to preach to the Africans. Maybe that's why Governor McCarthy made him superintendent of a new recaptive village."

"So he's not goin' with us to Cape Mesurado?"

"Don't think so. Would you if you were given a fine job like that?"

"Humph! Well, Lott Carey is going!" Carrie flounced away smugly as John tried to put his arm around her shoulder.

"We'll have one good preacher, at least," she said.

John ambled along beside Carrie, wondering why she was snapping at him. He'd been the only one around to listen and comfort her when she was lonely. John looked ahead on the path where Lewis and Charlie Johnson trotted excitedly beside their pa, and Lizzie rode on Elijah's shoulders. All three were chattering happily, proud that their pa was chosen to go on the expeditions to find land for the colony. Now Elijah was back and they would all move soon to the place he had helped to find. Dr. Ayres, the new agent, had said an advance party of men would leave tomorrow to clear land for the colony on Cape Mesurado.

John looked down at Carrie beside him, admiring again her lustrous coffee-colored hair braided and coiled round her head. Her smooth light brown skin molded a slender neck and shoulders. She carried herself with pride, her lithe young body moving gracefully. He watched the swelling curves of new womanhood strain against the bodice of her dress at every stride. Firmly rounded hips swayed her skirt bewitchingly, and the warmth of desire began within him. In the two years the colony had searched for land she was slowly becoming a woman--a beautiful one, too. He was swept by a physical desire that left him breathless, and suddenly he knew he must have for his own. Now was the time to tell her what he'd planned.

"We're leaving tomorrow for the Cape to start the colony. I'm going to begin my trading business as soon as we get the place cleared, and it won't be long 'til I'll be rich enough to build us a fine house--if you'll be my wife."

"Tradin' business? You ha'n't got enough money to start a hen house, John Bannon!"

Carrie meant her voice to be scornful, but she looked up at him with a fresh interest as the words 'fine house' caught in her mind. John had talked of merchant business so many times, but she'd thought it was just youthful dreams. Now she stopped in the path and looked at him in a new way. He was tall and beginning to fill out, with a 'high yaller' color that made it easy for him to be accepted by white people. He was healthier than most of the colonists, and had survived two fever seasons--one on Sherbro and the last one right here in Freetown. This time they'd lost three more white agents and seven colonists from the fever, most of them from the *Nautilus*.

But Carrie had seen what John could do when they'd needed a man who knew figures and could read and write. He'd helped Agent Wiltburger keep records of the supplies after Andrus and Winn died and Ephraim Bacon went back to the States sick. John had told Carrie that he'd learned storekeeping from his master, a river boat merchant in Maryland who'd allowed him to work extra hours to buy himself free. Now Carrie cocked her head and squinted at him in the noonday sun. John just might turn out to be a good store owner in the colony after all--and then he really would be able to build a fine house.

"Even if you know store business," Carrie demanded, "where you goin' to get the money for stock?"

"I made a deal with Mr. Sam Levy--he used to be my master. He's going to send out some goods to try me first. If I trade it right, and send him African stuff to sell, we'll make money both sides."

"Well, I got to see you do it first," Carrie said pertly. "Sounds like a dream to me. Besides, I got those three young'uns up ahead there to take care of."

John Bannon's face fell, but Carrie moved closer to him as they continued walking, and she didn't pull away when his hand finally reached for hers again.

####

Dr. Ayres had requested all the male colonists to meet on Sunday afternoon at the LeFevre manor house for final orders before leaving for the Cape. Elijah was there with the others, their excited voices filling the parlor. But all fell silent abruptly as the door from the study opened. Expectant eyes fixed on the three men who entered; Ayres was first, followed by Wiltburger, the surviving agent from the *Nautilus* expedition. John Bannon trailed behind them, holding paper, pen and ink in his hands. He barely had time to sit at the parlor table, sharpen a quill pen, and open the ink bottle before Ayres began the meeting.

"Gentlemen, we've planned the move to Cape Mesurado carefully, and will explain it now. But I must remind you first of the regulation I laid down when I arrived."

He turned from one side of the room to the other, peering keenly at every face, then put a stern tone in his voice.

"No insubordination or disobedience will be tolerated! We cannot have a repeat of the mutiny and sedition at Campelar and Yonie. Mr. Wiltburger tells me that while I was gone to seek land at Cape Mesurado, some of you broke the rules and had to be punished. I will ..."

"There's too much power in the agents' hands!" a voice from the group interrupted. "Mr. Wiltburger condemned some of us without any trial. That is in violation of the U.S. Constitution!"

"What's that?" Ayres burst out, turning in the direction of the voice. "Who said that? Stand up and explain yourself!"

Elijah saw a lean, scholarly-looking young man wearing eye glasses stand up calmly. Light-complexioned and obviously accustomed to freedom, he spoke out confidently.

"I did, Sir. My name is Colin Teague. I understood from the Colonization Society that we were to be governed by the law of the United States. But we're already been denied a right to trial several times. That is clearly despotic."

"Des--Desp--Despotic, you say?" Ayres spluttered. "Why, young man, you don't--you can't really--that is preposterous! The final authority in all matters, both for the Government and the Society, lies in the Agents. That was made clear to you in the beginning!"

Teague flinched, but stood his ground. He quickly drew a paper from his coat pocket and began to read in a loud voice.

"To provide an Arbitrating Body to act in disputes between the Emigrants and the Agents, we have formed the American-African Union Society, which will also assist in the government of the Colony and the ..."

Ayres had walked over and now stood directly in front of him.

"Who is this 'we' you speak of?"

"We--we've got a full slate of officers for the Society," Teague explained, pointing to the bottom of his paper. "That comes at the--the end of our--our statement," he mumbled, his confidence beginning to fade.

"Oh, you have, have you! Well, let me tell you now, Mr. Teague! I don't need, nor do I want, any help in carrying out my duties!"

Ayres paused, turning to address all the colonists.

"I was commissioned by President Monroe and by the Colonization Society as agent in charge of both the station for recaptives and the colony of freedmen. We already have a Justice's Court in the regulations which, at the prerogative of the agent, may punish those who need it. Now, I don't want to hear anything more about it!"

Pointing to where John Bannon sat, Ayres explained that the system for distribution of land at the Cape required them all to register now for the town lots and ten-acre farm plots the Colonization Society had promised.

"Gentlemen, the time has come for you to decide! The first ship leaves tomorrow. All those who accept the rules of the Society and want to move to the new land we've purchased, come up to the table and sign for land allotments now. Those who object, like Mr. Teague, should remember that nobody goes without signing."

Elijah signed up as soon as he could and then found Joseph Blake.

"I'm goin' to slip out now and go see Reverend Coker over at Hastings before it gets dark. Tell me about Ayres' orders when I get back, will you?"

Blake was surprised.

"Yeah, sure, Elijah. Is that the place the Freetown Gov'ner appointed him to? You goin'to say goodbye, or somethin'?"

"I want to know why he isn't goin' with us. After all he's been through, he ought to be our main leader at the Cape."

Blake's look turned from surprise to disbelief.

"He wasn't popular with a lot of us after what happened at Yonie--you know that, Elijah!"

"S'that so? I heard he was made Correspondin' Secretary of the American-African Union Society Teague was talkin' about. That sound like he was unpopular?"

Blake's eyes opened wide.

"He was? Well, I'll be damned! Then why is he stayin' here?"

"That's what I'm goin' to find out."

Elijah left the mansion, walking quickly and was soon passing through Regent Town, the first recaptive village that the British had set up south of Freetown. He was amazed to see the fine church and school, but then recalled hearing about the hard-working English missionary, Willliam Johnson, who was in charge of the town. Elijah smiled as he ascended hilly country, thinking of what he, himself--a second Johnson, but black--might someday do for Africans at Cape Mesurado. A school and a church, he mused. He could preach and his sons could teach!

Sweating as he walked steadily on in the late afternoon heat, Elijah knew it was another mile to go--through this low pass between two mountains, and he'd be there. Hastings was a new recaptive village, recently started by Governor MacCarthy because the Royal Navy was capturing so many slave ships that Freetown and Regent Town couldn't hold them all. Elijah felt a surge of pride as he thought of Daniel Coker specially appointed to be in charge.

But was that really why Coker was staying? What had happened to Coker's dreams of bringing light to the darkness of Africa in the American colony?

####

"This is my wife Maria, Elijah. And here is Samuel--he's eight years old."

Elijah noted Daniel Coker's quiet pride as he introduced his family. They'd come on the *Nautilus*, but Elijah had been so busy with the expeditions to find land that he'd never met them. Maria was younger than her husband, a smiling, round-faced brown woman who doffed her kitchen apron and fussed with her hair before stepping up to shake Elijah's hand. But the boy stayed back of her long skirts, too shy to speak.

A silent figure shuffled into view from the back of the house. They all turned to see a tall, thin teen-ager as pale-skinned as his father.

"And this is Daniel, Jr. He's having a hard time with the fever. Meet Mr. Johnson, Daniel."

"Hullo," the young man said, slowly offering a limp hand and staring vacantly.

"Hello," Elijah replied cautiously, puzzled at the boy's manner.

But at the shock of his cold hand, Elijah's mind whirled backwards to his wife Mary's struggle with fever on Campelar. It was the same icy, lifeless touch as hers before she died in his arms! Elijah shuddered, and eyed the young man closely. How long did he have to live?

"Better get back to bed, son," his mother said. She took his arm as he swayed unsteadily on this feet. "You come, too, Samuel."

The men waited for Maria to guide her sons out the door, and then Coker motioned Elijah to a chair by the table, sinking despairingly onto one himself.

"You and I know what fever does," Coker said, his voice very low, "but Maria is too new."

Elijah looked at Coker keenly.

"You mean--your son? He--he might make it."

"Don't pretend with me, Elijah. I saw you when you felt his hand."

Elijah was ashamed and looked down at the table. Coker sighed, leaned both elbows on the table, and covered his face with

99

his hands. Elijah waited, unable to think of any words of comfort. From within his hands Coker's voice came hollow and muffled, but Elijah heard the anguish.

"I feel like Abraham--sacrificing his son Isaac! Does God really expect me to?"

Finally Coker dropped his hands and Elijah saw his tortured eyes.

"But I have two sons. At least I'll have the second one to keep."

Elijah saw the truth of it. Coker would have to face his loss, just like he himself had done when Mary died. Now Elijah knew what to say.

"It makes you empty inside, Reverend. But you go on, and it's not so bad after awhile ... a long while."

Coker thought about it, and then smiled faintly through teary eyes.

"Thanks, Elijah."

Coker drew in a long, rasping breath, then spoke with a forced heartiness.

"Well, my friend, I suppose you've come to say goodbye!"

"I hope it won't be goodbye. You should be goin' with us, Reverend. We need you to--you know--be between the agent and us, like you did on the *Elizabeth*. You understand both sides."

"Why, you can do that, Elijah."

"No. It isn't the same. You're educated and so--so white they think you're almost like them. It helped smooth things over plenty of times on the ship."

"Yes. But after the agents died and they left me in charge, nobody would listen to me when I had to be tough like the agents."

"Some of us did! It was Peter Small and Ed Wigfall and some of that kind that were rebellin'. Some of 'em have even gone home now. Wigfall and Adams went back on the *Nautilus* and Peter caught a ship to England--said he's goin' to the West Indies, or someplace over there. Good riddance, I say."

Coker shook his head ruefully.

"It was more than that. It was most of them--even good people like old man Terra Hall were fooled by Kizell and Wigfall."

"But that's all over with, Reverend! I hear you were 'lected an officer of that new American-African Society. That proves they're beginnin' to change their minds about you, doesn't it?"

"'Fraid not--that's the new people from the *Nautilus*."

Elijah threw up his hands, desperate now.

"Dr. Ayres tromped on them, too! Don't you see--he's too hard--gonna get himself in trouble soon. You're the only one who can be between us! Why are you quittin'?"

Coker's patient voice held a tinge of sadness.

"I'm not quitting, Elijah. I'll be doing what I came to do, right here at Hastings. It just won't be in the American colony, that's all."

"That's right! You preached to us all about the Africans needin' help, and how it was our destiny to do it. But it was goin' to be in our own colony--not the British. Now we finally got land, you're desertin' us!"

"No, no, Elijah ... you don't understand."

Elijah caught his breath as he saw Coker's stricken eyes.

"I'm not allowed to go with you."

Coker's voice nearly broke on it. Elijah was stunned.

"What ... How could that be? The Navy officers--even the new agents--they all commended you! And the Colonization Society sent you a special note of thanks for holdin' all the colony together until the new agents arrived! They all understood the conditions that caused the rebellion. They didn't blame you!"

"No, they didn't ... But you've been gone on those expeditions to find land. You don't know what happened when this second group of agents began to die of fever."

"Wha--what happened?" Elijah gasped.

"They usually asked me to advise them, and I became close friends with Andrus and Ephraim Bacon especially. But Winn and Wiltburger took the opposite view from us on things, so the agents were often split. Bacon caught fever and went home, and Andrus and Winn died of it. That left Wiltburger, and he began to break under the load--got moody, suspicious, and angry at every colonist who disagreed with him."

"So that's why they called him despotic!"

"Well, not then. But later the tension got worse when a few colonists disobeyed the rules. He hit one man who talked back, and had another tied up. That angered a lot of our people."

"So what did you do?"

"I tried to intercede, but Wiltburger was so high strung by then that he accused me of wanting to take over, and I had to back off."

"That's why the *Nautilus* crowd 'lected you an officer of

101

their American-African Society--because you stood up for them?"

"I suppose so--it was a surprise to me. But I agreed to be in it because I thought it was important to have some way to protect against Wiltburger's excesses."

"Did Wiltburger know about the new society?"

"He heard that the *Nautilus* people, specially Lott Carey and Teague, were getting up a protest group, and that I was on it, so he came and said he would see I never got a place in the colony again. He did--it would take months now to get it all cleared up in Washington."

Coker shook his head.

"You shouldn't rely on me to stand between you and the agents anyway, Elijah. My color is not the right reason for that. Maybe ..." He paused to think. "Maybe the *Nautilus* people have begun to show the way."

Elijah exploded with helpless frustration.

"But they didn't get anywhere! Ayres tromped on their new society--I told you that!"

"Yes, you did. However, if they're using United States law as the basis of their protest, that's something solid to build on."

Elijah snorted.

"We weren't protected by it in the United States--why would we be over here? The agents are the law here!"

"That's only temporary, Elijah. I had to have that power, too, just like the agents did, to hold everybody together. Later, when we learn how to work together, that power can be shared like the whites do in America."

Elijah was silent a moment; then it began to come clear to him.

"They were plenty mad at you at Yonie ... partly because they didn't like someone tellin'em what to do when they thought they was free ... and partly because you're almost the same color as the whites they were expectin' to be free of."

Coker sighed, but waited for Elijah to go on with his thoughts.

"But the *Nautilus* crowd haven't been that bad, has they? They haven't made any mutiny or rebellion--they're just pushin' the agents for sharin' power more fair-like, wouldn't you say?"

"Yes, Elijah, yes! That's my point. And even if they didn't succeed the first time, they should keep on pushing whenever the agents get too bad."

102

Coker raised a warning finger.

"But they still have to learn to work under the agents until the colony is going well. The Colonization Society will turn it over to them when they show they can handle it."

"All right, I see what you mean. We don't need a go-between like you've been. We have to get along with the agents and they have to get along with us. Both sides have somethin' to learn, I guess."

Elijah took a deep breath. "But I'm sure goin' to miss you, Reverend."

"The same here, Elijah."

They stood up and walked to the door. But before he said goodbye, Elijah had one more thing to say.

"I hope you'll like it here in Hastings, Reverend. They're all recaptives, aren't they? Will it be the same as preachin' to the Africans like you wanted to do?"

Coker looked surprised.

"They're Africans, too, Elijah--just torn away from their villages by the slavers. Thank God the British Navy caught the ships and brought them here. Half of them would have died going across to America."

"But aren't they mixed up and confused, comin' from so many parts of Africa? How can they hear your preachin' with all they've been through and havin' so many languages?"

Coker changed before Elijah's eyes. His eyes suddenly sparked with excitement and he smiled.

"It's wonderful, Elijah! They're learning English fast, and they're so hungry for our Christian religion. It's as if they've come up from the hold of a slave ship--like Jonah from the belly of a whale--cut off from the old life and ready to be born into a new one!"

Elijah felt envious as they shook hands one last time.

"I want to preach someday myself , after I get some trainin' in it. I hope it'll be like this at the Cape. Goodbye, Reverend."

12 Uncertain Bargain

Cape Mesurado
January 16, 1822

Elijah, working with a dozen colonists building temporary mat-and-thatch shelters on the island, stopped and wiped his sweating face with a worn-out bandana. They had arrived at Cape Mesurado nine days before, expecting to clear a place for their settlement on the heights of the cape. But the Africans had warned them off, finally allowing them to land temporarily on the little island in the middle of the river, almost in the shadow of the Cape.

Dr. Ayres walked over to speak to Elijah.

"Mr. Johnson, I want you to get up a party of five men to go with Mr. Nicholson and myself. We've got to go palaver for the Cape, and the natives will have their weapons. Bring your muskets and bayonets--I want to show them we have some, too."

"Dr. Ayres, beggin' your pardon, but you hadn't ought to go to any land palaver. We bought this island and the Cape fair and square."

"We haven't a choice in the matter, Mr. Johnson. Look."

He pointed with his short wiry arm.

"See all those canoes? The chiefs have been coming down the river all morning. It started right after the *Augusta* left for Freetown. They mean to have their palaver, and if we want to get over to the Cape soon, we've got to meet them."

Looking across the Mesurado River, Elijah saw the crowd of Africans assembling on its north bank. A few had spears and war knives, but some wore the flowing blue and white robes of chiefs. Almost every chief was heralded by his own small band of men dressed in leopard skin caps and vests trimmed in bits of bright red cloth and shiny metal, with plumes of long white goat hair on their caps. They carried carved wooden horns and short sections of bamboo with a slit in each, beating these hollow reed drums furiously with small sticks. Hooting horn blasts and rattling drum rhythms carried noisily across the river to the island. The rest of the colonists stopped work and joined the agent and Elijah, staring at the strange spectacle.

"Whooee!" Nathaniel Brander exclaimed. "There's more

kings and chiefs and whatnot over there than you can shake a stick at."

"Yeah. See this one comin' close here?" John Lawrence pointed out.

A broad-beamed canoe with a narrow strip of red, white, and black designs painted around its sides had swerved over near the island. The occupants sat silently, as if commanded to ignore the colonists, and the oarsmen paddled swiftly by, a bare twenty yards away.

"Look at that chief sittin' up there like he owns all of Africa," Lawrence said, his voice soft with awe. "Ain't he the cocky one!"

All the colonists stared. Elijah noticed the young chief sitting erect on a raised, box-like seat. Something about him looked familiar, and as the canoe came directly opposite, he saw the chief turn and carefully examine the colonists standing on the edge of the little island. Elijah's heart jumped as he recognized the man's face.

"Zoda!" he whispered. "That's the chief who signed the treaty! Remember him, Dr. Ayres?"

Ayres watched the canoe's oarsmen turn it toward the river's north shore, waiting until it was out of earshot.

"Yes, I believe you're right. That's one of the chiefs who sold us the land."

Blake gave a low whistle.

"He sure looked us over, didn't he?"

A strange foreboding passed quickly through Elijah's mind. Why would they send Zoda to check us out? Did his name really mean he was a *Zo*--a big man in the Poro? Elijah decided not to say anything about the mysterious African society. He didn't know enough about it yet.

Ayres cast a worried look at the crowded river bank and then turned to the colonists, raising his voice.

"All right. I'd better tell you the latest. King Peter sent another urgent message yesterday--said some other kings are holding him a prisoner for selling land to a white man without consulting them. He fears they will cut off his head if I don't come to another palaver. The rumor is that the other kings are saying the Cape can't be sold to anyone."

"Well, King Peter and five other kings sold it to us!" someone shouted.

Elijah burst out, "I saw it myself and you signed it."

Ayres raised his hands, stilling angry voices.

"Hold on, gentlemen. We'll find out why they don't want to sell it when we go to the palaver. We have to be patient with these people--the Colonization Society wants us to be fair in our dealings."

"Where is the palaver to be?" Elijah asked, resigned to it now.

"On the beach at Krootown--tomorrow morning. Have your men ready and we'll go over at eight o'clock."

Elijah remembered about the weapons.

"The muskets are pretty bad. Ever'time we move'em from one storehouse to another they get rustier. Some need repairin'."

"Well, fix something up," Ayres said. "We've got to get this palaver over with. This island won't be very healthy when the rainy season comes."

Fred James' eyes grew big.

"That's right--the fever! It'll be just like Campelar all over again. We've got to get off'a here!"

He looked up to the top of the Cape anxiously and all their eyes followed his.

February 16, 1822

"That's an American flag she's flying, gentlemen!" Ayres called weakly from where he sat on an empty pork barrel, his brass spy glass trained on a strange vessel in the harbor. She'd lowered her small boat, which was being rowed through the surf toward the island. Shouts from the colonists almost drowned out Ayres fever-ridden voice.

"The ships' name is *Calypso*!" Ayers said. "Doesn't look like a slaver. Probably a merchant vessel. That's an American flag all right."

The little party of colonists had been waiting eagerly for the *Augusta* to come back from Freetown--she was long overdue and their supplies of food were running low. They were anxious to hear from loved ones waiting in Freetown on the LaFevre plantation.

"There's a man standing up in the boat," Ayres said, squinting through the spy glass again. "Looks like ... it is! It's Wiltburger. They're from Freetown!"

"Yaaaaaaaay!" everyone cheered, throwing hats and bandanas in the air.

This was what they'd thought of every waking hour, lately. They rushed to the edge of the island where they'd fixed up a small dock out of stones and logs, straining to catch a glimpse of the boat's occupants. When it finally docked, the new men were helped out, and Wiltburger rushed over to where Ayres was still sitting on the barrel.

"Don't stand there gawking, Wiltburger--get me down," Ayres said. "Everyone's so excited they've forgotten they had to put me up here. He smiled faintly. "Yes, I'm sick. We've had an epidemic of some sort--it laid all of us low for a week."

"Are you all right?" Wiltburger asked.

"I'm afraid it just about did me in. Careful! Get me over to the bench in the shade there."

Wiltburger supported his frail superior officer to the bench and watched in silence as the agent lay down on it.

"Don't look so shocked, man!" Ayres chided. "I'll recover in due time. I haven't even told you the bad news yet."

In tired, halting sentences, Ayres told Wiltburger about King Peter's change of heart and the new palaver about the Cape.

"There's a sacred place at the highest point of the Cape that King Peter wasn't supposed to sell. They call it a 'Devil's bush.' When I found out about it, I went to King George--the Cape is in his territory and he lives at the foot of it. He and I made a deal for all but the sacred grove. Then we started clearing some space on our part of the Cape."

"Thank God! So it's all cleared now?"

Ayres shook his head, a wry grimace on his face.

"No, it's just begun. We were all sick for a week--but that's not the real reason."

Ayres sighed and shook his head.

"The colonists were so happy when the deal was finally made with King George. But when we went over to clear it, the place wasn't divided so each one could work on his own land, and they dragged their feet. I couldn't get them to work for the common good."

"So have you given up?"

"No. I hired some Africans to assist them. That helped for awhile. But then they got discouraged when the *Augusta* didn't come back. It really depressed them."

Ayres looked up at Wiltburger.

"What happened to the *Augusta*? Why the new ship?"

"The Navy has taken it over to capture slave vessels," Wiltburger said. "I hear it's up in Rio Pongas north of Freetown catching quite a few. So I had to buy the *Calypso* for transporting our people, even if it is a little small."

"How many more trips will it take to get them all here?" Ayres asked.

"Just one more, for the women and children. But you'll have to go to Freetown to settle up with the authorities before we leave there. Are you well enough for that?"

"If you'll have me carried on board, I'll leave tomorrow. I need a doctor who knows about these tropical illnesses."

"Should I stay here and be in charge?"

"No. I want you to help in Freetown. I'll leave Elijah Johnson in command here."

Wiltburger looked incredulous.

"You want a colonist to be in charge?"

"We have to give them a chance to learn to govern. Why not now? We'll be back soon, anyway."

But Elijah was not happy with the assignment when called to Ayres side.

"Beggin' your pardon, Doctor, but I need to go back, too. My family's still there. I've been on all those expeditions for findin' land, and this one to clear it. I haven't had a chance to take proper care of my own chillun, and I sure want to be there when we bring 'em this last trip."

"All right. You have somebody else you can recommend?"

"Yessir. Joseph Blake or Fred James could do it."

"Good. We'll try them both--make it a joint command."

March 20, 1822

"Blake! Blake! Wake up!" John Fisher and a Kroo man were standing by Joseph Blake's cot. Fisher was trying to shake him awake.

"What'sa matter? What'ya want?"

Blake rubbed his eyes and sat up. Moonlight streamed in the open doorway of the shelter, and he recognized Fisher.

"John! Is somethin' wrong'"

"Plenty!" Fisher said. "King George is out for murder tonight, for sure! He and his people is 'round there where the ships always run aground in a gale. They're whoopin' it up somethin' fierce. Listen!"

Gusts of wind brought faint sounds of a horde of warriors chanting and dancing, driven by the furious rhythms of small drums. Blake got up and walked out of the shelter to hear it better. The eerie sound of the drums made him shudder.

"Enough to drive you crazy! What're they after?"

"This Kroo man says he saw one of King George's men swim out after dark and cut the anchor cable of that British prize vessel--the one that came in today for fresh water. Now the captain's trying to sail out of the bay, but the wind is pushing him back towards the rocks."

Blake remembered something.

"Oh, oh. The captain had a big argument with King George about the price for the water, and sent a letter addressed to Ayres this afternoon. I read it and sent back word that Ayres is gone and King George own's the waterin' place so we can't make him change his price."

"Yeah, well this Kroo man says the King refused to let the ship get water 'til tomorrow mornin' and ..."

"God a'Mighty!" Blake said. "So George fixed it so the ship could bust up on the rocks tonight! Why would he be so mean?"

Fisher was almost bursting with his information.

"There's 35 slaves on that prize ship and the British are takin' it to the Freetown court. This Kroo man says King George wants those slaves 'cause he has a contract to supply the French slaver sittin' out in the bay since yestiday. So he's goin' kill two birds with one stone!"

"You mean he's going to rob one ship to give to another?"

"Don't you get it, Blake?" Fisher shouted. "Not just rob--murder! He'll have to murder the British crew to get the slaves!"

Blake rushed back to his cot and began putting on his pants and shirt.

"John, go wake up Fred James and call all the men. Tell'em it's an emergency! I want everybody here right away."

Blake called for volunteers when everyone had mustered out in the dark and he'd explained the situation to them. Only four others besides Blake and Fisher were willing to go to the rescue of the slaves and the prize crew. But Joshua Webster and John Wiley were big and husky, and Jonas Carey and George Washington were both hard workers, so Blake knew they all had the strength to fight. He unlocked the storehouse and issued them muskets, all cleaned and repaired now--that had been the last thing Ayres had assigned Elijah Johnson to do before the *Calyspso* left for Freetown.

"Don't fire your musket unless you really have to," Blake warned them. "The Africans bluff easy, so you might not need to shoot. We don't want to start a war if we can help it."

The Kroo man got a fellow tribesman to assist him and they took the six volunteers in their canoe across the river, hugging the north bank closely until they came to the sea. They heard the surf boiling as the high waves, driven by the wind, broke on the submerged sand bar guarding the river mouth. But the Kroo men seemed to know just when to buck an incoming wave and ride over the bar. They were free of it quickly and turning north toward the rocks when they saw the wrecked prize vessel in the moonlight, about a hundred yards ahead.

"There she is! She's got a big hole in her!" Blake shouted.

They saw the jagged break in the ship's hull and the huge black rocks the ship had foundered on, but it was still standing upright, about fifteen yards off the beach. The Africans were dancing gleefully on the beach, sporting their knives and spears, but making no effort yet to swarm the ship. The sailors on the ship were maneuvering a large cannon into shooting position.

"Why aren't the warriors goin' to the ship?" Blake asked the Kroo man.

"Plunder-mens wait for waves to break ship and push to beach. Then it be their part."

Blake asked the Kroo man to get them close enough to hail the captain. The canoe rose and fell in the heavy swells as the two paddlers struggled to keep the canoe on course without being swamped. Gradually they moved closer.

They paddled furiously, judging each wave, backing and turning, then pulling mightily at the right moment, avoiding disaster. Fisher marveled at their skill, but he was so scared he managed only to shout "Whooee!" every time they escaped another wave. Blake cupped his hands and shouted at the British prize crew.

"Don't shoot, Captain! Don't shoot! Bring your boats this way and we'll protect you! We're friends! Don't shoot--bring your boats this way!"

Heads appeared at the ship's rail and Blake called again; the captain bobbed his head in agreement.

"They've stopped workin' on the cannon," Fisher said. "Movin' to their boats."

Blake spoke to the Kroo man.

"Where we goin' to land them?"

Speaking in Kroo language, the paddlers argued it out. Finally the lead man pointed to a break in the rocks.

"We go for that place many times. This time waves make plenty palaver, but we try."

The vessel began to lower its boats, and Blake asked the Kroo man to show the way to shore. When the canoe got through the break in the rocks, the surf was easier than the Kroo men expected. But King George and his warriors were waiting for them on the beach. Blake marshalled his group as they climbed out of the canoe.

"We'll charge'em and drive'em back on the beach. Shout at them as loud as you can and hold up your muskets like you're goin' to shoot if they come back. That'll keep'em off. Remember, don't shoot."

The bluff worked and Blake drew a line in the sand with the butt of his musket, shouting at King George to keep the warriors from crossing it or he'd not be responsible for what happened. They obeyed the order until the first boat approached from the ship. Then some of the warriors rushed into the surf, snatched out guns and ammunition, and ran off with them. Blake restored order with much bluster and threats. The second boat was loaded with slaves, and the warriors rushed forward again, carrying away five slaves before Webster, Wiley, Fisher and Blake muscled into the fray, pulling other slaves back.

A shot was fired close to Blake, and he turned to see a British sailor in the boat put down a smoking musket and pick up another one.

"Stop!" Blake shouted. "You'll start a war!"

The sailor looked at him in disbelief.

"This is a war!"

Before Blake could protest, the sailor fired the second one, and two warriors lay dead in the shallow water. A shout went up from other warriors and they came to carry the bodies away. King George rushed to the boat, saw what had happened and began to

111

rage at the sailor.

"We have guns, too! Now we go get'em and come shoot you!"

He shook his fist in the sailor's face. "We can shoot as good as British!"

He stomped off, muttering angrily, and his warriors went with him. Blake and the colonists spent the rest of the night and the next day helping the British prize crew unload the ship, securing the cargo and slaves on the island. All day they expected an attack, but strangely none came.

The next day King George came along the south bank of the river and stopped opposite the island, hailing the colonists. Blake was called by his men, and he stood on the edge of the island to listen.

"You make plenty palaver for yourself, fighting my people and helping British!" George shouted. "That ship belong to me--all ships who break on my rocks belong to me! Don't come over on my side to get water again. No more water for you or for British!"

Blake didn't want to argue by shouting across half the river, so he lifted his arm to signal he'd heard, and turned away to talk with Fred James.

"Now we're in trouble! Besides getting water for us we've got to have enough for the British crew and the slaves, too."

"Don't pay any attention to George and this threats," Fred said. "Let's go get the water at his spring as usual. His people haven't used any guns for a whole day since they stole them. Either they don't know how, or they don't have any gunpowder."

Blake agreed because they needed the water desperately. When the colony's regular boat for carrying water was ready to go to the spring, Blake asked Fisher and Wiley to go along with muskets primed, just in case. Then he stood with McLean, the British officer, and watched the boat pass upriver along the south bank, heading into the cove where the spring was.

"Blake! I saw George's warriors in the bush over there," a colonist warned. He pointed directly across to the heavy foliage at the base of the Cape.

They could see black figures squatting low, dashing from bush to bush, heading for the spring.

"How many are they? Do they have any muskets?" Blake asked.

They watched the warriors' flitting progress, but no colonist spoke. McLean cleared his throat.

About a dozen men, I'd should say. Just a few firearms," he said coolly. "Shall we go support the water crew?"

Blake turned to the officer, appraising him.

"A second boat? Yeah--they might need our help."

McLean ordered two of his sailors to launch a boat, and he and Blake armed themselves with new breech-loading British muskets before jumping in. Rowing quickly, they soon rounded into the cove, where they met the water boat with full casks coming back out. As Blake hailed it with relief, muskets suddenly blasted from the bushes.

McLean and Blake returned the fire rapidly with their new guns. But Fisher and Wiley in the water boat labored feverishly to ram and prime their muzzle-loaders after getting their first shots off. Wiley was hit in the neck by a chunk of brass fired from an African's old blunderbuss, and he stopped to staunch the bright red blood that poured down his chest.

"Back us off the shore!" McLean ordered.

The British sailors turned the boat smartly, but one took a shot in his right side and crumpled to the floor. The other sailor grabbed both oars and pulled hard. In the water boat Fisher swore as he was nicked, but went on firing and loading as the colonists pulled away, too. Both boats withdrew a short distance, the men aiming where they saw powder smoke rising from the bushes. After a few minutes that still hadn't stopped the firing from the shore.

"We're sitting ducks out here," Blake said. "The way to stop it is to chase'em."

"Chase'em? Oh--have a run at them!" McLean said. "I'm game, old fellow. Here, the bayonet's a bit tricky. I'll show you how to clip it in attack position."

"Fisher!" Blake called over to the water boat. "Load both muskets--we're going after them. Whoop it up a little!"

The boats moved shoreward and Blake startled McLean with a loud war whoop. They all joined in, shooting and reloading as they hollered. Ready to jump as soon as the boat grounded, Blake suddenly realized the shots from the bush had stopped. He put up his hand for quiet, and they heard the warriors scrambling up the back side of the Cape in a wild flight.

That ended the gun fight. Fisher and Blake were only slightly wounded. But life ebbed away from Wiley and the British sailor before the boats reached the island, in spite of frantic efforts to save them. On shore, Blake and McLean gave orders to their own men and then stood silently watching as the bodies were carried off to the center of the island. The enormity of what had happened hit Blake--he was in charge of the island while Ayres was away, and now he'd let one of the colonists get killed! He turned to McLean, his face beginning to twist with remorse and grief, straining for control.

"Wiley was a good man--I didn't want nothing like this to happen. It was to be all bluff!" His eyes widened. "He's the first of us to get killed fighting the Africans--our own black brothers. It wasn't supposed to be like this!"

The next day a colonist saw King George's men climbing up to the top of the Cape where the clearing was. Blake and James were called and everyone gathered on the edge of the island to see what the warriors would do up there. A few muskets were fired down at the island, peppering it ineffectively from that distance. The colonists laughed, but Fred James saw nothing funny.

The warriors began to break up one of the new houses the colonists had built, taking rafter poles off and pulling smaller poles and sticks from the walls, ripping out the vines that tied them together. None of the walls had been plastered with mud yet, nor the roofs thatched, and the colonists watched helplessly as the first house was picked apart easily. The Africans gleefully shook pieces of it at the colonists, shouting down to them what sounded like insults.

Fred James, outraged at the injustice of it, turned to Blake.

"Shoot'em with the cannon!" he shouted. "That'll teach them! Get the cannon!"

Blake was willing--anything to chase the warriors away from destroying the houses. After two years of waiting for land and getting it and finally building on it--it would be too much to see it destroyed before their very eyes.

"All right. Let's do it!"

But none of the colonists had ever used a cannon, and they'd left the heavy iron barrels just where they'd dropped them off the boats when they first arrived. Blake called on McLean's help, and the officer directed them in mounting a rusting six-pounder on one of the carriages they'd put in the storehouse. They opened a keg of gunpowder, a box of balls, and a tin of wadding, and were instructed in the art of loading the cannon.

McLean showed them how to aim it, and took the honor of touching off the first shot. It was wide of the mark, but the roar of it startled the warriors on the heights. The ball from the second shot crashed into tree limbs close to the clearing, and the third routed the warriors completely. The colonists cheered wildly, vying for the privilege of loading the next one.

"Better save your powder and ball for a real fight," McLean advised.

Blake finally prevailed on the newly-vetted gun crew to hold the next shot in readiness, and they settled down to preparing the evening meal. Just as the sun began to lower to the sea's horizon, the British sailor who'd killed the two warriors spied a band of King George's men plundering the shipwreck. Calling two other sailors to turn the cannon around quickly, he aimed it out toward the ship and ran to the cooking fire for a burning stick. He raced back to touch off the shot, but the powder being damp, it blew at the touch hole. Flame spewed out like a geyser, catching the mat-and-thatch storehouse on fire.

"Fire! Help! The storehouse is on fire!" he called.

Colonists and sailors rushed toward the storehouse, but previously spilled gunpowder had turned it now into a raging conflagration, eating away the colony's supplies of food, clothing, and tools. They struggled to save what they could, but then Fred James remembered the kegs of powder.

"Get back! Hurry--the fire's almost to the powder barrels!"

Frantically he and Blake pushed and shoved, driving everyone away. They stood far back in the shadows of the night watching the blazing pyre, feeling its intense heat and waiting for the powder to blow. Four earsplitting explosions blew the flaming mass apart, and pieces of crates, boxes, and even parts of muskets rained down on them.

Blake stood in the gaping crowd, hearing their noise and shouts, but he felt alone. The awful weight of responsibility for this was on him and Fred. Now the supplies were gone, blown to bits except for a few barrels and bags they'd saved. They might run out of food before Ayres could get back from Freetown with the women and children. What would Ayres say when he saw this mess--and a house gone--and a man killed?

13 Learning to Palaver

Krootown
April 24, 1822

Seventeen kings, thirty-six half-kings, and a large assortment of princes and head men had been meeting for three days. It was the biggest palaver some of the Africans could ever remember. Krootown on the beach was like one big market day, alive with people stirred by the rumors. "Doctor Ayres" was on everybody's lips--the big white man who had come back from Freetown and found the colonists and King George's people at war. But when they did catch a glimpse of him the crowds of villagers who'd followed their chiefs to the Cape to ogle and bask in the exciting days were shocked at the puny size of the agent, now a victim of dysentery. Thin and dehydrated, he was not their idea of a powerful man.

The palaver was the wonder of their days, and there were all sorts of predictions on how it would come out. But the smart native traders who had upped their prices for the roaming crowds knew the kings would prolong the palaver as long as possible, extracting daily stipends of tobacco and rum from Ayres for their presence at the deliberations. The traders also knew their profits would be skimmed by the chiefs--a 'market fee' that the local chief shared with his brother rulers for bringing so much business to his town.

Most of the kings were quartered at King Peter's town, afraid to get too near Boatswain's encampment on old Carrey's island, just upriver from the colonists. Boatswain, always enjoying his reputation as a powerful warrior and the head of the Kondo nation--a ruthless band of outlaws and renegades, some said--still had the good sense to lodge his warriors twelve miles away on the St. Paul river so they would stay out of trouble. But rumor had it that he would order them into action if he couldn't succeed in settling the palaver peacefully.

On the fourth day the palaver got down to Ayres' business and he was asked to state why he had called the palaver. He gave the kings a brief account of the recent affair with King George and accused him of making war on the colony. Then King George was called to answer the charges against him.

"That 'Merican black man there, Blake, he killed two of my people on the beach. He's the one who started the war!" said George, pointing squarely at the nervous colonist. "He shot at my people with a big fire stick and that's how their storehouse got burned up."

Ayres stood up to protest, angry at the outright lies.

"That's a lie! Blake didn't do it--it was a British sailor from the prize crew who did it! The sailor was only trying to stop the slaves from being stolen and the ship from being plundered!"

But the horrible truth dawned on Ayres even before he took his seat--the case would rest on whether Blake or the British sailor killed the two warriors at the beach. And he could not provide witnesses the chiefs would accept. The British prize crew was gone, picked up by a British Navy schooner a week before and carried to Freetown along with the 30 slaves they still held for the Admiralty Court. And any statement by a colonist involved in the incidents would be disbelieved. King George's lies might be accepted by the chiefs!

Stunned at this turn of affairs, Ayres turned to his party in the palaver circle and asked them to think of any witnesses. All their faces were blank, until Elijah Johnson asked Blake if any other vessels were in the bay at the time, and Blake remembered the French slave ship. Elijah almost shouted at Ayres in his excitement.

"Doctor! The captain of the French slaver is on shore today! I saw him in Krootown this morning!"

"Good! Go find out what he knows and, if you can, bring him here quickly."

An hour later, through an interpreter, the French captain stated to the chiefs that the British sailor who shot the two Africans and fired the cannon at the plunderers had bragged about it to him personally.

Furious at losing face, King George wildly accused the women of the colony of firing the cannon. Ayres pointed out that the women had not arrived from Freetown at that time, and, in any case, the absurdity of the king in charging one person, and when that had been disproved, charging another showed that he was trifling with the kings and hiding the truth. The logic of this was enough to engage the kings for the rest of the day in endless debates, only part of which were interpreted to Ayres and the colonists. Finally King Brister, in charge of the palaver, raised his elephant tail fly whisk and the circle fell silent. Brister spoke directly to Ayres.

"Doctor, the palaver be finished for today. We come tomorrow and say what we decide."

He turned and looked around the circle, and heads nodded in unison. Laying the elephant tail whisk on his mat, he waved a hand, dismissing them all.

But outside the palaver, Ayres' interpreter told him that most of the chiefs already favored telling Ayres in the morning to go away and they would set a time for another palaver. Elijah heard it and stepped up to warn Ayres as they headed for their boat to go back to the island.

"They'll keep on stringin' out this thing 'til it costs you a fortune in tobacco and rum, Doctor. You better do something right away in the mornin' when the palaver opens."

"Yes, but what? I've been wracking my brain to think how to impress all those chiefs. I see now they won't decide on the basis of proof--it'll be some kind of feeling they all get, I guess."

"I think I know why Stockton won out when we made the first treaty with King Peter."

"Let's hear it, Mr. Johnson. We need something badly."

"Well, he just plain got mad. Then they started respectin' him. He used a little force--you remember?"

"You mean the pistols?"

"Maybe. But it doesn't have to be that. Just some kind of force. Looks like they kind'a admire a strong, forceful person."

Ayres smiled.

"I'll think about it, Mr. Johnson."

####

They all seemed to be there in the morning. Ayres started to count the chiefs and half-chiefs in the palaver circle as he listened to King Brister get things going. Finally Ayres caught the end of preliminary remarks and focused on Brister's words.

"Doctor Ayres called this palaver and we come sit down to hear him. Now we have sat plenty. We listen plenty. We talk plenty. This war business he brings is a big, big thing--too big
for one palaver. Our decide is for him to go away and we make a time to talk again."

My God! They're doing it already! Ayres jumped up, chagrined that he'd been caught off balance. Better get angry with them right off, he thought.

"I came here with Captain Stockton and we bought the land from King Peter and five other kings, and paid the first part of it! Then I came again, ready to pay the second part, but others said take it back. So you did, and then I paid King George for all but the Devil's bush, which you wanted to keep for your people. That's twice I paid for the land! I will not go away and come back for another palaver ..."

They're all listening now, Ayres saw. Better make it louder.

"If King George or any of you think you can drive me away you can try it anytime! I haven't made war yet, but if you try to drive us away from the ..."

Ayres' face felt hot. I'm really worked up. Brister is looking worried now. Boatswain is chuckling--he likes it!

"I will show you what fighting really is! I'll bring ships and batter down all the towns from Cape Mount to the Line that want to oppose us. You heard our cannon--our fire stick--we have more and bigger ones ..."

They're talking about me--white man getting mad! It's working. Just a little more.

"Commodore Mends is coming with four Navy ships anytime now from the south! If you ..."

That did it. They're all whispering--really worried. Boatswain is standing up! He must want to talk--will he back me?

Ayres finished and sat down, watching the warrior king stride boldly to Brister's place in the circle. A huge man with wide shoulders, well over six feet, Boatswain's loose robe exposed hard muscles rippling beneath a velvet black skin. Casually held in the crook of his left arm, his short chief's spear had a stained dagger-blade head and a shaft bound with leopard skin and red leather. Ayres shuddered at how deep the spear seemed to have been driven into enemy bodies. Boatswain's eyes seemed penetrating and cruel, but there was a humorous twist to his smile now. A hard man, but true to his work, Ayres guessed. Boatswain spoke calmly to the chiefs.

"One thing we hear for true in this palaver be how the 'Mericans not to blame for this war. They bought land and paid for it, so it be theirs. They have right to fight anyone who breaks down houses they put on it."

119

He paused. They watched him with nervous glances, and no one said anything. He reached down and offered Brister a hand. Brister hesitated, took it, and was pulled up.

"Fine!" Boatswain said. "We go settle this thing one time. All chiefs come with Brister and me."

Taking Brister by the elbow, Boatswain guided him outside to a huge cottonwood tree and the kings and half-kings followed, leaving the princes and head men in the palaver circle with Ayres and his party. The kings stood about under the shade of the tree listening to Boatswain, in plain view of those still in the open-walled palaver hall. Ayres could see some of them objecting and suddenly Boatswain raised his spear above his head in combat position, speaking angrily to them. Their talk stopped abruptly. Boatswain finished, offered his hand again to Brister, and led the way back to the circle. When they were all seated Brister raised his elephant tail whisk, and in the sudden silence he cleared his throat. He solemnly addressed Ayres.

"If your people like the Cape, Doctor, it be yours. We not take anything more for it. Your people can go there now."

He looked at several of the chiefs and cleared his throat again.

"We make questions for you, Doctor," he said, and nodded to one of the chiefs.

A keen-eyed man with a greying beard asked the first one.

"Doctor, what your people do when next ship is wrecked?"

"We'll protect the crew and property. Our idea is to help all people in trouble, no matter who they are."

Brister nodded to another chief, who looked at Ayres sharply.

"S'pose slave ship come in bay and be attacked by British, would your people proteck this ship and property?"

They're testing me about their slaving, Ayres thought.

"No ... all the countries of Europe and America have condemned the slave trade. We wouldn't protect any ship trading contrary to the laws of its own country."

A long silence hung in the air like an oppressive cloud, the chiefs staring at Ayres relentlessly. Finally a third questioner received Brister's nod and cleared his throat.

"We have our own laws about slaves--old laws before white man come. Will your people respect our laws?"

He's trapped me! Ayres realized instantly. Steady now.

"We ... we don't know your laws about slaves ... but we'll study them and see if they are what other countries agree on."

Ayres held his breath, but the questioner didn't have any more to say. Brister seemed to be waiting for other questions, but none came. Ayres began to breathe again--his answers must have satisfied them. Finally Brister spoke again.

"Doctor, we say something about the war thing. Listen to our oldest chief."

He nodded to a balding, white-haired old man whose voice quavered as he began.

"I remembers back to old, old times ... we never see such thing as war between black man and white man."

He pointed a shaky finger at Ayres, his voice steady now.

"Doctor, if some of King Peter's people or your people do bad thing again, it must be put in front of King Brister. He the one to hear palaver between you, to settle it one time so no make war. There should be no war between black man and white man--never!"

Ayres wondered why the chief didn't speak to King George, but he nodded to show he understood the principle.

"I hear you, Chief. That is the way to settle things. We'll come to King Brister next time."

Ayres turned to Brister.

"I want to be sure now about the Cape. Do you have any other demand against me for the Cape, or will you have in the future?"

"No," Brister said, "it be paid."

He looked around the circle at the chiefs. They nodded in support of it. Then Brister looked at Boatswain, who was smiling broadly. The ceremonial elephant tail brush went up and Brister spoke the final word. "Palaver finished," he said, laying the brush on the mat.

####

Elijah, assigned by Ayres to the storehouse, was helping to lift the bundles of tobacco from the fragrant wooden barrel as Ayres counted them.

"Doctor," Elijah said, "I've been thinkin' this palaver isn't done yet."

"What do you mean?"

"Well, when you and Stockton bought the Cape, everyone

saw the treaty signed."

Ayres smiled wryly.

"I remember--but then they changed their minds. We don't need another useless piece of paper."

"Yeah, but I'm thinkin' of the people. We got a lot of people here for this palaver and now the Cape is ours for sure. We need to write that on their minds, not on a piece of paper."

"On their minds?"

"You know," Elijah said, "somethin' they can see and won't forget. Like a big ceremony with the big chiefs handin' over to us--to you--the land. Make it noisy and excitin' so they'll remember for a long time."

"I see. We have an American flag--we could raise that up on a pole up at the clearing. High up there with the wind blowing it out free and clear. It would be beautiful! They would remember that, wouldn't they?"

"Yeah ... and guns for a salute!"

"What about the six-pounder. Could we get that up to the top of the Cape by tomorrow?"

Elijah laughed. "That'll scare them clean away, Doctor! But we could fire some muskets, like we did at the military funeral at Campelar."

April 25, 1822

On the heights of the Cape, Boatswain, Brister, and all the other kings, together with their courtiers and people, witnessed the formal possession of the land by the colonists. The American flag was hoisted, a salute was fired, and Ayres and Brister spoke briefly.

Then the chiefs retired to King Peter's town to settle other problems and to try King George for his actions during the 'war.' He was given the choice of paying five slaves, twenty baskets of salt, and to move away from the Cape with all his people--or to have his head cut off.

"He's goin' to get back at us someway," Elijah said to Ayres when they got word of the chiefs' decision. "An ornery rascal like George can figure out a dozen ways, just sleepin' on it. Besides, I hear he's only goin' to move a few miles away."

14   Fire Bell in the Night

Washington
June 18, 1822

    Elias Caldwell sat behind his desk in the Society's small rented office and nervously appraised the young man before him.

    "The plain fact is," he said, "we've exhausted all of the Society's funds. Sending the first two ships to Africa has drained away every last cent!"

    Ralph Gurley, a handsome, neatly dressed recent Yale graduate, brushed aside his long black hair.

    "I didn't realize ... Mr. Key said there were wealthy auxiliary societies in all the major cities, like New York, Philadelphia, Baltimore. He helped start one in Annapolis, he said."

    "Yes, they're some of the original ones. But Rev. Meade organized many in the South, too--Savannah, Raleigh, Charleston. And a lot of small auxiliaries sprang up by themselves in Virginia."

    "And those aren't enough to support the colonization work?"

    Caldwell shook his head sadly.

    "Not even with the churches. We spent six thousand dollars for the colony's supplies last year, and have already used four thousand this year. Every expedition strains us!"

    "So we have to raise enough money to cover any new expeditions--that's what my first job is?"

    Caldwell smiled and his tenseness eased a bit. He liked the way this young man went about things. But there was more bad news to tell him.

    "Yes, that's the idea. But we'll have to raise funds for bills we haven't paid yet. Our income has tapered off drastically this year--only about eight hundred dollars so far."

    Gurley raised his eyebrows.

    "So the auxiliaries have almost stopped giving? Why?"

    "That's putting it mildly. They've not only stopped giving, in the South they've even reputiated us! We're under attack by leaders in Georgia and South Carolina especially."

    "What are they saying?"

    "We've been called abolitionists and a northern plot to

cripple the southern economy. Southern newspapers are full of it."

Gurley looked perplexed.

"If they were such enthusiasts for the Society, why have they changed now?"

Caldwell sat up straight and cleared his throat.

"It's the fight over Missouri coming into the Union as a slave state."

"But I thought that was over with--didn't they balance it by admitting Maine as a non-slave state? That makes thirteen of each now, doesn't it?"

"Yes, that's how they compromised it. But it went much deeper than that. I've been close to Congress here in Washington for years, and I've never seen such anger and sectional division." Caldwell shook his head again. "It was bad! Very bad!"

Gurley looked down at the floor a moment.

"Where--where exactly will I go, Mr. Caldwell? To the South?"

"No. There's no use going south--the auxiliaries there have almost died out, and thousands of dollars of pledges aren't being paid. We've actually been warned by our friends there to stay away right now. We're assigning you to New England--that's where the wealthy industrialists are."

"Are--are we giving up on the South altogether, sir?"

"Well--there are a few supporters of colonization down there who will carry on by themselves. General Harte in Virginia is one of them, I should think."

Ronda Plantation, Virginia
June 30, 1822

James Harte stepped eagerly out the front door of the mansion, enjoying the start of another morning round of the plantation. He called to the hostler waiting on the veranda.

"Sam, bring Roman around for me. Put on that saddle with the new-fangled thing on it--the pommel, I think it's called."

"Yessuh, Gen'rul. I sure will!"

Sam's eyes lit up at the news that Harte would ride the stallion. He went off in excitement, hoping that the General would give Roman a real run. The General was always trying something new, too--a better saddle, a new breed, or a different feed.

Harte, pacing on the veranda, thought of fields he wanted to check and the building projects under way. Laura had asked at breakfast how the chapel-schoolhouse for the slaves was coming and he'd promised to look at it. His mason was still using the bricks from the stock of bricks fired in the kiln last year. Would there be enough for the chapel and the dairy too? He didn't want to start a gang making new brick until next year, so perhaps he'd use stone on the dairy instead.

Sam came around the corner of the mansion leading Roman. He grinned broadly as he came up and handed the reins to Harte, holding the bridle until Harte would mount.

"Here he is, Gen'rul! He's spoilin' for a good ride!"

Harte stepped into the stirrup and seated himself, noticing the difference from his English saddle.

"Go pull some little carrots from the kitchen garden for Roman's treat when I bring him back, Sam. Be sure you ask Sukey, or she'll take after you with her big spoon!"

They both chuckled and Harte started the stallion off at a walk. It was a glorious morning and Roman was his favorite horse. He slapped the reins and urged him into a trot, heading for the old tobacco field near the river.

First problem of the day, Harte mused, was whether the overseer would put the right amount of marl and manure on that field. The soil was exhausted, but he could build it up and switch to grain for the next crop. That would be better than abandoning it like his father and uncles had done for so many years. Harte saw slaves and some wagons up ahead--that would be Greene and the marling gang.

Harte patted Roman on the neck as they came closer and stopped to watch. The wagon at the side of the field was half full of the whitish mixture of mineral and clay that he'd discovered in a rich deposit several years ago. That was a lucky find, he mused, pulling the reins to lead Roman over to the wagon. He'd started using it in place of lime and there'd been four years of trial-and-error before he'd learned how much marl per acre a particular soil needed.

"Morning, Mr. Greene. How's the marling going?"

The short, powerfully built overseer walking toward him turned and waved his hand at a smaller wagon slowly being pulled by mules back and forth across the field. Slaves in the back of it cast marl in a wide snowy path with their shovels, singing an old chant to keep in rhythm.

"Mornin', General. It's goin' all right, I s'pose. You said to put it on heavy, 180 to 200 bushels per acre, didn't you?"

"About that, yes."

"It's goin' to come out near that, the way they're throwin' it now."

Harte glanced at the marl left in the big wagon.

"How's it holding out?"

"It should take about three more loads this size. Oh--you mean the deposit? General, I think you've got enough there for years to come, unless you start using up a lot more land than we're cultivatin' now."

Greene took off his hat and wiped his brow with a big bandana. The sun was beginning to get hot, and so was his frustration.

"Trouble is, I can't trust'em to do it right on their own. Got to be here all the time! But I got some boys tearin' up trees on that new piece of bottom land, and I know they're sittin'down while I'm over here. Got the women and old men hoein'corn. I put that nigger, George, to watchin'em and told him to use the whip if they slack off any. But he ain't hard enough on'em--I have to go over there once in awhile, too." Greene's voice rose. "N'then we got some of the slave cabins to repair, and the corn cribs, too--got to get them ready. Usin' three men on repairs, but they're awful slow, too!"

"Well, do your best, Mr. Greene. I think George is going to be a pretty good field driver, and I don't want you to encourage him to be vicious with the whip. Every slave must do his work, but I don't condone any cruelty on Ronda."

Roman was pawing the ground and jerking his bit, ready for more action. Harte wanted to get on, but he had to be sure Greene understood him.

"You get the best work out of people when you're organized yourself and have tasks for each one to do," he said.

"That's what I do, General! Every morning when I wake up, I go over everything to be done for the day! But some days it all piles up. I could get more out of some of the gangs if we had another white man to supervise."

"I'm not in for more whites on the place, Mr. Greene. If you treat the slaves right, you'll find they'll go on working even if you have to go to another place."

126

Greene could hardly cover his snort of disbelief and scorn. Harte turned Roman around, looking towards the field, and gestured at the slaves pitching marl from the moving wagon.

"Who do you have in charge of the marling gang?"

"Nobody! They can't figure the number of bushels, or acres, or any of that!"

"It might help to have someone on the gang responsible for carrying out your directions, Mr. Greene. You do the figuring, but have a subaltern--a gang boss--to be in charge."

Greene was really disgusted now. It sounded like the General thought he was still in the army, directing sergeants and corporals.

"You can't run slaves like the army! There's no one smart enough to be a sub...a whatchacallit. Besides, I won't have any respect if the slaves think they're in charge of every gang. I'm in charge!"

"I suppose you're right for the field hands, Mr. Greene--it'll be a long time before we have any of them ready. But I want to move towards more responsibility for some of them, like the masons and the carpenters."

Harte turned Roman around, holding the horse in check for a moment longer.

"I'm going to check up on the building Jesse is working on in the slave quarters--that's the kind of slave I mean who can accept responsibility. He's one of the best bricklayers around this area now. When he gets the walls up to the ceiling height, I'll be calling on one of those carpenters you're using."

"Pretty fancy building for the slave quarters. What is it goin' to be for?" Greene asked.

Harte started to mention the chapel-school combination, but something warned him to be cautious. Greene wasn't in charge of building construction so he didn't know about the project. Harte decided not to speak about the school part yet.

"It's going to be a chapel for the slaves, Mr. Greene."

He heard the overseer snicker. Slapping the reins, he kicked Roman in the flanks and sped away before Greene could find out more. Laura had talked him into making the chapel suitable for schooling and he had agreed--it made sense for his long-term plans to get some of his slaves ready for freedom and going to the colony in Africa.

But people like Greene would be outraged about a school for

slaves. He wasn't afraid of his own overseer--he could fire Greene for insubordination if he had to. But Greene would angrily spread the word about a school for slaves in Richmond as soon as he found out. Then the public outcry would come soon enough. Harte pulled Roman to a walk, thinking about the trouble he'd meet in the city.

Harte eagerly looked out of the window of his phaeton as Sam turned the trim carriage into the sweeping curve of Ronda's mansion driveway.

"We'se home, Gen'rul," Sam called from the driver's seat.

Harte was getting back early from the trip to Richmond; he was tired, worried about the low prices his tobacco brought, and with some unspoken fear lurking at the back of his mind. But he suppressed it all, eager now to see if his family were out for their late afternoon romp in the garden. He caught sight of Laura and the two younger children. Jamie and Cissie were racing back up the hill to reach the veranda before the carriage did. Harte waved to Laura and saw her wave back, her face shadowed by the bonnet she used to protect her delicate skin. From memory he knew the smile that would be on her lovely face. He could almost sense the delicious warmth of her lips, the alluring fragrance of her soft embrace and her delightful laugh.

"Slow down, Sam," he said, breaking out of his daydream. "Let them get to the veranda first."

But the glow of homecoming hadn't buried the troubling thoughts that had been with Harte on his long ride from the city. Seeing Laura reminded him of the dangerous ground they were treading on now with their plans for the education of their slaves. He had to discuss it with her at the first opportunity.

Harte caught Laura around the waist as she took off her bonnet. Her shining auburn hair fell loose and she smiled, eyes sparkling as they embraced eagerly. They laughed when they broke away.

"Laura, you and the children look radiant!"

"We all feel good, James. It's so much better since Miss Meyersham came. The children love her teaching, even though she insists on afternoon sessions for the older ones. And I'm so relieved to be free of it!"

"So she's able to handle them all right--that's wonderful!"

128

He looked out over the garden and paused for a moment.

"Why don't we go and sit in the garden for awhile? I seldom have a chance to join you out here."

Laura called to Cissie and Jamie and they skipped happily ahead, glad to get another chance to dabble in the pond and its fountain. Harte chose a bench far enough from the fountain so the children couldn't hear their conversation.

"How was your agricultural meeting--the Albemarle, you call it?" she asked.

"Good and bad, I'm afraid. There were some reports on crops and fertilizers. I like the Albemarle, Laura--it's plantation owners who're serious about farming."

Cissie and Jamie were splashing in the pond and Laura called a warning to them, then turned back to Harte.

"So what was bad about it?"

"At the end of the meeting I was talking with friends and began to notice people pointing and looking at me. Finally, three men came over and broke in on our conversation."

"How rude! What was it all about?"

Harte shifted uneasily on the garden bench.

"Well ... They said they'd heard I had built a school for slaves on my place, and ..."

Laura put her hands to her face instinctively.

"How did they find out?" she gasped.

"I don't know, but they said I couldn't do that--they wouldn't let their whole economy and way of life be destroyed. Giving 'niggers' an education would make them dangerous ... Well, I won't go into it all, Laura. You know the language they'd use."

"Ohhh, James. What did you do?"

"Well, I couldn't stop them. The more they talked the louder they got, and a crowd gathered around us. It was pretty embarrassing."

"How awful! Didn't your friends stand by you?"

"The ones I thought were my friends drifted away before I knew it. I was alone."

"But didn't you tell them about the Colonization Society--about training our slaves for Africa?"

"I tried once to speak up, but they were hounding me and didn't intend to give me a chance. Finally I walked through the crowd and out the door. Nobody followed, but I had Sam take me to the inn quickly, just in case."

"What are you going to do about it, James?"

"What--the Albemarle meeting?"

"No, your plans for educating your slaves."

"Why ... Go ahead with them. We're doing the right thing, Laura. But we have to be cautious. We may be facing a lot worse things than the Albemarle unpleasantness some day. A lot of people are changing their minds about slavery these days--even Jefferson."

"Oh, did you see him about the university?"

Harte stood up to watch the children wandering through the garden.

"Yes--before the Albemarle. It's not my time to supervise construction until next month, but he's asking for my masonry gang right away."

Harte watched Laura closely.

"It--it means I'll have to pull Jesse off his work on our chapel-school, Laura. I hope you won't mind."

Laura's face clouded.

"Oh, James. We have so little time! Miss Meyersham's contract is only one year, you said. She'll teach the slaves at night, but what if the building isn't finished before she's ready to go home ... Oh no, James! I want her to be the one to begin the school for our slaves."

"I'll tell you what. Jesse's got the brick wall up high enough for the carpenters to put in the window frames. They can be doing that while he's gone. How about that?"

She smiled slowly and he began to breathe easier.

"Good!" Harte said before she could change her mind. "He'll be back and finish up the chapel soon."

"How is Jefferson?" Laura asked. "Can he really supervise the building of the university at his age?"

Harte laughed.

"He watches like a hawk from his hilltop at Monticello--says with his telescope he can see everything. We all believe it, too."

"He's planned everything carefully, I guess." Laura said.

"Even the curriculum! But I'm worried about the way he talks now. He wants Southern boys to come to the university rather than going north, because they'll be poisoned with anti-Missourianism up there."

"What's that?"

"Anti-slavery! The North fought the admission of Missouri as a slave state, don't you remember?"

"Why, Jefferson's the one who always said education was the means of liberating the human mind! And now he's going to use it to protect the interests of slaveholders?   James, what's happened to him?"

"I think the fight over Missouri shocked him. He told me it was like a fire bell in the night--waked him up filled with terror that the South might have to defend itself in a civil war someday. He really meant to protect slavery! He's lost all that democratic philosophy he used to have!"

Harte turned to look at Laura and she saw the fear in his eyes.

"Laura, I've always looked up to him! I know slavery is wrong and I know what I'm doing is the best way to end it. But if Jefferson no longer believes ... "

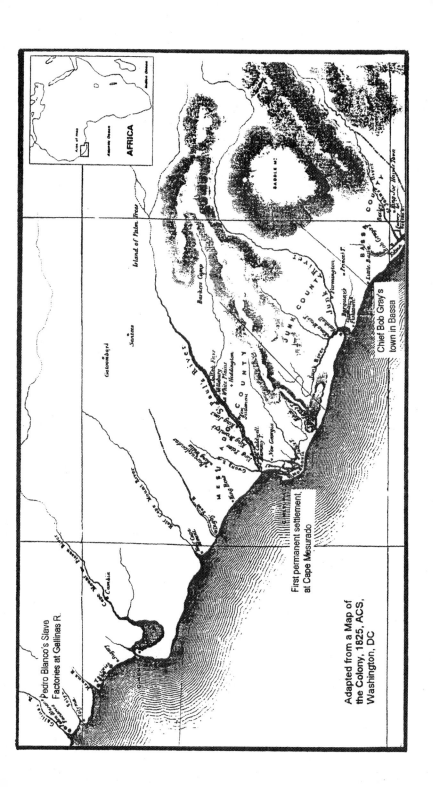

Pedro Blanco's Slave
Factories at Gallinas R.

First permanent settlement,
at Cape Mesurado

Chief Bob Gray's
town in Bassa

Adapted from a Map of
the Colony, 1825, ACS,
Washington, DC

AFRICA

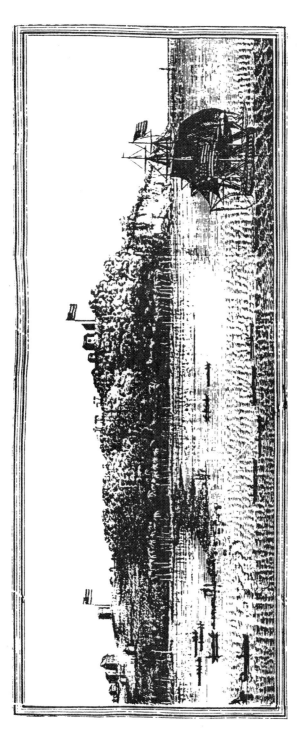

View of the Colonial Settlement at Cape Montserado

From the African Repository and Colonial Journal, Vol. III
(Washington: American Colonization Society, 1828)

Part 2

Birthing a Nation

A Memorial from the Free People of Colour to the
Citizens of Baltimore*

"We reside among you, and yet are strangers; native
and yet not citizens, surrounded by the freest people
and the most republican institutions in the world, and
yet enjoying none...If we were able and at liberty to go
whithersoever we would, the greater number, willing
to leave this community, would prefer Liberia, on the
coast of Africa ... already established there are many
of our brethren, the pioneers of African restoration ..."

Signed by:
William Cornish, Chairman
Robert Cowley, Secretary, at the
Bethel Church, December 7, 1826
Approved by:
James Deaver, Chairman
Remus Harvey, Secretary at the
African Church, Sharp Street
December 11, 1826

*American Colonization Society Papers, Library of Congress

15 The Clearing

Cape Mesurado
July 10, 1822

"That's a British warship out there, Elijah. Do you think they'd help us out?"

Blake was pointing to the schooner that had just dropped anchor about a half mile off shore in the shallow bay formed by the Cape and the land. Elijah, put in charge of the colony when Dr. Ayres and Wiltburger left for the United States, was as desperate as Blake for help. The colonists had completed the thatching of their houses in the clearing on top of the Cape, and moved in just as the heavy rains began. They were dry at least, but the food in the storehouse was running low, and the Africans had stopped bringing their produce to market on the waterside from fear of King George and his warriors.

"I don't like the idea of askin' the British for help," Elijah said. "Blast that George! I knew he would get back at us for winnin' the palaver about the Cape. We wouldn't have to go to the British if he'd just call off his runnin' dogs."

"Good name for'em, shootin' at us and then runnin' away," Blake said. "But now they're even shootin' at their own people at the market!"

"No--it's not his people bringin' the food in--it's the Mamba people from south of here. George is from the Dey tribe right around us. But I think he's scarin' everybody away, hopin' to starve us out."

"Is he just mad at us about the palaver?" Blake asked, shading his eyes to see the schooner better. "Or is he really tryin' to get rid of us?"

"I don't know, but we've used up most of the powder and ball for our muskets keepin' his men away. I hope that British captain out there'll spare us some from his stores--he must have plenty."

Blake turned and grinned at Elijah, gloating a little.

"So! My suggestion about that British ship isn't so bad, hey? You think maybe the first black guv'nor knows a little somethin'?"

Elijah laughed. "Governor! You!" he mocked, punching Blake on the shoulder playfully. "Why, you got us in this mess with King George in the first place."

Blake roughed him up in return, gleefully superior. "Well, I still was the first one!"

But Elijah's eyes lit up in triumph, and he chuckled. "You were only half of one. Fred James was equal with you--it was me that suggested you both to Doc Ayres 'afore we left for Freetown."

They both laughed, and sat down on a rock to look out again at the ship. Sitting on the highest point of the Cape, a mile-long peninsula thrust out into the water, they were suddenly awed to silence by the vastness of the ocean laying before them. Teal blue, its surface wind-ruffled and flecked with white caps, the Atlantic stretched to the horizon, unlimited. Lush green forests from behind them came down on their right and left to meet the ocean at golden sand beaches. A narrow line of creamy surf wavered constantly between land and water for miles in either direction, black rocks dotting it like markings on the back of a twisting snake.

Blake drew in a chestful of air sharply, and then turned to look down to the river at the foot of the Cape, and the little island they'd finally left.

"Perseverance Island--we named that right! It was worth it to stick it out down there, wasn't it. Remember when Doc Ayres wanted to quit 'cause the rainy season was startin' and we didn't have enough thatch for the houses?"

Elijah nodded his head, remembering too well. They'd sent an expedition into Stockton creek to cut thatch--ten men in the *Calypso's* long boat--cutting in the swamp all day, coming back exhausted but with a huge boat load of raffia palm branches. Then to discover the next day that it was only enough for one house up on the Cape! A whole day of learning to plait the palm branches into layers of thatch while balancing dangerously on the steep pole rafters of the house had tired them out like nothing else they'd ever done. King George had long since driven their African laborers away, so they'd had to learn this new craft by weary trial and error. Aching in their backs and legs, they complained loudly to the Agent when he called them all together on the island after their supper.

"Gentlemen, this can't go on!" Ayres had said. "You've only thatched one house in two days--it will take you another thirty days before you're in dry houses up there. By then the rainy season will have washed you away down here. This island is as low and unhealthy as Campelar, and half of you will be dead of fever. I can't allow it!"

Then he'd proposed that they return to Freetown for the duration of the rainy season and come back to the Cape to finish the houses safely in the dry time. Fred James and a half dozen others were for going back, figuring that by next dry season they'd be able to hire the Africans again. But Lott Cary had burst out in anger.

"I came to Africa to be free to make my own decisions, not to have some Agent telling me what I can or can't do! You wouldn't let me do my mission work all that time in Freetown. But I'm finally here in our own colony, and I'm goin' to begin my mission work now!"

Elijah had watched Ayres' tired face in the firelight, his reply heavy with sarcasm.

"We know, Reverend. We've been hearing a lot about your mission work. But I have to consider the lives of everyone. Now I want you all to think about this tonight and make up your minds by tomorrow morning. If we go back to Freetown, then I'll return to the United States in the *Calypso* to get more supplies and give the Society a full account of the situation."

Ayres and Wiltburger had slept that night on the *Calypso* as usual, and a violent storm had swamped the little island in the night, blowing water in sheets right through the flimsy shacks the colonists slept in. It was the second storm of the rainy season, and the next morning when the agents came on shore all the colonists were soaked to the skin, standing silently at the makeshift dock to meet them. Ayres stepped off the longboat, a triumphant look on his face.

"Ah hah! Didn't I tell you, gentlemen? This isn't going to work. That storm was just the beginning--but you'll all be safe and dry back at the plantation in Freetown. I'm sure we can rent it again."

Lott Cary stepped forward.

"We met last night and considered your proposal, Doctor."

Ayres frowned and looked to the others, obviously displeased that Cary was the spokesman for the group. But no one else spoke.

"Yes?" Ayres said. "What did you decide?"

"We've decided to stay. If we leave now, we might not be able to get the Cape back again. The Africans might ..."

"Nonsense!" Ayres cut him off. "We'll keep possession by

134

leaving some of our things here in one of these shacks. I'll ask John Mill to come stay on the island until we get back from Freetown."

"But the Africans have found excuses before to take the land back. We don't want to lose it again!" Cary protested.

"Confound it, Reverend! We're not giving up our title to this place just because we don't build on it right away!"

Lott Cary drew himself up, his rugged face scowling fiercely.

"But we say we don't want to take that chance again!"

Elijah saw they both were getting angry, and he moved closer. But Ayres and Cary stood toe to toe, eyeing each other fiercely, oblivous of anyone else.

"And I say I'm in charge here!"

Ayres, face red and eyes blazing, turned on his heels and walked a few paces away, turning back to look at the silent crowd. He pointed at Cary and shook his finger at him.

"This man has only one thing on his mind--his mission! But there won't be any mission if you die of fever! What do the rest of you say? I haven't heard anybody else talk!"

Elijah cleared his throat.

"Doctor, it's been two long years I've sought a home, and now we've found it, I want to stay here. But you might want to see somethin' over here before we decide."

He motioned to a small pile of green stuff, and walked over to pick something from it. Ayres hesitated, then followed, his red face fading to its usual fever-ridden pallor.

"What's that?" he asked gruffly.

"It's a roof leaf like they had at Sherbro," Elijah said, handing a broad green leaf to Ayres. "Allen James found it up on the Cape yestiday and showed it to us last night. He says it's all over the place."

"Roof leaf?" Ayres looked skeptical. "You mean you can roof all the houses with this? No boat trips to cut palm branches in the swamps?"

"That's right. Just pick it off the trees. And we don't have to plait it like palm thatch. Soon's we get the hang of it, we'll likely finish all the houses in a week or week and a half."

"You're sure about this, Mr. Johnson?"

Elijah turned and looked at the others. "We've all seen it at Sherbro, haven't we?"

They all nodded their heads, but Ayres still didn't look convinced.

135

"We started to do the palm thatch 'cause that's the way they do it here," Elijah explained.

"Well, who's right?" Ayres snapped. "Sherbro people or these people?"

"I guess it depends on what you're used to," Elijah said. "I saw some houses down at Bassa where they even used some kind'a grass for thatchin'."

So Ayres had given in and stayed with them until they covered all the houses and moved into them. Then Ayres and Wiltburger had gone back to the States in the *Calypso* for ...

"Well, Elijah, are you goin' out to that British schooner or not?" Blake shouted at him.

Elijah jerked his head up, the memory of the thatching shut off like turning a picture to the wall. He stood up and stretched.

"All right, let's go out in the longboat and see that captain. We've got to have some more powder and ball. Maybe he'll have a barrel or two of corn meal we can trade for, too."

But when they reached the British schooner an hour later and boarded her, the officer was stiff and formal, and Elijah felt an old anger begin to burn.

"No food, Mr. Johnson--we're short on rations ourselves. We've been cruising four months now and even the ship biscuits are full of the little crawlers. I was hoping we could get some fresh meat and water from King George."

"All right, Captain. I sure hope you find George in a friendly mood. He's had his men shootin' at us for quite a spell and we're almost out of powder and ball for our muskets. Could you spare us some?"

"Having a little war with the natives, are we?" the Captain said, assessing Elijah closely through squinting eyes.

Elijah stared back, almost feeling the calculating mind behind those eyes, hating the patronizing smile beneath them. It was just like the snickering British types he'd seen in the Great Lakes country during the 1812 War.

"No sir, we're just protectin' ourselves from George's snipers."

"Well ... we might be able to help you out. Can't let go of ammunition, you know, but we can send our marines ashore for a little action."

"A little action?"

"Yes, that's right. Our marines can run a fast sweep of the

coast here and scare the natives off for good."

It didn't seem to fit, and something warned Elijah.

"Why would you do that, if you can't even share a little powder and ball?"

The Captain smiled ingratiatingly.

"Well, there is one condition, Mr. Johnson."

"What's that?"

"You'll have to give us a place to put up our flag. We can't protect any land that's not British, you know."

The burn in the back of Elijah's mind exploded.

"No, by God! We want no flag pole here that'll cost us more trouble to pull down than it would to flog the natives!"

Elijah turned to Blake. "C'mon, Blake!" Angrily taking him by the arm, Elijah led the way to the railing. Before going down the gang plank to the waiting boat, he shot an angry glance back at the Captain.

"I fought your kind back in 1812 with Commander Perry on Lake Erie, and we licked you good! Might do it again someday!"

Neither Blake or Elijah spoke until the longboat pulled away from the schooner, and then Blake exploded, too.

"What'd you get so mad for! You took away our only chance! Some kind of gov'nor you are!"

"Oh shut up!" Elijah said. "Neither one of us is or was a governor--we just hold on 'til a new agent gets here."

"Well, whatever we are, you hadn't ought to get mad just when some help is offered!"

"Don't you know what he was doin'?" Elijah said with disbelief.

"Yeah! He wanted a place to put his flag before he sent his soldiers out to scare away George's men. So give him a little piece. There's lots'a land around here!"

Elijah looked at the backs of the colonists who were rowing the longboat, deciding not to argue anymore about it in their hearing.

"Only one more thing I'm goin' to say," he said. "It comes from what my Ma told me long ago--one of those African sayings her Pa taught her. Listen to it good now: 'Too late to take caution when the leopard got you in his mouth.'"

Blake laughed, repeating it scoffingly.

"Too late to take caution ... what was the rest?"

Elijah bore into Blake with angry, disgusted eyes.

"When the leopard got you in his mouth! Don't you ever let the British get a foothold on any land around this colony--you hear that?"

Blake recoiled from Elijah's angry shout. But his eyes narrowed in thought.

"Yeah ... yeah, I hear you, Lije. You may be right. But what're you goin' to do now about some powder and ball? King George don't seem to be runnin' out of his. And what about food?"

Elijah saw the other colonists rowing the boat turn their heads slightly to hear him, and he knew he'd better say something to keep their hopes up.

"Doc Ayres said when he left that he'd try to see to it that another ship comes out soon with more people and supplies. I think it'll be quicker than the last one."

But Elijah saw Blake shake his head, and he realized he had the same doubts. Now we're really in trouble, he thought. Sweat broke out on Elijah's forehead as he turned it over in his mind. There hadn't been time to start raising any food yet, and if George made good on his blockade, and a ship didn't come soon ...

July 29, 1822

John Bannon seemed to have come over to visit Carrie this evening, but she was still busy seeing that Elijah's children took their baths and went to bed. Elijah and John sat on the porch bench, hearing the noises through the woven mat wall of the house as Carrie dipped precious water into a big pan from the bucketful the boys had brought from the spring. But John revealed his real interest by asking for Elijah's permission to start his trading business right away.

"Sorry, John," Elijah said. "It's not safe to build stores on the waterside just now."

"But the Society said we'd replace the slave trade with honest trade--that's what I'm trying to do! And I've got to have my store down on the landing to do it."

Elijah smiled. John Bannon was smart--he knew just the right things to say. Crowding out the slave trade by peaceful means was an important thing. But the smile disappeared from Elijah's lips as he thought of their need right now just to survive.

"First things first, John. We've got to protect ourselves from

George's men. I can't let you or nobody else build down there just now."

"I thought you took care of that last week! I haven't seen or heard any snipers since."

"Yeah, we thought so ... "

Elijah didn't finish his sentence, remembering last week's action. For two weeks they'd been shut off so tight by a blockade of King George's snipers that Elijah had called a council of war. To a man, the colonists were for an attack on the snipers--even if it took all the remaining powder and ball. Elijah told the council about the British captain's idea of a sweep of the cape by the ship's marines. Blake reminded them of how George's men at the springs had turned and fled when the colonists whooped and hollered as they attacked. Fred James suggested the cannon, but everyone knew it was impossible to move it around fast enough. Charles Brander said that after the sweep of the Cape they should patrol the forest paths so the Mamba people could bring food into the colony the back way, instead of at the waterside.

After planning it, Elijah had called for volunteers. The sweep worked, and Elijah was as proud as the others that they'd carried out their first organized military action to protect the colony. The sound of George's muskets was gone from the Cape and the Mamba people had started bringing food to the market again. But now the colony was down to a half-keg of powder and one box of lead balls--not enough to patrol the forest behind the Cape or defend themselves from serious attack. Worse than that, this morning a secret messenger had brought alarming news to Elijah. So bad he'd not told anyone about it yet.

"You thought so?" John interrupted his thoughts. "Is King George going to send his men back to snipe at us again?"

"No, I think we scared'em off for good, but ..."

"But what?"

Elijah squirmed on the bench, hesitating to say it.

"I ... I haven't told anyone yet, John, so keep this close. But this mornin' I got word that George is goin' around to other kings to get up enough warriors to attack us for real."

"God a'mighty," John Bannon said, his eyes widening. "Who--who sent the message?"

"Some chief south of here, by the name of Bob Gray. His messenger says Bob Gray met me when I went with Andrus and Bacon to get land at Bassa. That was the deal that didn't work."

"I remember. But what did Bob Gray say? How many warriors is George going to get together?"

"I don't know. Bob Gray just said George had asked him for warriors, and he was lettin' us know because he was our friend. Maybe none of the kings or chiefs'll join George. But you see now why you can't build your store down there, don't you?"

"Yes. There would be no way to protect it, I guess."

"That's right. We'd have enough to do just to defend our little town up here."

Elijah saw a look of disappointment spread across John's face.

"But you could help the colony by beginnin' your tradin' up here, and you'd be safe," Elijah said.

"How? People wouldn't climb the Cape to trade!"

"If there were a market and store, the Mambas and others could come through the forest from the south."

Interest sparked in John's eyes.

"What would I trade for?"

"It'd be a big help for the colony if you'd buy rice and palm oil--food we'll need real bad if a ship doesn't come soon. Then later you could trade for things you want to send to America."

Carrie came out on the porch, overhearing part of Elijah's talk.

"When is the next ship comin', Elijah?" she asked quietly, resting herself on the porch railing.

Elijah saw John stare at her rapturously, a lovesick smile on his face.

"I wish I knew," Elijah said, sighing. "Why?"

"I'm hopin' to hear from my folks," she said, too wistful and tired to notice John's stare. "It'd be nice to hear from home some time."

16   A Powerful Need

Cape Mesurado
August 8, 1822

Rumors that King George was getting more warriors together to attack the colony kept everyone close to the little town in the clearing--now twenty-seven dwellings and a storehouse. The men formed a daytime guard to watch over all trips to the spring for water or for food at the waterside. No land had been cleared for crops yet, nor was it considered safe to work too far away. Confined in their little community, the women had little else to do besides feed their families and watch the children.

Although she did her usual tasks each day for Elijah's household, Carrie settled into a dull routine, moving around mechanically, acting from force of habit. Her mind seemed occupied and she went for long periods without saying anything. After two years of hoping to hear from her parents, her yearning for a message from home had taken over her life, and she thought of little else but the ship that would bring it.

Carrie took to walking up to a high point of the clearing with Elijah's three children after the morning rains were over each day, so she could search the wide blue Atlantic for a ship. Lewis and Charlie enjoyed the walks, but Lizzie, only four, tired soon and always had to be picked up. For Carrie the walk to the hill and the brief search of the ocean provided bittersweet moments of hope. She clung with an aching heart to the belief that the next ship would have news of her parents. Elijah understood and let them go, as long as they stayed in the clearing.

This morning the rain had lasted longer than normal, giving less time for the trip up the hill and the vigil. But when the sun finally broke through, they went as usual.

Lewis was the first to see something.

"There's a ship, Carrie!"

"Where?" Her heart fluttered as she anxiously scanned the watery vastness.

"I don't see it. Where is it?"

"Over there--it's just a tiny white speck!"

She ran to his side and had him hold up his arm to point so

she could sight along it. There it was, a small square of white against the blue, the mainsail of a ship way off to the north.

"Glory ... Oh, Glory be! It is one! A ship! A ship!"

They ran down the hill to tell Elijah and anyone else they saw. But the ship, tacking south against the blustering rainy season winds, did not make anchorage in the bay until near sundown--too late to send a boat to shore before dark.

"They'll be in soon's the rain is done in the mornin', Carrie. Then we'll find out who and what they be," Elijah consoled her at supper time.

Like Carrie, the colonists were all excited--hoping that the ship was from the Society, bringing mail and packages and more emigrants, possibly friends or loved ones. But Elijah, secretly desperate about the colony's survival, prayed fervently that night just for supplies.

"We've got a powerful need down here, Lord ..."

Only he and Blake knew they'd divided up the last barrel of salt pork yesterday, and were near bottom on the flour barrel. The few rounds of powder and ball left were useless, the powder so damp it wouldn't fire. There was now no way to defend themselves from the Africans' threatened attack.

"So we're restin' in your hands, Lord--dependin' on you."

A violent rain storm delayed the launching of the ship's boat until noon the next day. But the land was already steaming from a blazing sun when the longboat broke through the rough surf and reached the landing place on the river. A white couple were first off the boat, the man tall, spare, scholarly looking, and the woman slender and delicate, but with a determined manner. The man turned to Elijah, offering his hand.

"I'm Yehudi Asmun, sent by the Colonization Society. Is Doctor Ayres or Mr. Wiltburger here?"

"Didn't you know?" Elijah said, shaking Ashmun's hand. "They left here June 4th."

"No! We sailed from Baltimore before that--on May 20th."

"It took you from then to now in August?"

Ashmun grimaced. "Eighty-one days exactly. I'm afraid the *Strong* is a poor ship. We had to put in for repairs in the Azores. So who's in charge of the colony?"

"I am. My name's Elijah Johnson. I was left in charge. This is Joseph Blake and Fred James and Reverend Lott Cary. They're helpin' me."

Ashmun shook hands and Elijah turned to the white woman, offering his hand. "This is your Missus, I guess."

Ashmun introduced his wife, Catherine, and then turned to Blake.

"Your wife and children are on board, Mr. Blake. The surf was too rough to bring the families in, but we'll unload everybody as soon as we can."

Blake's mouth opened, his eyes lit up, and he dropped his musket.

"Whooee! Praise the Lord! Thank you, thank you, thank you!"

As Blake picked up his musket, Ashmun introduced the other emigrants stepping from the boat.

"This is James Benson, Major Draper, Daniel Hawkins, Thomas Tynes, Joseph Gardiner--and here are the Campbell brothers, Samuel and James."

They shook hands all around, and while they were talking Elijah stood back to count the newcomers. He motioned Ashmun over to his side.

"This is all the men?" he asked Ashmun.

"No, there are five or six more. Two are elderly and there wasn't space in the boat for the others."

Elijah's face fell.

"Why?" asked Ashmun.

"We're goin' to need plenty of men who can hold a musket. The Africans are gettin' ready to attack us, I hear."

Ashmun's face blanched, and he looked intently at Elijah.

"You're sure of this? When?"

"Don't know. Maybe not too soon. Way we hear it, not many've joined up with King George yet. But he's still workin' on it."

"Well, we have fifteen other young men on board, but they're recaptives from a Spanish slaver caught on the Georgia coast. They don't speak English."

Elijah looked doubtful. "Whose side would they be on?"

"On the colony's, I think. Have you got some place for us all to stay?"

"No. We just barely got ourselve fixed up. But you're all welcome to stay in our houses 'til some more get built."

Worry lines creased Ashmun's forehead.

"How about a storage space for supplies? We've brought

143

quite a bit."

Elijah smiled with relief.

"Sure glad to hear that! We're clean out of almost everything. Why don't you all come up to the clearing and see our town?"

The squad of guards formed up, and with Elijah and the Ashmuns in the lead, the crowd of welcoming colonists and newcomers struggled up the steep slope of the Cape. The children burst into happy chatter as the women helped them climb. Carrie picked up Lizzie and turned to the boys, pointing at one of the new men.

"Lewis," she said in a low voice, "I think I know that man. He's from Philadelphia, sure as a cat's got a tail."

Lewis craned his neck to see. Just then the man turned to look at Carrie closely. His weathered brown face crinkled around his eyes and he smiled.

"You--you're Martha Reeves child, ain't you!"

Carrie's heart hammered and she gulped for air.

"Yes'm," she managed to say, but had to catch her breath. Breathing hard, she tried again.

"Yes'm," she grinned. "I shore is!"

"Well, I'm Daniel Hawkins, and my wife's got a message for you, child. Right from your Ma'self. She'll tell you 'bout it when she gets on land, maybe tomorrow."

"Ohhhh ... my Ma done it! My Ma! My Ma! She sent me word!"

Carrie didn't know whether to laugh or cry, but tears flooded her face and she finally let loose the sobs she'd held back so long. Daniel Hawkins put his arms around her and patted her shoulders.

"Why's she cryin'?" Lewis asked. "I thought she'd be happy."

"She is, son. She's just been waitin' too long a time, I s'pect."

When they reached the top of the Cape, Elijah and his assistants gave the newcomers a tour. It took Ashmun two hours to survey the condition of the colony, asking them many questions and observing the Cape and its surroundings carefully. They showed him the little town with its main street and two short cross streets where the houses and storehouse were built. On the northeast corner of the clearing Elijah proudly pointed out the new market shelter John Bannon had nearly finished with the Kroo men he'd hired. Then he pointed to a well-beaten path that led to edge of the clearing.

"That's the way to the spring where we get fresh water. It's just over the edge of the hill."

Ashmun complimented them on building a fine little community in spite of many obstacles. "I'll be proud to join you in going forward from here. The Society authorized me to become the Principal Agent if Ayres and Wiltburger were gone." He handed a paper to Elijah.

Elijah smiled broadly and pumped Ashmun's hand.

"Welcome, Mr. Agent! We're mighty glad to have you come. Couldn't be any too soon, the way I feel."

Elijah gathered all the colonists at the storehouse immediately. Standing around in the late afternoon sun, they watched excitedly as he introduced the newcomers formally and read the Society's letter of authorization for the new Agent. After some more handshaking and congratulations, Ashmun asked Elijah, Blake, Fred James, and Lott Cary to make some plans with him. They moved to Elijah's porch for another half hour of talk and then listened, first with surprise and then growing admiration as Ashmun quietly began to issue a stream of directives in rapid succession.

Elijah was ordered to purchase 100 mats from the Africans for the walls and ceilings of new houses; he was to be the colony storekeeper of these and all other supplies. Fred James was to superintend the construction of a new storehouse opposite the first one. Blake would have the new market shelter closed in with mud-plastered walls as a temporary dormitory for the recaptive youths. Lott Cary would receive the medical kit and supplies Ashmun had brought and treat the colonists for their ailments.

"I'll work alongside you, gentlemen, in everything," Ashmun promised, standing up and shaking their hands. "We'll meet again tomorrow morning to plan locations for new houses and to hire some laborers to help the newcomers build them."

Then they would plan for the defense of the colony, he told them. But they should also think about friendly visits to the chiefs to counter King George's war-mongering. For now, Ashmun and his party would return to the *Strong* for the night. Unloading would proceed in the next few days as fast as accommodations for people and supplies could be built.

Still shaken by the speed of Ashmun's decisions, Elijah and

his assistants walked the newcomers down to the landing and the *Strong's* waiting longboat, watching as the oarsmen shoved off and began to row out toward the ship. From the dying sun a yellow-gold light glared off the calm evening sea, boat and passengers a dark silhouette against it, retreating for the night. Sounds of clicking oarlocks and splashing paddles faded, leaving only the surf's low roar.

Fred James sighed.

"Lord a'mighty!" he said, breaking into the thoughts of the silent group standing on shore in the twilight. "Can we keep up with him?"

Elijah laughed.

"We better try! The way he took hold, I believe we got us a man this time who's goin' to stay with us."

"Maybe you better wait and see," Blake offered. "He and his missus haven't been through fever yet."

"He'd better watch how he throws his orders around!" snapped Lott Carey. "I don't want to be told what I have to do all the time. I need to start my mission work."

17 Bad Fruit

Cape Medurado
August 16, 1822

"I hope Brister is goin' to be there, " Elijah grumbled, holding tight to the sides of the wildly pitching canoe as it thrust out from shore through the boiling surf.

"He will--I sent word yesterday that we wanted to talk to him," Ashmun replied, twisting half way round in his seat. "He sent back that he would see us."

Elijah knew it was important to get to the really big chiefs before King George talked them into joining a war party against the colony. Elijah and Fred James had gone with Ashmun to visit King Peter and King Long Peter earlier in the week, so Brister was the only other big chief left. At least that's what Fred and Blake had told Ashmun. But Elijah wasn't sure about that.

The canoe turned and followed the shore in a northern direction now, Elijah feeling the wind at their backs and a current pushing them along as the Kru men paddled steadily. He watched the powerful shoulders and arms of Prince Will paddling in the front, muscles rippling in tireless rhythm under glistening black skin. Suddenly Will jerked his paddle violently to thrust against a vicious cross-current. It was dangerous work needing a bold man who knew the treacherous waves. Elijah found himself admiring the skill of the man--in fact all of the Kroo men--who seemed to be fearless in good or bad weather. He'd heard they were the only people who did this work on the sea, hiring themselves out to ships and boats anywhere along the coast.

The sun came out and Elijah smiled to himself. Could it be that his own African ancestors were Kroo? Why had he liked the work he did in the Navy and working on the docks in New York? For the first time since landing on the African shore Elijah thought about where his people had come from back when his ma's grandpa was carried to America on a slave ship. Had her grandpa been a Kroo man? But Kroo people didn't make or take slaves, Elijah remembered hearing.They worked for slavers and non-slavers alike, so long as it was work on water. And they wore a blue tattoo mark on their nose as a sign they were free, not to be sold as slaves themselves. So Ma's grandpa couldn't have been Kroo ...

"There's Krootown!" Fred James called, pointing shoreward.

Ashmun and Elijah looked at the busy mat-and-thatch village stretched along the beach. Men were repairing fish nets and canoes, while small boys splashed at the edge of the water and women and girls tended racks of fish over smoking fires. Elijah and Fred had been in parts of Krootown, but never seen it just off-shore like this. Ashmun, new to it all, touched the lead paddler on his shoulder to get his attention.

"Are those your people?" he asked.

"They be Kroo," Prince Will acknowledged, "but no be my dako."

"Dako? What is dako?"

"White man say 'tribe'. My dako be Klepo people--we be fisherman, strong for canoe palaver," he said proudly.

"What are those people?" Ashmun persisted.

The Kroo man snorted derisively.

"They be Kabor! My dako no like Kabor people."

"But they look like fisherman, too."

"Klepo be better!"

Ashmun turned back to Elijah with a smile. "A little tribal jealousy, I guess. Which ones would we hire to help build the colony?"

Elijah didn't know that much about the different Kroo tribes. These names sounded strange to him. "Seems like there's other tribes in Krootown. The ones that John Bannon hired called themselves Wetu."

Ashmun tapped Prince Will on the shoulder again.

"What about the Wetu people? Are there some in Krootown now?"

Again the Kroo man snorted, this time in great disgust. "Wetu is bushman Kroo! No fishman--no canoe palaver."

He slapped his paddle on the water like a novice. "They be so-so bush people."

"But we need some people to work on the land," Ashmun said. "To help us make houses and other things. Are bushman Kroo good for that?"

There was a long silence, Prince Will paddling steadily, keeping the canoe headed north and slightly west against the incoming current.

"Wetu, Wea, Dufa--they all be good for that," he said finally. "Some Wetu people in Krootown just now. They go back home soon."

"Would they stay long enough to build some houses for us?" Ashmun asked.

"All Kroo people work for white man the same--British, 'Merican, Frenchy. You make book for time, he work that time for you, then you carry him home."

Ashmun looked back at Elijah, raising his eyebrows.

Elijah nodded his head, remembering what he'd heard at Freetown.

"The British Navy hires'em at Freetown," he said, "and then drops'em off down the coast when they're finished with the cruise."

"Where would we have to take them back to?" Ashmun asked Prince Will.

"Be for their own town, like Setta Kroo or NanaKroo. We call it Five Tribes place--white man call it Kroo Coast."

Again Ashmun twisted around, looking at Elijah and Fred.

"We need those houses built right away for the people we brought on the *Strong*. I'll hire about forty Wetus to help us, and afterwards take them down the coast on the *Calypso*. Does that sound alright?"

Elijah started to respond but something vague in the back of his mind made him hesitate.

"Mr. Johnson?" Ashmun prompted.

"Just wonderin' ..." Elijah mumbled, drawing it out of his mind slowly. "If the Kroo people are workin' inside our colony ... where do they stand if George's people attack us?"

Ashmun touched the lead paddler on the shoulder again.

"If Wetu people are making houses on the Cape, and King George makes war on us, what will the Wetu do?"

Prince Will answered immediately.

"If war come to Cape, Kroo people leave quick-quick! It be your war, no be for us!"

Elijah and Ashmun exchanged glances, and Elijah nodded.

"It figures," he said. "Up here they're for hire, and it's not their country. Might be different down on the Kroo coast, 'though."

They settled back on their seats, waiting now for the Kroo men to turn in at the mouth of the St. Paul river and go up it a short distance to King Brister's village. Elijah's mind was churning with questions. What would the Kroo do if war got to their own coast? But he knew immediately--who wouldn't fight for their own place?

Maybe that was what the Dey, Mamba, and Gola tribes around the Cape were so worried about now. But why can't they understand we're their brothers? This is our home, too--all we need is a piece of it! Suddenly he was fed up and he slammed the edge of the canoe hard.

"Damn their selfish hides!"

"What's that?" Ashmun said, turning his head to hear, but not looking back.

"Nuthin! Just thinking about this war talk," Elijah muttered. "They have plenty of land--weren't even livin' on the Cape itself! Why can't they share some of it without all this fuss?"

"It's strange, isn't it," Ashmun twisted around again. "When we visited King Peter and his young nephew Long Peter the other day, they were very friendly, but still insisted we owed more for the land and that another palaver would be needed to settle it. Are they just trying to get more goods from us?"

"I don't know," Elijah said. "There's something else going on, but I can't figure it out."

Ashmun looked at Elijah intently. "Please try, Mr. Johnson."

"Well, when we made the deed for the land I thought we were dealin' with the Dey and Mamba tribes who live around the Cape. But I just heard the other day that two of the chiefs who signed the deed were from the Gola tribe, and that the Golas didn't used to live so close--they've come down from the interior to settle around here and they're gettin' more powerful."

"What two chiefs is that, Elijah?" Fred James asked.

"One of'em is King Peter's young nephew, King Long Peter. He's part Dey and part Gola. And the other is King Zoda--he's young, too, but he's pure Gola. That'd make him more powerful in their tribe."

Elijah saw Ashmun's eyes squint like he was thinking hard.

"What does that have to do with the deed, Mr. Johnson?"

"I'm not sure. But those two young chiefs had a lot of say so when we were havin' the land palaver with Stockton and Ayres. Old King Peter seemed to be the boss, but Zoda and Long Peter did a lot of talkin' on the side. I think they must be havin' more say so now, too. Maybe that's why Long Peter was there the day we went to see King Peter."

"Are the Gola chiefs working their way into the places of influence in this area?" Ashmun asked. "Is that what you're getting at?"

Elijah hesitated. "Something like that, I guess."

"How is it going to affect us?"

"I don't know, but I have a hunch."

Ashmun's face darkened in frustration. "A hunch! What is it?"

"Well, Zoda looked us over pretty good one time when we were on the island as he went by in a boat. I could tell he was a pretty powerful chief, checkin' us out careful like, and ... and maybe he's what they call a 'zo'--some sort of big man in their secret society. They call it the Poro."

Ashmun sighed. "Good Lord! What is the Poro?"

"I think it must be some kind of a secret link between tribes--maybe ones that even fight each other sometimes."

"Whooee!" Fred James interrupted. "Where do you get all that stuff, Elijah?"

"Yes, Mr. Johnson, how did you learn all that? Is it really true?"

Elijah pointed to Prince Will's back. "John Mill told me some. But ask Will--I'll bet he knows. All the Kroo people seem to know about the other tribes--they work for anybody on the coast, y'know. And now that the Golas are coming down to get into the coastal trade, Kroos probably work for them, too."

Ashmun turned around to the front of the canoe, tapping Prince Will's shoulder lightly.

"You heard us, Will. Is it true? About the Poro, I mean?"

"Kroo people know plenty 'bout Poro. It be all over--Dey and Mamba and Vai got Poro, but Gola Poro be strong past all. Poro in Sierra Leone, too. Up there Mende Poro be strong past Gola Poro."

Ashmun turned back to Elijah.

"I still don't see what this has to do with us."

Elijah's mind was struggling for something--something he'd heard long ago--about Boatswain. It came out slowly, from what Ayres had said on the island.

"Boatswain--he controls the trade in the interior, both slaves and goods. He wants to be friendly with us because of trade. After the slave trade is over he'll want to trade with us for goods. That's what Ayres believes."

"He may be right," Ashmun said. "But what about the Golas?"

Now it was coming clear in Elijah's mind. Trade ... control of trade.

"The Golas are just beginnin' to take over on the coast from the Deys and Vais. And they won't want Boatswain to trade directly with us. I s'pect they'll want the coast trade themselves."

"I see ... so the Golas might want to get rid of the colony and control the trade themselves when they get powerful enough to dominate this whole area. But still--what about the Poro?"

Elijah thought about it a long time. Ashmun waited, his eyes squinted. Finally Elijah began to think out loud.

"If Zoda and Long Peter are part of the Gola Poro ... and if it's really a powerful secret society across all tribes ... then they not only can pass on messages, but orders, too."

Ashmun's eyes opened wide, his face turning pale.

"You mean, like orders for war?"

"Maybe."

"Come on, Lije!" Fred James said. "Zoda and Long Peter make orders for war? They're too young!"

"I didn't say they'd make'em--just pass'em on."

"But how can all these tribes get together to fight against us when they're usually fighting each other?" Ashmun asked.

"Maybe through the Poro? ... I don't know. But it looks like we could be up against a lot more tribes than just the Dey and Mamba like we thought."

"Good Lord!" Ashmun said. "Let's hope Brister can talk them out of war."

Prince Will and his paddler concentrated on catching a wave to pass over the sand bar at the river mouth. The three passengers held on tight as the Kroo men maneuvered the canoe in the choppy waves just outside the boiling surf. Suddenly Will shouted to his man and they paddled furiously, riding a high wave that pushed them through the surf, giving them the few inches of clearance needed to get over the bar. As soon as the canoe was safely over, Prince Will gave a warning in a low voice.

"We be coming close to Brister's town. Our people have a saying, 'When your hand be in lion's mouth, you take it out softly, softly.' Not good to talk Poro business now."

They understood, and silently watched the edge of a large village come into sight around the bend of the river. When they were fully round the bend, a breath-taking scene lay before them. About two hundred round huts covered a wide, gentle slope rising from the river's edge, their cylindrical mud walls painted with dazzling white clay and capped by nut brown cones of thatch.

Shining in the late morning sun against the azure blue sky, the village's rustic beauty glimmered in the dappled river water, a striking double image. "Whooee--look at that!" Fred James said.

"King Brister seems to be quite a leader, to have a place like this!" Ashmun marveled. Elijah nodded in speechless wonder.

Seated on three-legged stools, Ashmun's delegation waited outside the chief's large square house under a round thatch roof supported by poles. To Elijah the entire village seemed to be looking on from outside of this simple palaver hall, all talking exitedly. Children emerged at the feet of their parents and crept closer to stare at the strangers, suddenly jumping back and shrieking in terror when Ashmun jerked to balance himself on his three-legged stool. The grown-ups laughed at the childrens' fright, but Elijah saw uneasiness in their own faces. Everyone fell silent abruptly as five headmen filed solemnly out of the house, followed by Brister. They remained standing until he seated himself on a small, ornately carved black stool with four legs and a low back piece.

Brister was wearing the open blue and white robe of thick homespun cotton used by chiefs, but it had a single pocket sewn at an odd angle on the front. He wore cowhide sandals on his feet, and held the usual fly switch with leather handle in his right hand. Elijah could see the stiff black hairs of a real elephant tail in it and knew Brister was no ordinary chief, because most chiefs had only straggly thin cow tail hair in their switches.

The chief sat quietly, looking at the delegation with an unhurried dignity, his eyes surveying each person carefully. He showed no lordly airs or puffed-up pride, and Elijah observed the deep respect the villagers had for him. It was said that Brister was a son and grandson of chiefs, and Elijah noticed the calm way he wore this inherited mantle of power over his people. It seemed to be a power he used carefully and deliberately. The trust and veneration they gave him in return could be seen on their faces.

This is the way African kings should be, Elijah thought. After two years of meeting greedy, crafty chiefs like Sherbro and Ben and Peter who took our rum and tobacco, and deceived us with delays and more delays and ... Suddenly Elijah's faith in African chiefs was beginning to be restored, and he felt some of the pride

153

these people showed their ruler. It was like he had always dreamed of--Africa, a place where real wisdom and trust and respect stood high in the scheme of things. *If only Brister will help us ...*

A brief smile flickered across Brister's wrinkled, gray-bearded face as his eyes steadily continued to study the delegation. Elijah turned to see Ashmun's face, wondering if the silence was bothering him, but Ashmun was holding himself stiffly composed, trying to keep his balance on the stool. Finally Brister raised his fly switch, alerting everyone, and then he cleared his throat.

"You send message you want to talk. I say I be here today. Now you come. For what thing we talk?"

"I am the new agent of the colony," Ashmun said slowly and Elijah saw Brister nod in acknowledgement. Ashmun took a careful breath and continued.

"They told me you were friendly to the colony when Boatswain was called down to judge the palaver between King George and the colonists. I want to thank you for your friendship that time. We hope you will continue to be our friend."

Elijah, watching Brister's face closely, saw no response, and he felt his own chest tighten slightly. *It seemed a good way to start, but ...* Ashmun cleared his throat and began again.

"We hear that King George is going about talking up a war, trying to get the chiefs to bring their warriors and join him in attacking us. We do not want war. We want to be ..."

Brister's eyes glinted, his brows furrowing, and Elijah sucked in his breath. *Was Ashmun going too fast?*

"... peaceful and to trade with all our neighbors who want to be friends." Ashmun reached out with his open right hand toward Brister. "We can offer you fine American and European goods in trade for food your people grow--like rice, and corn, beans, yams--and other things. It will be good for both sides, this trade."

Brister's glare softened.

"I agree for black people from 'Merica to settle on Cape," he began. "I 'gree for it when Boatswain come down, and I 'gree for it now. It be good thing."

"And the trade? You will trade with us?" Ashmun pressed.

There was a long stretch of silence, and Elijah wondered what the chief was thinking about. Brister turned to the headman on his left and spoke quietly. Elijah knew it was the Dey language; he couldn't understand it, but he liked the respectful way the chief spoke to each headman and heard him out before going on to the next. Brister paused after all five had their say, and then he said something to them before turning back to Ashmun.

"We see your new people from last boat not settled and goods not all landed. When it finish, I be coming to pay friendly visit and talk about trade. We be glad to open trade with colony, and keep watch over our traders."

Ashmun smiled broadly, and Elijah's confidence in the agent's palaver skills went up.

"Thank you," Ashmun said. "We will guard this trade, too." He shifted his position on the stool carefully. "But how can we trade with you if there be a war? King Peter is said to be the leader of all the people around the Cape--the Montserrado country. He says he is our friend. But we hear talk of war all around us. Why is this?"

Elijah smiled inwardly at the smooth way Ashmun came back to the real problem. But Brister had already hedged about war talk a few minutes before.

"All this country be called Montserrado, for true," Brister said. "We say King Peter is father of whole country, but that be for respect to his line--plenty of King Peters far back in time. But we be different--different tribes with our own kings, own lands, own ways. You savvy?"

Ashmun's eyes squinted.

"You mean King Peter is not really in charge? Every king has a say, and can do what's best for his own tribe?"

Brister nodded. Elijah's heart leaped. It was part of the answer they needed. If King Peter were persuaded to join a war against the colony, that didn't mean the other kings had to follow him!

"War is not good for Montserrado." Ashmun pressed. "Peace and plenty of trade, that is what is needed. So why all the war talk? Who can we trust?"

Brister frowned fiercely, anger showing in his eyes. Elijah tensed his body, puzzled and confused.

"It be time you trust me!" Brister burst out, leaning forward on his stool. "I say I 'gree for the colony, I say I come to talk soon you get your people settled. I say my traders will make trade with you!"

Brister was staring angrily, his eyes boring straight into Ashmun's. Ashmun dropped his eyes in apology, and lifted his hands quickly to placate the chief.

"I didn't mean you, King Brister! I mean, who else besides you can we trust?"

Brister slowly sat back, and, satisfied with the apology, he relaxed. Then he raised his right hand, index finger extended to make a point.

"My people say, 'Two bad fruit no cause to chop pawpaw tree down'. Why you judge all Montserrado tribes by one or two kings, or some of their people? Wait and see."

Ashmun took it in, but Elijah saw his doubtful face and turned to look at Brister. The old chief smiled patiently at the young white man as he stood up to dismiss them.

"Ashmun, you be new to our ways. You don't believe me. It is good to walk softly-softly in strange place. Second time, you know better. When I come to visit, maybe you trust me and my people more."

As soon as their canoe crossed the sandbar and headed home toward the Cape, Ashmun turned around in his seat.

"Can we trust Brister?"

"Seems like a good man to me," Fred James replied. "Even 'tho he never said a thing about the war."

"Me, too," Elijah said. "I think he's a real African chief who says what he means. He doesn't want to talk about the war because he hopes it might not happen, I guess. But I wouldn't just 'wait and see' like he suggests."

"Why not?" Ashmun asked.

"King George is a powerful talker," Elijah said. "And he wants revenge. We can count on Brister, and maybe King Peter. But John Mill says lots of chiefs will follow George, 'cause he'll give them plenty of reasons why we should be done away with--specially the slave trade. They know we're against it, but most of 'em depend on it."

Ashmun squinted his eyes.

"So we'd better prepare for an attack--is that it, gentlemen?"

Both Fred and Elijah nodded their head

"We have to protect our people, just in case," Elijah said.

18   Love and Death

Cape Mesurado
August 31, 1822

    John Bannon sat down heavily on a long bamboo bench on Elijah's porch, exhausted from the day's work with a small crew of the settlers who had been ordered by Ashmun to cut down the forest around the little town of mat-and-thatch houses. John wanted to see Carrie, but as usual she was busy getting Elijah's children to bed, and he wasn't sure she'd come out afterwards anyway. She'd been so moody ever since she'd heard from Mrs. Blake that her ma wouldn't ever be able to come to Africa. He understood her despair and wanted to put his arms around her, hold her and comfort her--maybe even kiss her and caress her. His body warmed up just thinking of that, and he shifted on the bench. He wanted to make love to her so badly--but there was no way. Not now, with her sadness, and all the fear and preparations for war.

    "Out here all by yourself, John?" Elijah asked, coming out of his house to sit in the cool breeze.

    "Yes. Not much to do now in the evenings, with my market building taken over by Mr. Ashmun," John complained. "Thought I'd come see how Carrie's doing."

    "Well, Ashmun had to make a lot of decisions real quick, John--for the good of the whole colony. Havin' your building turned into a dormitory for those recaptive boys was a good move. I'm sorry you lost your business before you even got started. But there isn't goin' to be much business around here 'til this war palaver gets settled."

    "There's another one of Ashmun's orders I wonder about," John said. "He has us clearing all the trees and bushes around so the warriors can't surprise us. But why leave the stuff lay there if we need poles to make a musket-proof stockade around the town?"

    "It's a real good thing to leave the trees toppled over where they are so nobody can run through the clearing fast. Gives us time to take good aim at the attackers."

    "But he wants a stockade built, too. Where ..."

    They both saw a lantern light swinging toward them in the dusk, Joseph Blake's gleaming black face appearing as he lifted the lantern over the porch rail. Blake grinned as he set his lantern on an empty salt box.

"Where are we going to get all the poles for the stockade?" John continued.

"Don't know, Johnny," Blake answered. "Saaay--ain't that somethin'--all those plans Asmun has for the colony's defense! Stockades and cannon stations and clearin' away the forest. What was it he said on that paper he hung up on the storehouse wall today?"

"He declared military law," Elijah said, "and those things he wrote down are military orders which we all have to carry out, like it says on the paper."

Another lantern bobbed toward them, its feeble glow revealing Fred James's red suspenders. He took his accustomed place on the bench, and turned the wick down on his lantern.

"You still giving out orders, Elijah?" he jibed. "I thought we got a new man for that."

"Well, Ashmun did ask me to help him," Elijah admitted.

"Yeah, you two have it all figured out, don't you? So you say the cannon are supposed to be brought up the hill and fixed in place--just like that?" Fred said. "God a'mighty! They must weigh a ton apiece!"

"We'll just have to drag one up each morning, while the grass is still slick from the rain. Lucky it's rainy season now," Elijah mused, "probably only take ten or twelve men to do it."

"Where we going to put'em?" Blake asked.

"Ashmun says the big 18-pounder is to go on the west station, two 4-pounders on the east, and the other two 4's on the south. Those three stations will make a triangle that surrounds the whole town."

"Then where's my brass field gun supposed to go?" Fred asked.

"In the center on a raised platform of rocks and dirt. Your crew can back up the guns on the points of the triangle by shootin' on either side of 'em or over their heads."

"And my carpenters have to build a stockade around the guns on each point, right?" Blake said.

"Yeah, and then connect them so the stockade fence goes all 'round the town in one big triangle," Elijah said.

Blake shook his head. "Now I see what Johnny means. Where we goin' to get enough poles for stockadin' 'round the town?"

"Yes, Elijah!" John almost shouted. "That's why I said we can't cut down the forest and leave it laying there like Ashmun says--we need it for poles!"

They all looked at Elijah in the dim lantern light.

"Well, I don't know--Ashmun thinks that cut stuff is our first line of defense. But the stockade is important, too. I ... I'll talk to him tomorrow about it."

"Saaay!" Blake interrupted. "I heard from my house boy that King George is moving his town away from the foot of the Cape. My boy says they're moving down the coast to the Junk River, so he can't work for me anymore."

"Finally!" Elijah said. "George was supposed to move away months ago, as punishment for his men shooting at us and tearing down our houses. Remember? That's what the big palaver decided when Boatswain and Ayres were here."

"Why did he take so long to move?" John asked.

"I don't know!" Elijah said irritably. "You think I know everything? By the way, Ashmun said to find out from some of you what the Kroo workers are sayin'. They hear what's happening around the country, 'cause they work all up and down the coast."

"The ones helpin' me on the houses don't say anything, least ways not that I can understand," Fred said. "And three of them didn't even show up today. If they're not goin' to be dependable, I don't wa ..."

"What's that?" Elijah barked. "Three of them?"

"Yeah--three. Why?"

"Nobody said why they didn't come?"

"Well, I asked, but they just shook their heads and looked away."

"Dammit! Why didn't you tell me earlier?"

"I was busy! Besides, this is the first time I've seen you all day. What's the matter with you!"

Elijah stood up and walked to the porch rail, looking out into the darkness. No one said anything, waiting for him to answer. When he did, his voice was low.

"It's beginning to happen--I know it is!"

"What? What's beginning to happen?" Blake asked.

Elijah turned abruptly. "Don't you see? They're beginnin' to leave because the war is about to start. The Mamba and the Kru--they know something we don't!"

John shuddered, an ominous feeling coming over him.

159

"So that's why George is moving," he said slowly. "To get away from any counter-attack we could make on him."

They sat in stunned silence.

"God a'Mighty! I'm goin' to Ashmun right now," Elijah said. "We've got to set up a watch--startin' tonight!"

He grabbed Fred's lantern.

"Come on, Fred. You, too, Blake. John take care of the house 'til I get back."

They rushed off, leaving John sitting in the dark. He thought about Elijah's quick reaction. It must mean he thought the colony was in real danger--at least enough to have guards on duty. But Elijah had said he thought not enough tribes had agreed with George to have a war, so why was he so excited?

The glow of a lantern interruped John's thoughts, and he saw Carrie coming out of the house. She moved directly to the porch railing, not seeing him on the bench. Staring off into the night sky a moment, she sighed and then turned to sit on the bench. Both of her hands jerked upwards when she saw him, and she almost dropped the lantern.

"John! You still here? I thought I heard everyone go."

"Elijah wanted me to stay and watch the house. Are the chillun put to bed?"

"Thank God!" Carrie said, sitting down at the other end of the bench wearily. She was as far away from him as she could get, so he slid towards her easy-like.

"Stop right there!" she frowned at him.

"Awww, Carrie--what's the matter?" John said, stopping for just a bit, then moving closer. "You still thinking about your ma?"

"No! I don't want to think about her ever again!"

"Ever? That's a long time ... Why, Carrie? Is it her fault she can't come to Africa?"

"It don't matter! She shouldn't have said she would if she knew there was a chance she couldn't. I wouldn't have come out here if I'd known she wasn't comin'! I believed her, John--I trusted her!"

Carrie's voice quavered and John knew she was near to crying.

"Easy, Carrie. Take it easy." John reached to pat her shoulder, but she jerked away.

"My Ma lied to me! I didn't want to come to Africa--she was the one! Go to Africa! Be free! I'll come later after I see about

160

Pa--that's what she said. She lied to me!"

John put his arms around her and held her tight, feeling her wet tears soaking through his shirt, her body shaking. He wanted to hold her forever, comfort her when she needed him, be her protector always. She was still bound to her mother like a child, but now she was being pried apart from her as sure as if she'd been torn from her by slavers on the auction block. He tried to think of how to help Carrie see that her mother was just doing what she had to do.

"Your ma loves your pa, too, Carrie. She had to help him, didn't she? Mrs. Blake said that your pa was sold South by his owner because he'd run away. And your ma went South to look for him."

Carrie pulled back from John's arms and wiped her eyes on her sleeves.

"He's not my real pa! Just some black man she took up with when we got sent to New York from the plantation!"

"You and your ma were sent to New York? Why?"

"Can't you guess, John? You're so dumb! Look at me. Could my pa be a black man like you saw at the dock?"

He looked at her in the dim glow of the lantern, wanting to touch the light skin and slender mulatto features of her face. He loved every part of it, but 'specially her eyes.

"But your ma is light, too, so your pa could be dark and you'd still ..."

"My pa was the plantation owner--Massa Charles! His wife made him send us away--she couldn't stand the sight of me 'cause I looked too much like him."

"Oh. Well, no wonder ... I mean, I can see why your ma loves the man she took up with in New York. He is her choice, not like with the massa on the plantation. Carrie, she couldn't help herself when she was a slave on the plantation ... don't you see now why she would follow the black man, her real man, wherever he was sold to?"

Carrie sat with her arms tightly clasped around her breast, bending slightly forward like she were going to cry again but wanted to hold it in.

"Yes, but what about me? I'm her very own child--why did she send me out here by myself? Why? What mother would send away her only child!"

John felt he was on surer ground now.

161

"She wanted you to be free, Carrie. Like I wanted to, and all the rest of us who came out. We want to be free in a way we never can be in America. Africa is our homeland."

"Free! Like this?" Carrie flung out her arms in disgust. "Cooped up here on top of the Cape, afraid of our very own lives? Gettin' ready to shoot our African brothers and sisters with muskets and cannons? This is freedom?"

"It will be later. It takes time. They don't know us yet, or they've been told some wrong things about us," John explained. "We can work it out if we--if we survive," he finished lamely.

"If ! And my ma thought it was more important to send me off for this?" Carrie snorted. "That's what I mean, John--she sent me out here for some dream of freedom she or the rest of you knew nothin' about. You just guessed it was here for the askin'--if you could only get here. She sent me out knowin' nothing but a dream, John. Sent me out all by myself just to satisfy her dream! That shows how little she loves me ... no more than a dream!"

"No, Carrie! It's not like that. It's a dream, but we'll make it come true, and our whole life will be better because we did it. Your ma would have, too, but she had to make a terrible choice--and she gave you the best part of it, the chance to make the dream come true. She'll never have that chance now, but she made it possible for you by sending you out with the Johnsons. You can make your freedom be real. Right here in Africa--like it never could be in America!"

Carrie had straightened up as he talked, and now her hands were in her lap as she stared into the darkness.

"Well, I sure didn't ask her to."

"It was her gift to you, Carrie. She gave it to you and denied it to herself because she loved you."

She looked him full in the face.

"Really, John? Because she loved me?"

"I'm sure of it, Carrie."

"Ma's gift to me ... her love gift ... to come to Africa ... to find my own freedom ..."

She looked up at the starry sky, staring silently. He bent over and kissed her cheek, but she didn't notice.

"I'll do it, John," she said softly. "I don't know how, but I'll make my own freedom. Like Ma wants me to."

####

162

September 15, 1822

Elijah, Blake, Fred James, and Lott Cary stood around, hats in hand, waiting on the veranda of the agent's house for Ashmun to come out. Soaked to the skin, they stood in gloomy silence, listening to the steady hiss of rain falling in gray curtains sweeping in from the ocean on this bleak Sunday morning. Elijah knew none of them would have stirred from their homes this early except for the young Kroo boy who had come running through the rain with a sad message summoning them to Ashmun's house.

It was news Elijah had been expecting because the newcomers from the *Strong* were coming down with fever, and a few old-timers from previous ships were getting it once again. Their hope that the height of the Cape would spare them from the fever had been dashed within three weeks of the *Strong's* arrival. Twelve of the newcomers were completely disabled on September 1st, and yesterday's sick list posted by Lott Cary said all but two newcomers were now down. Everybody was saying that the white agent and his wife would be the first to die--and now part of it had come true.

Ashmun came out, haggard and gray-faced, his fever -wracked body slightly stooping from the fatigue of an all-night vigil.

"Catherine died this morning about three o'clock," he said quietly, leaning against a veranda post.

Elijah remembered his own vigil at his wife Mary's side, and he spoke the question on his mind.

"Was it bad? I mean, the chills and fever, were they too ... Sorry, I shouldn't've asked."

"It's all right. I think she resigned herself to it two days ago, but her body just wouldn't quit 'til this morning. She's gone home to the Lord now and looks very peaceful."

"We're sure sorry, Mr. Ashmun," Blake said.

Ashmun thanked them for their concern, then turned to Lott Cary. "Reverend, would you do the burial service later today?"

The two of them withdrew to the east end of the veranda to discuss the arrangements. The others shifted about uncomfortably until Ashmun returned.

"Gentlemen, I have some information about the war you ought to hear before you go," he said.

They gathered around again. Elijah was glad not to have to leave until the rain stopped, but dreaded hearing anymore bad news about a coming war with the Africans.

"A Navy ship patrolling for slavers has heard something going on to the north of us where there's a big slave operation--a place called Gallinas. Have any of you heard of it?"

They all nodded except Lott Cary.

"We heard about it on our way to Sherbro Island," Fred James said. "It's not far south of there."

"Supposed to be a lot of Spanish slave dealers there doin' business with Cuba," Elijah said.

"Well, I've just had time last night while sitting at Catherine's bedside to read a long report from the Secretary of the Navy sent out for Dr. Ayres," Ashmun said. He shook his head apologetically. "I should have read it earlier, but we've been so busy ..."

"That's all right, Mr. Ashmun. What is it?" Elijah cut in sharply.

"Well, a Captain Spence from the *Cyane* said a slaver named Pedro Blanco has slave pens at Gallinas from which he's shipping hundreds of slaves every month. But the shocking thing is he's got connections with chiefs all down the coast, and even has pens south of this cape."

"If the Navy knows that, why don't they stop him?" Blake asked.

"It seems Blanco's got such a good warning system that he never loads his ships until the British and the American patrols have sailed on by."

"We've kept the slavers out of our bay since we got here," Elijah said, "but we can't do anything about the river mouths north or south of us. So what's that got to do with the war?"

"Captain Spence heard that Pedro Blanco was behind the chiefs that almost got King Peter killed for selling the Cape to us."

"I knew it!" Fred James shouted. "There had to be somethin' like that to make them gang up on old King Peter! He was cryin' to us they would cut off his head if he sold it, and Ayres took the money back to save the King's neck."

"I'm afraid that's not all, Mr. James," Ashmun said. "Spence also heard that Blanco offered muskets and powder to any chiefs who would oppose us."

"God a'Mighty!" Elijah said. "Was that only when we bought the Cape, or is he still offerin'em now?"

"I don't know. The information from Captain Spence is

164

probably several months old."

"Well, Gallinas is a long way from here," Fred James said. "Maybe they can't get the muskets down this far."

"King George got some muskets from somewhere, remember?" Blake broke in. "Maybe that's what his warriors used on us when we were on the island!"

Elijah felt sweaty, in spite of the rain falling in sheets at the edge of the veranda. This war business was getting worse everyday, and he could feel it like a pressure in his head. He took a deep breath to steady himself and keep his mind clear.

"We don't know for sure if George got the muskets from Pedro Blanco," he said. "But if he did, then George will know where to go to get more for all the warriors he rounds up to attack us!"

"But we'll have the advantage of the cannon, Mr. Johnson," Ashmun said quietly.

His calmness irritated Elijah.

"With twenty-five or thirty men on our side and hundreds of musket-toting warriors on theirs? Will the cannon really stop them?"

Elijah knew he was close to shouting, so he turned on his heels and walked away to cover his alarm. At the end of the short veranda he turned around and stood facing them. He kept his voice as even as he could.

"If they have their spears and arrows and a few old blunderbuss muskets they've always had, we have a chance. But if they're supplied with good muskets from Don Pedro, we're in real trouble!"

"One good marksman is worth a dozen amateurs, Mr. Johnson," Ashmun replied. "New muskets in the hands of warriors used to spears won't help them much."

"But our men are no marksmen either!" Elijah protested. "Most've never used one before. And those recaptive boys are like bushmen theirselves."

"Then we'll just have to train them until their fire is accurate," Ashmun said. "You're one of our best shots, Mr. Johnson--I'm assigning you to start musket practice for all the men tomorrow."

Ashmun reached for the veranda doorpost, shivering slightly as he leaned against it.

"Please excuse me--my fever is coming on again. I'll see you all at the burial service."

19 Secret Ally

Cape Mesurado
September 15, 1822

At the southern edge of the clearing, the Reverend Lott Cary motioned for the men to lower Mrs. Ashmun's coffin into the ground. The crowd gathered around and he finished the last rites.

" ... and now we commend to Almighty God our sister Catherine Ashmun," he said. "We commit her body to its final resting place--earth to earth--ashes to ashes--dust to dust."

Lott Cary picked up a handful of soil and respectfully threw it down upon the coffin. Ashmun dropped a small bouquet of flowers in, and Elijah, along with others nearby, flung token bits of soil in before the men filled the pit with their shovels.

It was over and Elijah, waiting for Ashmun to finish his quiet prayer, idly watched the crowd turn and begin to walk back up the slope to the settlement on the ridge of the Cape. His eye caught a flash of blue and white striped robe in the shadow at the edge of the clearing, the dark figure wearing it beckoning to him. He raised his hand to shade his eyes, peering intently at the vaguely familiar face of a chief--someone he guessed he had not seen for some time. Then it came to him--it's Bob Gray!

Elijah remembered the joy and relief he'd felt when the friendly Bassa chief brought a group of his people from down the coast with food to sell to the colony. Left in charge of the colony by Ayres, Elijah had worried about dwindling food supplies caused by King George's boycott of the riverside market. As if in answer to prayer, Chief Bob Gray had guided his people through the forest on the ridge, avoiding the riverside altogether. They'd sold their foodstuffs and left right away, but Elijah had treasured Bob Gray's deep interest in the colonists and their reasons for coming 'home' to Africa. Suddenly Elijah recalled that it was Bob Gray who'd later sent a message warning about King George recruiting warriors to attack the colony.

Elijah turned excitedly to Ashmun, but saw with a shock that Ashmun looked as if he was about to faint in the heat of the afternoon sun. Ashmun smiled apologetically.

"Mr. Johnson, I can't make it back up to the ridge without

some help. Do you mind?"

They walked slowly toward the shade at the forest's edge, Elijah suppporting the thin, exhausted agent, who needed a rest before beginning the climb.

"See that chief waitin' over there?" Elijah said in a low voice. "That's Chief Bob Gray from the Bassa tribe down the coast. Looks like he's sort of hiding in the shade there."

"Hiding? Maybe the sun's too hot for him, too."

"I think he wants to tell us something. He was makin' a motion for me to come over to him."

They walked into the shade of the uncut forest, and Elijah pointed to a moss-covered tree trunk rotting on the forest floor.

"How's that for a seat, Mr. Ashmun?"

"Good," Ashmun said, sitting on it. "Invite the chief over and let's hear what he has to say."

Elijah walked over to the chief and ducked his head respectfully.

"You're Chief Bob Gray, aren't you?"

The dark brown man, lean and sinewy, barely filled his loose robe, yet he looked like a tough hand-to-hand fighter. He looked at Elijah calmly, and somehow Elijah felt an unspoken trust and admiration flowing between them.

"And you be 'Merican man called Johnson. I never forget what you say 'bout 'Merican black mens coming home to Africa."

"Thank you, Chief," Elijah said, and turned his head in Ashmun's direction. "This is our new agent. He's here to help us. You can talk with him."

The chief considered it, watching Elijah's face closely. Then he walked over to Ashmun, who rose to greet him.

"Mr. Johnson tells me you are from Bassa country, Chief Gray. We want to be peaceful with you and your people."

Again the chief considered the face behind the words; finally he spoke.

"Before your time I brought some of my people to show we want to trade. Johnson told us come back soon, but now King George move between us and Junk River. He making palaver about our trading with you--says we must join him and make war on you."

Ashmun nodded

"Mr. Johnson tells me King George is angry because the council of chiefs punished him for ordering his warriors to shoot at colonists after they protected a ship foundering in the harbor."

"It be more than that," Bob Gray said. "He lost his slave trade and wants it back. He tells other chiefs the same will be to them."

Elijah saw Ashmun squint his eyes, and he knew Ashmun would start asking questions.

"Have you lost your trade?" Ashmun asked.

Elijah sucked in his breath, but then realized Ashmun had not asked what kind of trade. Elijah watched Chief Gray, and saw him put his head down. Was he ashamed--or hiding his anger at being asked such a question? There was silence, and Ashmun said nothing to break it. Elijah barely breathed.

"I never like such trade," Chief Gray said, his voice low and husky.

"But you did make slave trade?" Ashmun's question was low, too.

"We ... all we chiefs make it. Our fathers make it before our time. And their fathers make it, too."

"Why?"

It was said softly, like a gentle push, and Elijah waited, wondering if the tough warrior chief would be pushed any further.

"It be quick way to get plenty of goods from slave traders. We give most of it to our people--they like it. Women like pretty cloth and beads and mirrors. Men like rum. Rum makes every man feel good. No bad thoughts 'bout people we sell to slavers if we drink plenty rum."

"You sell your people and don't feel bad?"

The chief sighed, and moved to sit down on the log facing Ashmun. He motioned Elijah to sit, too, so Elijah sat behind Ashmun in order to watch the chief's face.

"I feel bad when there's no rum. That be why we chiefs keep on doing it."

"What do you say when there's no rum to make you feel good?"

"Say? Say to who? I can't say bad things 'bout slave trade--my people would want to get another chief who could give them all those goods!"

"No. I mean, what do you say to yourself?"

Elijah was afraid Ashmun had gone too far, but he watched the chief's eyes close and his mouth twist down as he thought about it.

"I say ... I say we chiefs be slaves! For true! We keep doing it, so we be slaves to white slavers. Ever' year we have to go more into back country to get slaves. Ever' year our land have less and less people. Coast lands cry out for more people--nobody to grow food! Villages be empty, burned down ... only wind howling there. Lonely, empty places in our land--people all taken to slave ships!"

Elijah and Ashmun were stunned.

"Whole villages?" Ashmun's voice whispered.

The awful sadness in Bob Gray's face was terrible to see, and Elijah wanted to look away. But he knew it would be wrong to turn from a man who was baring his soul. Bob Gray sighed heavily.

"In olden times we fight plenty wars--it be our way. We win war and take captives. That be our right--they be our slaves, to do work, live in our compounds, be part of our village life. It be our way ... it be good!"

Elijah saw the appeal in Bob Gray's eyes, but could only stare back in fascination as the chief continued.

"White man called Portagees come to get workers so our grandfathers giv'em captives or bad people who must be sent away or killed. Trade goods and rum begin to satisfy our fathers. Other white men come--English, Frenchy, 'Merican, Spanish--and they give us guns to fight more tribes for captives. My father be the one to do that. His warriors surround whole village in night, move in at first dawn, burn ever'thing, kill old people and chillun, save young strong ones for slavers."

The chief sighed again, pointing to himself.

"My time come, there be no slaves left to fight for on coast, so I fight more upcountry. But Mandingos and Golas and Kpelles say that be their business. So now I start to trade for slaves they send down to me, and I make trade with white slavers waiting on beach."

They sat silently, awed that the chief would trust them enough to tell all this. Elijah felt sure that Bob Gray would be killed by his fellow chiefs if they knew he had betrayed their secrets.

Finally, Ashmun asked another question.

"But you don't like this slave trade?"

"I want good trade like before white slavers come--for salt, palm oil and food, and iron pots, leather, cattle--no more killing for slave trade!" Chief Gray stood up, anger in his eyes.

169

"Why we destroy our land and people for white slavers? Why we fill up their ships with our strong young people? But the chiefs won't hear me! My people won't hear me! So I come to Johnson now--and to you. Before, he tell me black 'Mericans come back home to be free, so no slavery be allowed in colony. I want to help colony do this. Someday it help me be free, too!"

Ashmun was speechless, but he reached out his hands and the chief offered his, and then Elijah grasped both of theirs in his, and they smiled as their minds soared with this newly discovered brotherhood and common cause.

"Amen!" Elijah burst out. "Let the brothers say Amen!"

They looked at him, accepted it as fitting, and said it loudly. "Amen!"

Bob Gray looked thoughtfully at both of them.

"Kwi woh, dyeapo!" he said huskily, and they knew it was something in his own Bassa language. "Kwi woh, dyeapo!" he repeated. "Kwi woh, dyeapo!"

"What is it, Chief?" Ashmun asked. "What are you saying?"

There was a strange glow in the chief's eyes, and he repeated it once again. "Kwi woh, dyeapo! It be my 'Amen' to you. You come in freedom ship, we be saved. You bring ship of freedom."

They nodded at the truth it could be if they worked for it together. Elijah felt lifted up and marveled at its double meaning--'ship of freedom' for American blacks and for Africans, too--both of them getting free of slavery from different sides of it!

Elijah felt a tremor in Ashmun's hands and it broke the spell of their handshake. He glanced at Ashmun, who was beginning to shiver again.

"I'm sorry, the fever's returned," Ashmun said. "I'm afraid I'll need your help again, Mr. Johnson."

Bob Gray looked at Ashmun's shivering, then spoke hurriedly.

"I be coming to King Peter's place. He sent for all chiefs of Montserado country to talk King George's war palaver."

"How--how many chiefs will be there?" Ashmun asked.

"All chiefs got to go. There be plenty."

"Can you--ahh--can you tell us what they decide?"

"That be why I stand in bush to talk to you--I want to help colony. I give you secret-like ever'thing chiefs talk in palaver, but you never-never say who tell it. You savvy?"

He looked at them both with a piercing stare.

"Never!" Elijah said.

"It will never be told, Chief Gray. You can be sure of that," Ashmun affirmed.

"It be better if I send message at night," the chief said. "You know Bassa boy who carries water for colony--name of Kekleh?"

Ashmun shook his head.

"I know him," Elijah said. "I'll point him out soon's we get back."

Ashmun smiled weakly, and then turned to Elijah.

"We must go, Mr. Johnson, before you have to carry me."

The chief anxiously watched Elijah put Ashmun's arm over his shoulder and grasp Ashmun's waist. As they walked toward the clearing, Ashmun fainted. Elijah lifted him up in his arms and continued.

Bob Gray called out. "King George be telling chiefs colony white man sick and soon be dead--then they attack. I send medicine for fever. You help him live so more freedom ships come. Amen?"

"Amen!" Elijah called back.

####

October 2, 1822

Chief Bob Gray took his accustomed place in King Peter's palaver hall, noticing that something was different this morning, the end of a second week of palaver. Shifting on his own mat to find the most comfortable spot, he looked around the circle of kings and chiefs, checking them out. Proudly he noted all of the Dey and Mamba chiefs who were beholden to King Peter, by tradition the patriarch of Montserado country. He straightened himself into a more dignified pose, because he was one of them, his Bassa lineage linked to the Mamba aristocracy.

Bob Gray saw King Long Peter and King Zoda sitting very close on either side of Peter--that was the difference today! But what did it mean? He frowned at the sight of the two young Gola chiefs in seats of prominence, resenting that the Gola people, late-comers to the coast, were in so strong with King Peter. He recalled stories of the sly way the Golas had done this--for years giving their women as wives to Dey chiefs, and later those wives demanding that their boy children be trained only in the Gola bush school for Poro. When the boys had grown older and inherited seats of authority, these Dey-Gola men insisted that they were Gola and began to bring more Golas to their villages. Finally the Gola had taken over villages and trade routes right down to the sea at Digby Town.

Bob Gray was dismayed and disgusted--he felt like spitting! King Long Peter was one of those rude Dey-Gola boys, a nephew of Peter. And King Zoda was an upstart young Gola, already with high rank in the Poro, a *Kanda Jia*. Were they sitting close to King Peter to influence him to do something today? It alarmed Bob Gray and he didn't want to think about it. He turned to look at others in the palaver circle.

King Governor, King Bromley, King Konko, King Jimmy, King Brister, King Willy--these older chiefs might balance the young ones. Bob Gray smiled as he spotted Ba Caia still in the palaver circle. The only chief in the council who was a friend of Boatswain, Ba Caia and his people were protected against attacks from other chiefs because of this friendship. Is Ba Caia a spy for Boatswain in this palaver, Bob Gray wondered. If so, why did the chiefs allow him to stay this long? Maybe they wanted him to let Boatswain know what they were thinking about and ...

A sudden disturbance at the entrance to the palaver hall interrupted Bob Gray's thoughts. King George was finally walking into the council and everyone turned to see him stride arrogantly to his mat. He made a show of sitting down and adjusting his flowing chief's robe. It was a fresh, new one, just off the weaver's loom. To impress us on his big day, Bob realized with a twinge of jealousy.

"King Willy has something to say," George announced. "He heard it from Sherbro people--that be where those black 'Mericans tried to settle first, before they came here. They made plenty trouble in Sherbro and people there be too glad they left from that place."

George waved his hand at Willy and everyone settled back with a sigh to hear the windiest chief in the country. A short man with a deep voice and a gift for oratory, King Willy brought his hearers up straight with a stern warning.

"Revenge!" his voice boomed out. "That be what one Sherbro chief say he fear from those black 'Mericans! He say the slaves he sold to slave traders going to 'Merica could come back in this colony thing and make a revenge on him! He fear plenty 'cause one such man already come back to Freetown, and he be making big talk about revenge on some Sherbro chief who sold him!"

It stunned them all. Bob Gray sat in shock, recognizing the unspoken nightmare that had lain in the back of his mind, never coming to light because of the guilt that overlaid his thoughts on any night these last few years when there was no rum. Could a slave he'd sold off to Cuba or 'Merica really come back to threaten or kill him? He looked around the circle at grey, ashen faces, mouths arrested in unvoiced surprise, fear, or doubt. Doubt--Bob Gray's mind grasped at that. No single man by himself would dare come back and challenge a chief--certainly not a slave sold away in disgrace, no matter when he came back.

"We talking about one man, self!" Willy emphasized. "But those colony people be plenty, and more to come in other ships. Soon their town grows big, they want more land. They make their own laws and you all know they don't agree for slavery business!"

Now Bob Gray understood what George and Willy were doing--playing on the fears of the chiefs. It was something they must have cooked up last night.

"No! When their town gets big it will be all right for we!"

Everyone turned to see who was standing up to challenge George and Willy. It was Brister, his hand raised in protest.

"They need to grow big, so their town can do plenty of business and get strong! They not be enemies--they be friends. Look at their color. That prove they be our countrymen and have a right to live here with us. They bring plenty of new things for we. They come back not to revenge, but to show what they learn in 'Merica. They be civilized people now. When we see such things we learn, too. We get better ways to ..."

"No! No! No!"

King Governor was shouting Brister down and shaking his head and hands in strong disagreement. George waved for him to stand up.

"That be all wrong! Those 'Mericans not friends--they be strangers, black or no black! They forget they be from Africa. They forget their forefathers come from here. This be prove by their connection to white men from 'Merica. They not respect us, not trust us, not ready to live under our rule like real Africa people!"

Governor sat down with a triumphant look on his face. Like a lion who ate the whole carcass, Bob Gray thought. But

173

Governor had missed Brister's idea about what the 'Mericans could bring us. Now George pointed to Willy, and Bob could see how the palaver was being controlled by George.

"These friends of Brister have take over the Cape! Will they take over your land next?" Willy thundered.

That brought them up straight again, and Bob Gray's thoughts jumped to his own land near the mouth of the St. John river. He allowed the French and Spanish slavers to keep their slave pens there because he brought the slaves down to them from upriver. Would the colonists ever come down to Bassa country and take over his land?

He saw the signal from George to Willy. Willy sat down and George rose quickly, stepping off his mat into the center of the circle.

"We stop them now before we lose our land!" George cried, whirling around to all of them with a clenched fist. "In few years, they be kings of whole country if we not *stop* them!"

He swung his fist down like a knife slash, voicing the warriors grunt, "Unnnh!", to drive the knife deeper into imaginary flesh. "*Stop* them!" he shouted, turning around, fixing them with his burning eyes. He raised his arm again.

"Now be the time!" Down came the arm--"Unnnh!" "The Navy ships be gone!" "Unnnh!" "First two agents ran away!" "Unnnh!" "New white man be sick!" "Unnnh!" "And soon he die!" "Unnnh!" ...

Bob Gray swung his arm with the rhythm of the long curved war knife, cutting down his enemies in battle. From the corner of his eye he saw the other chiefs doing it, grunting hypnotically at the end of each stroke. George led them on, chanting the story in mounting fury, driving it into their minds.

Suddenly they sprang up shouting their victory cries, arms brandishing imaginary war knives overhead, the ecstasy of victory flooding their bodies and minds. Bob Gray saw the slaves he would collect after the battle, and the goods and rum that soon would be his to give out to his admiring people, hailing him as a hero once again.

Tears came to his eyes, but the other chiefs thought he was so happy he couldn't hold them back. Only Bob Gray knew he cried because he was trapped in a life he no longer wanted.

20   Fever Medicine

Cape Mesurado
October 5, 1822

Lott Cary came out of Ashmun's door, a worried frown on his face as he joined the colonists waiting on the veranda.

"Well, how's Ashmun doing?" Elijah asked.

"Might poorly. I'm not sure he's going to survive the fever. I've tried everything I know, but nothing seems to work."

"What did you use?"

"Lemon grass tea, and then a powerful lime drink. And finally some fever leaf tea." Cary sighed. "Looks like his fever's too strong for any of them."

"Don't you have any of the stuff we used in Freetown ?"

"That bark and wine concoction the British had?"

"That's it. My wife used it on me and the chillun before she ..." Elijah's voice broke. After a long pause, he cleared his throat.

"Before she died ... I guess it doesn't work on everybody," he finished lamely.

"We don't have any," Cary said. "Dr. Ayres told me about it, but said he never had a chance to buy some in Freetown before we left."

"So there's nothing we can do?"

The anxious crowd on the veranda drew up close to hear Cary's words.

"I'll keep on using the fever leaf tea. That's the strongest thing I've got." Cary shrugged his shoulders. "It's all I can do. But he's so far gone now, he doesn't even move."

The colonists standing around shook their heads.

"What are we going to do, Lije?" Fred James asked.

Others nodded and voiced their fears. "We're nowheres near ready if the Africans attack!" "Yeah, the cannons aren't all mounted." "What about the stockades--they aren't even started!"

"All right, all right!" Elijah said, raising his hands. "While Ashmun's sick we'll just keep on doin' what he laid out for us to do!"

Elijah saw the doubt in their eyes and knew he had to boost up their spirits.

"Some real good fever medicine is comin' from down the

coast. Won't be long now--then he'll get well."

"Coming with the Navy?" someone asked.

"No. Some friendly chief is sendin' it."

"Friendly chief!" "That'll be the day!" "We don't want Mr. Ashmun poisoned!"

Fred James raised a hand to quiet the crowd.

"African medicine, Elijah?" he asked. "You sure it's not some of that juju business?"

"No. I figure it'll be the best in the country. The chief wouldn't send it otherwise--he really wants to help us. Now let's get back to work. And remember, we have musket practice for an hour at noon!"

They all began to leave, but Elijah touched Blake and Fred James on their shoulders, signaling for them to wait. When the others were out of earshot, he drew Fred and Blake over to Lott Cary.

"Reverend, how bad is he really?" he asked in a low voice.

"He's so weak he hasn't said a word for two days. If something doesn't change soon, I don't think he has much time left."

"God A'Mighty!" Elijah said, "If he dies we don't have a chance!"

Lott Cary frowned.

"Why do you say that, Mr. Johnson? We don't need a white man to tell us everything to do! You were in the 1812 war on Lake Erie, I hear. You can lead us through this war!"

Elijah looked with disbelief at the preacher-turned-doctor. It was plain that Cary knew nothing about a war.

"Oh, I've been through a war all right--and I stood up to it, too." Elijah said. "I only stopped when I got hit and couldn't see."

Elijah fixed his eyes on Cary with a hard stare, anger beginning to boil inside him.

"But I'm not a fool, Reverend! Black or white makes no difference! Commandin' the defense of this colony calls for more experience than I've got. I was just a deck hand--carried the powder and ball from the ship's magazine to the gun crews--and never shot a gun the whole time. Ashmun commanded a local militia and knows about forts and battles. He's the man we need! Just forget what color he is--get him on his feet again!"

Elijah walked off, embarrassed he'd gotten so angry. Cary was a good man--just upset that they still had to depend on white men in Africa. Elijah turned, softening his words.

"Oh, Reverend ... I'll send the chief's fever medicine as soon as it gets here."

They had been chatting quietly on the bamboo bench of Elijah's porch for nearly an hour, only a feeble yellow halo from one lantern dispelling the black velvet darkness of the tropical night. Now Fred James yawned, tired from the day's work, and Blake responded with a yawn of his own. But the younger John Bannon was alert and on edge in spite of his weariness.

"Boss man!"

It was a low call from the darkness to the east of the porch, and all their heads turned sharply towards it.

"Who's that?" Elijah called.

John expected to see somebody emerge from the darkness, but there was nothing. They waited in silence, everyone alert now. It was the soft speech of an African, and they tensed in fear.

"Who be that?" Elijah said again, louder.

"This be Kekleh ... I be the water boy."

But no figure emerged from the deep shadow, and John exchanged worried glances with the others. How had Kekleh gotten through the guards? John wondered. The low voice came again, this time closer to them.

"I bring something for boss man. But my chief says I stay in dark place to give you."

"It's a trap, Elijah," Fred whispered.

"No, I reckon not," Elijah replied, getting up and stretching.

"Be careful, now," Blake warned.

Elijah walked casually off the porch, pulled a piece of broom grass from its stalk, and picked his teeth with it as he strolled to the corner of his house. They lost sight of him in the dark, but then heard his voice.

"Kekleh? Where are you? What do you have for me?"

"Here be fever medicine, boss. It have two parts."

There was a pause.

"What! This is a big bundle of something!" Elijah exclaimed.

"Yes, boss. That be bundle of sticks from *maw ah yidi* bush. Take three sticks, cut off bark 'self, and put in small pot of water

177

for cook on fire. Makes plenty bitter thing to drink ... wait small, boss. This be other thing to go in bitter drink."

There was another pause, and everyone on the porch listened intently.

"Feels like a cow's horn, Kekleh."

"For true, boss. White powder be in there. Put small, small pinch in pot after you take bark out."

"All right, Kekleh. How much drink you give each day?"

"Medicine man say one cup morning, one cup night."

"Kekleh--this be strong medicine for fever?"

"Oh yes, boss! It be strong past all!"

"Thank you plenty, Kekleh. Tell your chief ..."

"Wait, boss. I not finish yet."

"Oh--sorry. What else you have?"

"This be 'bout war council, boss. It be plenty secret thing ..."

Another pause made everyone on the porch draw in their breath. But they heard a crackling in the bushes behind the western side of Elijah's house.

"I got to go, boss! Somebody coming!"

"Wait! What did--what be the message?"

"He say nine for war, three for peace! Goo'bye, boss!"

Footsteps pounded around the west side of the house and Nathaniel Brander rushed into the lantern light.

"Where's Elijah? There's somebody inside our lines! We need more men to find him!"

Elijah appeared from the darkness on the east side and walked calmly to the porch entrance, setting down a large bundle wrapped in banana leaves and a cow horn with a wooden plug on it. Then he straightened up and faced Brander.

"What's the trouble, Nathaniel?" he asked.

"Somebody's been seen walkin' around sneaky-like inside the lines and we got suspicious! We need some more lanterns and men to check it out."

Elijah fixed everyone on the porch with a stern glare, a clear warning not to talk, and then turned back to Brander.

"It was only Kekleh, the water boy. He brought some fever medicine for us. Just tell your men to forget it."

Brander's eyes opened wide, but something in Elijah's tone warned him not to argue.

"Whooee! We were going to hunt him down and shoot! All right, we'll watch out for him next time. But you better arrange some kind of signal, Elijah."

He shouldered his musket and walked off into the darkness.

After a moment John asked, "Elijah, why'd you want us to keep quiet while Brander was here? You told him it was Kekleh and what he brought."

"Not all of it, John. Did you hear his message about the war council?"

"Something about nine and three, wasn't it?"

"Yes, and I think it means we're in real trouble. Sounds like King George has talked nine tribes into joining the war and he only has three more to go."

They were stunned. No one spoke while they each thought about it. Finally John broke the gloomy spell.

"Does it have to be unanimous?" he asked.

They all looked at Elijah. He shook his head in exasperation.

"How do I know? I'll talk with Ashmun. We've got some good fever medicine now, and he'll be on his feet soon. Maybe there's still time to do something else before the Africans get organized--they haven't all agreed yet."

He stooped and picked up the bundle and the cow horn.

"John, take this right away to Lott Cary and tell him to cook up a pot of fever medicine.   You heard how to make it?"

John nodded, grasped the makings for the medicine, and started off the porch into the darkness.

"Tell the Reverend not to wait for morning," Elijah called after him.

CHAPTER

21   War Doctor

Cape Mesurado
October 17, 1822

Chief Bob Gray settled on his mat quietly, listening to the idle talk of fellow chiefs sitting around him. This was the ninth day of war council meetings and he had become a close friend with King Governor, the chief on his right. He leaned toward him.

"Morning Governor. You hear about King George making secret deal with those two young Gola chiefs?"

"You mean with Zoda and Long Peter?" Governor said. "They be related to King Peter by marriage, not so?"

Bob Gray nodded his head.

"That be why George could make a deal with them to shut up King Peter."

"So that be why Peter not saying anything all this time! What did George promise to give them?" Governor asked.

"I don't know and I can't find out--it makes me plenty vexed!" Bob admitted. "It be sad thing to see George take over. His mouth too loud, always shouting at us, making secret deals behind our backs. I think he hates colony because 'Mericans shamed him in big palaver."

King Governor's eyebrows went up.

"Speak softly, my friend! George be in charge now--you better be careful what you say."

Bob Gray spit angrily. It felt good, and he did it again, a mighty one, blasted clear into the center of the palaver circle. Maybe George would step in it the next time he got up to shout at them! A little calmer now, Bob took stock of the situation facing the council this morning. In spite of the noisy chatter, his mind cut through to the main thing. George was about to wear down the last three chiefs holding out for peace.

"You think George will get all the chiefs on his side today?" he asked Governnor.

"Maybe. Who's left?"

"Brister, Ben, and KunoKree," Bob said.

"Well, George say they have to decide today, so we see soon."

180

Bob was glad he'd already promised to join the war party. He could spy on their war plans and keep the colony informed. But when the council was over and the official call went out for warriors, he would go back to Bassa and not send any of his warriors up for the attack. No other chief was near his territory to make him change his mind at the last minute, so he'd be safe for ...

There was a sudden stirring at the entrance to the palaver hall. It was King Zoda. George rose to his feet.

"I say this palaver now be open!" he called out, and the chiefs' conversations ceased abruptly. A few scurried to their mats, scowled at by George as he waited impatiently. He cleared his throat.

"King Zoda be back from trip we send him on to find war leader with strong medicine. When he be settled, we listen to him first."

All eyes stared at the young Gola chief being ushered into the hall by three headmen, who were treating him with more deference than they ever had before. Bob Gray wondered why, until he saw that Zoda carried under his arm a leopard skin rolled tightly and bound by a leather thong.

"Look, Governor!" Bob Gray whispered. "Zoda be one of the *Ki La mi* now!"

"Ay, yah!" Governor exclaimed. "He come back from Gola country a big 'skin man'!"

Bob Gray knew that only powerful men in the upper level of the Poro were privileged to sit on a leopard skin--it was the special sign known by all members of the Poro. Bob felt a twinge of jealousy. There was a low murmur of suppressed awe and excitement from the chiefs as King Zoda asked a headman to remove the raffia mat from his accustomed place in the palaver circle. Then he calmly unrolled his leopard skin, seating himself with conscious dignity under their watchful eyes. Bob ducked his head politely in his turn as Zoda nodded to each of them around the circle, a new aura of power in Zoda's penetrating stare.

"King Zoda, we ready to hear you know," George said.

Zoda stood, drawing his robe around himself proudly.

"I come back from Kongba, ancient homeland where my Gola forefathers begin at Mana Bla," Zoda began. "Mana Bla be old town--first town--founded by ancient chief who come from East long time ago. Kongba chiefdoms all be from sons of this one man 'self, and be powerful brotherhood to keep sacred tradition of Poro safe

181

and true. Konga be place where Poro be strong past all in this whole country!" Zoda swept his arms out proudly.

Bob Gray's mouth almost slipped into a scornful leer, but he held his face straight with a strong effort. The Golas always want us to believe they are the best, he thought, and we swallow it like taking medicine from our mothers. Zoda is going to give us a good dose now!

"You, my brother chiefs of Montserado country, send me to find war leader with strong medicine. So I talk plenty with all *zo's*--all high doctors of war--in Kongba land. They say one man be higher than all the rest. His name be Zarbo. I find him and bring him here."

"What make him big man for war?" KunoKree asked. "What he do for that?"

Zoda gave the questioner a brief stare as if he was interrupting, and then turned to address the whole circle again.

"Jarbo be son of great warrior, taught by his own father before he go to Poro bush school. In bush school he be best fighter of all boys. When he come out, he lead his age group. In few years they be Kongba's best warriors. Then Jarbo be asked to be war leader for Tungele chiefdom. He be famous for his victories and then he become head war doctor of all Kongba chiefdoms."

There was complete silence while the chiefs pondered it. Bob Gray marveled--it was a masterful and clear explanation. If it was all true then no one could object to Zoda's selection. Zoda himself nodded to another questioner's signal, ignoring George's role as today's council leader. Bob Gray was surprised--this was overshadowing George.

"You say he be high-high *zo* in war business," King Ben asked. "How he get to be so?"

Bob Gray kept a straight face, but knew the question was impertinent. Zoda had already said Jarbo was a high priest of war--it was almost like doubting his word. But Zoda nodded calmly.

"All true Africans be members of Poro," he said, and searched their faces carefully, his eyes sweeping slowly around the circle as he checked them out. Bob heard each one affirm it and nod his head. It was the ritual test, and no one dared fail it. Bob made sure his own affirmation was loud and clear. When the circle was rounded, Zoda nodded his head. He raised his hands to form the Poro sign for secrecy, and they all made it. Two men stepped to the door to guard it. There was a sudden stillness in the palaver hall. No one moved or breathed, waiting for Zoda to tell them the secret news about Jarbo.

"Jarbo made the big sacrifice for high-high doctor of war," Zoda began, his voice low and husky. He raised his right hand, stabbing the air with his finger. "First son! There be no sacrifice bigger! I talk to high *zo's* who made this ceremony for him and ate heart and flesh of his son."

Zoda raised his voice, his finger still jabbing at them.

"There be no doubt! Jarbo be highest *zo* for war! Azowa!"

But Zoda raised a warning hand.

"Remember, brother chiefs, this palaver still be under Poro oath," he said, looking at them sternly. "Jarbo be waiting outside, and I send for him now. You can ask questions, but all he say must be secret. You know what happen if Poro oath not be obeyed."

Jarbo was escorted in and Zoda motioned him toward the center of the circle. Startling to his beholders, he stood a head taller than any of them, the effect heightened by a fierce war helmet with a pair of horns jutting forward. A bold ruff of eagle feathers was on top, with white cowrie shells across the front headband, side flaps of leopard skin with a leather chin strap, and a long white mane of ram's hair trailing to his shoulders behind. Stripped for battle, he wore only a black loin cloth and short war vest of leopard skin that set off his massive chest and shoulders. The muscles of his powerful arms and legs rippled as he strode forward. He carried a spear tipped with a deadly iron lance in his right hand, and a mysterious bundle wrapped in black cloth in his left. Reaching the center of the circle, Jarbo swung around with the easy stealth of a panther and faced Zoda.

Bob Gray quickly totaled up the insignia on Jarbo's helmet--horns, feathers, cowrie shells, and leopard skin--by his calculations it meant seven enemies slain! He looked at Jarbo closely, noticing there was no gray in his short, jet-black beard, and then saw with admiration that a healthy red glow showed through his deep black skin. But Jarbo's intelligent eyes in a calm face impressed Bob even more. Here is not only a fighting man in his prime, Bob thought, but a great war leader, for true! Bob's heart lifted as Zoda raised his hand toward Jarbo, introducing him proudly.

"Here be Jarbo, mighty war leader of all Kongba chiefdoms, high-high doctor of war in Poro--and now the Azowa of our

Montserado country!"

The response was immediate. The entire circle of chiefs rose as one and shouted their confirmation.

"Jarbo! Azowa of Montserado country!" "Azowa!" "Azowa!" "Azowa!"

But something echoed strangely in Bob Gray's mind as he and the other chiefs fussed with their robes and settled on their mats again. His mind repeated it: 'Azowa of our Montserado country'? Wait. Our country? Zoda, a Gola and a newcomer to the coast, can be part of our country--and choose our war leader for us? What other decisions would he make for our war? Whatever deal George struck with Zoda, it was plain that George was losing ground to Zoda fast. Did George sell us out in order to get help from the Golas for the war? What were the Golas after--what did they want in return?

Zoda and Jarbo were still standing as the others sat down. Bob saw that George was standing, too, his face beginning to swell up again. He's getting mad about Zoda taking over--and it's about time!

"Thank you, King Zoda, for bringing us Jarbo," George said. He bowed to Zoda and swept his arm down to show that Zoda was to sit down--that his part was finished. Without waiting to see if Zoda did it, George turned to the center of the circle. Bob smiled at his tactic.

"Jarbo, we welcome you to our war council! You be famous war leader, so our chiefs be happy you come. Our council be under Poro secret oath now, and we make questions to ask you. If anything you say be Poro secret, it will stay in our ears only. We all be Poro, so let your heart lie down 'bout that."

"Brother chiefs!" George continued. "Now be the time for your questions."

King Ben raised his cowtail switch.

"How we know Jarbo's special medicine be strong enough for this war?"

George scowled fiercely.

"You don't have ears to hear? Jarbo be high-high doctor of war in Poro! That mean his medicine be strong past all!"

"That be in Kongba--far up country--and with Kongba warriors," Ben said. "Here on sea coast it not be same. Maybe we better not fight colony with bush medicine. Maybe our warriors be too different."

184

Bob Gray saw what Ben was doing--he still hadn't agreed to join in the attack and probably hoped to stop it this way.

"I agree!" a voice boomed out. "How do we know how good Jarbo's medicine be?"

They hadn't heard Brister's voice in the council for days, and every chief jerked around in surprise to see the well-respected Dey chief come to life again.

"For true! Let's hear about Jarbo's medicine for our warriors. Will it work for our men?"

It was King KunoKree from Junk river. Now all three chiefs who opposed the war were raising doubts, Bob noticed. And other chiefs were beginning to nod their heads in agreement.

"I say he make the best medicine!" George shouted, desperate to squelch the detractors. "He be high-high doctor of ..."

George's angry voice choked off as Zoda caught all eyes by lifting his elephant tail switch.

"Jarbo, can you tell chiefs about your new medicine?" Zoda asked calmly.

There was dead silence in the hall. All eyes focused on Jarbo, and Bob Gray knew they were too embarrassed to look at George, who was gurgling helplessly in confusion. Finally Jarbo spoke.

"Mighty chiefs of Montserado country! King George be right. High-high *zo's* not be allowed to tell such secret things. But all of us now be under Poro oath, so I tell you about special medicine I make for your war. Then you know how strong it be."

Laying his mysterious black bundle down, he straightened and then lifted a thin black cord from around the left side of his neck, carefully pulling it over his helmet. He slipped it off his right arm and freed it from his vest, revealing a small ram's horn that had hung concealed under his arm. Holding it up high, he turned slowly around so all the chiefs could see the leather covered horn studded with polished cowrie shells. There was a murmur of appreciation for its beauty.

"This be the most powerful medicine I ever make--seven things to make your warriors win the war! Before, I use only five."

"Ay, ya!" the chiefs chorused approvingly.

But Ben was still skeptical.

"You going to tell us what they be?" he chided.

Jarbo nodded. George sat down quietly.

"First, small small piece of stone, it be best to make your

warriors strong!"

The chiefs nodded. Bob Gray did too--there was nothing stronger than a great stone, and a small piece contained as much of its vital force as the large one from which it was taken.

"Second, bark from *ba a yidi*--slippery tree so smooth even monkey can't climb. Makes warriors so nobody conquer them!"

Heads nodded again. It was true, nothing could go up that tree--nobody could conquer it. This was a valuable essence!

"Third, special leaf I catch floating in air, going so," Jarbo showed with his hand the leaf flitting quickly one way, then the next, as it glided silently down through the trees. "Makes warriors' feet go softly softly through the forest!"

"Ahh, hanhhh," some chiefs murmured, not quite sure. It was a new thing--but if you thought about it, warriors must quietly slip from tree to tree through the forest for surprise attack at dawn. More heads nodded. Jarbo was a deep one!

"Fourth, piece of squirrel skin, because he all the time turn and dip, hard to hit; makes warriors quick to dodge arrows and spears!"

"Ay, ya!" Some chiefs thought of the poisoned arrows, and the barbed ones that ripped you apart when someone had to yank them out. And the spears--nobody wanted to think about a long iron lance head ramming deep into his body! To dodge like a squirrel was very important!

"Fifth, small *vong* bush stays green forever, always plenty berries--makes warriors be fruitful, helps them win and bring home plenty of booty!"

"Yaaaah!" It brought them up straight on their mats. Bob Gray marveled with the rest--Jarbo brings something wonderful for true! Most of the forest turns brown and dies each season, but *vong* bush shows victory over this death. And the fruitful part--Bob liked that best. Every chief had to have booty to keep his people happy!

"Sixth, a piece of *gba yidi*, small tree we call 'black deer stick'. This deer be most cunning animal in forest--hunter can't catch it! Makes warriors be clever past all enemies!"

"Aaaayee!" Nobody ever catches black deer--all of them knew that. The crafty essence of the black deer was a great boon to a warrior! Bob Gray joined the others in nodding vigorously, sure now that Jarbo was the best *zo* of all.

"Seventh, piece of heart from last warrior I killed in battle.

186

He was great fighter! This be my strongest medicine! Makes all warriors great fighter like him!"

It stunned them all--the vital force of a great warrior's heart! Nothing had more power than that to help a warrior slay an enemy! And it was a gift from Jarbo of his very best medicine, so it carried part of his own spirit, too--a double force from two great fighters! It brought the chiefs to their feet.

"Aaaaaay, Yaaaaah! Jarbo!" They thrust their right fists into the air again and again. "Azowa! Jarbo be Azowa! Jarbo, Jarbo, Jarbo!"

After they calmed down, George asked them to sit.

"You be satisfied now!" he stated confidently. "I hear it and see it in your faces. So we move on. Three chiefs still not decide to join us. Today be the day! What do you say, King Ben, King Brister, and King KunoKree--are you with us now?"

George has them cornered, Bob Gray thought. They could hardly back out now. It was a clever move. King Ben raised his cowtail switch and George nodded. Everyone hushed.

"I join you with all my warriors," Ben said. "With Jarbo we will win!"

They shouted approval. King Ben was half Vai, Bob Gray suddenly remembered. Nobody had talked of the Vai people yet, but with Ben in the fold, he might influence the Vai to join them.

"King Brister, how you say now?" George asked.

Again everyone hushed. But Brister slowly shook his head.

"I say the 'Mericans be our brothers--that be feeling in my heart." He touched his chest, and they knew he really meant it. "I can't go against what be in my heart, but I won't stop my warriors from joining you if they want."

He stood up and looked around the circle.

"I leave you now, brother chiefs. You do what you must, and I do what I must."

He nodded solemnly and turned to go. They watched him in silence, respecting his honor and his decision. King George waited until Brister passed out of the palaver hall entrance, and then turned to KunoKree.

"What say you now, King KunoKree?"

The chief from Junk river stood up and shrugged his shoulders.

"It not be my war. I not trading in slaves anymore, so my people need trade with colony. I can't join you."

There was murmuring from some of the chiefs. Bob Gray could tell they didn't think KunoKree was showing the right respect for them. KunoKree quickly raised his hands.

"But! I go home now and tell my warriors they can do what they want. It be up to them."

He nodded to them and walked hastily towards the entrance. George was scowling again, but made no move to stop KunoKree.

He is getting out just in time, Bob Gray thought wistfully.

22 Poro Call

Cape Mesurado
October 17, 1822

"All right, we move on!" George shouted. "There won't be many warriors come from Brister and KunoKree's towns, so we get some from other places. King Ben, how about the Vai?"

"Wait small!" someone shouted over George's voice. "I just remember--there be something missing in Jarbo's medicine!"

Shock and disbelief shattered their mood and all eyes sought the spoiler. It was King Tom. Murmuring their displeasure, the chiefs gestured to shut him up.

"We all see Jarbo be greatest *zo* of his time!" George said. "What you think be missing?"

"Nothing there to stop the 'Mericans' guns!"

"You mean their muskets?" George asked. "The squirrel skin do that, not so, Jarbo?"

George turned to Jarbo for confirmation and the eyes of the entire council focused on the war leader. Jarbo nodded his head.

"You be right, King George. For arrows, spears, muskets--anything the enemy throw at you."

"What about 'Mericans' big, big stick that booms like thunder? They had one on island that shoots far up to Cape! Squirrel skin will stop that?"

Again the eyes of the council were on him. Jarbo shook his head.

"No! That be different, different thing--I carry special medicine for that in my body. Only high-high doctor of war can carry that one."

"Ah Hanh!" they said, not yet understanding.

"How so, Jarbo?" King Tom asked. "If you carry medicine for the big boom stick, who carry that horn you show us?"

"Medicine horn be for your warriors. I pound and burn all seven things to black powder in pot like making charcoal. On day before battle, you pick one high-born pregnant woman of your people who cook powder in her food pot with rice. Then she bury food in special place in path, I say secret words, and all warriors step over this place just so on way to battle."

189

He demonstrated the warrior's careful step-over.

"Yaaaaaah!" they chorused, admiring the way he would make sure the power of the medicine passed into each warrior.

"So--what about medicine to stop boom sticks?" Tom asked.

"I make special sacrifice to get ready to lead warriors--to go in front of them and stop mouths of big sticks."

"Ah hanh?" they said, not doubting his medicine, but wanting more details. Jarbo didn't say anything, so they waited respectfully. But Tom's impatience broke the silence.

"How you do that?" he burst out.

Jarbo shook his head. Then he wagged his finger slowly at them all.

"Medicine so powerful can't be told! I use name of enemy in my secret words, and if that enemy hear of it they can make stronger medicine to cancel mine."

He reached out his arm toward Zoda, palm upward in a silent appeal. Zoda raised his elephant tail switch and the murmuring stopped.

"Brother chiefs, Jarbo be in a hard place," Zoda said calmly. "He says there be a difference in medicine for warriors and for him. Let him tell us about that."

Jarbo nodded gratefully.

"Medicine for warriors be force from rocks, trees, and heart. I make it go into warriors. Now, for me, 'self--that comes from sacrifice! That be spirit business, not force from things. Spirit go into me, so I can do things like stop mouth of big sticks. Only high-high *zo* can do ceremony for that. I learn it in last step I take to be high-high doctor of war. It cost me great sacrifice--my first born son."

"Ah hanh," they said, nodding.

"Sooo, that be the difference!" Jarbo said, spreading his hands out, palms up.

"We thank Jarbo for telling us this," Tom said to Zoda. "But we sit here to judge his medicine for our war. We need something to stop the 'Merican's booms sticks. What is he going to use for that?"

Zoda looked to Jarbo standing in the center of the palaver circle. Their eyes met, and Jarbo barely moved his head, but everyone saw it meant the same 'no' he had said before.

"Jarbo can't tell that one," Zoda said. "It might spoil the power of it."

"That be just an excuse!" Tom shouted. "I won't send my warriors to be hit by 'Merican boom sticks! If Jarbo not tell us his medicine here now, I walk out of this council and not join war!"

Others took up the matter and the clamor spread around circle. King George stood up, scowling angrily and motioning for silence.

Jarbo's face was ashen. He closed his eyes and put his hands over them. The palaver hall hushed. They could see a tremor begin, starting with his arms, then his chest and trunk, and finally his legs. Bob Gray saw Jarbo's hands pressing tightly on his forehead and eyes and guessed he was seeking a vision. In a moment the tremors stopped and Jarbo lifted his hands away, opening his eyes.

"I have to ask my father's help to decide this thing," he said in a low voice. "His spirit be in his mask. There."

He pointed at the ground beside him, and their eyes followed his long black finger to the mysterious bundle. Bob Gray was as surprised as the rest--they'd been so interested in the horn they'd forgotten the bundle. Mesmerized, they watched Jarbo slip the horn and its cord back over his arm, through the armhole of his jacket, and over his helmet. When the horn was concealed once again under his arm, he knelt down by the bundle and began to unwrap the black cloth, talking to them as he did it.

"My father be great warrior who taught me all he knew before he died in war between Tungele and Zui chiefdoms. He be high *zo* for war and teach many boys in Poro bush school. They made fierce warriors when they grow up."

Laying back the black outer cloth revealed a white one inside, and Jarbo began to unwrap this also.

"When he die, he get plenty of respect. *Ki La mi* tell paramount chief of all Kongba to have mask made for my father's spirit to enter, so he be with us forever. When mask be finished, they tell me to sacrifice to it so my father know that I be the new high *zo*."

Jarbo lifted the mask reverently, turning it carefully for all to see. Bob Gray stared at it, amazed at the close likeness to Jarbo himself. The traditional set of ram's horns in the middle of the mask's forehead overshadowed the family likeness, but showed the power of a great warrior--a ram could smash anything with its horns! Looking closer, Bob saw the greasy, encrusted surface of the mask and knew what Jarbo had done to keep the spirit of his

191

ancestor alive. Only human blood and fat smeared over the mask could do that. How often did Jarbo have to do it? Bob wondered. His skin began to crawl as he thought of the secret ritual and a new victim to sacrifice for it each time.

"My father's spirit speaks to me with cowries," Jarbo said.

The chiefs were silent, hardly breathing. They watched him smooth out the white cloth and lay the mask down on it. Then he picked up a small leather pouch from the bundle and opened it. Four gleaming white cowrie shells fell into his hand. He turned to George.

"Two chiefs be needed to judge how cowries talk."

King George looked around the circle, scowling at them.

"King Willy! King Jimmy! Come see how cowries fall!"

Without a word they came to stand, one on either side of Jarbo. He cupped his hands together and raised the cowries up above eye level.

"O Spirit of my father, I follow in your footsteps! I be asked to lead this war. I will make sacrifice to go in front of warriors and stop mouths of 'Merican boom sticks. Secrets of sacrifice can be turned against us all if enemy hear them. So I ask if it be safe to tell secrets under Poro oath to chiefs. Let the cowries talk. If three or four be up, it be safe. Speak, O Spirit of my father!"

He threw the cowries down beside the mask. Everyone leaned forward, waiting for the call. Willy and Jimmy bent down to count.

"Three up!" Willy said. "That's right--three up!" Jimmy confirmed.

All the chiefs expelled their breaths with relief, and then grinning widely, broke out in loud chatter.

"All right! We move on!" George called out, waving his arms to quiet them. When they had settled down again, he turned to Jarbo.

"Tell us, now, how you going to do this sacrifice thing."

Jarbo covered the mask with the white cloth and, looking up, began to explain.

"It takes one white chicken, one white goat, and a young girl. First, I say secret words for sacrifice of chicken, hold it over girl, and cut its throat so blood fall on her. Next I do same with goat. Spirit power of both go into girl and make hers strong."

They had hung on his words, but now he was silent, and Bob Gray thought he knew why-- Jarbo probably didn't want to

192

say the next part. Bob didn't want to hear it, either.

"What you do next?" George asked.

"I--I put her on special altar made of elephant tusks. So her blood catch in bowl when I-- when I cut her throat."

Jarbo stopped again. The chiefs were spellbound. George almost forgot to prompt him.

"N-Next?"

"I take off my clothes and go to my medicine box with bowl of her blood, dip my hands in bowl, and rub her blood on all my medicine pieces, talk to them, and ask medicines to stop the boom sticks' mouths."

"That be all?" George asked huskily. No one seemed to breathe. Jarbo shook his head.

"No. I turn to north, south, east and west and say secret thing each time so power of all three bloods join mine. Then I--I drink part of girl's blood and ceremony be finished. I wash myself, put on helmet and war vest, and take my war knife and spear. Last thing, I pray to Spirit of my father in mask to help us get victory, and I go lead the warriors in battle."

"Aaaaaay yaaaaah!" the chiefs said in one long sigh of relief and wonder.

Jarbo nodded to George and then to the chiefs, turning around to face each one. Still beaming from their praise, he sat down by the mask to wait.

"We move on!" George said. "But now we have another big thing to talk."

The chief's chatter stopped instantly.

"What thing that be?" King Willy asked.

"We need more warriors if Brister and KunoKree's warriors not come," George said. "Maybe we should make Poro call for all chiefs on coast to join us. That way, no one can say no."

"Poro call! There never be one in my lifetime!" King Jimmy said in surprise and alarm.

The words went around the circle like a grass-fire in high wind. "Poro call!" "George talking Poro call!" "Poro call on coast." "Aaayee! This be big thing!"

King Ben raised his cowtail switch, but didn't wait for George's nod.

"Why we need more warriors? With Jarbo's medicine we get victory for sure!"

George rounded on him angrily.

193

"Strong medicine be important, but we need plenty of warriors to swarm over 'Merican's war fence! Must be like army of driver ants moving through forest and villages to kill and eat everything in path."

"Ya! Driver ant be small, but when he come by thousands nothing stop him," Willy said. "Besides we need plenty warriors to carry away booty."

"Booty!" George shouted. He'd forgotten that. "For true-o! Last ship for 'Mericans bring so much goods they build second storehouse. All that be for you! For you! And you!"

George went around the circle, jabbing at the chiefs with his finger. He's poking at our weak spot--our greed, Bob Gray realized. Greed for booty is really what drives us all. Booty buys us support from our people.

"So to get booty we need more warriors," George continued. "Remember the saying, 'water not run over sunken log twice'--now be time to attack colony. 'Mericans be sick with fever and there be no ships in harbor to protect them. But if ships come back again we lose our chance!"

He turned to Zoda.

"We have to make Poro call for warriors now! King Zoda--can we do this thing quick-quick?"

Zoda inclined his head to think, and all conversation ceased.

"It can't be done while Poro or Sande bush schools be in session--that be Poro law," Zoda mused out loud. "And Gola schools going on now."

"But those be up-country. They not have anything to do with our palavers down here on coast!" George protested, his face beginning to darken. "We don't have to look out for them. We must have more warriors now!"

The chiefs saw the conflict coming and sat up straight.

"Only the *Ki La mi* can decide a big thing like Poro call," Zoda said. "I just saying why they not call one now."

"*Ki La mi*! What about us?" George shouted. "We're all chiefs! All of us be Poro, too!"

But Zoda shook his head. They saw George's face twist with rage, his eyes bulging, and they nerved themselves for his next blast.

"Your Poro in Kongba is for Gola people! We Dey people have our own Poro and bush schools on coast. We don't need Gola

Poro leaders to tell us what to do!"

Horrified looks passed between the chiefs, and Bob Gray shuddered. George's anger was making him heedless of the dangerous waters he was entering! Only the highest ranks of Poro officials in different tribes could meet with each other about such grave matters as a Poro call. Bob was only sure of one man of such rank in this palaver circle--Zoda. George was over-reaching himself and almost defying Poro law!

Zoda stood up slowly and straightened his robe, every move dignified and deliberate, his face rigid as stone. Only his eyes belied his calmness. The chiefs saw redness in his eyes and knew he was furious. They sat suspended on their mats, not moving a muscle--not even to blink.

"I be *Kanda Jia*, inspector of your Poro groves," Zoda said in a deadly flat voice. "King Peter be *Kpopla Kan*, owner of land and priest. But you!" Zoda's upper lip curled as he stared at George. "You be nothing! Nothing! You hear?"

His eyes bored into George's, but George drew himself up and stared back.

"Nothing! I be Poro! I be chief of Cape! I have big trade with slavers! Nothing, eh! That be same thing you Gola come down to coast to get!"

"Watch what you say! Your tongue be like fish flapping on beach, about to die!"

The palaver hall was deathly quiet, the chiefs cringing inwardly. Bob Gray winced--they all knew Zoda could make good on his threat if George broke any Poro law. Bob wished the argument would stop before George said too much. But nobody dared to caution him.

"Sons of Poro, be silent!"

Heads turned at the command, given in a voice almost too weak to be heard. It was King Peter, silenced himself by some secret deal for nine days. But the old patriarch was still in his honored place in the palaver circle.

"Both of you be flapping fish!"

Bob Gray suddenly remembered that Zoda had just revealed Peter as *Kpopla Kan*, which meant he was not only traditional 'owner' of Montserado country, but also high priest of Poro! Bob sucked in his breath. A rare thing, this being both a public official and religious leader--and Peter could even condemn Zoda, in spite of Zoda's highborn Gola connections!

Chastened, George and Zoda stood silently in their places in the circle, Jarbo crouching by his mask in the center, almost forgotten. Finally George appealed to Peter with both hands outstretched, his voice plaintive.

"We must have more warriors now!"

King Peter straightened up on his mat, taking in a deep breath and composing his face. He cleared his throat.

"You be asking for Poro call, King George?" he said.

"Yes. Maybe just along the coast," George said. "A small Poro call, if there be such thing."

"Mmmhunm," Peter said. He turned to Zoda.

"You saying we 'self can't make such call down here on coast, King Zoda?"

"That be right. Gola brotherhood keep Poro straight for all tribes--only *Ki La mi* can make Poro call."

"Mmmhunh." Peter turned to Jarbo in the center of the circle.

"Jarbo, Spirit of your father in mask can say something for us about this thing?"

"Yes." Jarbo stood up. "He say yes or no with cowrie shells, and he give direction with kola nuts."

Jarbo picked up a small grass bag from the folds of cloth by the mask, shaking out five white kola nuts and one red.

"Aaah hanh!" the chiefs chorused, smiling with relief.

Peter looked around the circle at all the chiefs, and then at the headmen sitting in the corners of the palaver hall. He raised his weak voice as much as he could to address them all.

"You all be satisfied to ask great war leader's spirit in Jarbo's mask where to get more warriors?"

It was one unanimous voice, and the hall shook.

"We be satisfied, King Peter!"

Peter nodded, and waved to Jarbo to begin.

"It take two people to read what direction kola nuts say," Jarbo said.

"King Governor and King Bromley, you can read kola nuts for us?" Peter asked.

They nodded and went to Jarbo's side. Bob Gray's heart was happy with the wise old man's way to get others to serve without shouting at them.

Jarbo spread out the black cloth and stood up, taking the red kola nut and biting off some to chew. Then he spit on one of the white kolas. He bit off some more of the red and repeated this for all five white ones. He put the rest of the red kola nut on the mask, between the horns. Cupping the white kola nuts in his hands, he lifted them over his head.

"Spirit of my father, great war leader and teacher of warriors, maker of strong medicines for war, show us what direction to go find more warriors for this battle. Speak through kola nuts. Three or four kola nuts face one direction, that be way to go. If less, we try again. Speak, O Spirit of my father!"

The five white kola nuts landed on the black cloth, and the chiefs leaned forward anxiously. Governor was the first to read the kolas, and he cried out as he pointed.

"Three--in that direction!"

King Jimmy twisted his neck in different positions, but came back to the same one three times.

"Three-one-one," he said, and pointed almost in the same direction as Governor.

"North!" they cried in unison.

"Aaah hanh," the chiefs cautiously approved. Bob Gray knew which tribe it meant, but no one dared say it. King Peter nodded his head and cleared his throat.

"That be Vai people," he announced. "King George, King Zoda--you be satisfied with that?"

They both nodded.

"The paramount chief of Vai people be one man called Massaquoi," Peter said. "Zoda, will you go to him and ask for his help?"

All eyes focused on Zoda. He smiled and drew himself up proudly.

"Yes, King Peter. Massaquoi be big man in Poro like you and me. He will listen to us."

Bob Gray saw George scowl, and guessed he was being eaten by jealousy.

"Massaquoi be next to Don Pedro's slave pens at Gallinas!" George burst out. "He could ask Don Pedro to send us muskets to fight the 'Mericans!"

King Peter ignored it.

"When you be leaving for Massaquoi's place?" he asked Zoda.

"It take one day to get ready. Then I leave."

"We thank you for your journey. Go well," Peter said.

197

He turned to the chiefs. "What does council say to our brother who travels long journey for us?"

"Go well!" they said.

Peter turned to George.

"King George, our people have a saying, 'Hunter who talks loud in bush can't find meat.' Another thing they say, 'Elephant can't grow in one day'. You savvy these things?"

George's face looked stricken. Bob Gray thought, for once he is speechless! George looked down at his feet, and the chiefs knew he had been properly shamed by proverbs even children knew. Then George looked up at Peter and nodded.

"Fine," Peter said, "I turn this council back to you."

CHAPTER

23   Last Minute Warning

Cape Mesurado
October 23, 1822

"Companeeee--Halt! At Ease. No! You can't walk away! That means stand still!" Elijah shouted, nearly at the end of his patience. "Hold your gun down at your side and stand there like this ... easy like, but watchin' me."

Elijah demonstrated the 'at ease' stance, his eyes scanning his new musket company recruits with a stern face. He stabbed his arm toward a man in the second row, pointing in outrage at him.

"You! Get back in line! I didn't dismiss you!" He rolled his eyes in despair and motioned John Bannon to go to the recaptive youth standing in confusion in the second row. "Show him how, John."

Everyone waited while John stepped over to the young man and put him through the drill. Elijah knew that the main problem was language. The recaptives had been in America for over a year before being returned by the Navy to Africa, but they hadn't learned much English, Elijah thought. In fact, they hadn't changed much from the way they'd come out of the bush in the first place. But at least they'd stayed in the colony right here on the cape and were eager to learn. Could he train these thirteen raw bush youths and a dozen colonists into a company of sharp shooters? There was so little time! And there wasn't much powder and ball to waste on practice shots. Sweat broke out on Elijah's face. The colony's future might depend on their aim. He took in a deep breath and barked the commands again.

"Ten-shunnn! Present arms! Right face ... March!"

Elijah called the cadence, waiting until the company passed, and fell in behind them, matching their stride.

"Left, right! Hip, haw! Left, right! Hip ..."

He would drill them until they learned to react fast, disciplined to his commands, and only then would he put them to target practice. But how to save powder and ball?

"Hip, haw! Pick it up! Left, right! ..."

He would train them to draw a bead on their target, and pull the trigger. Draw and pull-- on running targets. But only load

199

their muskets every--say every tenth time, to save ammunition. But they needed practice on loading powder and ball, too! They'd have to be able to do it fast, as the warriors attacked. Could they hold their ground behind the stockades, reloading in the face of hundreds of shouting warriors rushing at them? Would the stockade even be ready?

"Column right ... March! Wait! The other direction, you damn fools! Halt! Companee halt--dammit!"

Elijah ran to the front of the group, waving at the confused ones, wiping his face with his bandana, shouting to restore order. When they were all facing the right direction and lined up squarely, he looked them over. Tired, ready for their noon meal, and facing a heavy afternoon's work cutting bush again--he knew he'd put them through enough for their first drill.

"Disss-missed!"

They broke ranks and Elijah mopped at his face. Fred James walked by, having discharged his Kroo workers for the noon break. He grinned wickedly at Elijah.

"Havin' a good time giving orders, Lije?"

"Oh, shut up!" Elijah said, glaring over his bandanna.

"Pretty sharp bunch you have there," Fred teased. "Taught'em which is right and left yet?"

"They're learnin'. How about your Kroo boys--I don't see any stockade poles goin' up yet. What's the matter--you haven't taught'em how to use our axes yet?"

Elijah hid his own grin behind the bandanna, knowing he'd caught Fred in his own game.

"They don't like our axes," Fred complained. "They want me to get them some long knives--machetes, they call them."

"That so? You gon'ta make'em some?" Elijah said, dropping the bandanna from his face, his grin as wide as he could make it.

"How can I do that? Where am I ..." Fred saw Elijah's face, and he narrowed his eyes to glare at him.

"You knew!"

"Guess you're just gon'ta have to teach'em how to do it with the axes. Good luck!"

Elijah laughed and walked toward his house. Fred's jibes were just what he needed--it took the place of the way he and Mary used to joke each other. It always seemed to relieve their worries.

####

John Bannon proudly pointed to the cannon emplacement in the center of the town. "See, Carrie, that brass cannon is what's called a backup. Being higher, it can shoot over the cannon out on the points of the triangle and back them up."

He pulled her up on the earth-and-log mound that stood on a high point of the ridge.

"Now you can see the triangle the town makes."

His arm swept to the east and west points along the ridge and then to the third one lower down on the slouth slope.

"We'll be putting a stockade around it all, if we have enough time. And the cannon at the points will be the first ones to shoot at the enemy when they attack."

She didn't reply and he turned to see her face. She was staring at the ocean beyond the cape's end on the west, and then she took in the wide expanse of the ocean to the south and the forest in the east. Her eyes opened wide and he saw a new look in them. Her face was changing, too.

"Look, John, the Atlantic--it's so blue now--and the forest so green. It's beautiful!"

She was right. It was beautiful, and he hadn't looked at it that way for quite a spell. But they couldn't take time for that right now--the noon rest period was over and he had to get back to cutting trees. Carrie had fed Elijah and the children their usual noon meal and this was her time to rest briefly from household chores. So he'd brought her to look at the one part of their defenses that was completed, sure she'd be proud of what they were doing to protect her and the other women and children in the colony. But she hardly saw it. He tried again.

"Look down there, Carrie. The south slope's all cleared of most of the trees now, and we'll soon ..."

"I didn't know it could be this beautiful, John!" She turned and smiled up at him. "My Africa! I'm glad you got me all straight about my Ma givin' me this chance to be here."

She turned and waved her hand toward the northeast.

"That's the way into the heart of Africa, isn't it? See the forest stretchin' away for miles and miles. Oh, I'd like to go in there and find out what Africa is really like!"

"Whoa! Wait a minute! You're forgetting what's going on--you can't go anywhere yet! We're stuck up here on this cape, waiting to be attacked."

He turned her slightly to the north and pointed down to the

Mesurado river at the foot of the cape and the land beyond it.

"There's a war about to take place--you got that? And most of the tribes that are talking about attacking us are out there north of us somewhere in all that forest you think's so beautiful. They'll probably have to come across the river there and up the hill--and we've got to be ready for them. When they come over the hill we'll blast them away!"

"I can't believe it. The forest is so peaceful and calm. Look at it, John. And now all this commotion on the cape, choppin' down trees and spoilin' the forest for your big fence. And piling up dirt for your cannons. Why does there have to be a war? It doesn't make sense!"

He threw up his hands in disgust.

"Where have you been all this time, Carrie? You act like you've had your head in the sand! Ashmun and Elijah and Fred have been trying to make peace with ..."

"Well, maybe they haven't tried hard enough! Or they should try again. Anything to stop us from shootin' them down with these big cannons! We shouldn't be killing the Africans--they're our people, even if we don't understand each other yet!"

She was right, he thought. A lot of people could be killed--both them and us. But ...

"We're not the ones going to start the war, Carrie. This is only protection if they attack us. We tried to talk them out of it, but we hear they're getting all the tribes stirred up to make war on us."

"Well, hasn't anybody told them how terrible it'll be if they come in front of those big cannons? Maybe if they knew, they wouldn't come."

"No, of course not! You don't tell your enemy what you're going to defend yourself with. It'd be like telling them where or how to attack you. Carrie, you don't know what you're talking about. Just stay out of it."

He took her arm to help her down from the mound, but she jerked her arm away and climbed down herself.

"Well, this is my Africa, too! And this is no way for us to start makin' a home in it. I'm going to talk to Elijah about it!"

John was shocked by the boldness she was suddenly taking on. And so saucy about 'her' Africa! He was amused and turned his head so she couldn't see his smile.

"But Carrie! At least you'd better wait and see Elijah

tonight when he gets home. Don't go speaking to him in front of all the men where he's working now. You'll be the laughing stock of the whole ..."

She turned on him, her eyes furious.

"Laughing what? What's that mean?"

She turned towards the eastern point of the triangle where they'd seen Elijah from a distance supervising the next cannon emplacement, and she began marching toward it with a determined stride. John hurried to catch up.

"I mean, you'd look kind of funny, being so smart about war when you've been in the kitchen all this time."

But she didn't slacken her pace, and he felt desperate, wanting to spare her from embarrassment.

"Carrie! Wait! Wait until tonight! You'll have time to think about what you want to say-- and Elijah will have time to listen!"

She slowed down.

"You'll come and be with me when I talk to him?"

"Yes. Just leave it for now!"

There was a sound and everyone sitting on the bamboo bench in the dim lamplight turned to the door as Carrie came out.

"Carrie!" John said, his eyes lighting up. She had fixed herself up and looked really nice. She smiled and nodded at each one of the usual nightly visitors on Elijah's porch.

"Mr. Fred--Mr. Blake--Mr. Johnson--Mr. Bannon."

It took them by surprise, and John could see she'd gained their full attention, all of them smiling widely at this pretty intrusion on their evening talk.

"I have something to ask you gentlemens. Would now be the right time?"

She was so polite and charming, John could hardly believe this was the Carrie he knew.

"Why, yes, Carrie," Elijah said, "What is it?"

She looked at Elijah, her eyes searching his carefully.

"You were there when my mother said she was sending me to Africa to be free, Elijah?"

"Sure was."

"You believe she wanted me to make my home here, like the

rest of you gentlemens and your families?"

"Yes."

She took a deep breath. John saw her mouth twitch faintly with uncertainty.

"Then I want to say I don't believe this is the way to start making a home in Africa--this getting ready to kill the Africans with your big cannons. They don't know cannons, do they? Maybe if they knew how many of them would be killed with each shot they wouldn't make war on us."

John watched their jaws drop with surprise. But before they had time to reply she ask another question.

"Have you gentlemens honest and truly done ever'thing you could to stop the war from coming?"

She looked reproachfully at each of of them. John knew from his own feelings it had stung them deeply--and he'd already known she would do something like this! He marveled at her simple,direct challenge. Awkwardly silent, they finally turned to look at Elijah.

"Well, Carrie ..." Elijah began slowly, "we've tried to talk with the important chiefs." He sighed. "But maybe that's not enough. Maybe we should try something else."

"Yeah, but we'd better be careful what we tell'em about our defenses," Fred said.

Elijah nodded.

"I'll talk with Ashmun. We've got some good fever medicine now, and he'll be on his feet soon. Maybe there's still time before the Africans get organized--they haven't all agreed yet to make war on us."

"Thank you, Elijah," Carrie said softly. She turned to face the others and dipped a brief curtsy to them.

"Thank you, gentlemens."

John caught her eye and smiled. He hadn't believed she could do this, or even if she should. But now it seemed right that she'd tried. His heart swelled with pride as she said goodnight and left them.

October 25, 1822

"Mr. Ashmun, I think maybe Chief Ba Caia could take the message to the other chiefs."

Ashmun sat bent over his writing table, his head in his

hands. But at least he had gotten up this morning and was trying to do his work, Elijah noted. Lott Cary must have made the fever medicine right--it was beginning to work.

"What message?" Ashmun said.

It was more like a moan than a question, and Elijah realized that Ashmun couldn't think on anything very long.

"What I just said--something to warn the chiefs that if they attack us, a lot of them could get killed."

"Oh, yes ... a last minute warning ... something like that?"

Ashmun was pressing his temples and Elijah guessed his fever was in the headache stage.

"Yes. Some of our people asked if we shouldn't warn the Africans about our cannon-- how it would kill so many with one shot. But I said we couldn't let'em know how we're goin' to protect ourselves."

"That's right. Surprise is an important ... important ... it's an important tactic ... mustn't lose surprise."

Ashmun put his head down on his arms and Elijah wondered if that would be the end of their conversation. He waited a minute, but there were no further words. Elijah tried once more.

"So could we just warn them--just general like?"

Ashmun sat up slowly and opened his eyes, taking in a great breath. He shook his head as if to clear it.

"All right ... Ask Chief Ba Caia to tell the other chiefs we know they are making plans for war ... even 'though they've been trying to hide it from us ... If they try to make war on us, without ... without even asking to settle their differences in a friendly manner, they ... they will find out ... they will learn ..."

His head started to fall forward again, but Ashmun caught himself and jerked upright.

"... they will learn what it is to fight Americans!"

"That's good, Mr. Ashmun! It's a good warning--I'll ask Ba Caia to deliver it himself. He's one of the best friends we've got in that whole council goin' on over there."

Ashmun let his head ease down with a sigh.

"Maybe the only one," he mumbled into his arms.

"No, sir. You're forgettin' Chief Bob Gray--he's there, too."

"Oh ... We haven't heard from him yet, have we?"

"We have, but you were so far gone with fever you couldn't hear anything goin' on. First time, he sent fever medicine--that's what's gettin' you well. Second time, he said the chiefs voted for war, got a big war doctor to lead it, and they sent to the Vai tribe to come help them."

"The Vai? ... Why them?"

"Bob Gray didn't say. But we're guessing they're part of that Poro business that covers so many tribes, or maybe it's 'cause they're right close to Gallinas and that big slave trader, Don Pedro."

The name seemed to penetrate Ashmun's fogged brain. He sat up straight.

"The one who gives out muskets for tribes that will fight us?"

Elijah nodded.

"Oh, Lord!" Ashmun's voice was only a whisper. "Did you get the defenses ready like we planned?"

"We're workin' on it. Got the trees and bushes cut down on the south side. Got the brass cannon up on the center platform. We're workin' now on the two eastern guns, gettin'em mounted on carriages and makin' a platform there. That's about all, so far."

"Nothing on the western side yet?"

Elijah shifted his feet.

"We'll be gettin' to it soon. It's wearing everybody out keepin' night watch and workin' in the day--and drilling the musket corps at noon."

Ashmun's slack, fever-ridden face came alive, the forehead creasing as his eyes widened in alarm. His voice squeaked out.

"No gun, no platform--not even clearing on the west?"

"Not yet. You wanted the long 18-pounder, remember? It took a lot of men to drag it up the hill and we haven't got it mounted on a carriage yet."

"But that's the main way to come up from the waterside! It might be the first point of attack! We must have something there to stop them right away. Don't wait for the gun, Mr. Johnson--get the men out there chopping trees right away!"

"All right, we'll shift some men over soon's we can. But about all those trees bein' cut down-- we'll need some of 'em for buildin' the stockades."

"No! Don't you understand? The trees and bushes are to be cut and tangled first so the warriors can't rush through them. If we have nothing else ready, at least that will slow them down. Do that first, Mr. Johnson!"

It was the sharpest outburst Elijah had heard from the new agent and he felt his face flush with resentment at the blunt order. But *Ashmun is in charge, and he knows military tactics better than the rest of us.* He shrugged.

"We'll try to get at it right away. But more of the Kroo and Bassa men we hired are quitting on us, so everything's goin' slower."

"Quitting?" Ashmun said, struggling to his feet. "More of them? You think they're getting out because the attack is coming soon?"

Elijah nodded his head. Their eyes met, but neither one spoke. Ashmun shivered and Elijah thought it was fear, but the shaking continued and he knew it was the fever chills coming back again.

"You better get back to bed, Mr. Ashmun. It takes time to get over the fever, even with good medicine. I know."

Ashmun sighed.

"You'll carry on? Just as we planned?"

"Yes. We're all workin' hard on it."

As he turned and headed for his bedroom, Ashmun reached for support from a pole that framed one side of the doorway in the mat wall. He paused before passing through into the dark room, leaning heavily on the pole.

"I ... I dread going back in ... Catherine died in there ... You lost your wife to fever, too, didn't you?"

Elijah's throat tightened. He started to speak, but couldn't make any sound. The picture of Mary dying in their bedroom after the last violent cycle of her fever came into his mind. He tried to banish it with a shake of his head, tried to swallow, and rasped heavily to clear his throat.

"I shouldn't have let her come," Ashmun said, his head sagging on his chest. "But she wanted to, and I couldn't say no ..."

Elijah's eyes began to brim and the pain tightened his chest. Mary had come with him, too, because she loved him. He swallowed hard, turning to leave quickly, to get out before it all rushed on him again. But--he had to say something to Ashmun--couldn't just walk off.

"You can do it, Mr. Ashmun. You can carry on. It'll be hard at first. I had to keep going, 'cause I had the children to take care of ..."

He should bite off his tongue! Ashmun and his wife had no

children! But then it came to him.

"The colony is your children, Mr. Ashmun. And we need you very much. We can't make it if you don't help us."

He turned and got out as fast as he could.

24 Review of Troops

Cape Mesurado
November 7, 1822

Carrie took a deep breath after letting John pull her up on the earthworks of the central cannon.

"This is nice, John, to see everything from up here again."

But when she looked across the wide expanse of virgin forest simmering in the noon day sun, she saw that the sea of beautiful green leaves stretching for miles to the northeast was dull and strange looking. They didn't glisten fresh and clean like the last time--instead they were limp and still. The fierce sun burned down on her face and arms and she could feel the oppressive heat. Now she understood why the forest leaves sagged.

"The leaves--they don't look so beautiful anymore, John."

"Of course not. The rains are getting shorter. It's been dry and hot all mornng. Anyway, look over there. We've cleared some on the west point now."

Carrie jerked her head sharply around to where he pointed.

"Not more chopping, John! I thought you'd stop all that if the war wasn't coming. Didn't Elijah say they'd try again to send a warning?"

"They did try it, Carrie. They sent a message, but the chiefs didn't answer it. They're just ignoring it."

"So you all are going to go on chopping and putting up more cannons to kill them?"

"Yes! We're going to protect ourselves any way we can! And that's not all. The Africans are about ready to attack us, so we've got to work faster."

Carrie wanted to hit him but instead she put her hands over her ears.

"Stop it! Stop saying that! You all are just talking yourselves into a war!"

John took her by the wrists and forced her hands off her ears.

"Let's both calm down, Carrie," he said quietly. He looked her carefully in the eyes.

"Today we got a secret message from a chief who's in the

war council. He said in a few days the attack will start--soon as the rains slack off."

Her eyes widened.

"I don't believe it--you're making that up!"

"No. I wish I was. It's the truth, Carrie, and you have to face it."

She shut her eyes tightly in protest, not wanting to think what it would mean for her dream. She broke away and turned to look out across the forest.

"No! It's my Africa, too! I won't let you--I won't stay here and let you all chop it down and ... and blow it away! I'll go somewheres else!"

"Carrie, that's ridiculous! You're not going anywhere now. We'll all have to stand together and fight for our right to stay here. It'll take everyone--even you and the other women."

"Not me! I won't have anything to do with this killing business!"

"Yes you will! Elijah and Mr. Ashmun have called the whole town to an emergency meeting when the work's all done this afternoon. It's to review the troops--a checkup on everyone. Men and women both. You'll have to be there, too!"

"Ten-Shun!   Eyes right.   Line it up there, men. Ready--Front! Present Arms!"

Elijah nervously eyed his little company of musketmen--three were down with fever again. But the rest stood up pretty smart, waiting for Ashmun to pass in review. Ashmun was now calling it the 'Lieutenant's Corps', and that meant Elijah's rank had become lieutenant. Only seven of the recaptive boys had proven out in the drills, so the rest of them had been posted to guard duty. Elijah sighed as he watched his rag-tag bunch of recaptives and colonists--at least they now knew how to shoot and load their muskets fast, and to obey his commands. John Bannon was the best of the lot, but Elijah wasn't sure how he'd stand up under fire--or the others.

Richard Sampson walked beside Ashmun as he passed slowly in front of the corps, one hand leaning on a cane, the other on Sampson's shoulder. Ashmun kept a stern eye on each of the musketmen, checking them out carefully. Elijah watched the agent closely, hoping he wouldn't fall and cause everyone to lose confidence in his leadership. His face was still white as an egret from weeks on his bed in the dark room, but Elijah knew nothing would stop Ashmun from making sure that all was in readiness for the attack. The agent finished his review, and Elijah barked a command.

"Ten-Shun! At ease!"

Ashmun paused, took a new grip on Sampson's shoulder, and walked on toward the gun crews waiting their turn. Fred James' crew was first in line--he was captain of the brass field gun at the central station. Everyone thought it was the main cannon for protecting the colony, and Fred was a little puffed up about it.

Fred and his crew saluted as Ashmun passed by and Elijah shook his head in wonder that short little Fred, with his round belly and red suspenders, could command Ralph Newport, a huge, strapping soot-black man who looked like he could lift a cannon barrel by himself, and William Meade, a pale, skinny six-foot pole that also towered over Fred. But they'd learned to charge and fire their cannon so fast it was like watching a whirlwind.

Ashmun stumbled and Elijah sucked in his breath, but Sampson steadied Ashmun and they continued on to the next crew. Allen James, captain of the long 18-pounder for the western station, called his men to attention. All six of them stood beside him, but young Benson's half-closed eyes and slack body alerted Elijah. Only sixteen, Benson had come on the *Strong* and wasn't really over the bout of fever every newcomer had to go through. Hawkins looked the same way. Ashmun should put them on sick list, Elijah thought, but he probably wants everybody who can stand on his feet to be up for the attack. Elijah had seen to it that the long 18, most powerful cannon of all, had been mounted to point squarely at the path that came up from the waterside on the west. It needed a large crew like this, but could this feverish bunch handle it?

The crews for the southern and eastern stations stood at attention as Ashmun, hobbling slower, inspected them. Elijah craned his neck to see Jesse Shaw's group--five good men in their prime years, who served two four-pounders at the southern point. Jesse was the youngest--too young maybe. Would the older men obey him in a crisis? Daniel George, captain of the eastern crew, saluted Ashmun smartly as he passed, and Elijah admired the brisk, handsome dark brown leader with a touch of white hair in his sideburns. But Daniel had only four men for two four-pounders. Was it enough, if hundreds of warriors would swarm up the rocky slope on the east? Elijah began to sweat as he thought about it.

Finally Ashmun approached the last little group, Charlie Brander, captain, with Thomas Tynes and William Butler, in charge of two small swivel cannon on a single wooden-wheeled carriage. Elijah knew it would be hard to roll the clumsy carriage quickly to different places for back-up. But the colony would need everything it could muster when the warriors came swarming in--like the ones who had come after him at Sherbro! An image flashed in his mind of the blood lust he had seen in their eyes as they rushed him, swishing their long vicious knives at him. He shook away the image and focused on the agent.

Stopping to ask Brander a question, Ashmun frowned as Brander shook his head. Ashmun pointed to Sampson and then turned and headed back to the center of the little parade ground. Elijah could see he was almost exhausted, but when Ashmun stumbled again and Sampson moved to lift him up in his arms, the agent protested and shooed him away. He made the last few steps with just his cane.

Someone brought a chair, and then two wooden crates were put side by side, and the chair placed on top. This time, Ashmun let Sampson lift him up to the makeshift platform and help him sit on the creaky, hand-made chair. Finally settled, the agent looked at the crowd of women and children and then waved the men on line to come closer.

"Dismissed!" Elijah shouted to his musket company, and the captains released their men, too. When all had gathered in front of the agent, he began to address them, his voice so weak that they hushed the children to hear him.

"My friends ... the war is coming. Our visits to chiefs and our message asking for talks have only delayed the inevitable. Word has come now that the tribes will attack within four days."

Ashmun rested his chin on his hands as they gripped his cane. He closed his eyes for a moment, then drew in his breath, straightened up, and began again with a louder voice.

"The protection of your property, your settlement, your families, and your very lives depends, under God, on your firmness in acting together to defend this place! You must obey your officers--and each one do your duty as if the whole defense depends on you!"

Now his voice rang out in warning.

"There can be no place for cowards among you!"

The crowd stood rooted by the foul word, everyone murmuring their denials. Silence spread as his eyes slowly swept across them all. Then he spoke to them calmly.

"Your cause is just. You have returned to your homeland and God will bless your success if you do your duty faithfully. All of you will be needed--men, women, and children. Let no one give less than his or her very best in the coming battle."

He looked down at Elijah.

"Mr. Johnson has the orders for both the men and women. Listen to him carefully now."

Elijah walked to the simple platform and stood in front of it, raising his voice.

"Beginning tonight, every man must be on line from dusk 'til first light in the morning. Then report fast to your cannon or the corps! The recaptive young men on guard duty will patrol all night in the bush outside the lines and points. Women and children must sleep in houses inside the triangle. After full dawn, if no enemy is reported, the women and children can go back to houses outside. But check with me first!"

"What about ammunition," Ashmun prompted. "The swivels don't seem to have any."

Elijah's heart jumped, partly in anger at Brander, and partly because it was just what he feared--something would go wrong.

"Every gun crew that doesn't have some fixed ammunition get to Sampson right away!" Elijah shouted. "He'll make up some for you quick. And keep it dry--we don't have any to waste. And remember, no useless firing!"

Elijah turned and nodded to Ashmun. The agent raised his hands for prayer and children were hushed again.

"God, our Father, help us all work together so that every post and every person will have the firm support of every other in whatever comes. Watch over us now as we go to our places, and keep us safe through the night. Amen."

Fred James called out "Amen!" and other men echoed it. Then they went to find their wives and children. Elijah couldn't find Carrie or his children and supposed they'd gone home before he could get free to say goodnight. He saw John Bannon and called him over.

"Did you see Carrie and the chilluns?"

"No, I didn't. I ... I thought maybe ..." John didn't finish it and Elijah saw something flicker in his eyes before he looked down.

"Maybe what, John?"

"She probably stayed home with your children. She's been hoping the war wouldn't come."

"Didn't you tell her the bad news this noon? I saw you and her goin' up to the gun platform."

John still wasn't looking him in the eyes and Elijah tensed.

"Yes, I told her, but she doesn't believe it--she wants to stop it from happening to her Africa. She keeps calling it her Africa like she's got it all figured out what it'll be like--some kind of dream she has, I guess."

Elijah sighed. He'd never seen Carrie take on like this--she was always so quiet and hardworking. Why didn't she tell him how she felt instead of John? John was too young to advise her about life.

"Dreams, eh? Well, she's got to watch out for Charlie and Lizzie, at least. Lewis can look out for himself. I can't go lookin' for her now--got to meet with Mr. Ashmun quick before dark. Check and see if she and the chillun are safe before you come back here to the corps, will you John?"

Elijah hurried toward Ashmun's house for a last minute talk. The review had shown they only had thirty-seven men able to fight, and they hadn't put up a foot of the stockade yet. Four days wasn't enough time to even get well started on it, but somehow he'd have to convince Ashmun to use at least part of the trees they'd cut down to protect the gun platforms. How could the crews handle the cannon if they weren't protected by some sort of stockade?

25 Choices

Cape Mesurado
November 11, 1822

Elijah stood on the hard-packed earth of the center gun platform, peering into the darkness. It was the fourth night, and if Bob Gray was right, tomorrow the Africans would attack. It was his turn to be on watch on the platform, but there were no stars or moon showing. Why did the clouds hang on when the rainy season was practically over? He heard a faint sound, like footfalls, and strained to hear, staring helplessly into the black void. His skin prickled as he heard the swish of someone's legs coming through tall grass. Stepping quietly over to the new log breast works that now protected the gun, he aimed his musket down where he heard the sound.

"Who's there?" he called, listening closely.

If the reply wasn't in English, he'd better shoot. They hadn't allowed any African workers inside the triangle at night for weeks.

"Stop or I'll shoot!" He really would have to pull the trigger if ...

"It's me! Fred James! For God's sake, Lije! I'm coming to double the watch--Ashmun's orders."

"Why didn't you signal? You could've got yourself shot!"

"We didn't have any signals worked out for it--Ashmun decided only a few minutes ago to double every picket. He just got word from Bob Gray that the warriors have started to move across the river a few miles up above us."

"Did he say when they'd attack?"

"No. But they say Africans never attack before dawn."

"Yeah. We've all heard that. But they might try somethin' different once."

Fred climbed up on the platform and Elijah moved towards his voice, touching him on the arm. He could barely distinguish his outline against the dark sky. He pressed Fred toward the west.

"You stand over there to watch the west point, and I'll watch the east one," Elijah said, and they parted, sliding their feet slowly across the platform's uneven surface to the log breastworks on either side.

"All right, Lije. I'm over here," Fred announced.

"Good. Keep your ears open--they're the only thing we've got, unless the clouds move on and we get some moonlight."

They stood quietly, looking into the dark and listening to the sounds of the night. A long time passed, and Elijah asked Fred if he heard the faint roaring sound when the breeze blew from the south. What did he think it was?

"That's the surf crashing on the beach over on the south side of the Cape," Fred said. "I heard it two weeks ago when we were clearing trees around the south point of the triangle. A Kroo man took me down to the beach and showed me. It was powerful--the waves pounding on the rocks, and swishing up on the sand, like the sea is licking at the beach--and then drawing back before it comes to crash again and again. He said it'd be louder at night when the moon was full or there'd been a storm out to sea."

"Seems like the sea wants to eat the land," mused Elijah, smiling at Fred's image of it licking the beach.

Elijah's legs tired of standing still, so he moved around a little, still trying to stare into the blackness. The moon came out briefly through an opening in the clouds and they both looked southward. The forest gleamed darkly in the moonlight, and except for the clearing they'd made, it stretched toward the beach and southeastward along the shore of the Cape. Beyond it the sea glimmered, acres of sparkling jewels spread before their eyes. It seemed calm--but they could hear it chewing noisily at the beach when the south breeze blew. "It makes me wonder ..." Elijah started to say.

"Wonder what?" Fred asked.

"Oh, this peninsula we're on ... reaching out like a protecting arm ... guarding the bay and the land, saving it from the hungry sea. Saving it for all of us--the black people--Africa's people."

Fred snorted with disgust.

"If it was saved for all black people, why are we having to fight so hard to get some of it to live on? What have Africans got against us? Aren't we their blood brothers? They refused us at Sherbro, and now they're trying to do it here!"

He kicked in anger at a log in the breastworks, and Elijah understood his bitterness.

"Well," Elijah said, "that's just the way I felt about

America. Even some of the whites who were against slavery and worked for our cause didn't want us around when some of us did get free." He sighed. "But there were a few who were all right--just like here with the Africans."

Resting his musket on the breastworks, he leaned his hands on the top log, listening for a while to the night sounds and the surf. The moon disappeared behind the clouds again, and he knew they had to be more watchful. He spoke softly, pondering their situation.

"Chief Bob Gray is on our side, and King Brister, and old man Ba Caia. And a couple of headmen called us their brothers one time, remember?"

"Yeah, but that didn't stop all the others! King George didn't have too much trouble stirring them up against us. There's plenty of land around here--every black in America could come back here and the land wouldn't be crowded! Why can't he see that?"

Elijah started to reply but saw something different in the night sky. His eyes strained to detect it. A faint change in the darkness? Was it starlight? Over there! His head snapped around to the east.

"First light, Fred! See it?"

"Maybe ... Yeah ... Guess it is. First light! I hope my gun crew gets here quick!"

They heard sounds of the town waking up, and as the light increased they could see the dim shapes of men beginning to come in from their picket stations on the line. But none was headed for the central gun. They waited tensely and still none were coming toward them.

"Those warriors will be on the move soon," Elijah fretted. "Probably be here right at dawn, and all hell will break loose! Their war cries scare you out'a your skin! Where's your gun crew, Fred?"

Pounding footsteps turned Elijah, and he saw two dark shapes racing toward them just as Fred shouted.

"Who's there?"

"Newport and Mead here, Sir!"

"Good! Get up here and stand ready!"

Fred grabbed Elijah's arm in the dark and squeezed it.

"Good luck, Elijah.. Now you can go to your own men. Lookout for those African spears, 'though. They can't hit you with their muskets, but they sure can spike you with those long iron-pointed sticks. Go right through ya, the way I hear it."

Elijah grinned in the dark and clapped Fred's shoulder roughly before moving to the log steps. He turned back to give his own parting shot.

"Don't ram those charges down the cannon too hard. It might blow when you touch it off. Sprinkle you all over the town if you're not careful."

Elijah walked quickly toward the parade ground where the musketmen would be forming up. He stumbled once in the semi-darkness, but saw sunlight beginning to show faintly on the horizon. Got to hurry, he thought--they'll attack soon's the sun comes up--howling for blood. Dammit! We bought this place fair and square! And by God, we'll keep it--this is our home, too!

The corps was almost ready when he got there. John Bannon was passing out the powder horns Elijah had ordered him to fill and keep dry.

"Ten-shun!" Elijah called. "Has everybody got their shot pouches?"

There was a general murmur and nodding of heads.

"You finished giving out powder horns, John?"

"Three more to go."

"All right, listen to me while he finishes! If we're sent to a certain spot, you listen to my orders. Don't move or pull a trigger without my command! You got that?"

They called out their assent and he glanced at Bannon, who slammed his tin box shut and stood up, nodding to Elijah.

"Ten-shun! We'll report to Mr. Ashmun at the central gun station. Line up! Left face! Forward march! Hip, haw, hip ..." Elijah marched them off as fast as he could in the dim light.

Ashmun was there on the platform with Fred and his crew. There was someone else--he had a satchel in his hand. That would be Lott Cary, Elijah knew. Ashmun had made Cary the chief health officer, and he'd have to bind up their wounds without much help or supplies. Elijah didn't envy him. He called up to Ashmun, reporting in for the corps.

Carrie had gotten up in the dead of night, determined to do something this morning before the fighting started. But what could she do? She had no power to stop the war. All she could decide was whether she stayed here and became a part of it, or went away, like she'd told John Bannon she would. But should she leave Elijah's children? Lizzie and Charlie needed someone while Elijah was out fighting.

But she wanted no part of the war--it was the wrong way to begin life in Africa to kill the very people you'd come all this way here to live with! She was as sure of this as she was about the wisdom and love of her Ma, who had given her the gift of Africa. She agonized over it for what seemed like hours and finally decided she had only one choice. Lewis would have to do it--he was old enough now to take care of his little brother and sister. She waked him and told him she had to go somewhere quick and he'd have to be the family man 'til his father got back from the war.

"Don't let Lizzie or Charlie go outside 'til he comes back, you hear? No matter what kind of commotion goes on out on the line or the gun stations, you keep'em in here!"

"But where're you goin' Carrie? Can't we go with you?"

"No! I'm ... I'm just goin' to the Hawkin's house, outside the lines, to help her this morning." It was a lie, coming quick to her lips to ease Lewis' fears. "I won't be far--and while I'm gone you'll be the man of the house. All right?"

She grabbed the bundle she'd made up in the dark--a little dry food, an extra dress and underwear, her comb and hairpins, and a piece of lye soap. Bein' clean was always important. If she was to go out and meet Africa--meet some young African man, a chief's son, or someone like that, or some women of a big village, she'd have to be as clean and smart as any of them. But she had to go quick! Now! She shook off the dream and turned to kiss Lizzie and Charlie, still sleeping in their beds. They didn't wake from the tender brush of her lips.

"All right, Lewis!" She put her hands on his shoulders and looked at him fondly. "You're the best man I can think of to leave in charge. You'll do everything just right and your daddy'll be proud of you when he gets home."

He smiled uncertainly, basking in her praise, but some questions were in his eyes. Forestalling him with a quick hug, she turned to get out the door while the dim morning light would still cover her escape. But she called back one last instruction.

"There's plenty of jollof rice in the covered pan and the water bucket is full, so none of you need to go outside. Take good care, Lewis!"

Tears wet Carrie's eyes as she stepped out of the house, turning quickly to head north toward the Hawkins' place. Last night Mrs. Hawkins had declared she wasn't going to sleep any place but in her own house, in spite of official orders. It was a good excuse to use now to pass through the guards on the line, and Carrie rehearsed it--she was just going out to check on Mrs. Hawkins to see if she needed anything.

Then, after checking her, she'd slip away to the north edge of the ridge and into the bushes. From there she'd move eastward toward the high forest, going careful-like to avoid the warriors, wherever they were. Then she'd be free to go into the heart of Africa--to find the real Africa--her Africa, where there wasn't any fighting over slave business or land palavers! That was really what her ma would want her to find--the good way that Africans live, and become part of it herself. Maybe some day she'd find a handsome young man, a chief's son, say, and marry him and have her own children to take care of, and be somebody important.

Three men passed in front of her, hurrying toward the eastern gun platform. Quickly she stepped back around the corner of a house hoping they woudn't notice her, but one man turned half-way around in his stride.

"Who's that? Carrie? Better go back to Elijah's house--the attack will probably start soon!"

It was Daniel George's voice, but he didn't wait to see what she did, so she paused until they were gone and then continued north, watching carefully for others. There was no guard on the line--maybe the men were all heading to their gun stations now. Three of the houses north of the line were familiar to Carrie--homes of the Bensons, the Drapers, and the one nearest the edge of the ridge, the Hawkins. Carrie walked swiftly past the first one, hoping the Benson family had slept inside the line and wasn't here. But the door burst open and the whole family of Benson children began to spill out, stretching and lining up sleepily at the rain barrel for a face wash. Mary Tynes came out, too, helping the littlest ones. Mary was so recently married, she had no children herself.

"Morning, Carrie," Mary called. "Where you going?"

"To see how Mrs. Hawkins is doing. Why didn't you sleep inside the line?"

"Well, Tom hired me out to help the Bensons, so I had to sleep with her and the chilluns. She couldn't move all these into somebody else's house now, could she?"

Carrie nodded and walked on quickly, thinking of Tom, who'd hired his new wife out as if she was a slave. Elijah sort of treats me like that, Carrie suddenly realized. She looked at the sky in the east. The sun is about ready to come up--if the warriors show, it'll be soon. She moved faster, passing the Drapers and hearing the squawl of a baby inside the house.

Minty Draper had two children from her previous husband, who'd drowned last month in the bay. And now she was already married again to Major Draper who came on the *Strong*. She had to do it for her children's sake, Carrie thought. To be a mother of two out here in the colony without a husband was a quick way to starve. Everybody is so busy trying to survive, they don't have much time for others. In a village in the heart of Africa it'd be different--the Africans would care about each other better than we do. Before she had time to think anymore about it a horrible noise started up at the western point of the triangle.

Carrie stopped dead still. It was a wierd howling of some animals--no, it might be the warriors! The noise chilled her as it increased to an ear-splitting yell, and she knew it must be coming from hundreds of throats. Looking westward she saw in the early morning light what looked like a dark river pouring up over the edge of the ridge. They came out of the bush into the first rays of the sun, hundreds of black warriors clad only in loin cloths, madly waving their spears and muskets. They ran toward the western gun station, hopping over the tree trunks and cut bushes lying in their way. Suddenly stopping and raising their muskets, they fired on the men clustered in confusion around the western gun. Carrie saw some of the gun crew fall, and the rest turn and run wildly toward the central gun platform.

Frightened out of her trance, she ran toward Mrs. Hawkins' house, holding her bundle tightly in her left arm. A great shout of triumph came from the warriors, but Carrie had no time to watch their next move. She reached Mrs. Hawkins' door, and began pounding on it.

"Miz Hawkins--let me in, quick! The warriors are coming!"

Waiting for a response from her knocking, Carrie turned back to see the warriors arguing, some pointing toward the central gun and others toward the houses north of the line, including Mrs. Hawkins'. She pounded desperately again.

"Miz Hawkins! Miz Hawkins! Please! It's me--Carrie!"

221

The door latch was lifted and Carrie pushed in, almost knocking Mrs. Hawkins over.

"Lor' sakes,child! What is it?" Mrs. Hawkins said, tying her wrapper around her waist.

Carrie knew she was hard of hearing, and probably hadn't heard her warning. Carrie slammed the door and shoved the latch pin through its hole.

"The warriors have come, Miz Hawkins! They were pointing this way! You've got to come with me--out the back door to the bush. Quick!"

"Why child, I don't see why I should run from those ignorant bush people. They don't know enough to ..."

"Miz Hawkins, it's hundreds of angry warriors with spears and muskets! Didn't you hear them shooting?"

She reached for the woman's arm to pull her toward the back door, but Mrs. Hawkins shook her off with an angry look.

"Nobody's goin' to come in my house, child! I can take care of those so-so warriors!" She reached behind her and picked up her husband's axe, her eyes glinting fiercely.

Carrie knew there was no use. It was the same stubborn streak that made Mrs. Hawkins refuse to sleep in a house inside the line. Carrie sighed--she had tried to help. But now she would get on with her own plans.

"All right, Miz Hawkins. I'm going now. You be careful!"

She patted the woman's shoulder and ran to the back door, determined to reach the bushes on the ridge's north edge before the warriors decided what to do next.

26   Plunder

Cape Mesurado
November 11, 1822

Arguing heatedly at the front of the column of warriors, the war leaders ignored those behind them. The column, nearly fifteen men wide, grew wider as those behind pushed into the clearing. No orders had been sent back down to the waterside to halt those still coming up, so the orderly column was rapidly becoming a pool of pushing, jostling warriors. Jarbo shouted angrily at the war leaders, motioning for silence.

"Listen to me! I be the one in charge of this war!"

Nine of the war leaders, handpicked by each of the chiefs of Montserado country, fell silent. But Quajah, leader of the Vai warriors and an outsider, ignored Jarbo and turned to watch the colonists who had retreated from the western gun.

"I told you my medicine would stop mouth of big boom sticks!" Jarbo boasted. "You saw 'Merican men turn and run--they be afraid of us! Now we go quick to next boom stick in center of town and take it, too!"

Quajah turned back with a faint leer on his face.

"It not be your medicine that do it. We surprise them and make one helluva good war cry--that be what make them run! But look at them now--they getting ready to shoot the center one at us."

Shocked by this mocking of Jarbo's medicine, the other war leaders watched closely. Only a high-born man could talk like that! They knew Quajah was a prince, a son of the Vai chief Massaquoi, and he'd brought a large army of warriors to join the attack--so his voice carried weight.

"My medicine be strong!" Jarbo defended. "I prove it to you--we go attack center boom stick and I be in front for second time. Then you see how its mouth be stopped!"

Quajah shook his head, leering in contempt at Jarbo's boast.

"My people say, 'frog who croaks loud makes snake to follow him.' Be careful how you talk, Jarbo."

Jarbo's eyes narrowed, his face stiff and controlled.

"We have a saying, too, 'dog trusts his belly when he

swallows bones.' I know what I be doing--I train for war since I be boy. You be high *zo* for war?"

The chiefs hid their nervous smiles. The prince was too young to have gone through the upper levels of learning in any kind of work. But Quajah sneered.

"I know one thing that only chiefs know! Booty is most important part of war. Chief Massaquoi tell me to bring back plenty of booty to satisfy his people. 'Merican man leave houses outside his line--we go there for booty, one time!"

"Yaaaah!" the other chiefs cheered. Some of them had already argued for this, and now with Quajah's support they clamored even louder for it.

"No!" Jarbo shouted, furious at Quajah. "True warriors go for heart--they not stop for just one leg, one arm! We must go to center boom stick--that be heart of 'Merican man's war!"

King George and King Willie's war leaders headed toward the houses, ignoring Jarbo. The others followed, and Quajah joined them with a surging lust for plunder, visions of returning to his chief with rich gifts, and of the great honor this would win for him. Jarbo had no choice--they were already spreading out to the four houses, eager to get whatever plunder came to hand, forgetting any idea of a central leader. Jarbo moved near the houses, aware that he was not needed until their lust for plunder was satisfied and they would be willing to renew the attack.

He turned and watched the colonists at the central gun station. They had run to it in confusion, and if his warriors had attacked it immediately, they would have easily over-run it. But if the colonists got themselves organized before his warriors finished their plundering, it might be plenty hard to attack. His medicine would really be needed then to stop the boom stick's mouth.

Carrie, hidden by thick bushes just a dozen yards away from the Hawkin's house, watched some of the shouting warriors run toward it. Their muskets already fired, they swung their war knives or spears in their other hands. Carrie saw that she hadn't closed the back door and she wanted to call to Mrs. Hawkins to close and block it with something, but it was too late. She could see directly through the house to the front door, and now it was shaking as the warriors beat on it from the front. Mrs. Hawkins

224

lifted her axe and stood by the door, waiting for any intruder. The latch gave way with a splintering crash, and a warrior fell inwards, sprawling on the floor. Carrie glimpsed the flash of the axe head swinging down on the back of his neck and heard Mrs. Hawkin's shout of rage.

"Get out of this house! Out, I say! Get out! Out, out, out!"

Aghast, Carrie saw the warrior jerk once and then lie still. Mrs. Hawkins went on screaming, hysterically demanding that the dead man pick himself up and get out. Other Africans leaped in the door and held her off with their jabbing spears while they dragged the dead body away, blood spurting from severed arteries in the neck. She swung at their backs, and screeched at them.

"You cowards! Get out! Get out! And don't come back!"

But others rushed in upon her and began to slash the air with their long, curved war knives. Heedless, she raged at them, swinging her axe until one warrior's knife hacked her arm such a terrible blow that she dropped the axe and reeled backward in pain.

"Daniel! Oh, Daniel! Where are you?" she shouted. "Help me Daniel!"

Carrie's heart broke and tears flooded her eyes, but she clamped her mouth tight so no sobbing could start. Daniel Hawkins had been on the western gun crew, and if he hadn't been shot by the warriors, he'd already run to the central gun station where he'd be no help to his wife. Carrie wanted to leap out of her hiding place and beat on the warriors tormenting Mrs. Hawkins, but it would be useless to fight them with just her hands. Jabbing at Mrs. Hawkins with their spears, the warriors forced her backwards until she fell over a bench. Carrie turned her head away, unable to watch them poking their spears at the fallen heap still moaning for Daniel.

Carrie saw Minty Draper running from her house with both babies in her arms, heading directly for the bushes in which Carrie crouched. Wanting Minty to make it to the bush, but realizing that her own hiding place would be revealed, Carrie started to turn and run, but saw a warrior leap at Minty with a wild swing of his knife to her head and she fell to the ground. He stooped to get her babies, but Minty, blinded by blood from a gash above her right eye, hung on to them, kicking at him furiously.

Three other warriors came to his aid, pulling the screaming infants from her arms and shouting in triumph. The first warrior gestured with his knife to show that he wanted to cut off their heads. Carrie watched in horror as the warriors argued over who would do it. But a shouted command from Jarbo stopped them. He pointed to the path on which they had come up from the waterside and barked an order. The infants were handed over to two other warriors who carefully carried them toward the path.

Carrie saw warriors streaming out of the Hawkins and Draper houses waving their booty, exclaiming over pots and pans, table coths, curtains, dishes and spoons, pictures, saws and hammers, hand rugs, sheets ... they were taking everything. She remembered the Benson children and turned quickly to see if they had escaped to the lines. But Rosa Benson and Mary Tynes were wielding axes, screaming fiercely at five warriors, holding them away from the Benson front door. Carrie saw Mary turn to Mrs. Benson and shout a warning.

"Run, Rosa! Take the children out the back way! I'll hold them off. Run!"

Rosa disappeared inside her house and Mary kept swinging at any warrior who dared step forward, roundly telling them off. But one of them dodged her swing and quickly stepped in, plunging his short spear at her heart. The long iron lance point was buried to its hilt in her breast and she fell with a scream. Carrie felt like the spear had pierced her own heart and she uttered a low cry, cringing at the pain Mary must feel. The warrior pulled the spear out and the others trampled over her in their rush to get to the booty in the house. The horror of it gripped Carrie's mind, but it was interrupted as she saw Rosa climb out a back window with her baby. A warrior reached out and snatched it away just as Rosa planted her feet on the ground to run. Other warriors came around the corners of the house, and she darted away, heading for the line to get help.

"Boooom!" The loud noise of a cannon reverberated across the clearing.

All five of the young Benson children were still inside the house, and Carrie's heart ached for them--what would become of them now? She felt helpless, unable to do anything about the murder and plunder before her eyes. But it was nothing compared to the killing that would begin now that the cannon had begun to boom. She could take it no longer! She turned and began her escape, rushing deeper into the bushes, heading east along the ridge. She was going towards her Africa, into the vast forest where people lived the right way--there would be no wars and killing.

####

Fred James's crew at the center gun platform had fired the first shot of the war! The earsplitting boom had announced that they were ready to fight back, and the colonists around the platform all cheered. Fred knew his crew was so excited they'd aimed too high, and the charge of small balls went way beyond the warriors. But at least it restored some confidence after the retreat of the western gun crew, who'd panicked without firing a shot. They'd come running back to the center platform carrying four men injured by the warrior's musket fire.

"Hold your fire, Mr. James!" Ashmun called from his position at the central cannon's breastworks. "Remember, there are women and children in those houses they're plundering. Put in a double charge--both ball and grape--and tell me when you're ready to fire."

He turned and called down to Lott Cary who was treating the wounded from the western crew.

"How are the men, Reverend?"

"One dead--young Benson. Three wounded--Hawkins, Benson Senior, and Billy, a recaptive."

"Alright, fix up the wounded and talk to the rest of the crew. Settle them down and get them ready to go back to their gun."

Elijah, standing by the musket corps, watched Cary with his basket of cloth strips torn from old sheets and clothes. He was binding up Daniel Hawkin's thigh first, and Daniel's face was gray with pain. But he gritted his teeth, uttering no sound.

"Aren't you going to dig the slugs out?" Elijah asked Cary.

"No time, Mr. Johnson! Billy and Benson are bad hit, too! I can dig the stuff out later."

"Mr. Johnson! Are your men ready for a flank attack?" Ashmun called.

"Yessir!"

"Come up here and I'll show you where to do it."

Elijah climbed the log steps and moved to Ashmun, staying away from Fred's crew ramming a charge down the cannon's still-smoking barrel. Ashmun's left arm and cane were propping him against the breastworks, and Elijah knew he was struggling to stay on his feet for the battle. Looking to the western point, Elijah saw the huge mass of warriors collecting as more came up from the waterside. Perhaps fifty of them had broken off to loot the four houses.

"God a'Mighty!" Elijah said. "There must be six or seven hundred of them over there, and more still packin' in behind!"

Ashmun nodded.

"Yes. And when they get through plundering those houses they'll probably come toward this gun. If we can't get our men back to the western gun to support us, all those warriors might be too much for us. They could run right over us."

"I've only got thirteen men in the corps. We wouldn't be much help, would we?"

"If you surprise them on their flank, it could divert their attention long enough for us to do more damage with our cannon."

"All right, we'll try. Where should we hit them?"

"Go south behind that row of houses, then work your way west to the end of them."

They looked west along the main row of houses.

"How about coming through there about where Nace Butler's house is?" Elijah asked.

"Yes. That would get you in a good position to attack their western flank. Keep your men under cover as much ..."

"They're comin' now!" Fred shouted. "And the gun's all ready!" He blew on the long, smouldering match stick, eager to touch it to the cannon's fuse hole.

Ashmun put his hand on Elijah's shoulder.

"Take your men and go quickly, Mr. Johnson. We're depending on you. God go with you."

Elijah felt a flow of strength coming into him.

"And with you, too, Mr. Ashmun."

He scrambled down the steps and led his men away.

Ashmun turned to Fred and his gun crew.

"Aim right at the leader, Mr. James."

Fred's crew looked at the tall, powerfully-built man in front of the warriors wearing a fierce-looking helmet with horns, its cowrie headband flashing in the rising sun, and a long white mane of goat's hair flowing behind it. The giant black war general gestured toward the central gun station and shouted his orders. Then he raised his stabbing spear, beginning a war cry as he started forward at a run. From hundreds of throats the cry swelled to a blood-curdling yell and the mass of warriors surged forward.

Fred shouted his orders, pulling the cross-block from the carriage, and the crew swung the gun's barrel down. He slammed the block in so the barrel settled at the proper angle to point squarely at the oncoming warriors. Ashmun raised his hand, and Fred held the glowing match close to the fuse hole, waiting for his signal. They stood tense and half-crouched as the warriors raced towards them. Ashmun held the crew a minute longer. Then his hand slashed down.

"Fire!"

Touching his match to powder at the fuse hole, Fred stepped back.

Ffffft! BLOOOM!

The blast of the double charge whomped their ears, slamming cannon and carriage backwards. Ball and grape flew from the gun's mouth, wreaking their awful havoc on a solid mass of racing black bodies. Three rows of them fell screaming to the ground, writhing in agony, and others behind stumbled upon them, piling body on body. The war leader, in front of them, was blasted backwards, falling headless, helmet and head severed from his powerful shoulders. Still tightly gripped in his right hand, the stabbing spear pointed skyward.

####

Stunned by the horror of it, the warriors in the front ranks stopped their war cry. But those behind had only heard the blast and knew nothing of its consequences. Their cry died out only as a message went back, jumping from man to man with disbelief and shock.

"Jarbo be dead!" "Boom stick blow Jarbo's head off!" "Jarbo's medicine fail!" "No war doctor to lead us now!"

Chaos in the front ranks gave way to instinct--the deeply ingrained habit of carrying off their own fallen warriors. Wounded or dead, they were pulled to their feet or lifted to someone's shoulders and carried quickly off to the waterside. Jarbo's head, helmet, body and spear were carried back by a special guard. But only after searching the ground to find any of his war medicines that might have fallen off--those couldn't be left for the enemy! None of the chiefs' appointed war leaders in the front ranks were still alive, except for Quajah, the Vai prince. He took charge at once, seizing his chance for glory.

"Get them out, quick-quick!" he ordered. "Clear the way! Send for war leaders to come to me, one time!"

King Willy's and King George's second leaders were found and came forward at once, eager to assume command. Disappointed to find the Vai outsider already in charge, they objected.

"We the ones to be war leaders now!"

Quajah sneered.

"No man be taller than his head! I be prince, what you be?"

King Willy's man countered with his own interpretation of the old proverb.

"We not need prince business to measure heads today! Your head be short in war palaver. Mine be three times taller!"

Quajah smiled, turning to give orders to warriors who'd already accepted his command.

"Get your men ready for battle! We attack when I call!"

The warriors turned and passed the message, eager to fight again now that a forceful leader had shown himself. Quajah turned back to the other two leaders.

"My people say, 'never strike at snake after it be past you.' I be here when warriors need someone. You be too late. Now you take my commands! Get back to your warriors!"

He turned and lifted his spear, signaling for attention. The other two leaders grudgingly accepted the situation, turning back into the horde of warriors now nerving themselves for Quajah's signal to start the battle again.

Ashmun had ordered another double charge of ball and grape, hoping he would not have to use it. But he saw the new leader shouting at the warriors, marshaling them to his command.

"We have to stop them before they attack again, Mr. James! Are you ready?"

"Ready!"

Ashmun hesitated, still hoping the new leader would turn the great body of warriors around to retreat. But the man turned and pointed at the gun platform, shouting fiercely. Then he began the horrible war cry. Ashmun had no choice.

"Fire!"

230

The blast drove small ball and grape shot into the warriors before they even had time to move, cutting down those in front with the violence of a hundred slashing knives. The war cry had travelled back to the rear ranks, just beginning to swell to a full-throated yell, and again only those in front heard the screaming of falling warriors. But the cannon's boom was an instant message to the entire horde that the same sudden slaughter had come again from the mouth of the boom stick. The war cry died in their throats, fear and confusion gripping them. Some in front tried again to pick up bodies, but panic seized others and they turned to retreat, pushing in vain against the leaderless, milling crowd.

Ashmun shouted down to Lott Cary.

"Reverend! Is the western crew ready to go back to their gun? We need them now!"

Cary looked at the five men left from the crew. He'd been trying to get them to forget their fallen crew members and to try again. Allen James stood up.

"I'm ready," he said quietly.

John Barbour looked at Tom Spencer and they both nodded.

"We're in, too," Barbour said.

"Me, too," piped Eddy Smith, the fifteen year old.

They waited for the last member, Bill Holanger. Finally he stood up.

"Count me in."

Allen James put his hand out and they all slapped it.

"The colony is counting on you," Cary said. "You'll do fine--just like you did in practice!"

Ashmun leaned over the breastworks, looking them in the eye.

"Get to your gun on the double, men! Go behind the houses to the end of the row and then run for it. Turn your cannon around and start shooting as soon as you can. We've got to blast them until they retreat!"

Allen James turned and ran, calling for his crew to follow. The sound of musket fire began, and Fred James pointed to Nace Butler's house.

"It's Elijah's corps! They're attacking the way you said, Mr. Ashmun."

They heard the steady musket fire and saw smoke, but Elijah's men stayed under cover. Warriors on the western edge of the horde began to return the fire with their own muskets. A few began to fall and Fred's crew cheered.

####

Stupified, the warriors in front realized that Quajah was dead before they even started to attack. The second war leader gone! The boom stick's mouth had spoken again with its terrible voice. No powerful medicine or high *zo* or big prince could protect them from its evil blast. They picked up the fallen and cried for direction.

"Where be the war leaders?" "Call war leaders!" "Bring war leaders quick-quick!"

King Willy's and King George's second leaders were summoned from the horde, but the warriors saw their gray faces and shaking hands. Whispers and then outright talk spread the shocking word.

"War leaders tremble!" "Ooooh Woooh! Fear live in leaders' hearts!" "It be time for snake to uncurl!"

Consternation swept through the mass of warriors, setting it buzzing. In front, the order to retreat was given by King George's leader, and those who had seen the destructive power of the boom stick pushed frantically to move the unwieldy mass of warriors back from it. The more they pushed, the greater became the anger of those compressed, and they pushed back. Waves of pushing and shoving moved through the horde, but no one could go anywhere.

The western gun now boomed out, the charge of small balls spending itself in the western flank of the body of warriors, near the rear ranks. Warriors at its edge fired their muskets at the gun, but had no orders to attack it. Again and again the cannon raked the rear flank, every shot burying itself in a solid mass of human flesh. Suddenly, the warriors' musket fire ceased and a horrendous cry went up from throats on the western side, travelling across the entire horde until it shook the air of the whole cape.

The great crowd of warriors seemed to explode outwards in a wild scramble, retreating in every direction! The colonists watched the frantic exodus, dumb-founded that it took but a few minutes for every warrior to disappear.

27 Kwi People

The Forest
November 11, 1822

Panic drove Carrie racing through the bush. Crouching low, flitting across open spaces, she watched anxiously for the warriors. Could she escape along the ridge of the peninsula without being seen? She heard more booms from the cannon as she ran. Now the killing of Africans would begin--they would be blasted away--that's what John had said. It would be a slaughter because they didn't know what a cannon could do to them! She wanted to stop up her ears at each blast but there was no time. She must run and run. There was no sense to it--both sides killing each other--she would escape from it all! Her dress caught on a broken branch and tore as she dashed on. Twisting and turning, dodging bushes and trees, she reached the end of the ridgeback and began to descend to the mainland.

Here was the real forest she'd seen from the Cape! The trees were taller and she looked up at the giants, awed by vines as thick as her wrists looping downward from the high canopy of leaves and branches. She slowed as the foliage thickened, the leafy mass overhead filtering the sun's rays to a dim, greenish light. The dense tangle of vines and bushes grabbed her tighter with each step. She pushed them aside, fighting to make headway, realizing that she should have brought Elijah's cutlass--she could be slashing her way through it easily. But it would make noise. Exhausted, sweat streaming down her face, she stopped to get her breath.

She had to find a path through the forest or go to the river and travel along its banks. Panting hard, she tried to think. It could be dangerous to go running along a narrow, twisting path--she might suddenly meet a warrior face-to-face. But on the riverside there might be crocodiles or worse! She remembered the rumors of a thirty-foot python near the Cape--some recaptive youth saying he'd stepped over it in the night like it was a log. Would a python be near the river or in the forest? She couldn't remember which, and shuddered to think of meeting it. But crocodiles! She decided the forest was better, especially if she found a path and didn't make any noise. Then, if she heard anyone coming she'd be able to step off the path and hide.

Crack! It sounded like a small dry branch breaking, and Carrie stiffened, listening intensely. There was silence, and then something crunched like it was stepped on, only a dozen yards away. Carrie stopped breathing and crouched down, careful not to break any branches herself. She heard a soft swish--a branch sweeping back after somebody passed. Silence again, and then a twig snapped. Someone was stealing through the forest like a hunter, she thought. But who would be hunting with a war going on? Then she realized someone was hunting her! She crouched down as far as she could, ready to spring up and run.

Heart pounding, Carrie waited. A branch moved just a few yards behind and she wanted to scream. But she clamped her jaws tightly, hoping the hunter would pass by her. She forced herself to draw a breath and exhale it slowly. Another branch moved, on her right. Steady--he was almost past her. A cramp in her left leg begged for relief. She moved just an inch, but the tense muscle tightened violently. A stab of pain forced a moan from her throat and she bit down hard, cutting off the sound. It was too late--the forest erupted with the crashing noise of the hunter's rush Her eyes widened in fear as he got closer. The bushes above her were being spread apart by two dark hands! She fainted, falling backwards.

Sharp fumes stung her nostrils and she woke up coughing from something held close to her nose by one of those dark hands. Then she remembered--the hunter! But he was a young person, like herself. His brown eyes and worried face stared down at her as he knelt by her side.

"You--you're Togba, aren't you?" she faltered. "One of the recaptives?"

He smiled. "Yes, Miss Carrie. I know you from colony."

"You scared me!' she said, sitting up and twitching her nose to relieve the sting. "What've you got in your hand?"

He opened it and showed her some soft green buds, some of them crushed in his hand.

"It not be good to name medicine before person be cured," he said. Then he smiled. "But you already be cured, so I show you." He pointed to a small bush nearby and she saw the little green buds on it. "My people call it *lolo gbia*. It wake people up plenty fast."

He stood up and offered her a hand. Carrie grasped it and

was pulled to her feet instantly, surprised at his strength. She steadied herself and then appraised him. Tall, muscular, dark skin, gleaming white teeth showing in a friendly smile--he had an air of confidence she had not noticed the few times she'd seen him in the colony. The recaptives lived separately in their own building, supervised by a colonist, and she had not seen much of them. They had looked homesick and dejected to her, she thought. But since the rumors of war had started, they'd been assigned to patrol the outskirts of the colony. Maybe that had made Togba feel more useful and confident. She was about to smile at him, but then she remembered--he had attacked her! Or had he?

"Why did you hunt me down like an animal?" she asked.

The smile died on his face. He shook his head quickly.

"I not hunt you like animal! I see you leave colony and I be leaving, too. So I follow you for maybe you need help. You make noise like you hurt, so I come quick-quick to help."

"To help me! I was afraid you were going to ... " Then she laughed. "You were leaving, too? Why?"

"I live in this country before I be captured for slave trade and carried to 'Merica. Navy catch our slave ship by place called Georgia, and it take one year for court palaver before we be free. They bring us back here to Cape. But war palaver at Cape be too much, so I decide to go home. My village be eight days walk from here--that be how long the Gola people walk us to coast to sell us to slavers."

"But I thought you recaptives wanted to stay in the colony and learn English and American ways?"

He nodded. "That be true. But I think about my home and family--and my village--and I be homesick. My village be fine place, missy! We be peaceful, we measure life by seasons, and make feast and dance for each one. Forest gives us all we need. Boy learns in bush school to be man, to take his place in village, to build his house, to farm land chose for him by chief. Sometime he find girl who love him and give him children, and the ..."

Eyes shining, he talked on and on, and Carrie stared, transfixed by his voice and charming word pictures of an Africa she so desperately wanted to find. Finally he stopped, embarrassed.

"I say too much. But--maybe you see why I want to find my village."

"Oh yes! I do!" she said huskily. "That's what I want to find. I don't want to live on the Cape where people kill each other over

235

slave trade business! I ran away--to go upcountry to live in peace with people. Just like yours."

"Like my people?"

"Yes. My ma sent me to Africa where black people can live truly free. But I couldn't find it at the Cape--it's not the real Africa there." She hesitated, and then asked him boldly.

"Would you take me to your village?"

Disbelief showed in his face.

"But you be kwi!"

"I'm what?"

"Like white people. But your skin be better--more like we." He looked down bashfully, but then blurted out, "It look fine, missy."

His eyes sought hers, and she saw it was his honest feeling. He made no move to touch her or hold her like John Bannon was always doing. It was nice not to be pushed, and she found herself liking his simple compliment.

"Thank you, Togba." She smiled. "I'm not really 'kwi' am I? My grandpa was an African slave who came from somewhere over here. I got my light skin from my ma's owner, who forced himself on her. But he never raised me--his wife made him send my ma and me to the North. And when Ma got the chance, she wanted us to come back to Africa." She spread out her hands. "So here I am. Will you take me to your village? Please!"

He was silent, looking at her soberly.

"You--you want to live there long time?"

She nodded her head.

"To marry and have family?"

"Maybe. If I find the right person."

He shook his head doubtfully.

"African ways be different. Maybe too much for you."

"I've come back to Africa just like you! It's my Africa, too!" She felt herself getting upset. "I'm used to hard work, Togba. I've been takin' care of Mr. Elijah Johnson's children all by myself for over two years. That's proof I can be a good mother, isn't it?"

"Yes, missy. But ..."

"My name's Carrie. Please call me that, Togba."

"Carrie ... you can be fine mother. But to be part of my people, you must go to Sande--bush school for girls--like I went to Poro school for boys. No one be respected man or woman who not go to bush school."

"I can do that. I want to! I want to be African--that's why I ran away from the colony."

"Carrie, you know anything about bush school?"

"Well, no, but I know I can do it. I want to do it!"

"I tell you about bush school before you decide ..."

"No! I know I can do it," she said, determined now. "I don't need more talk!" Then she softened her voice and laid her hands on his chest. "Please, Togba. Help me."

It startled him and he backed away. Then he nodded solemnly, without saying anything. Any explanation now would be fruitless, he thought, and it would be better to wait until they got to his village where she would learn soon enough. He hoped she would listen to how difficult bush school was for girls who knew only village life, and would understand how much more so it would be for her from a different way of life in 'merica.

Cape Mesurado
November 17, 1822

Elijah woke up, stretched his tired muscles, and yawned. It was Sunday afternoon, the first time he'd relaxed since the battle six days ago. He got up from his nap and walked out to sit on the porch, reliving in his mind the relentless stream of orders Ashmun had issued, keeping them all working like madmen until the colony was ready to withstand the African's next attack. Within an hour after the battle they'd redrawn the lines, excluding a fourth of the houses. They borrowed fences and building material from every settler, and brought in trees from the clearing to make a musket-proof stockade around the remaining houses. By noon the next day they had enough done so they stopped and buried the dead. After that Ashmun and Elijah split the crews, half working on the stockade, some making the clearing wider, others mounting another cannon. At noon breaks they re-organized the gun crews, drilled them for more rapid firing, trained the musket corps to make faster flanking moves ...

"You awake, Pa?" Lewis asked, coming out of the house.

"Yes, son. Where's Charlie and Lizzie?"

"Playin' in back with Jimmy n' Hester."

"Who?"

237

Lewis twisted his face impatiently, and Elijah realized it was just like Mary used to look when he'd forgotten something. Sadness swept over him. Mary dead over two years and now Carrie has run off. How long could he carry on without a woman in the house to care for the chillun?

"Aw, Pa! You know--the Edmundson kids. That family that came on the *Strong*."

"Oh yes. Well, I'm depending on you to watch the little ones. We don't know what's goin' to happen next, so we've got to keep'em close to the house."

"Are the Africans goin' to fight us again?"

"Maybe. But we're ready for'em--don't worry about it."

Elijah looked at his oldest son with pride. Lewis was twelve years old, but taking on duties like a man. The boy turned to go around the house to the back yard, but then he stopped and faced Elijah with a wistful look.

"Pa, have you heard anything about Carrie yet?"

"She's been seen upriver by a trader. Word was brought down by a woman who sells food at the riverside market."

"Is Carrie all right?"

"I hope so. John says she wanted to go up-country to find the kind of Africa she's lookin' for."

"When'll she come back?"

"Don't know, son. Anyway, I don't have time to go lookin' for her with a war goin' on now, do I ?"

"No, Pa," Lewis said, disappearing around the corner of the house.

Slumping lower on the porch bench, Elijah closed his eyes, feeling the heat of the late afternoon sun slanting in under the porch's thatch. It was good just to take time to feel things again. He'd only had about four hours sleep some nights--not even time to think of the dead and wounded. Lott Cary had done most of that. Elijah sighed, counting them in his mind. They'd buried four dead--it was almost five, but Cary had saved Mrs. Hawkins, sewing up her thirteen spear wounds with needle and thread. Counting her, there were four wounded. And seven children missing, carried off by the warriors--Minty Draper's two babies and five Benson kids. And Carrie, too. Damn her! Running off like that! Elijah straightened up, anger and worry stirring him.

Fred James slapped the porch rail, startling Elijah.

"You wasn't at church this morning, you backslider!" Fred

238

said, sitting down on the bench in his usual spot.

Elijah yawned again and then smiled, cheered up by a chance to banter with his cocky little friend.

"I told the Reverend I couldn't make it after workin' night and day keepin' track of you lazy boys."

"Lazy!" Fred howled. "You're the big boss that stands around tellin' us what to do. That's real hard work!"

They kept it up until Blake and John Bannon moseyed over for the customary evening chat.

"Some Kroo man says the warriors are still campin' over near King Peter's town," Blake said. "Looks like they're not givin' up yet."

"King George is plenty mad, I bet," Fred said. "We beat him in the palaver and now we beat him in the war. I can just imagine what he's telling everyone--tryin' to get'em stirred up again."

Blake laughed.

"Yeah. He'll make the other chiefs so ashamed, they'll attack again just to shut him up!"

"How can you joke about such a thing!" John said. "It's not funny!"

"He's right," Elijah said. "We're sittin' up here on the Cape in a real tight spot. Think about it."

The silence was abrupt. They knew what he meant. It was a long time before anyone spoke.

"What about food," John said, and they stared at him. "The last time I was helping in the storehouse there was only about two weeks' provisions left, except for rice. And this morning the Africans stopped bringing food to the riverside market or coming up the back way through the forest."

"Another blockade!" Fred said. "They'll try shuttin' us off again, hopin' to starve us out. Can't we do anything?"

"Remember how we had to break their blockade last time," Elijah said. "It took all the powder and ball we had left to chase away the snipers. But now we'd have to chase a whole army away."

"How much ammunition do we have?" Blake asked.

They all looked to Elijah.

"I'm not sure," he said.

"You're stalling, Lije. You, Ashmun, and Barbour--you have to know. Tell us the truth."

"Well ... now don't tell the others about this ... Barbour has figured out we've got about one hour's worth of ammunition--if we're attacked pretty strong and all our guns are shootin'."

"One hour?" they echoed.

"Wait now!" Elijah put his hands up. "We're not sure they'll attack again. And even if they do, we don't all shoot at once, so ..."

"My god! Don't try to make it seem better than it ain't!" Fred shouted.

"Shut up! Hold your voice down or the whole town'll hear you."

"They have a right to know!"

"No! They'd go to pieces! We'll try to buy some more ammunition from the next trader who comes in the bay, or maybe a Navy ship will come along soon."

"But the Navy ships patrol the coast north of Freetown more than they do down here," John reminded them.

"Ashmun knows that!" Elijah snapped. "He's thinkin' of sending a message to Freetown by Prince Will to ask for help."

"Prince Will? You mean that Kroo man in a canoe?" Blake said. "It'll take him forever! Why him?"

"Because he can get out of the bay without anybody gettin' suspicious. Besides, he's been the boss of Kroo men who work on ships along this coast for years. Ashmun says the Navy captains all know him."

"So if he doesn't find any Navy ship up there, what do we do?" Fred asked.

Elijah sighed. "We just sit tight and do what Ashmun says--buildin' our defences and trainin' to shoot more accurate so nothin's wasted."

"Yeah, and doin' some prayin' too," Fred said, his voice husky. "You should'a been in church this morning, Lije."

####

Togba had wanted to stay away from well-beaten forest paths, and had chosen not to bring a cutlass because the noisy slash of it would reveal his presence when passing through enemy country. So they'd twisted their way through the tangled undergrowth, over hills, across creeks and swamps, through patches of open grasslands, and up rocky ravines into the ever-rising ground of the deep forest as they left the coast.

The first day Carrie had begged him to slow down several times, but he was deaf to all her pleas. Angry at being ignored, she tied up her skirt and plunged after him, determined to show him she could be a real African. He stopped in the afternoon to make camp and she thought he took pity on her because she was staggering with fatigue. But he used the time to make a bow and some arrows, tip the arrows with a paste from seeds of a poisonous vine, and kill a monkey. He built a fire to roast it, and she took over, sending him to find some bush pepper to make it tasty. He brought back also a strange, succulent root, and showed her how to roast it, too. She ate hungrily, falling into an exhausted sleep on the thatch he'd cut for her bed.

The sixth day of their journey through the forest they'd come to the upper reaches of a great river that was split in two by a long, narrow island. Togba said it was the Deng river but white slave traders on the coast called it the St. Paul. He planned to cross it at the upstream point of the island, which he called Dobli. He warned her that they were still in country controlled by slave-raiding Gola people--and he didn't want to be caught again. If he made it to the other side, he would be safe in Kpelle country and only one or two day's journey from his village. They waited until dark, when the ferrymen had tied up their canoes for the night. Togba swam silently between the canoes, untying one and floating it down to where Carrie waited in the dim light of a quarter moon. He paddled softly across the river, but when they passed the tip of Dobli island the stream on the other side was a rushing torrent and he lost control.

"Togba! We're turning downstream! Look at the rocks!"

"No talk, Carrie! Best to let canoe find its way."

She gripped the sides of the canoe, holding her breath and cringing at plumes of white water racing over submerged rocks. The canoe, dug out of a tree trunk, bounced and jerked through the rapids, floating over most of the rocks, banging and scraping against the bigger ones. Suddenly a huge rock loomed in the moonlight and Carrie opened her mouth to scream, but Togba thrust his paddle hard to the right and held it down to rudder the canoe sharply. Carrie, almost jerked out, shut her mouth and hung on desperately. The canoe whipped around the great rock, and suddenly they were in the dark, quiet pool behind it, eddying in a slow circle as the main stream rushed on past. Carrie heard Togba heave a sigh of relief, and then he guided the canoe to the bank.

Before they penetrated the forest a hundred yards they heard voices, and Togba turned swiftly to press his hand on her lips.   Light from many campfires flickered through the bushes ahead of them.

"Wait here, Carrie. I go look," he whispered.

He was gone a long time, and when he came back he said nothing, grabbing her hand and pulling her back to the river bank. For hours they walked along the bank, passing the upstream point of the island, turning inland on a well-worn path.

"This be Kpelle country," he announced. "Soon we make camp."

"You're safe now?" she asked.

"Soon it be safe."

But it seemed at least another hour before he left the path and found a place for their camp. He allowed no fire, and they ate cold meat and roots left from the previous night's camp. They both were exhausted, and he cut just a few branches of thatch before she insisted it was enough--that he stop and get some sleep. He protested that he should make two beds, but she pushed him down and then showed him there was room enough for her. It was the closest they had lain in the night, and to cover their embarrassment she asked him about the campfires they had seen at Dobli island.

"Warriors--Gola warriors--and others, maybe Bande people." He sat up. "Hundreds of them! They talk and laugh for battle they going to fight soon."

"Warriors!" Carrie sat up, too. "And we almost walked into their camp! Who're they going to fight?"

"I--I not sure. They talk about black men who come back white. They say such men forget they be African, and not fit to live in this country. That's who they go to fight."

"Men who come back white? Togba! That's us! I mean, all of us in the colony! The Bassa and Kroo who work on the Cape call us white people 'cause our ways are so different!"

She jumped up. "They're going down to the Cape to fight! Oh, Togba--what should we do?"

He was silent so long she wondered if he'd heard her question. Before she could make up her mind to speak, he began to reason it out as he talked. Somebody should warn the colony, he said, because he saw more warriors at the camp than he'd seen in the battle at the Cape. If there were still plenty of warriors left from the attack the day he and Carrie left, then the next one would be at least two times bigger! The colony's guns might not hold off that many. Whoever went down to warn the colony would have to go quickly by river, as fast as they could paddle. It was still dark and he could go back and find the canoe and start before dawn, so the warriors at Dobli island wouldn't see him.

"No! Not you, Togba! We came away from there because we didn't agree for the fighting and killing! Let someone else go--it's not our war!"

"But I owe something to colony. They take care of me when I come back in Navy ship."

She tried every reason she could think of, but he wouldn't sway from his obligation. Desperate not to lose him, and dimly aware that her admiration for his prowess in the forest had turned into something deeper, she made her final plea.

"What will happen to me? Are you going to abandon me here in the forest, Togba? I wouldn't last one day!"

He sighed, but said nothing. Finally he told her to get some sleep--they would talk in the morning. They lay down on the thatch bed. Relieved at his concern for her, she went to sleep quickly.

When chattering monkeys passing overhead announced the morning, she came awake in alarm, missing the weight of him on the thatch bed, and the now familiar sight of his muscular body. Sitting up, she glanced desperately around their campsite, only a hollowed-out space in the bushes. Where had he gone? She stood up, her heart constricting. Then she saw him, his back toward her, standing with his arms around a great tree.

He was almost invisible, his coloring nearly the same as the black-brown tree trunk. Motionless, half-turned face pressed against the tree, his eyes were closed. It gave her an eerie feeling to see him just standing there hugging a tree, not making a sound. She waited to see what would happen next, but nothing broke the silence, not a muscle of his moved. Slowly a quiet sense of something strong and serene enveloped her and she looked up at the massive tree he was embracing. Had it stood there a century or more, she wondered? How deep do its roots go? Look how far its branches reach! How many hundreds of animals and plants has it given life and shelter to in all that time? Is that why Togba stands pressed to its trunk--to draw strength and life from it, too?

She sat down, feeling a strange reverence for the place, content to wait for him. She gazed up into the tree's immense green canopy, trying to see all the life in it. She forgot time and when, without a sound, he dropped his arms and backed away from the tree, she had no idea how long it had been. He turned, their eyes met, and he smiled as he walked towards her.

"Come, Carrie. Today we go to my uncle's village. Garlo river runs by it and comes down to Deng river. Uncle will give me canoe to go down to colony to warn them. You stay in his compound 'til I come back."

She saw new strength in his step and heard the clearness of his mind. Following him back to the path with a widening smile, she felt happy--proud to be walking with him, learning from him, discovering the secrets of Africa--their Africa.

28   Final Battle

Cape Mesurado
December 1, 1822

"No pickets outside the stockade tonight, for sure," Elijah said. "It wouldn't be safe with the warriors all around us, watching every move we make."

"Yes. And they're just waiting for Captain Brassey to sail away before they attack us," Ashmun added. "When he leaves on the evening wind change, it will be their signal to attack."

"Tonight? You think they'll attack tonight?"

"No, no. In the morning at dawn--just like the first attack. But now there will be twice as many, if that recaptive boy is right."

Elijah stood up and began to pace, looking out the window of Ashmun's small house to the ship in the bay.

"Well, at least the Captain sold us plenty of ammunition and food," Elijah said. "Too bad he couldn't talk the chiefs into makin' peace."

Ashmun nodded, then pulled a page of notes from the corner of his writing table.

"He said he's traded with them for years and knew them well enough to try," Ashmun sighed. "Well, he didn't succeed, and neither did my message the other day. So we'd better check these assignments and prepare for the worst."

Elijah came back and sat down at the table, beginning to tick them off on his fingers.

"First, every man on guard inside the stockade tonight--spread out, one every five or ten yards."

Ashmun nodded, checking off the first item on the page, but then held his hand up.

"Wait a minute! We've only got thirty able-bodied men, counting the recaptives. Aren't there more muskets than that repaired?"

"Barbour's got two more fixed up, but nobody to handle 'em."

"Why not use women? A few look pretty strong."

Elijah tilted his head. "Well, some of the men trained their wives and chillun to reload muskets and fetch powder and ball. They all know we'll be fightin' for our lives now--won't be any

245

stubborn women like last time."

"Can any of them shoot?" Ashmun asked.

"I can think of a couple of em. How about Matilda Spencer and Ann Edmonson?"

"All right," Ashmun checked it off. "Now, what about the fire brigade? They may try to throw torches in to burn the thatch roofs."

Elijah ticked it off his finger. "Yep. We've got water and buckets collected in four places. And two women will watch the little kids in Butler's house. And two will help Lott Cary with the wounded."

Ashmun put his finger on the bottom of the page.

"And make sure every gun crew moves to their gun at first light and stays there!"

Elijah winced, remembering that the western crew ran away in the first battle.

"They're well trained this time," he said. "And they'll be protected behind musket-proof stockade."

"And your corps? Do they know about what they're to do?"

"Yes, I told them I'd call them all over to one place if the warriors attacked it heavy. Otherwise they're to stay spread out along the stockade on all sides."

Ashmun stood up.

"Good. I'll be on the central gun platform. You and Barbour and Cary will have to move to wherever you're needed. If there's nothing else, I'm going to rest now until dusk."

Elijah stood up, hesitating to leave.

"There's one more thing--the spears. If Togba is right, there'll be hundreds more warriors from upcountry, and they'll likely have spears. The kind with iron tips and tail pieces--so heavy they'll go right through you. A bunch of those rainin' down could be deadly, 'cause we're closed up in a stockade now and the women and chillun will be around helpin' us."

"All right, have the men call out if the warriors start heaving any over. And tell the women and children to listen and take shelter."

Everyone was in their place as the morning sun's faint glow in the east rounded into an orange sphere. It hung briefly in the mist above the forest, then rose higher and streaked the sky with its rays. Elijah was stepping up on the gun walk behind the northern section of the stockade when the war cries shattered the calm.

But this time the horrifying cry came from both the east and west--they were attacking from two sides at once! Screaming warriors came out of the forest and began their rush, shooting muskets and brandishing war knives and spears as they burst into Elijah's view. Cannon from both the eastern and western points boomed out immediately and the deadly hail of grape shot stopped the charge on both points.

Ashmun and Fred James, on the central gun platform, could see both attacks. On the west the 'long 18' had wreaked a horrible carnage as its lethal shot blasted into scores of black bodies, littering the ground with dead and dying. The attack seemed beaten off in one blast. But in the shocked silence some unseen war chief back in the forest shouted a command and more warriors appeared, joining the bewildered ones on the field, the whole mass surging forward again. Shouting their war cry, their musket fire splattered lead balls, copper ship bolts, and even bits of pot iron at the stockade as they ran toward it. The western gun crew worked feverishly, but were not yet reloaded.

On the center platform Ahmun spoke to Fred.

"Fire at the west side, Mr. James!"

The crew wheeled the cannon around, and Fred touched his match to the fuse hole. They stepped back and covered their ears as the cannon flashed and recoiled, sending its double shot of ball and grape into the advancing warriors. At greater distance, it did less damage, but it was enough to stall them for a moment. Knowing that the long 18 was now ready to fire again, Ashmun turned to see the action at the eastern point.

There a larger body of warriors had charged and retreated from the eastern cannon blasts, but now some warriors were firing their muskets from behind a ledge of rocks about forty yards from the stockade. The crew on the east was firing the two four-pounders methodically, keeping the attackers down behind the rocks. But the warriors were creeping from rock to rock on signal from one of their leaders. Timing his calls between cannon blasts, he was moving them steadily closer.

Ashmun pointed it out to Fred.

"They'll get under the fire of the cannon if we don't stop them! We don't have enough muskets to hold them off after that.

Send the swivel guns for close-in support."

"The swivels? Can they stop them?" Fred asked.

"Yes, but they'll have to get there fast!"

Fred stepped to the breastworks and called down to Brander's small crew waiting by the two small brass cannon on the wheeled carriage.

"Brander--take your swivels over to the eastern point. Hurry before the warriors get under the big guns!"

Tynes and Butler grabbed the ropes of the wooden gun carriage and began pulling while Brander pushed from behind. The small wooden wheels gave little clearance and the carriage stuck on clumps of weeds and half-buried rocks as it rolled along. Brander swore at every obstruction. Seeing the trouble, Elijah brought three men with him to the eastern point to help hold back the warriors.

"Hold your fire 'til they jump up to move to the next rock," he instructed them. "Pick off the front ones--we've got to stop them until the swivels get here!"

But the warriors ran from rock to rock so quickly it was hard for men with heavy muskets to hit them. One warrior was picked off the first time and the men cheered, but the rest of the daring warriors moved closer. They were almost within spear-throwing distance and Elijah knew someone might get spiked soon. A second warrior fell, sprawling on open ground, plainly bleeding from his right side. His musket was in his right hand, but he lay motionless for awhile and the men took their eyes off him. Ignored, he slowly aimed his musket at Joseph Gardner, who was pushing a rod down one of the cannon to pack the charge. The musket cracked, and Gardner slumped to the platform floor.

Jonas Carey stopped to lift Gardner and carry him to the back of the platform, calling for medical help. The inaction of one of the big guns lessened the hail of shot over the warriors, who grew bolder. One sprang up on the rock in front of him, shouting his defiance, and sent his spear over the stockade wall with a mighty throw. Elijah saw it coming.

"Spear coming!" he shouted. "Spear coming over!"

Other corpsmen echoed the cry, warning those working in the stockade, but drew a bead on the thrower. Three muskets went off together, and the spearman's body, following through on his great heaving throw, continued its own arc, falling lifeless on the stony ground in front of the rock. His spear cleared the stockade in its long arching flight, its point piercing the ground inside with a solid "thunk!" A few corpsmen turned to look for an instant. Together with the women and children huddled close to the wall, they stared at the upright spear, its shaft still quivering. It was horrible proof that the warriors could penetrate the colony's defenses even without muskets. They shuddered--whose child might've been spiked clean through by it?

Elijah marveled. "That's no ordinary spear! Look at it!"

The slender wooden shaft, its leopard skin hand-grip trimmed with red leather, was tipped by a deadly iron lance point, and its back end was a heavy iron fish tail. Someone whistled.

"Yeah, and no ordinary man threw it, either!" They turned back to the battle outside.

"He was the head spearman, I bet!" Elijah shouted over the noise. "There'll be others who have to do it now. Everybody look sharp--every warrior in the rocks may let loose soon!"

Just then Brander and his swivel gun crew arrived at the eastern point exhausted, and Elijah ordered two men to help carry the small two-gun carriage up on the platform. Pulling and shoving desperately, they got it up. Daniel George, captain of the big guns, figured out how to conceal the two swivels behind a loose breastwork, and Brander charged them with powder and shot. But while the musketmen and the gun crews were putting the swivels in place, the warriors again had a chance to move forward.

One of their leaders suddenly stood up, shouting commands, and in a few seconds a band of about sixty of them rose from the rocks and dashed forward fearlessly, yelling their battle cry. With a wild musket fire from their left hands to distract, they got close enough to loose a cloud of deadly spears with their other hands. A great shout from men on the platform and the gun crews alerted those inside the stockade, and the women and children ran screaming to huddle against the stockade wall again. In a few strides the warriors slipped beneath the fire of the heavy guns.

"They'll climb the wall next!" a musketman shouted in panic.

But atop the gun platform George and Brander ripped away the loose breastwork and Tynes and Butler touched off both swivel guns at once. The close-up blast of grape shot left the warriors screaming in surprise and agony where they fell. Those few who could escape scrambled blindly away, too stunned to think about carrying off their wounded comrades.

Three more times the eastern gun platform was attacked as Gola war chiefs ordered other bands of fighters into battle. Starting from below the rock ledge, the warriors were repulsed by the big guns without again getting as close as the fearless sixty had come. Ashmun was beginning to think his strategy of wide clearings on all sides was working. Fred James busily supported the western point from the center, assisting the long 18 in turning back another massive attack there.

Ashmun, glancing to the southern point, saw the low bush at the southeast edge of the clearing astir and thought it was a strong wind blowing. Looking again a few minutes later, the movement was still there, but it seemed closer. The scrub palm bushes were actually moving!

"Fred! Look over there! What do you see?"

"That's strange--looks like the bushes are moving. You don't think it could be ..."

"Yes! The warriors must have palm branches tied on them--probably so we won't notice their approach. They know they have to get closer somehow to start their rush."

"Look how long their line is!" Fred exclaimed. "Must be a quarter mile. Why, that's hundreds of warriors!"

"Five or six hundred, I'd guess." Ashmun's confidence was beginning to vanish.

They watched the long green line at the edge of the clearing grow longer and thicker as more warriors tied on palm branches and filled in behind and on the ends of it. The big guns on the western and eastern points were silent now.

"Sounds like the attacks have stopped," Fred said.

"Then they might be shifting what's left of their warriors over to this new attack on the south."

"Doesn't look like they're in any hurry," Fred said. "Why not? What are they up to?"

"They're just forming up," Ashmun guessed. "Probably waiting for more warriors to come through the forest to join them from the other sides. If they've given up trying to attack our big guns at the points, they'll try to hit us between them."

"You mean, between the eastern and southern points? Don't they know we'll hit'em with cross-fire from both points? They're crazy!"

"But if they attack spread out like that all our big guns can do is punch holes in their line. That won't stop them, unless they converge so we can ... Fred, send for the swivels!"

"But they're still up on the eastern platform."

"Get them down! Quick! Not you--send one of your men. Tell Brander to bring it right away. Hurry!"

Fred turned to his crew. Meade had the longest legs. He clapped him on the back.

"You heard Mr. Ashmun. Run, man!"

They waited anxiously and soon saw men on the eastern platform struggling to lower the swivel carriage to the ground. Elijah was helping with one of his corpsman. Fred looked back to the green line of warriors and whistled.

"Look! Maybe a hundred more already! How can we stop something like that?"

"We can't unless they converge," Ashmun said. "Fred, send two more men--one to the southern point and one to the eastern. Tell them not to shoot until the warriors bunch up as they run, then shoot at the bunches. But if the line doesn't bunch, start firing before they get within a hundred yards!"

Fred sent two more of his crew off, warning them to come right back or they wouldn't have enough people to fire their own gun. The swivel carriage was rolling slowly towards the central gun platform, and Eljah rushed ahead. Ashmun shouted down at him.

"Have Brander put the swivels on that little rise mid-way between the eastern and southern points. You take all your corpsman to man the stockade there. Shoot any warriors who make it through the cannon fire and try to breach the stockade. If you can't stop them get out of the way and let the swivels do it."

Elijah turned to run back to the swivels, but Ashmun shouted again.

"Have you got any women in your corps?"

"Still the same two--Matilda and Ann."

"We'll need everybody. Can they stand their ground?"

"They won't hang back. But I'll get'em out if it gets too bad."

"This may be the last attack--they'll put all their warriors in it! If they break through the stockade, get all the women and children into the gun platforms at the points."

Elijah nodded. "Anything else?"

"Encourage your people. God is with us!"

Elijah gave Ashmun a sober wave and rushed back to meet the swivels crew. Fred and Ashmun watched as Elijah pointed

Brander to the spot for the two small cannon. Then he arranged his own corpsmen along the gun walks of the stockade, facing the long green line of warriors across the clearing. Ashmun glanced at the eastern and southern points--both gun crews were ready, too.

"What's holding up their attack?" he asked.

"Maybe they're waitin' for final orders," Fred said. "Or maybe there's some palaver among the war chiefs."

At that instant they heard it. The howling war cry, faint at first, gained strength as all the warriors along the great line took it up, until the whole Cape resounded with it. The green line fractured in a dozen places as the warriors began their long run, some faster than others. But the line stayed spread out.

"Fred! Get ready to fire. If they don't converge ..."

They heard both of the eastern point's guns go off first, then one of the south's. Ashmun took in a great breath. It was started now--no more waiting.

"All right, Fred. Fire at will."

The other gun from the southern point fired before Fred's cannon blasted their ear drums. They could see warriors falling, but the green line's gaps closed and it came on. The big guns blasted away, and the line started to converge, as if every warrior wanted to get away from the guns at the points. Elijah and his corps will be there in the middle to meet them, Ashmun thought.

At the stockade Elijah was shouting his last instructions, moving the corpsmen toward the center of the eastern stockade wall where the attack seemed to be headed.

"Wait 'til they get closer. Pick one of the front ones and stay with him 'til you have a bead on him, then start on another. You can't get them all. If they break down the stockade, go to a platform on one of the points, but keep firing 'til your powder and ball runs out. Hold it! They're not close enough yet."

Black powder smoke from the three gun platforms was rising in the morning air as the crews fired round after round. Ashmun marveled at their steady team work, and their coolness in the face of the massive line of howling warriors coming closer and closer, perhaps to over-run their guns, and the stockade, and ... Ashmun looked again at Elijah on the stockade's gun walk. The green line was getting shorter as the cannon felled more and more warriors and the rest kept on converging. Suddenly Ashmun remembered that the middle of each stockade wall was the weakest, the colonists having built the stronger musket-proof sections out from the three points, joining them in the middle of each side with whatever material was still left. He began to pray for Elijah and the corpsmen.

Elijah was still holding the corpsmen back. "Don't fire 'til I order!" he warned.

Now they could see the black figures separately, the palm branches falling off as the warriors pounded towards them.

"Fire!" Elijah shouted, and the muskets barked, small sounds swallowed up by the cannon blasts and hundreds of throats at full cry.

Matilda Spencer, a heavy, full-skirted woman with a pipe clamped in her mouth, shot her musket with the rest. She took the pipe out of her mouth and spat.

"Missed him!" she said in disgust.

But she quickly set the musket stock on the gun walk, poured powder down the barrel from the horn hung at her waist, added a ball and wad from her pouch, and rammed them down with the rod. Outwardly calm, her fingers shook as she cocked the flintlock. Not since her first child was put in her arms by the midwife had she been so nervous. She wanted to be as calm as the men beside her seemed. She'd show them she could do her part in fighting for their new homeland!

Matilda raised the musket again, resting it on the stockade to draw a bead on another black figure racing toward her. It was hard to hold one in sight, but she pulled the trigger, felt the stock slam against her shoulder, and this time a warrior fell.

"Lord A' Mighty, we has to do it," she half prayed, half argued, but no one heard it in the noise of battle.

Now she noticed that Ann was gone, but the men were there, some on her right, some on the left, where Elijah stood. Reassured, she loaded faster, fired, and missed again.

"Damnation!"

Methodical and determined, oblivious of the warriors now so close, she opened her powder horn again as Elijah shouted at her.

"Matilda, go back! Go back with Ann! She's gone to the southern point!"

She turned around, but couldn't see Ann. The men weren't leaving so she wouldn't either, she decided. At least not until she had one more shot. Quickly loading again, she lifted the gun over the stockade to take aim. But it was almost knocked out of her hands by a warrior leaping upwards and swinging his war knife at her musket. Surprised and shocked, she held on to it, drawing back in anger at the warrior who'd spoiled her aim.

"Get out of here, Matilda!" Elijah shouted.

Swiftly he moved over to her, took her musket, and helped her get down from the gun walk. Feet on the ground, she turned and grabbed her musket back.

"I still needs that, thank you!" she huffed at him, walking off vexed that he would dismiss her as if she wasn't any use to them.

Other warriors reached the stockade, leaping at the corpsmen above them, throwing spears and swinging empty muskets to knock the corpsmen's muskets away. The corps' fire was deadly at close quarters, but the warriors now were arriving in swarms, climbing on each other's backs, reaching for the top of the stockade. The first few were shot as they leaped over, but the massive tide of scrambling black bodies couldn't be stopped.

"Fall back to the points!" Elijah shouted.

He swung his musket butt to deflect a huge curved war knife whipping down at him, and pushed the warrior backwards off the stockade. The corpsmen jumped off the gun walk just as the stockade wall began to crack and waver under the weight of warriors pushing up and over it. Every man ran for the nearest gun platform.

The big gun crews had stopped firing, not wanting to blast the stockade itself. Ashmun and Fred watched Elijah and his men retreat.

"They did their best--couldn't hold that horde back very long," Ashmun said. "But we still have the swivel guns down there to stop it. Don't fire from here, Fred, until the swivels have had their chance. We don't want to hit any of our own men."

Down the hill, Brander's crew was getting ready to fire both swivels. But a section of the stockade wall collapsed inward under the weight of the warriors. They tripped and fell over the broken logs and poles, scrambling to their feet inside the stockade. A war chief among them raised his arms and shouted commands while he turned to survey the scene. He pointed at the swivel carriage and its crew, just a short distance up the slope, and then moved toward it cautiously, the others surging after him.

Brander, Tynes and Butler stood transfixed at the sight of this bold warrior striding towards them so calmly. On the central gun platform Ashmun cupped his hands and shouted down to them. "Fire, Brander! Fire at them!"

He watched in disbelief as the swivel crew stood staring at the flood of warriors pouring through the gap in the stockade and following the war chief directly toward them at a walk. A musket cracked from the top of the next section of stockade and Tynes crumpled to the ground. Startled into action, Brander and Butler picked up Tynes and fled toward the southern gun platform, leaving the swivel guns without firing a shot.

The corpsmen, women, and children had all retreated into the gun platforms on the points, except for a few stragglers. Ashmun could see that the gun crews were frantically working to turn their cannon around to fire inside the stockade at the warriors.

"Fred! You'll have to use your gun on the warriors! Quickly before the other gun crews try to shoot. They'll blow us all up and destroy the houses!"

"I can't deflect it down that low!" Fred said.

"You've got to! Work it out somehow!"

"Well, maybe we could tear out part of the breastworks and prop up the rear of the carriage."

"All right! Do it!"

Ashmun watched the warriors reach the swivel gun carriage and gather around it, the war chief and his aides talking excitedly as they realized that these were two of the magic boom sticks that had killed so many of their warriors.

"Hurry up, Fred! They're staring at the swivels now, but they'll renew their attack from inside in a minute. If you don't blast them before they spread out, it will be all over for us!"

Fred and his crew were frantically pushing and shoving in the morning heat, moving the heavy cannon to a new position and tearing away part of the breastworks. Ashmun turned back to watch with consternation as more warriors poured through the gap in the stockade.

A movement at the southern point caught his eye and he put up his hand to shade his eyes from the bright morning sun. A woman was leaving the gun platform and walking slowly up the hill toward the warriors standing around the swivel guns. He could just barely see that she had a pipe in her mouth, and that meant it was Matilda Spencer. He wanted to shout at her to go back, but that would alert the warriors.

Matilda shuffled up the hill slowly. Got to go peaceful-like, she thought. She blew gently through her pipe stem and felt the warmth on her face from the pipe bowl. She took her pipe out carefully to spit. Keep the fire coals glowin' and they'll be hot enuf to light the fuse. She was going to show them all what a woman could do! Brander and his crew had left the swivel guns charged and ready to fire, they said. The warriors wouldn't bother a woman who just came by casual-like, would they now? Maybe ... maybe not.

I is scared! she admitted to herself. But keep on walkin'. You knows you can do it. She put her pipe back in her mouth to blow the coals to red heat again.

Ashmun was dumbfounded. "What is that woman doing? She's walking right toward the warriors at the swivels--directly into our line of fire!"

"Fred, are you ready yet?" he fretted.

Fred didn't answer, figuring Ashmun could see for himself that they had a long way to go. He worked furiously to build a wedge the right size for the back end of the carriage, sweat almost blinding him.

The warriors crowding around the swivels were perplexed--the magic of the 'fire sticks' was still a puzzle. The colonists had been making these and all their others boom out rapidly, like thunder and lightning. It was a mystery the warriors couldn't understand; they had examined the swivels until they were tired of them. Nothing was happening--the sticks were dead. So the war chief stepped back and turned to talk of the next battle maneuver to his aides, letting other warriors crowd around to satisfy their curiosity.

Matilda reached the edge of the throng of warriors, growing more tense, but determined she wouldn't show it. She kept her mind on her plan. All she had to do was get next to one of the swivel guns, hold her pipe to the fuse, and step back for the blast. She began to talk to herself again in her mind, taking it step by step.

Got to do it real slow now. Look like you's goin' about your business, not int'rested in the guns. Steady now. Nobody even cares you's here. Listening' to their big chief, ain't they. A little more now. You's just a no-account woman nobody's watchin'. Get around that little man. He's watchin' you. Turn your back casual-like. Blow on the coals. Take out yore pipe like you's goin' to spit. Spit a little. Where's the fuse? *They said there'd be a fuse!*

Steady. The warriors could've took it out. You can put the littlest coal down the fuse hole. Pipe in the mouth. Blow it good an' hot. Out to spit again. Knock the coals out'a yore pipe. Goin' to burn your fingers. *That's the right one.* It's goin' in the hole. Step back.

BLAAM!

The explosion in the midst of the warriors was a ripping concussion of soundwaves and hot metal that blew them down for twenty feet in front of the cannon. The grape shot bore holes through the bodies of those directly in front of the gun's mouth. Even Matilda and those at the sides of the cannon felt the searing impact of the blast, so confined was it by the crowd of bodies around it.

But the physical shock of the blast was nothing compared to the mental terror unleashed in the following seconds. Those not hit realized the firestick had spoken in horrifying, death-dealing violence--even after they'd fingered and watched it safely for a long time! They'd even ignored it because nothing could happen--it was dead. But it had come alive, and they could not believe what rang in their ears and tore at their hearts as they saw the carnage from its evil mouth!

The power of its terrible magic was too great to combat! There was only one thing to do--escape as fast as possible! Those in the rear turned and fled back through the gap in the stockade, shouting the call to retreat. The front ones, stunned by the sight of their dead war chief and his aides, were overtaken by terror and, abandoning all reason, ran screaming out of the stockade.

The colonists crowded on the gun platforms watched the warriors go, hardly daring to believe it was all over. Elijah, on the eastern platform, heard Daniel George call to his gun crew.

"There they go! When they get outside the stockade, start firing at them!"

"Wait!" Elijah said. "It's all over--we've won. Don't shoot them in the back. Their chiefs put them up to this."

"No! We should kill as many as we can--those bastards were going to wipe us out!"

Elijah put his hands on Daniel's shoulders and looked him squarely in the face.

"Get hold of yourself, Daniel. Think! In a few days you'll be dependin' on them all to sell you food and make trade. We'll need friendly people around us in the future. Let them go."

"I--I can't do it, Elijah! This is war! They have to pay!

They're the enemy!"

"Not now they aren't! It's over!" Elijah shook Daniel's shoulders. "We've won, Daniel. Calm down. Maybe now we can make neighbors out of them."

29 Bush School

Zuwoluta
December 2, 1822

Carrie sat on a low bench just outside of the round mud-and-thatch hut, leaning back and wriggling her toes in damp, cool dust. Unable to sleep, she had come out before dawn, quietly waiting in the dark for another day to start. It was all she could do--wait while the days and hours passed until Togba returned. She was a guest of Togba's uncle, Chief Zuwolu, while Togba was gone on the trip downriver to warn the colony. He'd promised to be back as soon as he could, but Carrie was missing him intensely.

Their horrible journey was fading from her mind, replaced by the exciting knowledge that Togba loved her. She had seen his eyes following her when he thought she wasn't aware. He'd watched her body move when she walked, and she knew he liked her figure. He had peeked at her bosom when she'd bent over in front of him to pick up something, and stolen glances at her long slim legs more and more. She enjoyed his secret attention and knew he wouldn't touch her as John Bannon often tried to do. But he would make her his wife, she was certain. She'd seen Togba's uncle judging her slyly from behind lowered eyelids--maybe it would be his word that cleared the way for Togba to wed her. She could be Togba's wife and raise a family with him! She quivered in ecstasy at the thought of it.

Carrie smiled to herself as she watched the sun rise slowly, penetrating dark fringes of palm trees above the huts at the village edge. Small shafts of orange sunlight winked at her as a breeze stirred rustling palm branches, wafting to her a soft scent of forest undergrowth, faintly perfumed by flowers. She breathed deeply, relishing the quiet, peaceful village, picturing it in her mind as a possible home. It was true, wasn't it--this was her Africa, the one she wanted? There were no wars or fighting about slavery--just the village, forest, and river; and all the animals and people living in perfect harmony? And yet ...

Carrie tried to resist the images that crowded into her mind ... a woman with a baby sucking at her breast while children played beneath her feet and clung to her legs ... the shock when she heard that the woman shared her husband with two other wives! Could she share Tobga with another? And could she labor on Togba's farm, and sleep in a separate house with her children until the nights when he came to her? Carrie had watched other wives walking behind their husbands on the path, carrying a head load and a baby in a sling on their backs--while the men carried nothing! She'd learned that these wives had all been bought with a bride price which could be returned to the wife's family--along with the bride--if the man didn't want her anymore. And wives were expected to be obedient and submissive ... can I really be like that, she wondered?

A rooster's loud caw broke the early morning stillness, disturbing her thoughts. Carrie watched the bird flap its wings and fly down from the thatch roof above her, landing close to her feet. Twisting his neck, he inspected her with one blinking eye and then the other, finally blasting her with such a raucous caw that she sat up.

"All right! So morning is here!" she said aloud, stretching her arms.

Suddenly from thatch roofs throughout the village other chickens fluttered to the ground, flapping and cackling. A shaft of sunlight warmed Carrie's legs as she watched them begin the day's round of pecking and scratching for food.

People began to come out of their huts, women and children sleepily heading for the river's edge with empty gourds and water pots, while men stretched and yawned in the sun. Coming back from the river, wet black legs glistening, the women and children carried water to mat-enclosed bath places. Happy noises of splashing, chattering families struck Carrie to the heart. This was the Africa she wanted! But ... in the hut where she stayed with two women, Carrie had seen strange scars disfiguring their private parts that no one would explain to her. Now she wished her ma was here--she needed someone to tell her about these things. Did love-making with a man make these scars? It must hurt bad. But Togba wouldn't hurt her, would he?

Carrie saw some old women coming toward her and wondered if she could ask them. Lakali, a young married woman in the chief's compound, was her only friend, but she wouldn't talk about the scars and she'd disappeared somewhere this morning. The women walking toward her looked directly at her, advancing with determined steps, and Carrie suddenly felt alarm. She scrambled quickly to her feet, but their strong hands grasped her and began to walk her forcefully towards a hut on the edge of the village. She felt like screaming, but no one seemed concerned.

"What are you doing!" she shouted, struggling against them. "Why can't you tell me!"

They said nothing, and while they pushed her forward she remembered who lived in the hut--people had said the woman was the zoe, the head teacher of the bush school. What were they going to do to her? She found out quickly--inside the hut they pulled off her dress, laid her on her back and spread her legs while the zoe examined her private parts, even putting her hand inside! Her surprise and shock were changing to anger when she saw the zoe nod and signal to the women to take her away. They pulled her up, put her dress on, and walked her back across the village to where she had been sitting at the chief's guest hut. Stunned, she slumped to the bench and watched the women return quickly to their own huts--all without a word to her!

Lakali startled her by suddenly showing up with a water jar.

"Some water for you, Carrie."

Drinking it thirstily, Carrie blurted out, "What're they doing?"

"Togba want you to be his wife," Lakali smiled. "For that you go to Sande bush school and learn to be proper African woman. Dry season be here, so Sande begin school soon. This be what you want, Carrie, for true?"

"Yes. But why did they ...?"

"Togba's wife have to be virgin. They come to find out for sure. You all right now."

Lakali patted her shoulder and left, but Carrie was still shaken by the old women's rude inspection. She thought of Togba's trying to warn her and wanting to explain the Sande bush school before she decided to go into it. But she'd refused because she was already eager and didn't need to be talked into it. She shivered even in the morning sunlight, fearful now about all the unknown things she would have to face next. It seemed that the old women were in charge, and could force you to do what they wanted. Lakali had called them the Sande and would say nothing about them, so it must be some secret women's society. Was Lakali a member herself?

####

261

For two weeks the men had been building a special mud and thatch house at the edge of the village, rectangular and large enough for all the girls to live in briefly before they were to be moved to the forest for the bush school itself. There was a fringed raffia curtain over the front door, and a mat-walled corridor from the back door to the edge of the forest. Carrie kept asking Lakali why they would stay in this house first.

"Don't ask such things, Carrie--I can't talk about it!" was her only reply.

Finally, with the house finished, and the village alive with the smells of cooking and bustle of preparations for a celebration, Lakali relented.

"Tomorrow be the day, Carrie!" she said, her face aglow with anticipation. "All families make a big feast for their girls who go to bush school. It be big thing for their life. Chief Zuwolu say I should be like your ma 'cause she not here. You come to my hut for feast tonight!"

Carrie was overwhelmed by Lakali's happiness for her.

"Thank you, Lakali. You're so good to me! I'm tryin' to follow your ways to be a good wife for Togba. But I worry about what the old women will do in the bush school. And ... and why you won't tell me about the Sande house."

Lakali's face sobered and she looked to be sure the other women who stayed in the guest hut were not around. She put one finger to her lips and spoke softly.

"No one speak such things, Carrie. The zoe and her helpers are best of our old women--they know plenty past all others! They teach our girls to be good wives and mothers and to know our own ways."

"What about the Sande house before we go to bush school?" Carrie pressed.

"No, Carrie," Lakali shook her head. "It not be for me to say. Sande house is first step--to get girls ready. Don't be afraid. That part soon be over."

"Afraid? Is it something bad? Will it hurt? What is it--tell me, Lakali!"

"Sande is secret! Don't worry, I be your ma now, and I give fine present to zoe for thing she will do to you. Carrie, you mustn't fight this first step--it make you look bad in eyes of all our women. They come get you anyway if you don't go with me to Sande house first thing tomorrow."

262

Carrie came slowly to conciousness from a nightmare she was having--something chasing her through the forest. It never stopped and there was no way to escape. She had nothing to protect herself from it--she ran and ran. At first it was a black leopard and then it changed to an old woman and finally it was a group of women bearing down on her. She cried out to Togba, "Togba! Help me!" He grabbed her shoulders and he was ...

"Wake up, Carrie!" Lakali was shaking her shoulders "Your time has come! Bush school make you proper African woman now. Wake up!"

Carrie stared into Lakali's eyes, trying to make sense of it.

"I thought you were Togba," she said, sitting up and shaking her head.

"He came last night, " Lakali smiled. "Chief Zuwolu told him not to see you 'cause it spoil your time in bush school."

Carrie's heart leaped. "He's back! Ohhhhhh...Togba's back! And we can't see each other?"

"No, but he say to tell you he love you and he be waiting for you to come out of bush school."

"He will? Oh, that means he really wants me? To ... to be his wife?"

"It look so," Lakali laughed. Then she shook Carrie again. "Get up! We be late. Most mothers already at Sande house with their girls. They come for you if you too late."

The horrible dream flashed in her mind again. She reached up and grasped Lakali.

"Tell me, Lakali! Where do those scars come from on the women's private parts! Who does that to them! Do their husbands do it? You've got to tell me!"

Lakali took pity on the frightened kwi girl.

"No, no, Carrie! Not from their husbands! Scars come from bush school. Every girl is cut--it be best for marriage. It be done in Sande house so they get well before going to bush to learn other things."

Carrie's nightmare was true! It was the old women--this evil thing was part of the African way! And they were doing it to their own girls! No! It was a big mistake! But they would not do it to her! Never!

She shook Lakali's shoulders fiercely.

263

"Go to Togba, Lakali!" She saw women coming in the door with that determined look on their faces. They were coming for her! She lowered her voice, whispering to Lakali, "Tell Togba to come to me. I won't let them cut me! Ever! Tell Togba he must come!"

The old women surrounded them, lifting Carrie to her feet and guiding her out the door.

"Lakali!" she shouted back. "Tell him! Please!"

#####

All the girls were sitting in the Sande house, most of them waiting in terrified silence--only a few whispering anxiously to each other. The house was hot, crowded with many naked bodies. Carrie saw that they were of different ages, some just beginning to show their puberty; others, like Carrie, already well-formed and ready for marriage as soon as they finished bush school. Their clothes had been taken from them by the zoe and her helpers, and Carrie felt humiliated, trying to cover her nakedness. Like the girls' mothers, Lakali had handed Carrie a bundle with a loin cloth and some dried food just before the ceremony for the bush school had begun. Carrie sat quietly now, remembering the ceremony and what Lakali had said about it.

It had seemed like a happy celebration, with all the villagers singing and dancing, full of joyful anticipation for the girls. Carrie had joined in with the clapping and swaying of the crowd, yet she'd seen on the girls' faces the same anxiety and fear she felt. Even the mothers couldn't always cover their worry, she noticed. With beating drums and furiously hooting wooden horns urging them on, the zoe and her three helpers each danced their own special Sande dance, to wild applause. Then the women who had gone through the school in past years paraded around the mothers and girls in the dance and song of all Sande members.

Finally, when the crowd had quieted, Chief Zuwolu handed to the zoe a tall staff with a carved head on it--the symbol of her office as leader of the bush school. He charged the zoe and her helpers to pass on the tribe's traditions and make the girls good wives and mothers. She moved in front of the raffia curtain of the Sande house and signaled her helpers to bring the girls forward. One by one, they had been thrust through the raffia curtain into the house with a ceremonial chant.

264

The heat during the day of waiting was only relieved by a faint breeze at the front door stirring the raffia fringes of the curtain. Below the fringes Carrie could see the woman guarding the front door, sitting just outside on a stool. At the back door the Sande guard stayed in the mat-walled corridor that led to the bush. Carrie could not figure out a way to escape and finally left the matter until the day they would go to the bush. She had little appetite, but just before dark ate some of the boiled cassava Lakali had given her. Sleeping fitfully on the hard dirt floor, the nightmare returned, and she was running through the forest pursued by the black panther,which became a woman and later still a group of women bearing down upon her. She woke twice during the night, and by morning was crying silently for Tobga to come take her away from the old women who would cut her private parts.

In the morning the zoe and her helpers took them one at a time through the mat corridor and into the forest. When Carrie's turn came, she knew from those who had already been brought back that this was the day of purification. Two of the zoe's helpers kept firm hands on her, guiding her along the forest path to a creek. She tried to get away from them, but their hold on her was too strong. At the creek three women washed her, and then rubbed her entire body with a mixture of white clay and water, rubbing it in carefully. She'd asked Lakali earlier when she'd seen white clay on a woman's skin, and Lakali explained that it was to purify and protect the woman from evil spirits. It felt good to Carrie after the previous day's sweltering in the Sande house with all the girls. But she felt sure that tomorrow would bring something worse--probably the cutting. When they walked her back to the Sande house when she watched the path carefully for connecting paths or other places to run, if she could escape tonight through the corridor.

The other girls had fallen asleep long before Carrie dared to try slipping past the guard in the corridor. She stepped over their bodies carefully, working her way to the back door. But in the corridor the moon shone brightly and she could make out the drowsy form of the guard slumped against the mat wall half way to the forest. Waiting at the door for a long time, she was rewarded when a cloud covered the moon completely. Now it was pitch black and she started forward carefully, sliding her feet over the smooth dirt, touching the mat wall lightly at short intervals. Getting close enough to hear the guard's breathing, Carrie held her breath and slowed her approach. She was moving by her when the cloud's edge suddenly passed, flooding the corridor with moonlight. Startled, her hand caught on a piece of the matting, snapping it off. The guard's eyes opened.

"Yaaaah! Yaaaah!" the guard screamed, leaping at her.

Carrie ran toward the forest end of the corridor, but just as she reached it two women stepped in, blocking her path. She ran at them with a burst of speed, trying to break through. No match for their sinewy arms, they all fell in a heap, locking Carrie between them. The guard helped them up, and they marched her back to the Sande house, screaming their anger in their Kpelle tongue. Bruised and hurting, Carrie was glad she couldn't understand them. They forced her to lie down just inside the back door where some moonlight shone on her, and two of them spent the rest of the night sitting within arm's reach.

It was the second morning, and Carrie rummaged hungrily in her food bundle, finding the pieces of cassava and edoe, and one remaining banana. She would need her strength because she would fight them with all she had if they tried to cut her today! Where was Togba? Did Lakali have the courage to tell him of her cry for help? Would Togba dare to defy the rule about men coming into the Sande's bush school?

The other girls were eating their food, too, when the zoe came in to speak to them. Carrie couldn't understand what the zoe said, but she felt the old woman's scorn as she pointed at Carrie and angrily made an example of her to the other girls. After a few more words, the zoe gave an order and one of her helpers called out a name. Then it began--the women had come to take the first girl to the forest, and Carrie knew it was for the cutting. The girl stood up, grim-faced, trying not to show her fear. Everyone stopped talking as she left with two women holding her tightly. No one said a word, waiting for the time it would take the girl to walk through the corridor, down the path to the creek, and stand before the zoe. Carrie recalled the walk from yesterday--now the girl has stepped into the forest--she is halfway down the path--there is the creek--would the girl's blood flow into the creek?--three old women would take hold of her--the zoe would raise her evil knife...

The scream pierced the air of the Sande house, constricting all the girls' hearts.

"Eeeeeeeouwwwww! Eeeeeeeouwwwww! Eeeeeeou ..."

They were jolted upright, reaching for their hearts to stop

266

the wild beating. The hysterical screaming was shut off quickly like a hand clapped over the girl's mouth. Carrie had covered her ears, but it was too late. She would never forget that high, piercing cry of agonizing pain. They heard the zoe shout an order, and beating drums flooded the air with a frenzied, distracting rhythm.

Three more girls were taken out before the first one was returned. When Carrie saw the girl come back, walking stiffly with an awkward bundle of crushed leaves pressed to her private parts, she guessed that the juice of the leaves had stopped the bleeding. She'd learned that much from Togba, who knew the medicinal power of the forest's leaves and roots. But it would take some days before things healed, and Carrie knew the danger of infection would be high. It was wrong to take such chances with their girls--they could die from this! Why do they do it! Lakali had said it would make marriage better, but it seemed a strange and unnecessary African belief to Carrie. She would not submit to it herself! She would make her break at the creek when they took her there! Oh, Togba, her mind pleaded, where are you? Please come for me! Please!

It was a long day for the zoe and her helpers, but every girl had finally been cut and her blood flow stopped, at least for now. The girls sat about in various positions in the Sande house, moaning and moving restlessly to ease the pain; some crying, others ridiculing the cryers, but all sick to their stomachs and unable to eat. Carrie had grown restive while waiting, and more nervous by the hour. When she finally realized that they were keeping her for the very last so they could all work on her together, she became desperate. The guards had been vigilant all day and there had been no chance for her to escape. Now it was her turn and all three helpers came for her. She decided to act submissive and hope they would let down their guard on the walk to the creek or just as they prepared to cut her. It would be her only chance. She stood up meekly and held out her arms for them to grasp. Two of them held her arms and one was behind her as they moved through the corridor toward the forest.

Carrie noticed that the sun was going down. The drummers had stopped and the forest seemed strangely silent when they entered it. They walked down the path, Carrie watching out of the corners of her eyes for a break in the undergrowth or a bush she could run around. She was faster than any of them, but not stronger, she knew that. Something back in the foliage on her left moved slightly, but it could have been a bird or animal. They were half way to the creek when she saw the movement again and slowed to check it out without turning her head. But the woman behind her pushed her to keep up the pace and those at her side tightened their grip on her. She saw the path begin to slope down to the creek and steeled herself for her escape. Wait! Don't tighten up, she thought--be submissive or they won't loosen their grip!

Forcing herself to relax, she walked meekly to the zoe standing by a large flat rock in the middle of the creek. It was covered with blood, and Carrie knew she was expected to sit down on it to be cut. She nodded her head and helped them seat herself on edge of the rock. The zoe was surprised that she wasn't struggling, and smiled. Motioning to the helpers to stand back, she reached toward a bowl on another rock, lifting the crudely made razor and explaining in Kpelle what she was going to do. Carrie didn't understand, but the zoe motioned her to lay back, so she nodded. This was her chance! As she lay back, she flipped on over in one movement, landing on her feet on the other side of the rock. She was free to run up the creek bank on the other side and into the forest!

The zoe screamed at her helpers and they came for Carrie. She turned to run, but saw something black in the bush behind them and lost her concentration, stumbling on a rock in the creek bed. They were on her before she could get up, and were dragging her back to the rock when she realized who was in the bush.

"Togba!" she shouted, gagging on creek water. "Togba--help me!"

In a great leap from atop the creek bank, he landed with a splash and an animal-like roar in front of them and the old women fell backwards in fright. He lifted Carrie from the water and plunged ahead to the opposite bank, setting her feet on the ground.

"Run, Carrie!" he urged, pulling her up the bank and into the forest.

They had traveled together through the forest before, but this time it was a frantic race to escape the bush school and the power of the Sande. Togba's strong arm urged her forward, helping her over, under and around all obstacles in the forest, repeating his urgent command in her ear--run!--run! Carrie ran, her feet pounding through the underbrush heedless of cuts and bruises, lungs beginning to burn. Finally, sore and gasping for breath, she begged him to stop.

"No, Carrie! If Sande zoe go to Chief Zuwolu, he send plenty people after us! We must be outside Zuwolu clan before we stop."

But darkness soon forced them to go slower, allowing Carrie to favor her sorest foot and breathe normally again. When they reached the small river that marked the boundary, Togba stopped, looking up at the night sky for clouds.

"Moon have plenty of room to shine tonight," he said. "We hunt for place to cross before we sleep."

They crossed where the river spread out over a wide rocky bed, shallow enough for them to walk most of the way no deeper than Carrie's waist. But they took a moment to bathe in the deepest part of the river, and Carrie, conscious now that she was wearing only the loin cloth Lakali had given her, sank up to her neck in sudden modesty. In his usual shorts, Togba came up out of the water, his wet black chest and arms gleaming in the moonlight right above her. Her heart skipped a beat, and she stood up boldly beside him, their bodies touching. Carrie looked up at his face and smiled. Togba wrapped her in his arms and kissed her tenderly, then broke away.

"We go to other side and make camp, Carrie."

In the bushes near the river bank Togba found some berries that he crushed to ease the pain of Carrie's cuts and bruises. Finding a secluded place in the forest nearby, he broke off leafy boughs and made their sleeping place. Carrie sank gratefully on her side of it and was asleep before he finished securing it from animals with some thorn bush.

Carrie waked just after dawn hearing the sound of voices, and she crawled carefully out of their sleeping place. Crouching low, she moved toward the river bank and saw through the bushes a short, wiry man talking to Togba. He was pulling a green packet out of a bag tied to his waist. Handing it to Togba, he turned to head back across the river, shouting a burst of Kpelle words that sounded to Carrie like an angry warning. She stood and walked to Togba's side.

"Lakali send this to you," he said. "It be your dress--put it on quick-quick! We must go fast. We did a bad thing."

She unwrapped the banana leaf packet and took out her dress, putting it on hastily.

"What bad thing, Togba? We can be married without bush school, can't we?"

He lifted his hands to his head in horror as he thought of what they had done, pressing his temples and moaning.

"We broke sacred law--Sande law and Poro law! Ohhhhhhhh! I go in Sande bush school to get you and I spoil a sacred place! Ohhhhhhhh, Carrie! My people kill us for this thing! They sending messages to all tribes to kill us if they find us! Lakali say we must go fast and far away--the Poro has long arms to reach out everywhere."

Carrie, stricken dumb by the death threats, put her arms around him. He hugged her close, and they clung together long enough for Togba to make his plan.

"We go back to colony on coast. They can't catch us if we go now--I know forest as good as any country man. It be hard for you, but I know leaf medicine to make your feet tough. Soon you run all day. Come, Carrie!"

30 Trade Town

Monrovia
March 15, 1826

Elijah waited on the veranda of the new Agency House, looking off into the distance. Ashmun had asked him to come this morning to talk about the nest of slave traders at Trade Town. But when he arrived, Ashmun was just starting his breakfast and invited Elijah to join him. Elijah knew he would be eating some of the strange African foods, like fried plantain and cassava, so he'd declined. The only thing Mary had really gotten him used to before she died was rice, and whatever she put in the spicy gravy.

Smiling as he enjoyed the view from the veranda, Elijah reflected on this new move by Ashmun. He was now preaching to them about eating African foods so they wouldn't have to import so much expensive American food. But who would give up things like corn meal, flour and salt meat? Not for the tough, tasteless African stuff! Ashmun was preaching agriculture, too, but the soil on the Cape was so thin and rocky ... Elijah sniffed the strong aroma of roasted coffee coming from Ashmun's kitchen. Now that was something different! John Bannon, on one of his boat trips down the coast to buy rice for the colony, had come back with some wild coffee beans. Soon everybody was having their African cookboys roast it. And John predicted that coffee might some day become as profitable an export as camwood or palm oil nuts.

Elijah looked across the Mesurado river to the shoreline of Bushrod Island. Only one ship lay at anchor, sails furled in the vaporous morning mist. A month before there were sometimes three ships in the bay, but they had been slavers. This one was a merchantman that would soon be loading camwood and ivory. Elijah remembered with pride the second meeting of the colony's Council--as an elected member he had recommended that they drive the slavers out of the bay as soon as Ashmun completed purchase of the island. With the help of an English brig's guns and two companies of the colony's new militia, they had succeeded in closing down the slave factories at Mama's Town and Digby, and this had gotten rid of the slavers' ships.

"All right, I've finished breakfast, Mr. Johnson," Ashmun

called, coming out on the veranda.

"Good morning. You sure got a good view from up here," Elijah answered.

They both leaned on the railing, looking northward, up the coast.

"Yes, isn't it," Ashmun said, pointing to a low blue mound barely visible on the horizon. "That's Cape Mount, almost fifty miles a way."

"That's where King Peter gave us tradin' rights?"

"Yes, and with the Sesters Territory from King Freeman south of here, that makes our coastline about 120 miles long."

Elijah whistled. "How many trading stations are in that?"

"Four." Ashmun turned to Elijah. "Come in to the council room. I want your best military advice on how we can stop the slave trade at our other stations."

When they had settled into the creaky, handmade chairs, Ashmun pulled out a Navy dispatch.

"The last Navy ship that stopped here for water said there are sometimes fifteen slave ships at once along the coast between Cape Mount and Trade Town, making contracts with chiefs for slaves. This dispatch from Navy officers in the African Squadron says they've heard of contracts for eight hundred slaves to be picked up in the next few months!"

Elijah's chair creaked loudly. "Lord A'Mighty! Maybe those slavers we chased out of Mama's Town and Digby just moved on to someplace on our own coast!"

Ashmun looked at the dispatch. "You're right. It says Kroo people have reported that the Spaniard from Digby has gone down to Trade Town and joined a Frenchman and a Cuban. They have three factories there, guarded by two ships with big guns on them."

Elijah's chair creaked again. "We ought to be chasing them out, too!"

"Listen to this!" Ashmun said, reading the dispatch again. "While the Spaniard waits for his barracoons to fill up with slaves, they say he's pirating along the coast. And now he's bragging he's caught eight of our men!"

"Ours? You mean colonists?" Elijah couldn't believe it.

"No, they're recaptives--some we took away from Mama's Town slavers. I suppose they just wandered off from our new farm on Bushrod Island. A Kroo man said he'd seen them and knew they were our people."

Ashmun threw down the dispatch and raised his hands in disgust.

"If they can raid down around Trade Town, they'll soon be raiding our other trading posts and boats. How can we replace the slave trade with legitimate commerce if we can't protect ourselves? And the recaptives--we have to protect them, too!"

"How many armed men do the slavers at Trade Town have?" Elijah asked.

Ashmun squinted at the dispatch. "About fifty or sixty on the two ships and twenty on shore. But they're also giving out free gunpowder and rum to the chiefs. So they'll have some armed Africans helping them."

"What a mess!" Elijah said. "Right in our own territory!" But his chair creaked in his excitement. "Well, we can get up the militia again, with Barbour as captain. That's about fifty men. If you could get a Navy ship to carry us down there, it could drop us on the beach to attack the factories while it goes after the two ships."

"So you think we could do it?"

"Why not? Those Spaniards aren't much fighters--you saw how they gave up without a fight at Digby."

"But they would be much bolder this time with all their men and guns."

"All right--ask the Navy for some marine squads to help us out."

Ashmun was silent, thinking about it, but his chair squeaked, too. Finally he spoke.

"Yes, that's a legitimate use of the Navy, isn't it--to protect the rights of the eight recaptives and to combat the slave trade. All right, if the Council approves I'll send a message to Freetown to see if a Navy ship is cruising up there and could come down our way."

"Hope it doesn't take too long," Elijah warned. "The Spaniard could take off a load of slaves before we get there. And do a lot of pirating meantime."

####

Monrovia
April 12, 1826

Elijah stood on the new dock with the rest of the townsfolk,

273

watching the Columbian oarsmen rowing a squad of the colony's militia out to the warship *Jacinta* anchored in the bay. Beside him was Carrie, with her baby girl, Elizabeth, in her arms. Elijah held a squirming two-year old, John Bannon, Jr.

"Wave goodby to Daddy, Elizabeth! Johnny, wave!" Carrie prompted.

Two Columbian warships, the *Jacinta* and the *El Vincidor*, whose government had recently declared the slave trade illegal, were now patrolling the West African coast. Because Ashmun couldn't locate any U.S. Navy cruisers, he had accepted the offer of help from the Columbians. At the last minute, Ashmun had asked Elijah to stay behind with Company B and protect the Cape, or "Monrovia", as they were supposed to call their town now. And the militia belonged now to "Liberia", the two names having been bestowed by the Society recently. Elijah remembered that the Council had accepted them gladly, but it was hard to get used to, when "the Cape" had always covered them easily. Things were changing fast, Elijah mused. He turned to follow the crowd back up the hill, now a series of wooden stairs with landings at intervals.

Stopping at the gate of the Bannon home, Elijah put John, Jr. on the ground and watched Carrie nudge the boy through the gate while she shifted the baby to her other arm. She made a wonderful mother, Elijah thought. He stood looking at her--she had matured into an attractive young matron, as well-dressed as any woman in the colony, making a good wife for one of the colony's most successful traders. But there was a worried look in her eyes sometimes, and he often thought he detected a restlessness about her. He'd never know the real story of what happened to her upcountry in the forest. Could she have loved that native boy? Elijah shook his head. Impossible! She must love John Bannon--she was his wife!

"You want to come in, Elijah?" Carrie interrupted his thoughts. "Just for a little?"

"Well, I'm supposed to be in charge of the colony's defenses while Ashmun is gone. Thought I'd go up to the Agency House for awhile." He saw the plea in her eyes. "But I guess a few minutes wouldn't hurt."

Elijah sat on a porch seat and Carrie excused herself to see to the children. In a few minutes she was back with a basket of wood blocks for Junior, settling herself in a rocking chair to nurse the baby.

"Guess you're worried about John," Elijah remarked. "Don't worry--we sent enough marines and militia to fight a whole army. Trade Town's just got a small bunch of Spaniards left to defend it, and they'll turn tail and run when they see our men."

"I know you and Mr. Ashmun planned it good," Carrie said. "John told me so ... but something could always happen."

They were both silent with their own thoughts, ignoring Junior's chatter and banging of blocks.

"You've got a good provider, Carrie. John's probably got more money stashed away than any of the rest of us. You did the right thing when you married him." Elijah couldn't resist saying the rest of it. "A lot better than that native boy, Togba."

A soft moan escaped Carrie's lips and Elijah turned to see tears welling in her eyes. She shook her head sadly.

"Elijah, he wasn't a boy. He was a young man. And smart, too--in ways you'll never understand. He was brave and he had honor! And someday he could have been a chief. That night when you came to take me away from my--my 'adventure' as you called it--I was frightened and confused. I followed you back to the colony without protest. But now here I am, facing the thing that drove me from the colony--the fighting over slavery and trade! When will it ever stop? It was so peaceful in the deep forest and villages. I can't help but wonder ... did I lose Togba only to have John killed fighting slavery at Trade Town?"

"John's not going to be killed, Carrie! We've got them outnumbered three-to-one!"

Elijah stood up impatiently.

"I've got to get up to the Agency House! Stop worrying, Carrie. It'll come out all right. I know it will."

Elijah's calm had returned by the time he walked up Main Street to the Agency House and sat on the high veranda overlooking the bay. He could see the two Columbian schooners tacking across the wind, slowly working their way out of the bay. Now John Bannon would have the thrill of sailing on a warship. But with the chance of death, too ... it was a sobering thought, with John and Carrie just starting their family, and John succeeding as a merchant on the waterside. No, it shouldn't happen to them--not after all the trouble he'd gone through to get them together!

He remembered how Chief Bob Gray had sent him a message three months after the battles with the Africans, saying that Carrie and Togba were fleeing from the Kpelle people and the

275

Poro, and must be punished by death as soon as they were found. They had escaped all hunting parties but were known to be heading toward Bassa country--Bob Gray's territory--and he would try to find and protect them until Elijah came.

Elijah stood up abruptly, stirred by the remembered shock of it. He walked to the end of the veranda, following the white sails of the Columbian ships as they wheeled in a half circle, heading south-southwest for Trade Town. Elijah recalled how quickly he had jumped aboard a passing trader's brig and arrived at the mouth of the St. John river, hailing a Kroo canoe and going upriver to Bob Gray's village, arriving in the night. Awakened, Bob Gray took him secretly to his slave barracoon, where Carrie and Togba huddled in a corner hut, blinking with terrified eyes at the lantern light. Elijah had arranged through Bob Gray to pay a large sum of money for Carrie's breaking of sacred African law, but exacted his own price from Carrie--that she would marry John Bannon as soon as they returned to the colony. Togba was never seen again ... maybe he had paid the final price.

Elijah sighed. The schooners were disappearing in the distance. He stood on the veranda staring into the empty sea. How long would these battles continue? That was what Carrie had asked. Would John survive this one?

Trade Town
April 13, 1826

The bright sun of a tropical morning glittered on choppy waves as they stood on the heaving quarterdeck. Captain Chase of the *Jacinta* looked through his telescope, describing what he was seeing.

"There's a sandbar where the river meets the sea, with pretty heavy surf--and rocks on either side--passage only eight or ten yards wide--looks rather risky to go in there."

He handed the telescope to Ashmun, who had to lean against the rail to steady himself.

"A lot of thatched roofs behind that tall stand of palm trees," Ashmun said. "It looks like the whole village is out on the beach to welcome us. But we don't want innocent people involved in this--Oh, oh! There's the Spaniards with their muskets!"

"How many are there?" Barbour, the Liberian militia captain, asked.

Ashmun handed him the telescope. "See for yourself."

"Looks like a coupl'a dozen--just like the ones at Digby, only more of'em."

He handed the telescope back to the Captain Chase

"I count thirty armed men," Chase said. "They're within half a musket shot of where we would go in over the bar. That must be the village on the right side of the river and the barracoons on the left. If we start firing our carriage guns at the beach, at least it would scare off the bystanders--maybe the Spaniards, too."

Chase focused the telescope on the river mouth again.

"It's too small an opening to use our barges. We'll have to use the smaller boats. But with that surf, it might capsize them. Do you want to take the risk?"

Barbour spoke up.

"It's just what we have all along the coast--we're used to it. If we can't make it over the bar, we can go around the rocks on the right side and land on the beach there."

Chase consulted his marine officer, sent a boat over to the *El Vincidor* anchored a short distance away, and in twenty minutes both ships were firing their heavy guns at the beach. The villagers fled into the bush and palm trees. Two boats were loaded by the time the firing stopped, and their oarsmen headed for the narrow opening in the rocks. Captains Chase and Cottrell, Americans serving the Columbian navy, with eighteen marines in each boat, made it over the bar, the boiling surf soaking some of their muskets. Spaniards fired on them, but those marines with dry guns were forcing the Spaniards back toward the village. Ashmun and the marine officer followed in the flagboat with more marines and a few militia.

A huge wave lifted the flagboat up, but a crosswave slewed it violently, so that it settled on top of the rocks on the left, balanced precariously for a moment, and then spilled everyone onto the slippery, barnacled rocks. They scrambled awkwardly through the rocks to the beach, soaked by the pursuing surf. Ashmun, always weak from fever, was slow in getting a foothold, and another wave dumped its flood upon him. He fell into a crevice in the rocks, both of his knees wedged together tightly by the V-shaped fissure.

John Bannon turned to see Ashmun just as another huge

wave rolled inward toward the rocks. Bannon raced back, desperately leapfrogging from rock to rock, hoping to reach the feeble Ashmun before he was submerged again. Ashmun grasped the slippery rocks at his sides, digging his fingernails frantically at the hard, unyielding stone. The rolling mountain of sea water smashed upon the rocks, and Ashmun took a deep breath, hoping to outlast its flood until it sank away between the crevices. As the wave engulfed him in its cold, green water he glimpsed a dark uniform that seemed to leap down from the sky and straddle the crevice above him. He felt strong hands reach under his armpits and pull him upwards, his knees coming loose from the crevice and his head emerging from the flood.

"Are you all right, Mr. Ashmun?" John shouted as they struggled to maintain their balance in the swirling water.

"Is it you, Bannon? Thank God you came!" Ashmun shook the water out of his eyes and ears, gasping for breath. "I couldn't get loose--you saved my life!"

"Let's get to the shore before another one comes," John said, guiding the older man.

One more big wave swashed around their knees, barely slowing them, before they fell gasping on the beach.

"Where's Barbour and the rest of the militia?" Ashmun finally asked.

Bannon pointed seaward. "They're not coming in here--going around to the right."

When Barbour's boat hit the beach they saw him jump out and urge his men forward, pinching the Spaniards between themselves and the marines. The Spaniards fled into the bush with the villagers, and the landing party took possession of the village. Ashmun quickly assumed command, sending a message to King West to bring in all the slaves held in the barracoons, with a warning that if there was too much delay, the town would be burned down. That afternoon, the Bassa chief sent in thirty-eight slaves and promised he would catch others who he said had broken out of the barracoons during the attack.

But the next morning only fifteen slaves were sent in, and these were the weak ones, left over from several hundred that had been in the barracoons. Before Ashmun could decide what to do, the Bassa warriors joined the Spaniards, pouring musket fire into the unfortified town. Barbour, deciding they'd be better off counter-attacking, eagerly ran to Ashmun's command post for permission.

"No, Mr. Barbour--let's try to settle this without killing a lot of Africans," Ashmun said.

"But they've joined the Spaniards to attack us!"

"Some are, but I don't believe most Africans have much say in it. The Spaniards are preying on the chief's thirst for rum, and he sends his warriors out to get more slaves from weaker neighbors. We're only trying to break up the Spaniard's evil business--not kill people."

Barbour's astonishment showed in his eyes. Then he nodded slowly. "You're right."

"Can you defend us while I send another message to King West?" Ashmun asked him.

"We'll hold on," Barbour promised, his voice husky.

At sunrise the next morning, musket fire started up again, wounding the surgeon of the *Jacinta*, together with three Liberian militiamen. By noon Ashmun decided to move the slaves to the ships. Barbour led the marines and militia on a whooping, hollering charge into the bush surrounding the village, scaring the attackers away. Ashmun hired Kroo canoes to take the slaves through the surf to boats standing outside the breakers. In the midst of this, John Bannon approached Ashmun.

"I've found the goods the Spaniards trade for slaves--mostly rum and cloth. If we took it back to Monrovia, I could sell it at low cost to the people."

Ashmun was surprised at the young merchant's greed.

"You're a shrewd trader, John. But you can do more for the colony than that."

"All right. I'll share fifty-fifty with the colony."

Ashmun squinted thoughtfully at him. He could insist that the goods belonged to the colony, not John. But John had found them. Ashmun felt awkward, realizing that John had saved his life. Was John counting on that?

"All right, John. But leave the rum to burn here. Hire your own Kroo men, and give the Council a correct accounting when the cloth is all sold in Monrovia. But don't delay our getting off today."

By three-thirty that afternoon all the slaves, the militia and the marines, and the cloth goods were on shipboard. Ashmun and the officers left last, after the village was set afire by the rear guard. As their canoes pushed off, flames leaped swiftly across the thatch roofs, fanned by the sea breeze. Then they heard small explosions.

279

"What's that?" Ashmun asked.

"Sounds like casks of gunpowder," Cottrell said. "They must have hidden a few up overhead in some of the huts."

"The Spaniards should have had a lot more than that somewhere," Chase said, "but we didn't find it."

Just before the canoes reached the boats, a thunderous blast erupted from somewhere in the village. The earth shook and even the sea swells seemed to hold still for a brief moment. They looked back in awe, their ears ringing. All trace of what was once Trade Town had blown away, and the surrounding country and sea were strewn with burning thatch. Sticks fell from a height of more than a hundred feet. Some pieces fell among the boats, and they could see wood floating out beyond them.

"My God! They did have a powder magazine hidden in the town!" Chase cried.

"Lord A'Mighty! How big was it, you s'pose?" Barbour asked.

Cottrell, the armaments expert for the Columbians, made a guess. "Maybe 250 or 300 casks. Good powder, too. I can tell by the smell of it."

They watched the black smoke drifting high over the town's ashes. Ashmun thought of the day he and Elijah had talked about coming to Trade Town. He would be able to tell Elijah how complete the job had been done--blasted from the face of the earth! Word of it would travel rapidly along the coast, he knew. The blast of it would be good for a hundred miraculous tales among the Africans. But hopefully it would impress upon their minds that the colony was serious about stamping out the slave trade!

The next day at Monrovia, Ashmun publicly extended the Council's thanks to the two Columbian captains, and the slaves were officially entered into the colony as recaptives. In an expansive mood, Ashmun wrote to the Colonization Society's Board of Managers that the Trade Town affair would "make every slave trader along the coast feel the insecurity of his commerce."

31   Taking Sides

New York City
March 7, 1829

"Traitor! He's selling out to coli'zationists!" "White lover!"
"Beat him up!" "Betrayer! We ain't never goin't to no Africa!"

The mob was beating a dummy stuffed with straw and rags,
pounding it furiously, throwing garbage, sticks and mud at it. Rev.
Samuel Cornish, used to mobs at Five Points venting their anger at
an effigy of someone they hated, pricked up his ears when he heard
the word 'Africa.' There was only one street lamp at this sprawling
intersection in New York's densely-packed black neighborhood, so
he stepped off the curb for a closer look at a sign hung from the
dummy's neck. But a handful of mud flew up and splattered the
sign as a mud thrower shouted in outrage.

"He's desertin' us just when we need him most! Let him go
die in Africa!"

Cornish saw the sign's remaining letters, "JOHN B.
RUSS...", and he knew that his friend and former newspaper
co-editor, John Russworm, was the mob's target. He shook his head
sadly, and walked on toward the office of *Freedom's Journal*, just a
block down the street, where he had worked until last month.

A month ago it had been a friendly place where admirers
hung about to cheer the two famous editors of the nation's first
black newspaper. Heroes of the black community's fight for
equality and freedom, both Russworm and Cornish had been
outspoken critics of the Colonization Society, which blacks in the
street feared would expel them from the United States.

Cornish trudged up the steps to the second floor loft,
hearing the thump of the old hand press above him. He knew
Russworm was shorthanded now that he had resigned. They had
fallen out over editorial policy, Russworm beginning to take a
moderate stance on the Society when the majority of New York's
blacks were totally against it. And so were black community
leaders in Philadelphia, Boston, and other cities. Anti-colonization
was the prevailing mood of blacks everywhere, and *Freedom's
Journal* was expected to lead the fight! Why couldn't Russworm
see it? Cornish sighed as he reached the landing and pushed
through the pressroom door.

"What have you written this time?" Cornish shouted over the noise of the press, startling his friend with a slap on the shoulder. "There's a mob at Five Points burning you in effigy!"

John Russworm, looked up with glazed eyes, rubbing them on the back of his sleeve. "What? What's burning?"

"You! The mob's burning you! Let me see the paper."

Cornish carried one over to the lamp and turned quickly to the editorial page, squinting in the dim light. Suddenly his dark face paled, and he looked around at Russworm in shocked disbelief.

"My Lord, John! You can't mean it!"

"Mean what?"

"This--this giving up! Listen to yourself: 'We consider it a waste of words to talk of ever enjoying citizenship in this country.' And then you say it's a hopeless cause...and that whites will never grant true equality to blacks...so you've changed your mind...now you see colonization as the only means by which we'll ever get to live as free people! You're *mad*, John! How many copies of this are on the streets? They'll burn you in the black quarters of every big city!"

Russworm walked wearily over to the pressman.

"That's enough tonight, Richard. We'll run the rest tomorrow. See that the boys clean up."

Russworm motioned Cornish to follow him, and they moved to the office where a pot of tea bubbled on a charcoal brazier. Cornish warmed his hands around a mug of tea, and prepared to start up their old argument. But this time might be their last, he thought angrily.

"Why, John? Why? You've shattered all the things we stood for! We were partners in the only black newspaper in the land--breaking the monopoly of white newspapers! We gave black men a voice, and a place to express their viewpoints. And now you're going to throw it all away! *Why?*"

Russworm's elbows rested on his desk, his hands covering his eyes. Cornish could barely hear his tired voice.

"I can't take it anymore, Sam--I'm pressured on every side since you've quit. Every single word I write is criticized, either by the abolitionists or colonizationists. They both want me to take their side."

"So now you've decided for the colonization people, just like I thought you would! That's why I quit, John--I don't trust *any* whites to defend my rights! Only we blacks know what's best for ourselves. And sending us off to Africa is not it!"

Russworm shook his head sadly.

"There you go again, Sam. The Colonization Society is *not* sending people off without their consent! You're so suspicious of whites, you're getting irrational. There are good whites, too. And some of them are in the Society--they sincerely want to help us find true freedom. And that will never be possible here in America."

"You're the crazy one, John!" Cornish shouted, standing up so suddenly tea slopped out of his mug. "Just because you had a white father and he put you through college, you think all whites are like him! I'm telling you, those Society people are a bunch of slave owners. They're trying to weaken our antislavery movement by sending free blacks out of the country so there'll be no one to speak for our brothers in slavery. You can't ignore that!"

"Sit down, Sam. I think we've been looking at it all wrong. Slave owners will be more likely to free their slaves now that there's a place for them to find freedom and dignity in Liberia. They're doing it more and more! Every ship going out to Liberia now has an increasing percentage of manumitted people."

"And so they're going out there to die of fever! Some freedom!"

Cornish wasn't sitting down. Wanting equal footing now, Russworm stood up, too.

"I know they have to get through the fever season and they have some hard times getting started out there, Sam. And some don't make it, but those who do are glad they stuck it out. They take part in their own government, serve on juries, are officers in their own armies, have their own businesses and farms--wait a minute, I want to show you something."

He rummaged in his desk drawer for a minute, then lifted out a printed statement.

"Listen, Sam. It's an 'Address of the Colonists to the Free People of Colour in the U.S.' It says:

'The first consideration which caused our voluntary removal to this country is liberty...Now our sentiments and our opinions have their due weight in the government we live under. Our laws are altogether our own: they grow out of our circumstances, are framed for our exclusive benefit...'

Cornish interrupted sarcastically.

"Oh, isn't that fine--all those good laws! But they're still

283

under the thumb of a white agent over there!"

"Wait, Sam. Here's the real meat of their statement. Listen:

'Forming a community of our own, in the land of our forefathers; having the commerce, the soil, and resources of the country at our disposal; we know nothing of that debasing inferiority with which our very colour stamped us in America...The burden is gone from our shoulders: we now breathe and move freely; and know not...the empty name of liberty, which you endeavor to content yourselves with, in a country that is not yours..."

"It *will* be ours if we fight for it!" Cornish shouted, drowning out Russworm's voice. He jabbed his finger at a copy of *Freedom's Journal* lying on the desk.

"That's what we were doing with our paper--fighting for our people's rights! If you'd join the abolitionists we'd win our freedom right *here!*"

Russworm shook his head emphatically.

"Never! Not in a thousand years! Sam, don't get mixed up with those abolitionists. David Walker is advocating violence and revolution. Attacks on slave owners will only provoke retaliation against slaves--you don't want that, do you?"

Frustrated for always being outreasoned by his friend, Cornish slammed down the tea mug.

"You *do* talk like a traitor to the black man! We helped build this country by the sweat of our backs, and fought in wars for it, too! We were born here! This is our country! We have a *right* to stay. I'm going over to the abolitionists!"

"Sam, don't! The South won't give up its slave system without a bloody fight. We can be free, without dying for it, by going to Liberia. Don't you see? It's the best plan because there'll be no violence."

Cornish turned abruptly and stomped toward the door.

"I'm not listening to any more of your 'white' mind! You don't even think like a black man anymore. You'll be burned in every black community in America, John. Goodbye!"

Colonization Office, Washington
July 23, 1829

"Russworm is going to Liberia? You mean the editor of that

284

black newspaper?" Elisha Whittlesey asked.

"Yes--and he's the best educated black man in America," Ralph Gurley said proudly. "He's already a graduate of Bowdoin College, and he'll have his master's degree by the end of summer. He's going to be Superintendent of Education in the colony this fall."

Gurley, now the Executive Secretary of the Colonization Society, pointed to a sheaf of correspondence on his desk.

"We wrote to him two years ago about going to Liberia, but he wasn't interested. Last March he changed his mind and applied for a post in Liberia. We suggested the education job. That top letter is a recommendation by Reverend Peter Williams, one of America's outstanding black Episcopal leaders. With *that* endorsement, the Board of Managers approved Russworm without question."

Whittlesey, always checking on things while he was in Washington, wasn't satisfied.

"Why did he change his mind?"

"He says he read everything he could about Liberia and finally decided it was the most practical way to bring freedom to his people--said it would speed up emancipation without violence. His editorials now say that blacks will have to find their own place in the world where they can develop free of racial hatred and oppression."

It brought Whittlesey to his feet with excitement. "So he's going to Liberia to find that place! Ralph, that's why I've worked for the colonization idea all these years--to give black people a *real* chance! And we've got enough auxiliary societies in Ohio now to raise substantial sums for it. When are you going to send a speaker out to us?"

Gurley got up and went over to a calendar on the office wall. "I've got it marked right here, Mr. Whittlesey. Let's see..."

He traced it out with his finger and then tapped the spot firmly. "That's him--Henry Bascom. He's going to Canton, Steubenville, and several other places in Ohio, and then down into Kentucky. He's the best agent we have--a good speaker and organizer--starts new auxiliaries almost everywhere he goes and ..."

"When is he coming out to Ohio?" Whittlesey asked.

"Early part of September, I believe."

Whittlesey turned to go. "Thanks, Ralph. It looks like you're well organized yourself. There's one more thing. How is the colony doing?"

"The colony is thriving. We sent three ships last year so there are about 1700 colonists now, with churches, schools, courts, and many new houses. Three new settlements have been started on land ceded by nearby chiefs. In fact, quite a few chiefs have placed themselves under the colony's authority for protection from warring tribes."

"How about the medical situation?"

"You mean doctors?" Gurley made a sour face. "Our latest one, Dr. Mechlin, has just come home to recover. It was overwork, I'm afraid--he had to serve as both doctor and agent."

Whittlesey shook hands.

"I've got to go. But I'll be back for the Society's annual meeting, as a delegate from our Canfield auxiliary. And remember, our people will be generous when your Mr. Bascom comes out. I hope he's used to roughing it--it's still pretty wild country."

"Oh, he is. He told the Board he's been riding horseback since his early days on a country preaching circuit."

####

Ohio River country
September 12, 1829

When the river boat captain had dumped his passengers at the Marietta dock because the river level was too low, the stage coach company had made up an extra coach to Wheeling because some of the people couldn't wait for the regular mail run the next day. After a frantic search for a crew, the young man pressed into service hadn't completed his five training runs and didn't really know the dangers he was facing. The old hosteler to ride with him was pulled out of retirement and told to watch him.

Careening up and down the hills that morning on the narrow dirt roads jolted and swayed the seven passengers to near insensibility. Clattering wheels, pounding hooves and clanking harness made the rattling coach a deafening contraption. The driver kept his long rawhide whip biting at the horses' rumps on every down slope to gain momentum for the next hill's long incline. On one of the taller hills where the road was cut into the side of it in a tortuous, narrow ascent, the horses had slowed to an almost pleasant pace. With sighs of relief the passengers opened the

286

coach's curtains and gazed at the muddy waters of the Ohio River rolling quietly on their right, stretching out vast as a plain. Only the driver and the grizzled old hostler at his side on the coach's high box seat knew they were approaching a dangerous pass--the road so narrow that every rock threatened to jolt the coach into the abyss below.

A leafy branch of an overhanging tree, blown by a stray breeze, spooked the lead horse nearest the bank and it jumped away with a loud whinny, frightening the other lead. They both swung to the right, leading the wheel horses across the road. The driver stood to pull them back with the weight of his whole body, but they refused to follow his savage jerk of the bit, plunging headlong over the edge. Grabbing their seats, the passengers stared speechless at the scenery rushing past the windows as they went down.

The coach landed upright on a narrow bench of the hillside with a splintering crash. The axles broke, wheels flying in different directions, the coach bed crunched flat. The passengers' breath was expelled by the crushing stop and they were stunned senseless. Broken away from its bed, the coach body teetered on the edge of the narrow bench for a second, tilted slowly outwards, and then tumbled over and over down the rest of the hill, coming to rest on the grassy slope of the river bank. The coach body lay on its side, silent in the lush green grass.

Bascom was the first one to regain conciousness. Hearing a meadow lark singing, he became aware of his awkward position and pushed somebody's arm off his face. He was on top of a heap of bodies and reached for the coach door above him to heave himself up, clambering painfully out. Finding that he had only some minor cuts and bruises, he helped the others out as they came to. Jenkins, the newspaperman, was first; then the plantation owner Blackburn and his wife, and next two nuns named Sister Maria and Sister Agnes. The businessman McNamara was last.

Bascom filled his hat with river water and was reviving the Irishman when Jenkins saw the driver in the river slowly being pulled in over his head by two surviving horses. Jenkins and Bascom rescued him and one of the horses. When they all revived and were sitting in the shade of a tree, the old hostler hobbled to them with a makeshift crutch broken off the tree in which he had landed. The driver apologized to the passengers, rigged a makeshift harness for the horse, taking off for Marietta bareback, promising to return with another coach soon.

"I think its miraculous that none of us was hurt seriously," Mrs. Blackburn said. "I'm so thankful. Reverend Bascom, would you kindly thank God for us?"

Bascom looked at the two nuns, who nodded their heads, and then he began a quiet prayer. His soothing voice seemed at one with the peaceful surroundings of the river bank, and with their eyes closed he made them aware of the green meadow's beauty in the warm sunlight, the shade of an over-arching tree, a life-giving river flowing steadily beside them, and bird songs caressing their ears...all this, God's creation, for their rest and solace now...with His loving care. Bascom was finished, but they rested in the comfort of the moment, savoring it, hardy noticing he had stopped. They were at peace, the silence precious...

Jenkins, the hardened, cynical newsman, was startled when the spell was broken and they once more began to move around and talk. He'd never experienced such a deep, personal peace in his life. This man--this preacher who had hardly said a thing during the coach ride except to answer questions put to him--had given Jenkins a deep, serene moment that was almost profound. How could he do that? Who was he really? The reporter's instinct in Jenkins reasserted itself.

"Bascom! What about this colonization thing you're doing now? You sound like an experienced preacher instead of a money raiser."

"Well, I do both. But I've been released from the Methodist Church to do this work now."

Blackburn, observing Bascom's modesty, informed Jenkins that he had also been chaplain to the House of Representatives in Washington, a college president in Pennsylvania, and frequently drew crowds of four or five thousand to his preaching in the East before joining the colonization cause. Jenkins was shocked.

"Why do you spend your time on country stage coaches in the wilds of Ohio?"

"Don't underestimate the people of the rural areas, Mr. Jenkins. I was an ignorant Ohio boy from these wilds when I started out."

"No--I mean--it seems such a lowly task, out here," Jenkins finished lamely.

"Even the smallest villages have sometimes given three or four hundred dollars to help freed slaves who wanted to go back to

Africa, Mr. Jenkins. Some Eastern cities have done much less."

"But why do you do this when you could be a leader in Washington or in academic circles?" Jenkins persisted.

Bascom hesitated, choosing his words carefully.

"I think it's because slavery is the great evil of our time...one that our nation has not been able to solve. Yet it must be solved in some way that avoids bloodshed. I believe colonization is that way and I'm devoted to the cause, wherever it leads me."

Bascom's quiet sincerity penetrated the newsman's natural skepticism. Jenkins was strangely drawn to this enigma--a truly modest man! But could he really sway thousands, like Blackburn said?

"You say you're speaking in Steubenville tomorrow? I think I'll come and hear you."

Steubenville, Ohio
September 14, 1829

Jenkins was sore and stiff, and it was mid-day before he stirred himself. The inn-keeper's wife provided a greasy meal of fat middling, fried eggs, and coffee; he was not restored to his usual self when he set out to find the place where Bascom was to speak. But the day was beautiful, with bright sunshine and a soft, balmy air that revived him slowly as he walked. When he was a block from the church that had been designated for the Sunday afternoon meeting, Jenkins encountered crowds of people and, suspecting that the meeting had been cancelled, asked a bystander.

"Tisn't cancelled, sir. We came to hear the great preacher, Bascom, but the place is filled and the ushers won't let any more in."

"Why do you want to hear him--why all these people?"

"They say he's the greatest pulpit orator of his times, a giant among giants."

Another man joined in. "The newspaper I read says Bascom could 'wake the higher powers of the soul'--exactly those words!"

Now Jenkins knew he had a story. But how to get in the church? He hurried on, flashing his press card to three different officials, and got in on the outside aisle, standing up with others crowded against the wall on the side opposite the pulpit. There was hardly room to reach into his breast pocket for his notebook; he would only be able to see Bascom in profile. But at least he could hear him and keep an eye on the audience at the same time. Now he would find out if this oratorical wonder was true.

Mr. John C. Wright, president of the Steubenville auxiliary of the American Colonization Society, called on the Secretary, H. Everett, to read the minutes of the organizing meeting and the names of the elected officers. Jenkins dutifully noted the details, anxious for the business to be over. He realized he was waiting for Bascom's oratory as much as the dense crowd. Finally John Wright rose to introduce the speaker.

"...the Reverend Mr. Bascom, Agent of the American Colonization Society, who has come for the purpose of presenting his plea for colonizing our free people of color on the western coast of Africa."

Concealed until now by the mahogany front of the pulpit, the quiet form of the speaker suddenly emerged and stood for two minutes, erect and motionless as a statue. Jenkins was startled--the immense throng seemed struck with Bascom's immobility and the quiet eloquence of his attitude. From Jenkin's view of his profile, Bascom looked like a classic Greek scholar; his eyes, expressionless, appeared to be dwelling on his own inner thoughts.

Bascom raised his right hand, pressed his fingers to his pale forehead, and then his voice seemed to take wings and ride away on a whirlwind of fiery words. His voice rolled and pealed like an organ one instant, then crashed with tremendous power so that it seemed to jar the walls like thunderbolts. The sentences came like sharp zigzags of lightning. Jenkins was astounded at Bascom's mental opulence as thought piled on thought, and the rapid whirl of dazzling imagery almost overwhelmed, it was so rushing and ceaseless--so vehement!

Jenkins, caught off guard, started to scribble. Bascom had started out with 'ancient Africa, the country of the pharaohs' and, --what was it he said?--'parent of art and science, the great luminary of the world. When the soil of Greece and Italy were covered with primeval forest, only a shelter for wild beasts and roving barbarians, the valley of the Nile was occupied by a people who had already built temples honoring the gods and rearing columns to their kings,etc., etc.'

My God, thought Jenkins, how can I keep up? He wrote frantically, abbreviating more. 'As early as days of Moses, Egypt pre-eminent in laws, learning, art--later Thales, Pythagoras, Plato, etc., all acquired in Egypt elements of science they taught to their countrymen--even rudiments of Grecian art, which Greeks improved upon and raised to ideal perfection, is traced from banks of Nile--Egypt great empire, settled by Mizraim, son of Ham--45 kingdoms, 20,000 cities--in reign of Asa, King of Judah, Ethiopia could send great armies to field...'

Slow down, Bascom, Jenkins breathed, his pencil racing. '...offspring of Cush, Mizraim, Phut--reared pyramids, made most fertile country of the world, invented its hieroglyphics, gave letters to Greece and Rome...to us, gave bishops to the church, martyrs to the flames...'

Jenkins was losing ground to Bascom's mental creations, the cyclopedia-like scope, the quick succession of vivid pictures--it was too much! He jabbed a savage period in his notebook page and relaxed, letting the words flow over him. He looked at the audience, some openmouthed, all spellbound, hardly breathing. Bascom hadn't even come close to his main topic yet. When was he going to get around to slavery and colonization?

"Backward as the Africans now are, it will scarcely be believed that this condemned race, as to intellect, can exhibit a brighter ancestry than our own. But their ancestors are the offshoots, now wild and untrained, of Cush, Mizraim and Phut!..."

Bascom is finally getting around to it, Jenkins noticed, and looked at his watch. Nearly an hour! Where had all the time gone? He has entranced the audience with his magnificent conceptions all that time. By God, he himself had been entranced.

"But Africa has been degraded, insulted, wronged for many centuries. She has been robbed of her children to an immeasurable extent. What wind has passed over her plains without catching up the sighs of broken and bleeding hearts? Which of the sands of her deserts has not been steeped in tears, wrung out by the pang of separation from kindred and country..."

So this is how he prepares his audience, Jenkins thought. He must be ready now to detail the rape of Africa. Jenkins decided to get some of it down--just the main points.

'Africa has been rifled of her blood and treasure by every Christian nation--millions of her inhabitants sacrificed to European avarice--to every nation she has raised her cry of supplication--in reply she receives only an additional weight of chains. Every gale that blows over her, catches the sounds of her groans, and almost

291

every foot of her soil is strained and wet with blood, shed by Chrisitian steel...'

Again Bascom threw off a kaleidoscope of images, terrible pictures of the slave ships crossing the ocean, the infamous 'middle passage' in which many had died, chained to each other, lying on racks below deck only 30 inches high, the chains wearing flesh to bone. Bascom's voice sank to a wild wail, plaintive as a funeral dirge; then it swelled to the steady roar of a hurricane, suddenly breaking out into thunderclaps that caused Jenkin's hair to rise.

My God, Jenkins thought, looking at the audience, if he does this to me he must be making the very marrow of their bones creep! He saw their fixed, straining eyes, half-parted lips, and in Bascom's pauses, heard the deathly silence of their rapt attention. The cruelty and shame of the slave trade was bearing down on their hearts--the pity was in their faces. His pencil and notebook were useless now--it was fruitless to attempt to capture Bascom and his flashing eyes, the thunder and lightning of his words, the tremendous discharges of his intellect. This fiery transformation of the mild, modest man in the stagecoach was unbelievable!

But now Jenkins heard a new, calmer note, a reasoning tone in Bascom's voice. Sensing a shift, maybe to a conclusion, Jenkins put pencil to paper again, listening for clues. He would just catch the important phrases this time.

'the suppression of the slave trade---redemption of Africa from present degradation--can be effected only by colonization--the same way civilization and Christianity introduced into Greece, Europe, America--plea for African colonization--on grounds of justice--practicability already proven in colony of Liberia--on grounds of political consistency--our constitution--freedom to rise untrammeled by prejudice--to right the wrongs of the past --predictions of the scriptures on Africa--on grounds of final retributions of eternity...'

Jenkins was elated--he had captured the last part perfectly. What a masterful appeal! It was so clear that colonization would be the right thing to do for the Africans. He watched Bascom sit down and Wright call upon the audience to support the colonization cause generously. The collection plates were passed while the church's organist played.The people were turning out their pockets --everyone was giving! He'd put in, too--couldn't find a more just cause.

He had a front page story alright! Out here in the wilds of

Ohio, the greatest orator of the nation, leading the movement to halt the slave trade and make restitution for its wrongs. He'd send it by mail coach to Pittsburgh and New York both. Usually it didn't matter to him what his readers did about the subjects he wrote on, but this time he definitely wanted the colonization cause to get a boost from his story!

32 Manumission

Ronda Plantation, Virginia
July 8, 1833

"Laura, come here! Listen to this!" Harte shouted from his library desk, still squinting at the latest *African Repository* which had come up on the river boat. "Gerritt Smith has done it again!"

Laura sighed, put down her sewing, and went toward the library. She and Harte had settled into a quiet life on their isolated plantation because Harte's children were grown and either married or away at school. Exposed to wealthy society in Charlottsville, Richmond and Norfolk, all of his children had absorbed typical Southern attitudes, and were completely at odds with their father's independent views of nearly everything in the South.

She had stood up for him as he continued to take on new things and unpopular causes, usually fueled by his trips to the North on business. He was respected for his pioneer work in agricultural reform, and his long service on the county court and university board. But she knew that he was considered an eccentric for anti-tobacco views, and the mint-julep and hot-toddy crowd jeered behind his back at his temperance activities. She ignored most of it, but sensed that public opinion of his colonization work was hardening against him.

"Who's Gerritt Smith?" she asked.

She stood behind him, gently rubbing his shoulders which usually ached from his long hours of writing and correspondence.

"Smith is the millionaire in New York who pledged a thousand dollars for colonization."

"A thousand--that's unheard of!"

"Yes, but there's a catch to it, Laura. It's to be paid in ten yearly payments of $100--if a hundred other men will join him. He's just issued another challenge for people to do that."

"Amazing. And he's a Northerner--probably doesn't have any slaves himself. Do you know him? How did he get so interested in it?"

"Yes, I've met him. And Cresson, and Tappan, and Gaulladet. They're all Northern leaders who take the evil of slavery seriously, Laura. I wrote to some of them because there aren't many thinkers like that around here."

She finished massaging his shoulders.

"There. I hope you're not going to write anymore tonight. You spend so much time writing Northerners, you'll become a Yankee yourself."

"I've got to write two more. I'm going to get my draft for a hundred dollars off on tomorrow's boat for Gerritt's challenge. And then I'm going to write Cresson. I want him to know what damage Garrison's radical abolitionist newspaper is doing here in the South."

"You mean the *Liberator?*"

"Yes, and David Walker's vicious *Appeal* calling for blacks to kill whites. The whole South fears a general uprising! That's what's behind the new laws against teaching slaves to read and write--so they can't read such things."

Laura gasped. "So we won't be able to continue teaching our people for freedom in Liberia?"

Harte nodded. "Not reading and writing, anyway."

"Then it's time we sent the ones that are ready, James."

"I'm not sure there are any yet."

"But you wrote the Society several years ago that you had some almost ready, James!"

"They've been backsliding morally. You know I keep careful records, Laura. I'll know when they're ready."

Laura decided to press him--it probably was now or never. She changed her tactics.

"The *Enquirer* says this scare about an uprising has caused a lot of owners to free their slaves suddenly and send them to Liberia--without any preparation at all. But yours are much more ready than theirs, James. Don't you think the Society really needs some of yours to help the others?"

She could see he was thinking about it, so she waited.

"Well, there was something in the *Repository* about the Society needing to be more selective in sending emigrants to Liberia. Seems some recent ones weren't too satisfactory."

"There, you see? None of our people are like that."

She rubbed his shoulders some more, relaxing him. His eyes closed for a long moment, and then he reached for the slave ledger.

####

The next morning Jesse Belcor was summoned to the mansion. Harte was studying the slave ledger in the bright sunlight slanting in the library window. Jesse's mother, Sarah, a trusted house slave, brought her second son to the door. She coughed to get Harte's attention.

"He's heah, Gen'rul," the old woman said.

"Come in, Jesse, and have a seat," Harte invited.

He noticed for the first time a tinge of white hair in his chief mechanic's crinkly hair and beard. Years of work as a mason had changed Jesse from the young boy Harte once roamed the fields with, into a strong sinewy craftsman who had helped construct many of the buildings at Ronda.

"Yessuh, Gen'rul. Nothin's wrong, I hope," Jesse said, sitting in the wicker-bottomed chair Harte indicated.

Harte felt the trust between them as they looked at each other squarely. Master and slave--each born to his role, he thought. Raised by Sarah with strictness, Jesse had won Harte's respect by learning quickly from a hired white mason. And through the years Jesse had taught the skills to other slaves at Ronda, while maintaining the status of chief mason by outworking them all. Harte turned back to the ledger.

"Jesse, I see by the ledger you've been at Ronda for thirty-three years. Your wife and six children recorded here on last year's census ... I haven't heard of any of them being in trouble. How are they--all in good health?"

"Yessuh. They're all right. No trouble I know of."

Harte took off his glasses and wiped them with his handkerchief.

"I've decided to free you, Jesse--make you a free man--for all the years you faithfully served me, and because you, of all the slaves at Ronda, are ready for it. I believe you're the only one who could handle freedom and a new life in Africa."

"Me, Gen'rul? Be free?" Jesse was stunned

Harte closed the ledger and moved it aside.

"Yes, you," he said slowly. "Jesse, I've been working towards this for a long time, trying to help you and the others get ready for freedom. That's what the school was for, and the preachers, and the temperance society. But you're the only one so far who has made it."

"Made it? How, Gen'rul?"

"You've learned your trade well, you're a good Christian

man that's raised a decent family, and you've never backslid on your temperance pledge. And you can handle responsibility. I saw that when you did the schoolhouse. You're as ready for starting a new life in Africa as anybody I have."

"Africa?" Jesse hadn't really heard it the first time, but now he did.

His brows drew together. There had been talk in the quarter after Nat Turner's rebellion that the safest place for free blacks was Africa, because whites were seeking revenge, killing innocent slaves who had nothing to do with the rebellion. If a slave ever got free, it wasn't safe to stay around where you might get killed. And yet to go to Africa and leave the land you were born in--he wasn't sure he wanted to do that either. Besides, the talk about rebellion had died down now.

"Does my family--is they free to go with me?" he finally asked.

"Yes, that's the idea, Jesse. You and your family are the kind of people Africa needs. There's a colony--a town--already started in Africa for freed slaves from America. It's a place where blacks are to govern themselves when they're ready for it. There you can live free of the prejudice you'd meet everywhere in America. You can be your own boss and live in your own house on your own land."

"Under my own vine and fig tree..." Jesse said, wonderingly. It was a saying slaves always used when they dreamed of being on their own land.

Jesse asked for time to think about it, and Harte said he wasn't pressing for a quick decision. But if Jesse decided to go, arrangements would have to be made with the Colonization Society. In their cabin that night, Jesse revealed the news to his wife, Lida, after the young ones had gone to sleep.

"Freedom!" Lida almost shouted.

"Shush your mouth, woman! Want to wake the young'uns?"

"Lordy, Lordy, Lordy!" was all she could say at first.

It was a miraculous idea to Lida, who was like Jesse in his stolid acceptance of being a slave, obeying the master and mistress, working hard to get a few rewards at Christmas and avoid the anger of the slave driver. They had been resigned to slavery, but from then on they talked of freedom secretly every night, turning it over in their minds, wondering what it would be like to be free.

"Does we have to go to Africky to be free? Why can't we be

free in Virginny?" Lida asked when she finally understood that the offer was conditional.

Jesse was afraid to talk with the other slaves yet, not sure what they would say about his family being the only one chosen, so he was cautious in exploring for answers. But he found out soon enough. He whispered it to her the next night.

"They've made a new law--free niggers can stay only one or two days in the state, then they have to get out."

"Get out? What's that mean?"

"Go North! Can't go South--they makes you slaves again."

But they feared the unknown North. They knew the General had built his slave cabins better than on most plantations, and Jesse had one of the best of these because he was the chief mechanic. Hot in summer and drafty cold in winter, it still was their home. And the woods and creeks yielded fish or rabbits and squirrels when they could sneak away to catch them. In the North it was bitter cold. Africa would be better than that. But then they heard about the African fever that killed people.

Harte's oldest son, Richard, now in charge of one of the plantations, needed a mason and requested Jesse Belcor. Harte sent Jesse over to help out, and asked his son to sound out Jesse as to his decision about Africa. Harte had promised not to press Jesse, but he knew the time was getting short for the Society's next ship to go out if it were to avoid arriving in Africa during the onset of the rainy season and the fevers.

Not sharing his father's attitude toward slaves, Richard left the disciplining of them to his overseer, and expected it to be strong and absolute. Jesse noticed the difference the next morning when Dickson, the overseer, drove the field hands to work. It was harvest time and Jesse sized up the situation quickly when he saw some wooly white heads in the line of slaves straggling past Dickson for roll call.

"Come on, you lazy nigguhs! Move along! We ain't got all day!" he shouted, prodding the slow movers with a long oak cudgel.

Dickson put one end of the thick wooden stave down and rubbed the day-old stubble of red whiskers on his chin, his beady blue eyes watching for late-comers. Jesse could see that the short, stocky overseer had a powerful arm--a man to stay away from when he had a whip or cudgel and an excuse to use it.

Jesse guessed there were not enough hands to do all the work, so Dickson probably had pressed some of the old slaves back into service for the harvest. And in the hot days of August all slaves would be more exhausted than usual from long days in the fields. It would be a hard struggle to get up at four in the morning when the night patrollers coming off duty rang the bell. He was sure that the slaves barely had time to down some corn pone and molasses before the overseer was out of his house and waiting for them to line up for roll call.

"Damn your black hides! Gettin' out later every day!" Dickson shouted.

Jesse watched him growing more impatient, his eyes blazing. His freckled face grew red as he cursed and swung the heavy stave down on the back of a straggler. Jesse cringed as he saw the old slave knocked down and hit again until he got on his feet.

"Don't you play that old man stuff with me, you bastard! You been sittin' around the quarter all year like you don't have to work no more. I told you I'd roust you out come harvest, didn't I?"

The old man staggered on out of reach of the swearing overseer. The cruelty of it reminded Jesse of his own children who might some day fall under the power of a vicious slavedriver like this one. The sudden realization that even as a chief mechanic he was still a slave, and had no way to prevent such things happening to his children, was like a physical blow to him. Life under the General's rule at Ronda could be tolerated, but if the General were to die, Richard's rule would be like this. Jesse stared at the maddened overseer swinging the cudgel--every blow now seemed to pound at Jesse's own body. He flinched each time he saw the stave slam into someone's backside.

Abruptly he turned away, unable to watch any longer. The General was offering freedom and passage to Africa for him and his family, where they could be forever beyond the reach of whip and cudgel. What was he waiting for? It would be a way to give his children a new chance. Even if he and Lida died of fever, most of the children would survive to claim their inheritance in the land of their ancestors. It would set things right!

Resolute now, he returned when the job for Richard was done and told the General he would accept his offer. Lida understood--she'd been thinking about their children's future, too.

Jesse's mother, Sarah, gave her blessings, but she had no hankering to cross the ocean at her age.

"Make a shelter with some boards and that tarpaulin for Jesse and his family there, Amos."

"Here, Gen'rul?"

"That's it. Use those poles to hold it up. Here, I'll show you."

Harte moved to a space on the river barge's deck, between the bags of corn and hogsheads of tobacco, and gave instructions for the temporary shelter. He was sending Ronda's barge, loaded with tobacco and surplus corn, down the James River to his factor in the port of Norfolk. Jesse's family would go along and avoid a long, rough wagon trip to the port. Their ship, the *Jupiter*, was due to leave in a week and Harte had timed the barge trip carefully.

"Missy comin', Gen'rul!" a slave called.

Harte turned. A small crowd of his slaves were milling around the river dock, waiting for the departure of the Belcors. Over their heads he saw the carriage, with Sam driving Laura down from the mansion. He walked to the barge's gunwales, stepping down the plank to the dock to help her from the carriage.

"Oh, I hope everything goes all right." Laura looked around. "Where's Richard? Aren't any of your children coming to see?" Her voice trailed off in disappointment.

"He's busy--said he had to get his cornstalks chopped and laid by today, no later. I'm afraid Jamie is busy, too." He sighed. "Let's face it--none of my children is in favor of what we're doing."

She saw regret in his face, but they turned to look at the crowd. All of Ronda's house slaves and mechanics were there. The women clustered around Lida and the children, the men around Jesse. Dora, Lida's neighbor in slave row, was talking.

"You been like a sister, Lida. I'm sure gon'ta miss havin' you around to share my good times and bads."

"We're gonna miss you all, too," Lida said. "Won't see you no more--no more ever! Just as bad as bein' sold South." She dissolved into tears at the finality of it.

They moved to hug each other, both of them holding a child in arm, with others like stairsteps around their skirts. Wordless now, they moaned their anguish at cutting ties that had bound them through the years of raising families, surviving hard days in the big house, and the bittersweet life in slave row. They were best friends, had grown up and married on this same plantation, helped old Granny out with each other's babies, comforted each other in the death of loved ones. It was too much! They wailed and squeezed each other harder.

The men gathered around Jesse were out of earshot of the Hartes, joking and laughing nervously.

"Cato gonna be movin' in to your cabin. He's gonna be chief mechanic now!" Zeke jibed at Jesse.

"I didn't say nothin' like that!" Cato said, but he couldn't hide a pleased look on his face.

Jesse looked at Ronda's head blacksmith a long moment. Working with iron had always been higher up the scale in the slave quarter than working with rocks and bricks. This would be putting things right in the minds of most of the men. But he wanted them to understand what really counted.

"You're a good man, Cato. But iron's no mystery to white folks. The Gen'rul said he put me to chief mechanic because I learned my trade fast and I worked hard. I s'pect he'll look for the same thing for the next chief."

He glanced at the others, and then clapped Cato on the shoulder. They shook hands, smiling, no rivals now that Jesse was leaving.

The other men sensed the wise advice Jesse had just given them and dropped their banter, respecting once more the quiet, hardworking mason who'd shown them all how to be proud of the work they did, even as slaves. They stepped toward him one by one, saying goodbye and shaking his hand. Then they all moved to the Hartes and the river boat.

Jesse offered his hand to Harte.

"Gen'rul, I want to say for Lida and me, we know Africa will be a strange place, but God's gonna be lookin' on and we'll be in his hands. We thanks you for the readin' and writin' and cipherin' we learned, and for we bein' slaves no more."

33   Retribution

Ronda Plantation
November 15, 1833

News of the *Jupiter*'s sailing and Harte's manumission of
some of his slaves was reported in Virginia's papers. Laura thought
there was something ominous in the Richmond editor's comments
about Harte.

"I don't like his insinuation, James," Laura declared when
she spied it in the *Enquirer*.

"What does it say about me?" Harte asked, busy recording
yields on wheat and corn crops in one of his plantation journals.

Laura read it out to him:

"This is the man who has defied our laws in educating
his slaves--for the purpose of preparing them for freedom
in Africa, he says. There are other slave owners who
have done this, but they have sent all theirs to Africa.
The General has shipped a mere handful of his. Where
are the rest? It is rumored that he also hires Northern
preachers, and has built a school and chapel for his
slaves ..."

Harte was not perturbed. "Well, he's right in most of it,
isn't he?"

"But you're not breaking any laws or preparing your slaves
for some...what is he hinting at? An insurrection or something?"
Laura's voice rose."It's not fair! He's twisting your purposes! You'll
send the others when they're ready."

Harte looked up from his crop journal, wondering if he saw
anger or fear in her eyes. He closed the journal and went to sit
beside her on the settee, looking at the article.

"Ahh. I know that editor--he's in league with the politicians
who want to whip up the public again. They're either running for
election or wanting to justify more restrictions on slaves. Don't
worry--they'll forget about us. We're too far away from the cities to
be bothered with."

"But James, I'm afraid!"

He put his arm around her.

"Afraid of what?"

Her eyes began to brim, and she struggled to get the words out.

"You could get ... get hurt ... by some ... by a mob."

It was so preposterous he almost laughed, but instead held her close, chiding her gently about reading too many newspaper stories. Her tears still came, so he promised her he would watch out for the crowds on his business trips. The next one would be Court Day in Fluvanna County. She didn't want him to go, but he said it was a public duty he'd been doing for twelve years and he wasn't going to stop now.

A week before the county court session, Harte received a letter from Col.Thomas Bates, a friend who warned him that Matthew Corley, a local candidate for the legislature, had sworn to personally beat up Harte on sight on Court Day. Col. Bates promised to be there to protect Harte from the vote-hungry politician. Harte decided not to worry Laura about the letter. But another article in the *Enquirer* started up her fears again.

"It's about hiring preachers from the North for religious instruction of slaves, James. They want to make a law against it at the next ..."

"Confound it, Laura! Our last Northern preacher was a year ago--Jones is a local man. Now let me get out to the fields!"

Harte slammed out the door. Laura held the newspaper up to the light, rereading the article. A deep foreboding slowly possessed her.

####

It had been a routine day in court, and Corley hadn't appeared. Harte and Thomas Bates gave a last minute look at the courtyard before walking to their carriages.

"Guess the coward didn't show, General," the burly planter said, shading his eyes from the late afternoon sun.

Harte let out a sigh.

"Looks so, Tom. I wondered if Corley would really attack me. But I wouldn't have stayed home, even so."

"I knew you wouldn't. Why did he boast so much and then not come?"

Harte saw Sam pull the carriage out of the line and come toward them. He reached for the carriage rail, his foot on the step.

"Maybe he got carried away with his plans--thinking he could get elected just by beating on me. My ideas aren't popular,

303

but I don't think I'm that important."

"My family admires you a great deal, General. We know this Corley--he really hates the Yankees and their anti-slavery talk. Well, I'm sorry I got you worried for nothing."

As Sam slapped the reins on the horse's withers, Harte sat back, resting on the phaeton's padded leather seat. After all, he thought, it had been a good day, and the phaeton was his favorite carriage--he'd be home in a few hours. Sure of Sam's driving skill, Harte closed his eyes from the hot sun and relaxed to the sound of the horse's canter and the wheels spinning on the dirt road.

He dozed, but opened his eyes later as Sam slowed to ford the Rivanna river at a shallow crossing. The cool shade of the trees, water rippling through wheel spokes, and the splashing hooves made Harte smile with pleasure. He breathed deeply of the damp, mossy river bank and thought of his boyhood swimming hole. Suddenly he strained his ears, thinking he heard muffled hoof beats. But he could see no horseman on the dusty road behind, or the one that led into the forest ahead. It must have been his own horse's hooves thudding on the river's bedrock.

Harte let his mind wander as the carriage entered the half-darkness of the high forest. The trees formed a canopy over the road, shutting out the sun and making a gloomy, dark road running for miles through the low, rolling hills. The forest was like a great protecting fence around his plantations, and few people ever came through it. Ordinarily he liked it that way, but today the eerie light and wild growth pressing so close was getting on his nerves.

A half hour later he heard it again--a couple of hoof beats out of cadence. Strange. Was he imagining things? A look back at the meandering road revealed nothing. Sam, impassive in the driver's seat, gave no sign of anything unusual. Was it just the horse faltering in its rhythm? He tapped Sam on the shoulder.

"Stop a minute, Sam. I want to get down and stretch."

That was only a half truth--he wanted to listen a good long time and settle this hoofbeat thing. Making a show of stretching, he listened intently, finally bending down to the road. It was damp, with a cushion of pine needles--it would muffle any hoof beats. But he waited, not moving, and the silence of the forest was unbroken. He remembered a lesson of his boyhood, when he and the slave boys had the run of the forest--the animals always kept silent when a predator was near. He felt the same thing now.

"Sam, have you heard anybody following us?"

"No suh, Gen'rul, I hasn't heard nothing."

"Well, let's get going again."

Sam drove on. Still tired from the day in court, Harte was yet alert. He distrusted the forest's silence--an inner voice was trying to tell him something. The road wound through a stand of yellow poplars, not tall enough to arch over the road, and he was relieved to be out in the open. The sun felt good and the road was dry. There were even some of his favorite wildflowers along the side. Dogtooth, blue lobelias, and ... Then he heard it distinctly, the beat of a horse loping somewhere behind them on the hard road! But the bends in the road hid the rider as before. Now they entered the forest again.

Whoever he is, Harte thought, he's keeping just far enough back to keep out of sight. Why is he stalking me? If it's Corley, this is no place to win voters--nobody can see him beat me. Maybe he doesn't want an audience to see. Or perhaps it isn't Corley at all ...They were coming to another creek and Sam turned, interrupting Harte's thoughts.

"The horse is gettin' too hot, Gen'rul. Got to water'im."

"All right, Sam."

While the horse was drinking, Harte stood up in the carriage to listen. There were no hoofbeats, so he sat down and thought about the distance left to reach Ronda. About one mile to the fork, maybe, and then three to the northern edge of his plantations. He would be safe then. If he could just outwit this sneaking dog sniffing at his heels! The fork split the road, the right one toward Ronda and the other one to Columbia, not far from a bend in the James River. That was a notorious place for river pirates--his boats had lost more than a few hogsheads to them. Harte's mind leaped--that was it! Some of those Columbia river rats had been hired to ambush him at the fork! He sprang to his feet.

"Sam! That's enough water for the horse! Let's get going quick! We have to get through the fork in daylight!"

"Yessuh, Gen'rul. Gimme time."

"We don't have anymore! Move, Sam! Move!"

Harte reached down to help his slave up on the carriage. Sam fell into his seat, grabbed the reins and whip, and hollered. "Giddap! Hey there, giddap!"

They moved off smartly, gathering speed as Sam applied the whip. Harte's pulse was beating rapidly, his mind racing. So that was no hangdog trailing behind him--he was there to push them into a trap. No doubt he was armed and could force them to continue if they turned around. How much daylight was left?

"Faster, Sam! You've got to make him go faster!"

Harte gripped the rail of the lurching carriage, waiting anxiously until they came to an open stretch. Then he looked to the west where the sun would sink behind the Blue Ridge mountains. There was barely a half hour before the sun would touch the ridge, but it would be enough to get by the fork if nothing went wrong. From there to Ronda they could manage in the dusk better than the river rats, who wouldn't know the plantation road as well. He had to have a weapon, but there was not time to stop and pick up a stout branch. He'd use the whip. It wasn't much, but ...

The horse was at full gallop, the carriage bouncing along behind as they came down the last hill to the fork. Harte spotted the men waiting there, and his muscles tensed. He was right. Corley, or somebody, had hired a good half-dozen of Columbia's bully boys, and he could see they were paid to deliver a message with force behind it--they all had heavy clubs in their hands. Maybe this wasn't just Corley's work. Perhaps a group of men, like those at the Albemarle meeting that had been so angry at him.

The bullies must have seen the carriage come over the crown of the hill, because they were getting up from where they had been sitting in the waning shadow of a lumber wagon. It was parked crosswise in the center of the road. Harte took a quick look and decided what had to be done. He put one hand on Sam's back, gripping the hand rail with the other.

"Steady, Sam. Those are some of Columbia's bad boys and they're going to try to stop us. Keep the horse going flat out 'til we get to that shack there on the right. We'll surprise them by making a shortcut around the shack and getting on the road to Ronda before they know what's happening. They'll never catch us in that old wagon. You see where I mean?"

"Yessuh, I sees. Looks like that place by the shack ain't too smooth."

"All right, we'll take it slow. Make it look like we've decided to slow down and meet them peacefully. If they get close, I'll use the whip to keep them off."

Sam slowed the horse, coming down to a trot. The men in front of the wagon waited as the carriage approached.

"Now, Sam! Turn here!" Harte cried.

Sam yanked the reins and shouted at the horse, straining to pull to the right. The horse, confused at being guided off the road, lost its gait, almost stumbling, but finally followed the pull of the bit. The Columbia ruffians saw what was intended and some ran in back of the shack to intercept the carriage on the other side. Others headed straight for the carriage as it moved off the road.

"That's him! The nigger lover! Get him!"

The carriage was going too fast to be caught by the direct attack, and one man threw his club after it in frustration, but Harte fended it off. Sam guided the horse around the shack, and they were heading for the right fork when the other men came around the corner of the shack to face them.

"Go right through them, Sam!" Harte commanded, pulling the whip out of its holder.

But the shouting of the bully boys frightened the horse and it veered to the right, running the right carriage wheels over a hummock. Harte and Sam were heaved into the air by the upward jolt of the carriage. Both fell sprawling on the ground, the carriage going on without them as the frightened horse raced for home on the Ronda road. Before Harte could recover enough to sit up the river men were surrounding him. He saw them look to their leader, a bull of a man with a black beard and greasy vest too small for his huge belly. A cigar butt gripped in the corner of his mouth, his lips twisted in a triumphant leer.

"No killin' boys--just mangle'im good!"

Harte lifted his arm to protect himself and found he was still holding the butt of the whip. He managed to warn, "Stand back! Who sent you?"

"Who wants to know?" mocked the big man.

Harte looked up to see the man's fierce brown eyes glinting in the evening sun as he swung the first blow. Rolling sideways to get on his knees, Harte turned the blow aside with the whip butt, and then lashed the whip across the man's chest and arm. The man dropped his club and nearly choked on his cigar. Outraged, he shouted.

"You son of a bitch! Get him boys!"

Harte stood up, cracking the whip smartly. "Stand back! None of you has cause to attack me!" He looked quickly for Sam but couldn't see him.

The men backed away from the stinging rawhide, watching him carefully. One man rushed Harte's right side as the whip lashed to the left. He swung his club in a vicious arc, aiming at Harte's head. Harte saw it coming and ducked, bringing the whip back in a sweeping motion to the right, wrapping it around the man's leg. He jerked hard, pulling the man off his feet. But before the whip released, the rest of the men were at Harte, swinging their clubs in a frenzy. He tried to dodge the blows, but there were too many. A slam at the back of his legs brought him down to his knees and everyone cheered.

"We knows what to do with your kind, nigger lover!" one of them said from behind him.

Before Harte could turn, both his ears were struck with the man's cupped hands, and the concussion was like a blast in his head. Stunned, he dropped the whip and covered his ears with his hands. He saw a thin little Irishman with red hair and watery eyes shouting at him, but he could barely hear.

"Why don'tcha go North to the abolitionists, you traitor!"

Harte, his guard down and half senseless, was completely surprised when the cocky fellow boldly kicked him in the stomach. He doubled over, the pain so great that he stopped breathing for a moment, then fell to the ground and retched, conscious of other kicks in his side as they closed in.

"Got'im a good un!" "Let me at the bastard!"

He felt two clubs thud into his back, and other blows on his legs. Something hit his head. Then he was floating in a black mist, and there was a strange, hollow silence ...

When the horse and carriage rattled into the barn at Ronda an hour later without Harte or Sam, a startled slave ran to the big house. Laura was waiting dinner for Harte, holding only the cook to keep food warm. She had been unable to shake the menacing thoughts of angry mobs from her mind all day, and knew instinctively the meaning of the empty carriage.

"Robert! They've attacked the General--and Sam, too! Go call everyone up from the cabins. Quickly, Robert! Hurry!"

When they came, she ordered Sam's assistant to harness a wagon and to take three men and some lanterns to go search along the road to Fluvanna. She sent a fast rider to go for Doc Tyler. She had the house slaves light lamps in all the downstairs rooms and put some on the veranda. In the kitchen, she had Sarah and the cook boil some water, and sent the upstairs woman after sheets and blankets. They would be ready for anything, she vowed.

Doc Tyler arrived, saw the preparations, and joined the anxious group waiting for the search party to arrive. The house slaves stood on the veranda peering into the darkness, talking in low tones; the field hands clustering in the yard in the faint glow from all the lamps. Tyler and Laura waited in rattan chairs on the east end of the veranda where they would be the first to hear the wagon coming back.

When the wagon arrived, Harte was brought in bloody and unconscious but still alive, and put in a bed arranged in the downstairs library. Doc Tyler recognized the symptoms of a concussion, but couldn't be sure about broken bones and internal injuries until Harte became fully conscious. Sam's injuries were minor--he couldn't remember a thing after falling off the carriage. They concluded he'd been knocked unconscious by the fall and ignored by the bullies.

Harte was so maimed that Tyler feared he would not regain consciousness, and if he did, that he would never walk again. Laura stayed by his bedside day and night. The second night Harte mumbled something, almost inaudibly, but Laura excitedly reported it to the doctor in the morning. Tyler made her get some sleep then, but by evening she came back to sit at Harte's bedside again.

Harte became conscious on the fifth day, and after some probing questions Tyler soon saw that he had underestimated Harte's constitution. Once the pain from the deepest bruises abated and Harte could cautiously move all his bones and ligaments, there was no further doubt of his rugged health and his body's ability to mend. Recovery was slow, and the weeks in bed discouraged Harte. Laura read his journals and mail to him, and he gradually took a half-hearted interest in plantation affairs. But it was not until a letter arrived from the colony in Africa that he sat up in excitement.

"From the colony? Is it from Jesse?"

"Yes," Laura smiled, relieved to see him come alive. "It came to Norfolk by way of the *Luna*. Your factor sent it up on this morning's river boat."

"Let me see it. I'll read it out loud," Harte said, reaching eagerly for the envelope. His hands shook as he tore it open. "It was written last July!" He wet his lips, and began to read.

Dear General,

I hav this chance to write you and send by Joseph
J. Roberts coming on next ship if I gets it done in time.
He is one of our up and coming merchants here, a
mulatto man who goes back and forth across the
ocean sometimes and we met him on the Jupiter
coming out ...

As Harte cleared his throat and continued, Laura sat back
in the rocker. She listened to his voice growing stronger with each
line, saw his eyes light up and his rough-hewn face recover the
warm, animated look she had missed for so long. A profound relief
spread through her body.

We has had plenty of trouble sence coming here.
First off, the Jupiter took fifty six days on the ocean,
but we all landed safe on Jan. 1, new years day. All
took the fever and Letitia our six years old was lost.
My wife Lida seem like she would make it through
fever but she died too. She rest in peace now. As
Job says the Lord giveth and he taketh. But God has
make it possible for us to meet in heaven to part no
more. I thank God that the rest of us is on the mend.

Some people who trade hav got rich here and hire
the natives at low wages to do all the work. So poor
people who come from America hav no chance to make
a living. There is a new town of Caldwell for farming
but few favor it. When we shoud plant rice it rains too
hard and we dare not be out exposine our helth.

Most of us cant hire nativs like rich people. Stone
masons get a good price, three dollars and a half a
perch. But the sun is so hot people from America cant
stand it in dry season and in the wet it rains too much.
Most everything is barter here, and I being paid in
goods at high price. So when I sells them to buy food
I lose.

We had a white man name of Mechlin who was
colony agent. Old timers say none will ever be so good
as Mr. Ashmun. I think Mechlin was doing good, but
after five years he gone back, for his helth, I gess. The
new agent is Rev Pinney, but so many emigrants has
come there is not enough places in the receptacals for

*them, and not enough food and medicin. New emigrants
is suffering plenty. Gess it is wearing Pinney out and
fever has ketch him. He says he will go home soon.*

*One of our settlers, the Vice Agent Mr. Nathaniel
Brander will be temperery head, like before, such as
Lott Cary and A.D. Williams and Elijah Johnson early
on. This way black mens is learning goument.*

*My children will start school soon. Dina and
Martha can go to one Baptist school. The teacher is
Elijah Johnsons oldest son, Lewis. I teaches the rest
of mine at home ...*

The letter was a dream coming to life for Harte and Laura,
and they paid close attention to Jesse's thoughts coming off the
pages of his letter. Laura rocked slowly in her chair listening to
Harte's voice, realizing that once again they were sharing one of
the most important parts of their life together--the return of his
slaves to their rightful heritage in Africa. Tears of joy rimmed her
eyes.

*I got out of the receptacal with my family quick as I
coud and am on my own town lot now and building a
house slow but sure. Prices is too high so poor people
can't afford things. If you wants to send something let
it be a hoghead of tobacco. I can sell it to the nativs.*

*I have joined the militia that protecks our colony
and fights the slave trade. Captain Elijah Johnson is
our military leader. He know the nativs well from
treaty making after battles. They respecks him and
says he is fair but strong. I heard Mechlin went with
Johnson and the militia to fight Chief Bromley some
times ago because of his slave trading. Upshot was a
treaty signed by four chiefs and peace so we can now
trade with tribes behind Bromley's place.*

*Give my respecks to your family and all my people.
Pleas tell my mother Sarah you hav got a letter from
me. I will send her one nex time. Nothing more but
I remain yours truly,*

                                    Jesse Belcor

CHAPTER
34   Massacre

Monrovia, Liberia
May 10, 1835

Elijah reached the middle landing of a long series of stone steps wending up from the waterside. He stopped to rest, turning to look back down at the bustling trade going on at the base of the Cape. A narrow sandy street was crowded with settlers and Africans, hemmed in by warehouses, stores, and stone wharves at the river's edge. He could hear the crowd's loud haggling, most of them forced to barter because there were too few coins of any kind. African laborers carried boxes and barrels of merchandise from surf boats to stores as traders checked their cargo lists. Paddling a heavily loaded boat to the wharf, sweating Kroo men chanted loudly in rhythm.

"Wo-muta, wo-tah, wo-tah, sai! Wo-muta, wo-tah, wo-tah, deya!"

Other Kroo men, relieved of their loads, stroked their boats silently back across the river mouth to the "alligator." A long crooked sandbar, it left only one small, treacherous opening through which boats could pass to ships anchored in the bay.

The bay opened to the sea, which stretched to the horizon like a flat blue-green prairie, lying calm in mid-day. Once again Elijah was awed by the commanding view from the Cape. He turned to survey the long emerald finger of the peninsula, its forest now making way to the nearly two hundred houses on Monrovia's orderly streets and white picket fences.

The Cape had been his home for twelve years, a foothold on the coast of Africa that had expanded to three colonies and a coastline of two hundred miles--mostly free of slavery and beginning to enjoy a peaceful trade. And now Millsburg--another new town on the river--was reaching in towards the grasslands behind the coast. He drew in his breath, proud to be part of a growing new country in Africa. He felt strength in his chest and muscles as he breathed the air of freedom, exulting in what they had wrought in their struggle to find a home in Africa.

But his joy was for more than that--he felt renewed, a man once more! He'd finally married again, and Sarah had already given him two children, both girls, which they'd named Ellen and

312

Rebecca. And another one was on the way--maybe this one would be a boy! Elijah's loins stirred; Sarah was loving and enticing. They rejoiced in their good health and their ability to make babies, to start a new family which would grow up in their own land. Nothing could hold these children back.

Just like his first three children--Lewis and his wife teaching in a Baptist school, Charlie trading on the coast for John Bannon and being a captain in the militia, and Lizzie married to John W. Roberts. They had gotten their real start from their mother Mary, buried on Sherbro Island almost fourteen years ago. But they were on their own now, and he and Sarah were free to bring up a new family. All of them were sons and daughters of a new Africa, and maybe someday they'd be leaders of a black, self-governing nation!

His thoughts returned to the present. Got to hurry and get to Government House before the Council starts. Mechlin, the previous agent, had left exhausted and fever-ridden, and the vice agent, a colonist in a fit of independence from the Society, had led the Council in making new laws, expanding the number of council members, giving them veto-power over the agent, and adding a superior court that could over-rule the agent's judgments. Elijah chuckled. Anthony Williams and J.J. Roberts had even gone to the States to present these changes and to appeal for more self-government, but the Society hadn't approved. They'd sent out a new agent, Pinney, with word that the colony's laws would be completely redone later. So the only thing the upstarts got was some new titles and a few more council members.

Elijah strode up Ashmun street in a hurry. Pinney is the only one who can help now! He swung through the gate of Government House and took the steps two at a time. The messenger took him down the hall into the agent's office. He was shocked by the thin, pallid face of Pinney, who sat at his desk propped up by pillows.

"Sit down, General," Pinney said without attempting to rise or shake hands. "Never mind the formalities--I haven't the energy for them."

"Too much fever, sir?" Elijah asked, taking the chair in front of Pinney's desk.

"Yes, I'm afraid I don't have the constitution of an Ashmun or a Mechlin," Pinney smiled ruefully. "Dr. Todsen says I must leave soon, or be buried here. I really came to be a missionary, but

313

the Society asked me to serve as agent until they replace Mechlin."

"Better listen to the doctor. Todsen's good on fever."

"Yes, he seems to have helped most of the emigrants from the *Jupiter* and the *Argus* get through it."

Elijah shifted in his chair.

"That's what I came to talk to you about, Mr. Pinney. Todsen knows the fever all right, but there's another sickness he's not so good at."

"Oh?"

Elijah began counting on his fingers. "There are seven people from the *Jupiter* who have 'runny stomach', including three of the white missionaries. And Todsen is letting them die!"

"Oh come now, General! Todsen isn't letting people die. Many of the colonists have said he's the hardest working doctor the Society has ever sent."

Elijah stood up. "I mean his medicine isn't working for this kind of sickness! It's an African one, and they have something for it--it works, too!" Elijah threw up his hands. "But Todsen won't let it be used--says he won't permit any African juju as long as he's in charge of the colony's health."

"You know he can't let that black magic nonsense be used, General. We'd be the laughing stock of the civilized element along the whole coast."

Elijah's face contorted with anger, his dark eyes snapping.

"African medicine works--some of it, anyway! We used some on Ashmun, and it saved him! Africans know how to deal with their own sicknesses. If they throw in a little hocus-pocus to impress their people, what's the harm in that? You whites look down on everything black, don't you!"

"General, I was just saying ..."

Elijah interrupted him. "I visited one of the new emigrants sufferin' from it last night, name of Jesse Belcor, and he's almost gone now! Todsen claims he's takin' special care of him--a promise he made the man's former owner in Virginia. But the man'll die because Todsen's medicine isn't working! And we need Belcor--he's the best sergeant in the whole militia. The militia is going to have to protect the towns upriver from the tribal wars going on up there now."

Elijah pointed his finger at Pinney.

"And your missionaries are the same--runny stomachs. They could be cured if you'd get over your prejudice of everything

African! You want their deaths on your conscience, Mr. Pinney?"

They stared at each other, until Pinney looked away. The silence in the room was heavy. Elijah lowered his accusing finger, knowing he'd made his point. Finally Pinney looked up.

"General, I can't order Todsen to use such a medicine. You have to understand--it would be contrary to all he stands for to let a devil doctor with those revolting proceedings get at his patients. Even if there is some useful natural substance hidden in it, the evil magic some of them do..." Pinney shook his head. "No--Todsen would never allow it."

Elijah sat down, not willing to give up, but changing his tactics.

"It doesn't have to be like that, Mr. Pinney. I know of a Bassa 'leaf doctor' that's supposed to have some really good medicines, without the hocus-pocus."

They heard voices in the hallway and clumping of feet on the stairway. Pinney looked at the paper he'd been working on and sighed.

"They've come for the council meeting. Well, General ... I'm resigning at this meeting and going home to recover from the fever like Todsen advises. If I get well, I'll come back to begin missionary work."

Elijah's admiration for Pinney jumped--he wasn't just quitting, he was coming back to help through the church. Elijah had applied to become a preacher last year, but hadn't studied all the required books yet. He understood Pinney now.

"I hope you get well so you can come back soon."

"Thanks, General. I don't have any right to keep you from using that country medicine to help your friend. Just don't trouble Todsen about it."

Pinney struggled out of his chair, smiling weakly. "When you go out, ask the messenger to come in, will you? I won't be able to make it up the steps to the council chamber without him."

"Let me be the one. It'll be an honor, Reverend Pinney."

####

"Carrie, I need you to do something very important, but I want you to keep it secret."

"Secret, Elijah?" Carrie frowned from her rocking chair on the porch, where she was resting from a morning of caring for her

315

children and getting the house ready for a visitor John was bringing home to dinner tonight. "Shouldn't you be asking my husband's permission?"

"Oh, John won't mind. It's about some country medicine that one of my militia men needs, 'cause he's about to die. But everybody in the colony is so used to doctors the Society sends out, they'll start gossipin' about me taking up African juju if I do it."

Carrie's eyes widened in astonishment. She stood up, a cynical smile curling her lips.

"So you came to me because you knew Togba taught me about African medicine!"

"Well--yes. He did, didn't he? You believe in it, don't you?"

"Believe? I know it works! Togba used some on me."

Carrie shook her head in wonder.

"Elijah, you don't know how good it is to hear you say Africans know something we don't! That there's something we need from them besides their labor!"

Elijah felt his face burn. She was getting sassy with him again.

"Why d'you say that?" he demanded.

"Because you've always put Togba down like he wasn't equal to us!" Carrie felt her anger rise. "I was frightened and confused when Togba and I had to escape from the Poro, and you made me come back and promise to marry John! Don't you remember?"

"I was only doing what was best for you, Carrie! I promised your ma I would watch out for you. You wouldn't have lasted a year married to an African--you're too sassy for that. They don't accept backtalk from their women."

"Sassy! I'm too sassy? If you mean I stand up for what I think ..."

Then it hit her, the difference between African men and American men.

"I--I guess you're right. That's a good word for what I am, Elijah." She smiled. "And I'm proud of it."

Elijah smiled tentatively. "In fact, you're getting more sassy every year."

They both laughed.

"But I think it's good for us to hear your ideas, Carrie. There aren't too many women'll speak out. And you've had an experience that most of us will never have."

316

Tears came to her eyes. She hugged Elijah. It was a healing that she had needed for a long time. She couldn't hate this good man.

"All right, Elijah. What do you want me to do?"

He had it with him--wrapped up in a banana leaf. As he unfolded the soft green pouch, he gave Carrie her instructions on how to use it on Jesse Belcor.

"Start it right away--Jesse is desperate sick."

Her eyes brimmed, but she was smiling.

"Oh, I will," she said softly. "For Togba."

Elijah understood about Togba this time.

"Thank you, Carrie. This'll be our secret."

As Elijah rushed off, Carrie thought about another secret--but this one only she knew. Tobga was more than the youth she had met in the forest long ago when they were both fleeing the war on the Cape, and who had taken her to his village. And she had learned more than African medicine as they had fled through the forest from the girls bush school and the Sande initiation rites. Chief Bob Gray had hidden them in his empty slave pen when they had reached the coast, and then he'd sent for Elijah to come. Carrie sat down now in her porch rocker for a moment and relived it once again.

That night she and Togba had huddled in the darkness, fearing the anger of the Sande and the Poro, but hoping that Elijah and Bob Gray could somehow protect them. Exhausted, they had taken some old mats, piled them together, and gone to sleep curled up in the far corner of the empty pen as if it were the soft boughs of bushes like Togba had prepared for them each night of their flight through the forest. Their only security had been these secret lairs at the end of each day's headlong dash, when she had curled up next to him trusting his knowledge of the forest and his strength to keep them safe.

After a few hours on the dusty mats she had awakened, realizing that Togba had endangered his whole future and perhaps his life to protect her. Now their dream of marriage and a peaceful life in his home village might be about to end forever. He had tried to warn her about the girls bush school, but she had insisted on doing it--and then it was *she* who called him to come to her rescue! How stupid and ignorant and self-centered she had been--how blind to the ways of Africa. She owed him so much--how could she ever make it up to him?

317

Overwhelmed by her debt and awed by the enormity of his sacrifice for her she had turned on the mats and wrapped him in her arms, hugging him; wanting to thank him, not for being the African prince of her childish dreams, but for his goodness and faithfulness and his sense of duty to a girl he had chosen to protect simply because she had asked him. He had shown her honor and respect and his concern had been unfailing--he had not presumed or taken advantage of her eager dreams. Tears rimmed her eyes and as Togba awakened to her embrace, she told him all this, thanking him and saying she loved him whether they ever lived to see the next day or not--it was enough to have been shown such love.

In his cautious way he had listened to her, taking it in, and then found the English words to say that he loved her from the first day he saw her in the colony. But he knew the only way it could come true would be in the African way, because he needed the blessings of his ancestors and his people. He was proud of her bravery in trying his people's ways and going as far as she could. When she refused the Sande way of cutting a girl's private parts and called for him he knew she must not be forced to it. He loved her for living up to her own people's ways--it was the only way to be true to her ancestors. Now they had both shown they could be true, but they could be a man and woman and love each other tonight because it would be their way of ending what they both wanted but could not honorably have. She knew it was right, and they learned together for the first time how they had been created for love.

Carrie stirred in her rocking chair, knowing she must break away from the memory of it, and take the medicine in the green banana leaf pouch to Jesse. Only she knew that her first child was surely Togba's, and neither Elijah or her husband John knew it. Elijah had brought her back from Chief Bob Gray's slave pen and persuaded her to marry John Bannon. It had been the end of her attempt to live in the African way, but she had learned what true love meant.

Monrovia, Liberia
July 13, 1835

"Massacre! There's been a massacre of settlers down the coast!" "Where?" "At Bassa Cove--one of the new colonies called

Port Cresson!" "It's war! The Council has declared war!" "Who did the killing?" "King Joe Harris!"

People rushed out of their houses to hear the news, clustering on Ashmun Street wherever news-bearers could be stopped. Others hurried up the street to Government House where a huge crowd was collecting. Nathanel Brander, Vice Agent, and the other councilmen were standing on the veranda with General Johnson and Colin Teague, the Colonial Secretary.

"We have decided to take immediate action against this bloody killing," Brander was explaining to the crowd.

"Why did King Joe do it?" somebody called out.

"We hear that a Spanish slaver came back to Bassa Cove and found the new colony there, so he told the King that he couldn't buy any slaves so close to it. Joe got angry about losing his slave trade and decided to drive the colony out. He killed about twenty people and the rest fled to Edina across the bay. So now he's going to attack Edina."

"Murderer!" "Dirty slave-seller!" "What're you going to do about it?" "Yeah, you goin' to let him get away with it?"

Brander lifted his arms to calm the crowd. "Mr. Teague will read what the Council has decided."

Teague cleared his throat and started reading from his minutes. The crowd, shocked and fearful, listened intently.

" ... therefore it is Resolved, that War be, and the same is hereby declared against King Joe Harris, subject to the following three provisions:

1. That three Commissioners be sent to Bassa to demand from King Joe: an explanation of his conduct, reparations for all persons and property destroyed, and security for future peace and safety of the new colony.

2. That his delivery of the persons of the aggressors, and that alone will be considered reparation.

3. That in the event of failing to accomplish the above purposes, the declaration of war be rigorously prosecuted.

It is further Resolved, that the Acting Agent be authorized to accept the voluntary services of one hundred men, provisioned, and properly officered by the Acting Agent, to accompany the Commissioners to Bassa Cove. The Commissioners shall be:

319

Major J.C. Barbour of the Militia, John Day, Esq. from Monrovia, and John Hanson, Esq. from Edina."

Brander turned to Elijah, putting his hand on his shoulder and presenting him to the crowd.

"I'm asking General Johnson to lead the militia forces to Bassa for us. We have depended on him in all our wars, and know him to be a fearless military leader."

The crowd cheered and Elijah stepped forward, nodding and half-saluting them in acknowledgement.

"Thank you. All volunteers from Monrovia, New Georgia, and Caldwell, report at 6:11 a.m. sharp tomorrow! Those from Millsburg will take longer, maybe 12:00 noon. We'll sail on our Liberian ships as soon as everyone is equipped and provisioned. Men! It is our sacred duty to defend our colonies! The Bassa Cove colony had no guns because it was founded on Quaker principles. King Joe attacked it at night, without warning. Let us show this treacherous chief what it will cost him to slaughter defenseless people!"

While the crowd gradually dispersed, Elijah started calling militia officers together and issuing orders. Then he and Blake headed for the waterside with Brander's permission to requisition from merchants any supplies not in the colony's storehouse. As colonial storekeeper, Elijah knew its current inventory almost by heart.

"Figure on a hundred men for three days," he said to Blake. "Have the merchants send the stuff to the colony storehouse and I'll sign the vouchers there. I'm going to look for ship's biscuits in small boxes. They'll be just what we need if we have a long march away from base."

They split up, each going from store to store, hunting quickly for what they needed. Elijah had no luck on the ship's biscuits until he came to Dailey & Russworm's store.

"You mean 'cabin biscuits',Elijah," Russworm said, standing behind the counter wearing an apron and duster-sleeves over his white shirt. "I have a new supply that just came on the brig *Rover*--in ten ounce boxes."

"Good! What's the price?" Elijah asked.

Russworm bent to his invoices. It was strange to see John Russworm reduced to running a store, Elijah thought. He'd been superintendent of schools when he first came and then colonial secretary and editor of the colony newspaper. Now he'd lost all that in the recent turmoil over self-government.

"Five shillings, six pence," Russworm quoted.

Elijah thought it a little high. But then he remembered that Russworm and his wife now had a child to care for.

"A deal, John. I need a hundred for the Bassa Cove expedition. Send it over by noon to the colony storehouse and I'll sign the voucher there."

Elijah looked at Russworm closely.

"Are you all right, John? You look a little peaked."

Russworm grimaced, but said nothing until he'd instructed the store boys how to pack the cases of biscuits. Then he asked Elijah to come back to his office.

"I'm grateful for the colony's business, Elijah," he began. "With the tribal wars going on upcountry, the river trade is very slow. And Dailey and I just can't compete with the other merchants in the coastal trade."

Elijah nodded sympathetically.

"I know'em all. Roberts & Coleman, Bannon, Devaney, Sherman, Waring &Taylor--they're tough competition, aren't they?"

"It's more than that, Elijah. They've gotten an early start and now have a strong monopoly in the coastal trade. Most of them are Virginians who seem to hang together. And now they're beginning to have political power, too."

Elijah was startled. "What do you mean?"

"They persuaded the Society to expand the number of seats on the Council and make them elective. So now they can buy enough votes in Council to make the laws they want."

"Buy votes? How?"

"You really are naive, Elijah. Bannon is the worst--I think he's put some councilors on his payroll or extended them so much credit they have to listen to him when he wants them to vote a certain way."

Elijah's face blanched. He could feel his heart constricting. No--not John Bannon, the man he picked for Carrie!

"Bannon? Are you sure? What about the others?"

"I don't know, Elijah. Men like Roberts and Waring seem to be above that sort of thing. And yet they'll benefit from favorable tariffs and stiff license fees that keep other traders out. Maybe Bannon does their dirty work."

Elijah stood up abruptly.

"That's enough! It's all talk! What proof do you have? Are

you sure it's not just because you've lost out in politics and are getting bitter?"

Russworm threw up his hands.

"Lost out to whom? Elijah, I didn't lose out--I was fired by the agent unfairly! I warned Pinney that his proclamation declaring the superior court illegal would cause a riot. Prout led it, I didn't. But I was the one Pinney blamed because I didn't stop the mob from dismantling the press. Pinney thought I was the instigator, but I was caught in the middle!"

Elijah considered it. Russworm was kind of an outsider--not one of the Virginians and not close to the new agent. What was he really after?

"So what will you do now?

Russworm shook his head, his voice full of despair.

"It's like a nightmare, Elijah. I can't go back to the States--I came out here to find freedom, telling everyone at home that I would be free of white men! When Mechlin was recalled by the Society I thought sure they'd pick one of us in the colony to govern--maybe even me. But they sent Pinney--a missionary! And now Skinner is coming back to take over--a doctor! Who will they send next? They don't deceive me--we deserve more than just some stopgap person recommended by a Society member's friends. We need a competent leader! Why not a black man? One of *us!*"

He banged on his desk angrily, and Elijah saw the bitter frustration in his eyes. If any black man is qualified to lead the colony, Elijah thought, Russworm is. He was the first black in America to get a college degree. But ...

"Maybe it's too soon, John. Not everybody's as ready as you are. We still need the Society behind us."

"But the new colony being formed at Cape Palmas has planned for black leadership--its constitution guarantees it! Why can't our colony have it? Elijah, I'm fed up! If I could work it out, I'd go to Cape Palmas!"

"Well, it does sound like their constitution will be ahead of our set up. And the Bassa Cove colony is different, too ... Oh, oh! Bassa Cove--I'm supposed to be gettin' up an expedition for Bassa Cove--I've got to get out of here!"

But as Elijah left the store he was wondering how soon self-government should come.

35   Shame Palaver

Bassa Cove

Four ships, all owned by Liberian merchants, had carried the militia and commissioners down to Bassa Cove, arriving toward evening at Edina. There they heard that Chief Bob Gray had helped the Edina settlers drive King Joe Harris away. The next day the commissioners sent a message to King Joe's village for him to meet them about his attack on the new colony, Port Cresson. While waiting for his answer, a refugee from the colony, A.P. Davis, accompanied the commissioners and Elijah, with a squad of militia headed by Sergeant Belcor, across the river to see the site of the massacre.

Davis, a husky blacksmith from Virginia, stood in the center of the little town, now nothing but ashes. He pointed to the charred remains of his smithy.

"I was startin' to do some pretty good business. We built this town in a couple of months when we first came. We needed all kinds of iron stuff--I made it right here. There's my old anvil."

He kicked around in the ashes and uncovered a hammer and tongs, but made no effort to pick them up.

"No use now," he said, dismissing them with a hopeless gesture. Then his eyes lighted on a clump of charred bedclothes in the remains of a large house next door. He pointed.

"That was a big family, the Joneses, all of 'em killed except old Grandpa Milbro. He's in Edina now--lost his mind, I guess, watchin' his son and eight grandchillun all bein' hacked and speared and shot to death. His son's wife had already died of fever."

He shook his head. "Me, I'm single. As soon as I was waked up by the war cries that night and smelled smoke, I lit out for the bush. But I heard the Joneses screamin' and tryin' to fight back as I left."

The devastation was everywhere as they walked through the town, charred pole stumps standing mute among the drifting white ash of burned mat-and-thatch. Coming upon an unburned house, Davis answered their unspoken queries.

"That was Hankinson's, the agent. A friendly Kroo man

helped him and his wife escape--they were the first to reach Edina."

The commissioners had seen enough. By the time they returned to Edina, the messenger had brought word that King Joe Harris would meet them at the beach of Grand Bassa village "soon past noon." They ate hastily and crossed the bay with the same small squad of militia. A palaver shelter was in plain sight when their canoes pulled up on the beach, but King Joe was not around anywhere.

"Don't worry," Elijah said, "a king is always the last to arrive."

Another hour by Barbour's watch and the Bassa chief slowly approached with his courtiers, entering the shelter with a fierce scowl on his face. One of his head men put down a special mat for him, and after he was seated, they all followed. Elijah was content to watch Barbour cut his eye teeth in the frustrating art of palavering. To Barbour's demand for an explanation of the attack on the new town, Joe Harris' answer made it plain that he was a true unremorseful African slaver.

"This new town be bad thing! Spanish man say he no give me goods for my slaves if it be there. So new town must go! If it come back, I burn it same way. My slaves be mine by African law to do with like I say. How can I get goods for me and my people? This town be stopping my slave trade, spoiling African good life!"

John Day, one of the other commissioners, broke in.

"But we can make trade for rice, camwood..."

"Camwood!" Joe Harris interrupted scornfully. "I be fool to make camwood trade! I go to bush to get camwood, I got to pay plenty to other man to carry it down to coast. So I go to bush to capture slave, he carry hisself down!"

He waved his finger at Day, shaking his head. "No! King Joe no fool!"

It got worse as Barbour went through the other demands the commissioners were expected to make. Elijah watched patiently, sure that it all would come to naught, but respecting the council's desire to settle things peacefully, if possible. The first item, 'Reparation for persons and property destroyed', only caused Joe Harris to repeat his warning that he would drive away another settlement the same way. Barbour's demand for 'Security for future peace and safety of the colony' made Joe even angrier.

"You be the people spoiling the country, not me! Peace and safe business be gone if you stop slave trade. My people be plenty trouble if I not get goods for them from slaver!"

When Barbour got to 'delivery of the persons of the aggressors', it was the final straw. King Joe Harris shook his fly switch at him.

"My warriors be mine! How you can ask me to give to you? I be some kind of fool? Warriors be mine same as slaves be mine. African law say, if man be taken in war or be guilty of crime, he must die or be slave! I can only do two things--kill him or make him a slave. You want him killed? It be better way to sell him to slave ship!"

He got up and signalled his head men to pick up the mats.

"My way be best. It be true African way!"

"But King Joe," Barbour said, "we will have to make war on you if you don't meet these demands and stop your slaving."

Joe scowled, raising himself up haughtily.

"Never!" he said, and marched out, his head men following with as much dignity as they could muster.

Given clearance from the commissioners, Elijah prepared for war. Ordering the militia officers to have their men ready for a dawn march, he left them and went up the north branch of the river in a Kroo canoe with Barbour to consult Chief Bob Gray. Just as the river became a small creek and they saw the village on its banks, Barbour had doubts.

"Bob Gray was a big slaver himself. Why go to him for advice?"

Elijah smiled. "Bob Gray is a friend of the colony. He'll tell us how an old slaver like King Joe thinks. That's what we have to know to outwit him."

Elijah feared that Bob Gray wouldn't like his village council interrupted, but the chief's broad smile was a give-away.

"Johnson from Monrovia!" Bob Gray hailed, and came forward to shake his hand. "You the one they call General Johnson now? You be big man!"

Bob Gray introduced his elders, then closed the day's palaver session, sending them away.

"Come sit and we talk," he said, showing Elijah and Barbour to seats near his in the palaver hall. "How be your daughter Carrie?"

"She's married and has five children," Elijah smiled proudly. "She's a good mother and wife."

"Good! Maybe she learn how to be so from Sande bush

school."

"Maybe. Thank you plenty for saving her from the Poro's anger. Have you heard what they did to Togba? Did they ... ?"

Bob Gray shook his head.

"Kill him? No. I make them promise it not be so. They sell him to 'Spider' at Gallenas."

"The Spanish slaver, Pedro Blanco?"

"That be him. It better than killing, not so?"

"I--I don't know," Elijah said, not wanting to hurt Bob Gray's feelings. "It could be."

But Elijah remembered the Navy reports that a third or a half of of the slaves crammed into Blanco's ships often died before reaching Cuba. And the misery of life as a slave on the Cuban plantations--Bob Gray would have no idea of that.

"So what be the thing you come see me for?" Bob Gray asked.

"It's about King Joe Harris." Elijah explained about the commissioners trying to settle the matter peacefully and the king's refusal to do so.

Bob Gray shook his head. "So you go make war on him?"

"Yes, if we have to. You know what we're trying to do--stop the slave trade and make a home here in peace. How can we stop King Joe without killing a lot of people? What would make him change his ways?"

They waited in silence while Bob Gray considered it. Finally he cleared his throat.

"There be only one way. Make shame palaver for him."

"Shame palaver?" Elijah asked. "What's that?"

"Take away what he be most proud for--that thing he thinks makes him strong past other people. Then he have shame too much in eyes of his people."

"I see ... something that makes him feel strong past us? Well, he stood up and told us right to our faces that he would never accept our demands. Why was he so sure?"

Bob Gray smiled. "His village be like white man's fort."

"Fort! That's it!" Elijah shouted. "He's probably fortified his village so good he thinks we can't get at him. We'll take it away from him!" His face fell. "But how can we do that without killing a lot of his warriors--or our people, too?"

Again there was a long silence. Bob Gray looked at Elijah keenly, as if trying to decide something about him.

"Johnson, you be General now, with plenty men and guns. We Bassa people have a saying, 'When cow be here, goat no can dance in his place.' It not be for me to tell you how to make war. You must make answer for yourself."

He stood up and Elijah and Barbour rose, too. Bob Gray put his hand on Elijah's shoulder and smiled.

"Joe Harris be like two old animals--dog and turtle. Bassa man says 'old dog's tail not uncurl easy'."

They laughed at that.

"What about the old turtle?" Elijah asked.

"Old turtle not move unless fire be put on his back."

That made them laugh harder, and Bob Gray escorted them out of the palaver shelter, where a man waited to lead them back to the creek. Bob Gray waved as they moved off, calling to them.

"Remember, when turtle be stubborn, he pull in his feet and head."

Elijah nodded and gave a final wave. They moved quickly through the village and were launched downstream in the Kroo canoe before Barbour spoke.

"Well, that was funny. But was the trip worth all the time it's taking?"

"At least we know about 'shame palaver' now, and what we have to do to shame King Joe."

"Yes, but how?"

"I don't know," Elijah said, "but I think there's a clue in those Bassa proverbs."

The next morning it took an hour to get all the militia across the bay to King Joe's side of St. John's river in the merchants' small boats. Hanson and Day stayed back at Edina, content to let Barbour represent them on the march to punish King Joe. After about an hour of march along the river toward King Joe's village, they began to meet resistance--muskets firing from the bush on the right side.

"He's got guns!" Elijah said to Barbour. "So the Spanish slaver has decided to help the king after all."

"Yes, and he's probably given Joe all the powder and ball he needs."

Elijah turned and ordered his officers to split up the company into squads, each one taking turns in charging the bush where the firing was coming from, but keeping the company moving up-river in loose order. It worked, and they made steady headway with no casualties. But it was clear that King Joe's warriors were keeping just out of sight in the forest, moving along with them. Another hour and they reached a narrow trail that left the riverside, heading southeast.

"This is it," Elijah said to Barbour. "The trail to King Joe's headquarters--I can't wait to see how he's fortified it!"

"We aren't there yet," Barbour said sourly, "so you'd better figure out how we're going to move through the forest. They'll be able to shoot from both sides of the trail now."

Elijah slowed the pace, with two squads moving ahead of the rest, one on either side. But now the firing from the forest was close at hand, and more accurate--and there were some wounded to care for. He assigned one squad to protect them, helping them along and carrying one man in a makeshift stretcher.

"It's not far now," he shouted. "Keep them moving--we're not going to abandon anyone out here."

But it meant slowing the company's movement, giving King Joe more time to set up the outer defense of his village. The sniping increased on the right side of the trail as they got closer, so Elijah sent sergeant Belcor with a two-squad charge that made the warriors flee. But three men came back with strange puncture wounds, and one stabbed on his chest.

"Stakes with sharp points on'em!" Belcor reported to Elijah. "They're right in amongst the trees and bushes--a wide band of 'em, about ten feet wide. It must go all around the village. They'd go right through a man's bare feet!"

Though protected by shoes, three men had tripped and fallen on the stakes, but cried out to warn the others away.

"Stick to the path!" Elijah shouted to the company. "But watch out for an ambush. We must be gettin' real close!"

A short distance later a flurry of fire from both sides of the path confirmed it, but Elijah sent out squads to outflank the defenders, and soon they also fled. Pressing on, the company came around a bend to find a short, narrow gate in a row of tall, closely planted thorn trees. The spaces between the trunks were jammed with dense prickly bushes. Impenetrable without an hour's bloody hacking, the tight living fence forced them to consider the small gate and what lay in wait behind it.

"Look! It's hanging loose!" Barbour said.

"Stand back!" Elijah called. "It may be a trap."

The lead squad approached it cautiously, Belcor finally pushing it open. There was no gun fire or hail of spears, and no shouting, so he poked his head inside.

"Path's all clear," he said.

Bending low, they filed through one at a time.

"Looks like they've finally given up and retreated to the village," Barbour offered.

But Elijah was skeptical. The path was narrower, the forest pressing more closely. Around another bend they came to a small patch of ground cut out of the forest, planted with a grisly crop of skulls--dozens of them, each one atop its own short stick, two or three feet off the ground. The path went through the center of the patch, a mute but unmistakable warning. Everyone was silent, moving quickly through it.

Another tight, thorny fence gave them pause, but the gate was abandoned as before. There was no sign of any sentries or warriors around, and the forest was deathly silent as they submitted to the low, narrow entrance. It seemed to Elijah as if they were being forced to bow in tribute to the mighty chief inside, but he knew its more deadly intent--to make each person helpless for a moment as he stooped through.

"Looks like you were right, Barbour," Elijah admitted. "They've retreated to their fort. But it can't be far now."

Twenty yards away was a third fence, similar to the other two, but some strange source of light glowed above this one.

"Do you see that, Elijah? What is it?" Barbour asked.

Everyone was looking upwards, pointing to the bright light and exclaiming.

"It's so bright!" "Yeah, that's not the sun! It's coming from inside the fence!" "Whee-yeww! What God-Awful thing is that?"

Elijah waited until the whole company filed through the second gate and got over their wonder at the wierd glow above the next fence.

"All right! Let's have it quiet! Settle down--whatever's making that light is pretty bright, so protect your eyes with your hand when you go in--you have to see to shoot. Sergeant, go ahead and open the gate."

This time Belcor was even more cautious. He stood as far

away from the little gate as he could and reached out with his musket to nudge it. It was loose like the others, abandoned by defenders to retreat to the village somewhere inside. He moved closer, ready to swing it open with a strong push. Elijah's mind clicked. Had they abandoned the gates, or left them open to invite us in? Could this be the inner door to a trap?"

"Belcor! Don't open it!" he shouted.

Everyone turned to look at him. He raised his voice, explaining to the whole company.

"The village has got to be in there somewhere, but before we attack it I want to know how many other entrances there are. We're in the second inner circle and can probably go all around the village in it and be safe. We'll hold right here until two squads check any other entrances."

He sent one around in a clockwise direction and the other the opposite way. While the main part of the company waited, he went to the small door with Barbour.

"We'll push it open a crack just to take a look."

"I give you the first look," Barbour said grimly.

Elijah crouched by the door and eased it open an inch. The bright light showed through, but he put his eye to the crack.

"It's all white--nothing but white! No, there are some little black holes. Wait! There's a gate! It's a high white wall, and those black holes must be some gun or arrow ports. It's so bright it hurts the eye! Take a look."

Barbour squinted his right eye and spied through the crack.

"That's the noon day sun shining on a white wall! And the ground is bare, too. It's all covered with white clay. That's a mud wall, Elijah. Maybe eighteen feet tall, plastered smooth, wider at the base than at the top, and all covered with white clay! Amazing! A white fort so bright the enemy can't see to shoot at it!"

Elijah took another look and then stood up, turning to the company.

"We've found King Joe's fort!"

He explained its mud construction and the reflective white clay smeared on both the fort and the ground, saying they would wait for the two squads to report before making plans. Meantime, they would test out a few things.

"Sergeant, put your hat on your musket and stick it through the gate."

Belcor nudged the gate with his foot and shoved the hat

through as ordered. Three muskets barked and the hat jumped as lead balls perforated it. He jerked the gun back, almost falling over.

"All right--now we know they're watching the gate," Elijah said. "Everyone stay clear! Sergeant, stand back and push the gate all the way open with your gun."

Several more shots rang out, stirring the dust in the gateway, but now they could see how carefully the warriors had covered their tracks with white clay when they'd retreated into the fort.

"We would have been perfect targets going through and standing there in the glare," Barbour said. "Before our eyes could've adjusted, they'd have slaughtered us all."

"Yes," Elijah said, "and there's no way to scale that smooth wall quickly. By the time you chopped footholds, you'd be dead."

They saw the two squads coming back, and waited eagerly for their report. When Elijah heard that there were two other small gates, each about a third of the way around the circle, he called the officers together.

"We can wait for the sun to go down," one suggested.

But others countered that even the moon light would reveal attackers in the dazzling white corridor. Scaling the wall with ladders was proposed, but Elijah said to make enough ladders and bring them through the small gates in the two outer walls would take too much time. He warned that they couldn't stay very long in the inner circle where they were because it could become a trap, too. Desperate for a strategy, he turned to Barbour.

"What did Bob Gray tell us?"

"That King Joe had a white man's fort."

"He was right about that--real white! But there was something else. About a turtle."

"Oh. To move an old turtle, you put fire on his back."

"But Bob Gray called out something just as we left, didn't he?"

"He said that a stubborn turtle pulls in his head and feet. Wait a minute, Elijah. King Joe has pulled in his head and feet--he's retreated into his fort!"

"All right. So to move him out of it, we put fire on his ... That's it! This is the 'mid-dries' and there hasn't been any rain for weeks!"

"So that's why the sun reflects on the walls so bright?"

Barbour asked.

"Yes. But that's not what I mean. All the thatch roofs inside Joe's village are dry as tinder! And the houses are probably crowded so close that if one catches on fire they all do! We'll burn him out, and let everyone get out the two side gates!"

"How're we going to do that? We can't get close enough to his wall to throw a fireball over," Barbour said. "They'll shoot us down before we have a chance."

"Then we'll sling it over both this fence and his wall with a bent sapling!"

In a half hour they had a dozen bunches of palm nuts burning in fires, getting them red hot. Three saplings had been stripped of their branches and bent over, tied to stakes by strong vines, with a sling woven from green raffia fiber attached to each. When enough dry moss had been collected, Elijah inspected everything and gave some last-minute instructions.

"Take a red hot bunch of palm nuts, tie some moss around it, and when that flames up in a good fireball, put it in the sling and cut the vine. It should send it over the fence and the wall like a cannonball! It it doesn't go just right, change the bend of the tree, or where you tie the vine, or maybe the size of the bunch. Each time you should get better. All right men! Fire at will!"

Only one of the first three fireballs made it over the high white wall. Barbour, taking quick peeps through the gateway to avoid getting shot at, saw the two duds hit the white wall and fall useless in the corridor. But the first two crews were successful on the second round and a cheer went up when Barbour reported it.

"Only six bunches left!" Elijah warned them. "Fire one apiece, then we'll see. All crews fire at will!"

"Smoke! I see smoke!" Barbour cried.

Two more fireballs were heaved skyward, and everyone waited for Barbour's call. He took a longer peep and no gun fired at him, so he held his hat out. It was not shot at either, and he boldly squatted in the little gateway..

"Smoke's spreading! Looks like this whole part of the village is burning! No one's at their gun ports--they must be fighting the fire or leaving."

Elijah squatted in the gate, saw clouds of black smoke boiling up above the white wall, and turned to order two squads to move around the inner circle to the two other gates.

"Watch them escape and make sure none of the warriors

come back inside! We'll break in this front gate and then connect up with you."

The entire village cleared out through the side gates in about an hour, but the heat of the fire was so intense that Elijah's men couldn't enter the wall's front gate when it burned and fell inward. The massive white wall had turned the burning village into a giant cauldron, flames leaping high above it. Smoke poured out gun ports, blackening the pristine wall, and the swirling inferno lifted up great chunks of burning wood that littered the immaculate white corridor outside.

"No one will ever want to go back inside that village!" Barbour prophesied.

Elijah agreed with a sigh of relief.

"I think that is one big shame palaver for King Joe. Now it's up to the commissioners to settle the terms for peace. And maybe--just maybe--there'll be no more slave ships coming into Bassa Cove!"

36 Crucial Step

Washington, D.C.
December 13, 1838

The Twenty-Second Annual Meeting of the American Colonization Society was drawing a huge audience. But two days of tense debate between powerful new state colonization societies and the parent Society hadn't resolved their differences. On this final day committees were to present a compromise plan for the union of societies in America and a proposal for union of their colonies in Africa. Except for the Maryland society and its colony, which was going its own way with its new black governor, John Russworm.

Elisha Whittlesey, now one of the Society's vice presidents, was sitting in the front row listening to Charles Mercer, presiding over the third day's session. Both were members of Congress, quite at home with this kind of deliberation and negotiation. The large crowd of previous days had thinned out--illustrious speech making was over and it was time for committee reports and voting.

This is where the struggle really begins, Whittlesey thought. A report of the new amendments to the Society's constitution was first on the agenda, and it would re-define who had the power--the Society or the state societies, or perhaps just one or two of the latter, like New York and Pennsylvania. Mercer requested that Ralph Gurley, the Society's executive secretary, read the entire constitution as amended, and the crowd listened closely to the familiar wording, waiting for the fateful alterations. Gurley read Article 1, then 2, then 3, then 4--Here it is! Whittlesey leaned forward.

"...There shall be a Board of Directors, composed of delegates from the several State Societies, and Societies of the District of Columbia ..."

Yes, yes, get on with it, Whittlesey thought--we know the state societies are the new players. But why change the name of the Board from Managers to Directors? And how is the power going to be shared in the new Board? Gurley was reading on.

"...Each Society contributing not less than one thousand dollars annually into the common treasury shall be entitled to two delegates; each Society having under its care a colony shall be entitled to three delegates; and ..."

Oh,ho! You don't play unless you pay, Whittlesey noticed. Good--it takes money to keep the colonies going! Gurley read on to Article 5, and Whittlesey sat up, straining to hear it.

"...The Board shall have the power to organize and administer a General Government for the several colonies in Liberia; to provide a uniform code of laws for such colonies, and manage the general affairs of Colonization throughout the United States, except within the states which planted colonies. They shall appoint annually the Executive Committee of five with such officers as they may deem necessary ..."

What was that about a 'General Government in Liberia'? Whittlesey wondered. Would it be left up to the Board of Directors to create that government? What about the vice presidents --wouldn't we have a say in that? This new Board of Directors is given all the power and the vice presidents are becoming figure heads? No, by God, I haven't worked for colonization all this time to be put aside like that! Gurley droned on, but the moment he finished Whittlesey stood up, telling himself to be calm.

"Mr. Chairman!"

He had beaten them to the punch--he had to be recognized! Startled, Mercer raised his eyebrows slightly.

"The Chair recognizes the Honorable Elisha Whittlesey, Vice President from Ohio."

Whittlesey turned half-around to the audience, and raised his voice.

"It seems the Vice Presidents are now to be relegated to the back seat of the carriage, and the new Directors are to do all the driving! Before we give them power to create the new 'General Government' in Liberia, I think we should hear about this proposed union of colonies. Many of the Vice Presidents are members of Congress, with years of experience in government. Surely we can be of some use in this crucial new step for the colonies!"

Murmurs of assent rose from the crowd, and Whittlesey saw some of the vice presidents nod their heads. Mercer's sonorous voice rolled out smoothly.

"The point is well taken, especially because that is the next agenda item. Mr. Thomas Buchanan, delegate from the Pennsylvania Society and its former agent at Bassa Cove, was asked to make a draft of a commonwealth constitution. If you are

335

ready, Mr. Buchanan, please come forward and tell us about it."

Heads turned as a man of about thirty, of medium height, with a ruggedly handsome face set off by dark hair and neatly trimmed mustache, strode calmly up the center aisle, a sheaf of papers in his hand. Placing them on the dais, he faced the audience with confident ease, and smiled.

"This draft is based partly on existing constitutions in the Monrovia and Bassa Cove colonies, as well as recent revisions suggested by colonists themselves at the Board's request. It respects the separate colonies by converting them into counties under a commonwealth system with a common governor, council, system of courts, and armed forces; yet they retain some of their autonomy through elected representatives and appointed officials."

Buchanan paused, and Whittlesey could almost feel the crowd weighing the precise explanation. It's just what's needed, he thought. If the document is half as clear and diplomatic as the man himself, it's a winner. Heads began to bob as members indicated their tentative approval.

"Here, here!" someone called. Others thumped their canes.

Buchanan began reading a short preamble and the articles describing executive, legislative, and judicial powers of the commonwealth. Whittlesey noticed how quiet the room became, everyone concentrating on the details. When Buchanan finished and put down his papers, the audience sat back with relief.

But no sooner had the chairman cleared his throat than the clamor for recognition began.

"Mr. Chairman!" "Point of privilege, Mr. Chairman!" "I wish the floor, Mr. Chairman!"

Whittlesey wanted to challenge an article, too, but knew he would have to wait. Mercer recognized a Congressman from New York, Henry Foster.

"Article 9 seems to define citizenship in terms of colored persons only. Isn't this reverse discrimination? I believe this new commonwealth should be democratic!"

Mercer referred it to Buchanan, who said previous constitutions also limited citizenship to coloreds only, but outraged members in the audience shouted for democracy. They're new members, Whittlesey thought, and don't know what they're doing! He waited as more clamored to champion the popular word. Finally he could stand it no longer, and he stood up, raising his hand. Mercer chose him with a point of his finger, knowing it would end the shouting. "My friends," Whittlesey said, "we have forgotten the very basis of this great human experiment!" He felt himself getting angry at their shortsightedness.

"We knew when we began that our purpose was to provide a home for the dispersed and oppressed people of Africa! Not for any others! Only for the sons and daughters of Africa, torn from the soil of their motherland! We must preserve for them, and them alone, this opportunity to return, so they can enlighten and regenerate that benighted continent, raped and pillaged for centuries! White slavers and traders, who've built their nefarious factories and barracoons on Africa's shores for their ill-gotten gains, would be the first to claim citizenship! Their money would buy their way in through bribery and corruption and make a mockery of all our efforts!"

He shook his finger at them. "We must provide this built-in safety for their fledgling black nation! It is our duty--*we owe it to them!*"

Afraid he had become too angry, Whittlesey sat down quickly to cover his embarrassment, his face blushing. But cheers and cane thumping and calls of approval were coming from all parts of the hall. His outburst surprised him. Not the idea--he had lived by that since joining the Society--but the passion! He nodded his thanks to those around him, eager now to get on with the other articles in the commonwealth's constitution. Helping to devise a new stage in the colony's development excited him. This was a crucial step toward a full-fledged nation!

Monrovia, Liberia
April 4, 1839

The ship *Saluda* had arrived on April 1st, and Major Barbour had commanded the artillery in firing a long, thundering salute from Fort Stockton's battery. Elijah, striving for equal military dash, had assembled the best-dressed militia troops on the wharf, and officially escorted Governor Buchanan up the hill to Government House. Vice Agent A.D. Williams and the Council had received the Governor with impeccable courtesy. Now, three days later, Buchanan was presenting the Commonwealth Constitution and the Address from the Board of Directors of the Society.

Williams had requested that Buchanan read them to the

people from the veranda of Government House and answer questions from the crowd--an informal public hearing before the Council officially received and voted upon the new constitution in chamber later in the day. Buchanan read them through once, and upon a request from someone in the crowd, he began to reread Article 6 of the constitution slowly and clearly.

"The Governor shall preside at the deliberations of the Council, and shall have a veto on all their acts."

Elijah watched Colin Teague step forward. Now a middle-aged editor of the colony's newspaper and Colonial Secretary, Teague was one of their best informed and most articulate settlers. What was he up to?

"Governor, if we're to accept this new commonwealth constitution, it should offer us no less a degree of freedom than we already have in our existing constitution, don't you think?"

"Well, yes. That seems only right. What do you have in mind?" Buchanan replied.

"We already have the privilege in Council of over-riding the agents's veto, and this assures us that our own careful reasoning has weight in making our laws. Surely you don't wish that to be taken away from us now?"

Elijah marvelled at Teague's political skill. All of us missed that--it's important, too! He looked at Buchanan's eyes, but they showed no resentment.

"You mean, when your vote was over-ruled by an agent, and you then voted unanimously to pass it, it would become law?"

"Yes, that's correct."

"That seems reasonable," Buchanan said. "I'll recommend to the Board of Directors that they change Article 6 to correspond with the former constitution on that point."

Just like that! It was so sudden and unexpected--not like some of the autocratic agents they'd had before. Elijah looked around at his fellow colonists. The man was open and reasonable! Someone clapped, then another, and they all did it. But before the clapping died away Nathaniel Brander raised his arm up high.

"Governor, there's another article that bothers me."

"Which one?"

"Article 25, about who can vote. It seems too simple. We suggested in our draft that they had to be in the colony a year, take an oath, and own some property--twenty-five dollars worth, I think. Oh--and pay their taxes! But all this new constitution says is they have to be twenty-one years old."

Buchanan cleared his throat.

"Those qualifications might be more appropriate at a later stage. The Society feels that for now all emigrants who make the decision and sacrifice to come to Liberia should have the right to vote, providing they are twenty-one, of course."

Elijah saw Jesse Belcor raise his arm.

"That's right, Governor! There were too many rich folks who were on that draftin' committee over here. They didn't ask us poor people what we thought! Just because we come without nothin' doesn't mean we can't be good citizens and vote!"

The crowd pondered it. Elijah was proud of Jesse--most of the poorer emigrants would be afraid to speak up like that, he thought. So many had come in recent years--slaves straight off the plantations in the South, without money or equipment. They didn't have the experiences or skills learned from being free, like the earlier emigrants. But they knew how to farm and survive on the land, and some knew a mechanical trade, like Jesse's stone masonry. Jesse was a real asset to the colony--he'd already helped build a church, a school and some houses--besides being the best sergeant in the whole militia.

Brander stepped back in the crowd, shamed by Jesse's remarks. Buchanan asked if there were any other opinions or questions. Finally A.D.Willliams explained to the crowd that this public hearing of the Commonwealth Constitution would be followed with a meeting of the Council for a vote on it. And then he added:

"There will be an Inauguration of the Governor tomorrow at 2:00 p.m. in front of the Govenment House. All citizens are invited. Then the Governor will tour our settlements on the St. Paul River. After that he will go to the Bassa Cove colony and do the same down there. This meeting is now adjourned. Thank you for coming."

Elijah sent Blake to round up the militia officers and send them to his house for planning an inaugural parade, and then headed back to his house to ask Sarah to get ready for them. Carrie saw him striding rapidly down the middle of Ashmun street and waved at him frantically!

"Elijah! I've got to see you. Please!"

He swerved to the board sidewalk.

"Can't it wait? I've got to get ready for tomorrow."

"It'll only take a minute. I need your help tonight."

"Tonight?" he said, exasperated, wiping his face with his handkerchief. "What is it?"

"It's John, Jr. He's not learning in school, and always getting into trouble. I've decided to send him up the St. Paul river to the mission school at White Plains. The mission boat leaves tomorrow morning but John won't agree to send him ..."

She stopped, overcome and in tears. She pulled out a hanky to dry her eyes.

"Junior doesn't seem to fit in here in Monrovia! You know I've tried him in all three schools! He'll just get worse if we don't get him out of this town. The missionary will care more about his--his troubles."

"Troubles? What do you mean?" Elijah asked.

"He's different! The other children make him feel like an outsider and he fights them..." Carrie looked into Elijah's eyes, pleading. "Elijah," she said, almost whispering, "don't you know that Junior is ... is different?"

Suddenly Elijah understood. My God! Junior is not John's child--he's Togba's! No wonder he doesn't fit in with the settler children! Why didn't I see that before?

"Does John know that Junior is--that he's different?"

Carrie shook her head, tears flooding her eyes again.

"Whoa! Wait a minute," Elijah said. "White Plains--that mission is a vocational school for African children. Is that why John doesn't want him to go there?"

"Yes. But Reverend Wilson says they want both African and settler children to go to school together so they'll get to understand each other."

"Listen, Carrie. Tell John that will be a good school and that I'll be able to see Junior there often. I've just been certified for preaching and my first charge will be Upper Caldwell. That's just a short canoe ride from White Plains and I can see Junior every Sunday afternoon."

Carrie nodded. "I will, but you must come over tonight and talk with John after he closes his store. Will you please?"

"I doubt it, Carrie. We've got to get the militia boys sharp for the inauguration ceremony--have to drill'em all evening, I s'pect."

"Oh, Elijah! I was counting on you!" Carrie shook her head in despair, tears streaming down her cheeks.

"All right, all right! I'll talk to John tonight, but it'll have to be late."

"That's f-fine, Elijah. He--he doesn't come home ever 'til late. Says he's politicking after store hours and its important."

Elijah patted her on the shoulder.

"Yeah. Well, you tell him his family's important, too. Now, I've got to go. I'll see John, later."

He swung out to the middle of Ashmun street and strode down hill fast, muttering to himself. Politickin' is it John Bannon? What're you gettin' yourself into now?

Government House, Monrovia
March 20, 1840

"Have you protected the mission from further attacks by Gatumba?"

It was Governor Buchanan's first question when Elijah returned from Heddington, the remote mission station behind White Plains that had been attacked almost a week and a half before by Gola warriors. Gatumba had sent his henchman, Gotorah, to kill the missionary and the school children, but he had been killed himself by a lucky musket shot from one of the mission's defenders. Fearing another more massive attempt by the powerful Gatumba, Buchanan had sent Elijah with thirty men to set up defenses for the mission and nearby village.

"I think so," Elijah said. "We took three days to build a strong stockade around the mission and King Tom's village, set up a cannon, and train some men to use it. Reverend Brown and his assistants, Harris and Demery, will keep on training the villagers with the muskets. If Gatumba tries to attack it now, he'll get worse than Gotorah got."

Elijah winced as he twisted in his chair and lifted a dirty bag from the floor at his side.

"Is your wound still bothering you?" Buchanan asked. "I wouldn't have sent you to Heddington if I'd known."

Two slight wounds from a raid on a French slaver's barracoon at Little Bassa some months before hadn't completely healed, but Elijah didn't want it to show. He'd heard rumors that Buchanan was going to promote somebody younger to head the militia.

"It's all right, Governor. Nothing serious. Here's a present

341

for you from King Tom's men. It's kind of smelly."

He put it carefully on the governor's desk. Buchanan pinched his nose.

"Phew! What a smell! What is it?"

"It's Gotorah's head and his gree-grees"

Buchanan's mouth dropped open, his eyes aghast.

"His *what?*"

"It's an African custom. When they've killed a fierce enemy warrior, they make sure to cut off his head and take his powerful medicines, and show them to every one. Nobody can say it's a lie after they see them."

"I'll--I'll see them later, thank you. Could you--sort of-- remove them some place for now?"

Elijah smiled and stepped to the door, depositing the bag in the hallway, and returned to his chair.

"Mr. Johnson, what's behind these tribal wars all around the St. Paul river? Is it for getting more captives to sell to the slavers?"

"It's mainly the Golas attacking the Deys, but maybe it's for something bigger than just getting a few more slaves to bring down to the coast. Someday the slave trade will be finished."

"What's bigger than that?"

Elijah wasn't sure. He worked his mouth a little thinking on it, and then began to reason it out.

"We've been trying to make a trade route to Boatswain's because that's the jumping off place for the caravans that go to North and East Africa. The Deys used to be the middlemen to Boatswain, but I s'pect the Golas want to be the ones now. I think that's why the Golas are fighting the Deys--if they can get rid of them, we'll have to go through the Golas."

"Get rid of the Deys? You mean, kill all the Deys off?" Buchanan was shocked.

"Maybe. I s'pose that's why some of the Dey chiefs have been coming to us for protection."

"What about Gatumba. Is that why he raided the little remnant of Deys up at Millsburg?"

"He's probably trying to take over all the territory that Boatswain used to control before he died. That's everything around Bopolu and even across the St. Paul to some of our settlements. If we don't stop Gatumba soon, he'll kill some of our people. Heddington and White Plains are in his way."

"But after he raided near Millsburg I sent him a strong message to stop coming near our towns!" Buchanan said. "I still haven't heard from him."

Elijah shook his head.

"If you ask me, Governor, I'd say Gatumba murdered your messengers and that's why you haven't heard."

Buchanan turned pale.

"If that's true, then we have no alternative. We'll have to stop him."

Elijah nodded. "Now you understand, Governor." He eased his wounded leg to another position.

"I have a grandson at the mission school at White Plains, and many Africans have their children there, too. Same at Heddington. That's part of what we came to do--help the Africans. Someday we'll have mission stations all over the bush, teaching and preaching--even healing if we can get nurses or doctors. But not if we don't stop Gatumba and his kind now."

"How can we do that? What do you suggest?"

"Gatumba has put out word that he's going to take revenge for the killing of Gotorah and some of his warriors at Heddington. And he swears he'll wipe out Millsburg. We've already prepared Heddington's defenses, but if I were you I wouldn't go to Millsburg to defend it. I'd take my soldiers right to his home ground."

"Where is that--at Bopolu?"

"No. They say his head village is north of that--so deep in the bush and so well fortified that no one dares even try attack it anymore. But we've had some experience with that now. I'd sure try, if I were you--and soon, before he attacks Millsburg."

Buchanan was quiet for a long time, drumming his fingers on the desk. Finally he smiled.

"We'll start getting ready tomorrow. And this time, I want you to take it easy, Mr. Johnson, and let a younger man carry the burden of overall command. I'm going to put J.J. Roberts at the head of this expedition."

Elijah had heard rumors, but somehow it stunned him.

"You mean--you're casting me aside? After I just did so good on the French slaver at Little Bassa? And fortifying Heddington?"

"No, no! I'm not casting you aside. You can head up one of the militia companies. But give yourself a well-earned rest! Let Roberts command this time."

343

####

He'd showed them! Elijah was resting on the settee in their house in Monrovia, with Sarah running around propping up his leg and getting a big meal ready after he'd come back from the expedition to Gatumbah's village. Reviewing it in his mind, he almost laughed. Yes! It was his company that led in the final moments of the battle!

All right, J.J. Roberts did come up to the head of the column just as they reached Gatumba's village, and began to give orders to his own company to flank it and go around to the rear gate. And maybe that was the action that panicked Gatumba and made him flee out the back in a rush. But it was Elijah's own company first that routed the ambush just as the forest path widened to reveal the double-walled fort sitting in the midst of an open plain. And his company was the one that attacked the front of the fort while J.J.'s company ran around to the back. Yes, he showed them! And Jesse was his lead sergeant, who took his squad right through Gatumba's front gate!

But it was a sad thing to find that Charlie, his own son and Captain of the Artillery, was shot at the last minute as they pressed the attack. After things calmed down, he went to Charlie's side, praying as hard as he could that Charlie would make it. All the way back on the return march to the river, and down to Monrovia in a boat, he stayed by Charlie's side. Charlie did pull through--he saw to that. Now they both had war wounds. But more than that, they'd both given their best in battle for their own country!

344

37   Declaration

Ronda Plantation
August 16, 1846

"Come sit here, Cissie, and read some of Jesse's letters from Liberia," Laura Harte murmured faintly. "I want to hear them once more."

Feebly, she patted the bed beside her, where she had lain for seven weeks with the miserable fever that she'd always known would someday be the death of her. Weakened from twenty-one hard years as mistress of Ronda, constantly breathing the fever miasma that hung about the river, she knew this attack was the last. But she was relishing the joy of her life--James Harte's youngest daughter Cecily, now twenty-six years old and married, had recently inherited one of Harte's plantations.

"All right, Mama Laura," Cissie said, gently sitting on the bed and opening the Chinese lacquer box. "Which ones do you want to hear?"

Cissie was the only one of Harte's children who had absorbed any of his humanitarian concern for his slaves, and Laura was pleased with her husband's choice of Cissie over his other two daughters. He'd already bequeathed plantations to his two sons, but they callously regarded their slaves as mere property that came with the plantations. Both Laura and Harte had been deeply hurt by his children's disinterest in the colonization of freed slaves in Africa.. But Laura had hopes for Cecily.

"Just the last few letters, Cissie," she said.

Cecily lifted them out and opened a fragile envelope.

"H'mmm--Jesse wrote this in 1840. He says:

My helth being good, I took my musket and joined the militia to go up St. Paul River and drive out a feroshus Golah king by name of Gatoombah. Elijah Johnson led our company, me being sarjent, and we march through the forest, slept one night in raw bush, one night in abandon town, and on third day attacked Gatoombahs town. We broke into his

345

*front gate, at same time J.J. Roberts took men
around to his back. The King got afraid and run
out the back before our men get there. We slept in
his town, burned it next day, and marched back to
St. Paul with only five men wounded. Now there
is peace in the forest and other chiefs come to the
Guvernur to sign up to be under our colony.'*

"Oh yes," Cecily said, shifting to the second page, "here he tells about his girls. I remember them!"

*'My daughters improve themselves going to
school and Rebecca teaches in sunday school at the
Baptist Church. We have had a big case of murder in
our first superior court sitting with our own Judge
Benedict deciding it. I send our newspaper, Liberia
Herald, so you can read it yourself.'*

"That's about all in this one, Mama Laura."

Laura nodded slowly.

"You hear his pride, Cissie, how they have courts and a newspaper, and schools and churches, and Jesse is an officer?"

Cecily's eyes widened.

"Pride? He didn't say he was...well, I guess he doesn't have to say it in so many words, does he? That's a change for him isn't it, Mama Laura. When you read his first letters to us years ago he had such hard times."

Laura nodded.

"It was awful to hear," Laura said. "The terrible African fever that struck them down, and Jesse losing his wife and daughter. He had little work, and struggled to keep his children fed and a roof over their heads. He was cheated by merchants and sickened by the hot sun. But he kept on, because he was ready."

"Ready?"

"Yes. He had faith and hope from the Bible, and reading, writing, and ciphering from the books. Your father had a chapel and school for slaves built and brought teachers and preachers from the North. Do you remember it? You were only a child."

"Not much, I'm afraid. I went off to boarding school and got caught up in Richmond society."

"Read another letter, Cissie."

"All right. Here's one from 1841. Jesse says:

*'My apprentice Henry who come from you is
learning masonry trade and doing fine. I have*

*severel young men in training and boards them
at my house. My gang has finished masonry work
on the Methodist church, 33' by 60', and there is
talk by the Guvernur we will build a courthouse
and jail of stone, too. The British Navy has broke
down the big slave factory of Pedro Blanco north
of us. Took neerly one thousand slaves from his
barracoons and all his goods.*

*Wars between the Africans is declineing and
they are back to growing food Already we see it at
the market. My daughters is baptized and members
of the Baptist Church. I hope you send more people
from Ronda like you said in your letter. I been
preparing for them.'*

"Has Papa sent more of his slaves, Mama Laura?" Cecily asked.

Laura shook her head sadly.

"He only sends the one or two who meet his standards. It will take ages, the way he is doing it. Read another letter, Cissie."

Cecily fumbled with a sticky envelope and then began to read again.

*'We has more and more emigrants come without
no trade and see no way of making a living. Some
becomes so discuraged and shiftless they want the
colony to keep on feeding them after the promised
six months. We now have a poor farm where they are
put to raise their own food. For me, I am well
satisfied and say thankyou, Generul, for when I was
young and knew nothing you had your people teach
me. You sent me to this country where I am blessed
with a trade, where I can speak for myself and show
that I am a man.*

*The U.S. fleet has helped the British fleet stop
the slave traders somewhat. Peace has spread over
our savage neighbors, and our preachers can go neerly
a hundred miles in the interior to preach the Gosple.
Elijah Johnson is doing it at White Plains mission
station now. His family lives there and he goes out
to preach in the villages. We have been there for a
visit, even though its Methodist.'*

"Has Papa seen this--what Jesse says to thank him?"

"Of course, Cissie. It's what makes his work for colonization worthwhile. Your father is one of the strongest supporters of the Colonization Society in the South."

"I had no idea what colonization meant--their own nation! It must feel wonderful--like Jesse says--to be a man and show it!"

"They're not a nation yet, Cissie. They're a commonwealth --a group of colonies with some things they can do together."

"Can we--can Papa help them become a nation?"

Laura smiled, her heart full. Cissie was going to be a colonizationist, she could see it in her eyes. "Read the last letter dear. Jesse says something about that."

Eagerly, Cecily picked it up and opened it. "It's written just two months ago! Let's see, he says:

*You asked me to tell you what is going on now about
the commonwealth and the talk of independence.
Since Buchanan died and our own colonist J.J.Roberts
moved up from Lieut.Gov. to Governur, he has been
doing well. But theire is a problem about the common
-wealth that is making it hard for us. A British trader
at Bassa Cove refused to pay our anchorage fee and
port duties as per our laws. He says we are not a real
nation, because the Society that is behind us is private,
not a government. So he has a letter from the British
government that says we don't have a right to demand
fees and duties.*

*J.J. Roberts and our Council says we must become a
independent nation to collect revenues and pay for
government. The Society Board says yes, we should
do so, and they will send a new constitution. But we
are divided about it, and have much bitter argument
between Montserrado County and Bassa County. But
I feels we must be a people recognized by foreign nations
to enforce our laws ... '*

Cecily stopped abruptly, her eyes fixed on the rest of the letter, cheeks gradually turning pale. Laura turned to see why she was silent.

"Cissie, what is it?"

"B-Boys and girls--just like the ones on my new plantation!"

"What? What are you talking about, Cissie!"

"Yesterday, I went down to slave row and met all the families on my plantation...so many children coming of age to--work in the fields as slaves--forever!"

With stricken eyes beginning to fill with tears, she shook her head.

"Oh, Mama Laura, I can't do it!"

Laura put her arms up, and Cecily bent into them, crying with great heaving sobs. A sharp pain struck Laura's back, in the old place--between the shoulders, and she remembered when she first felt that deep pang of remorse for coming to Ronda to preside over slaves as their mistress. Now Cissie would have the same sadness in her life. Maybe not. She should help Cissie see what she might do differently.

"There, there, Cissie. I know what you're facing--I felt the same way when I married your father and came to Ronda."

Cissie sat up, drying her eyes.

"You did? And you didn't want to have slaves?"

"Certainly not. I'd never lived in a house with even a single one before I came here. But then your father explained to me how he had been training his people for freedom, and the Colonization Society would help them go to Africa and build their own nation. So I stayed--I loved him and believed he would do right by his slaves."

"He did, didn't he? Isn't that what we've just been hearing from Jesse?" Cissie asked hopefully.

"Yes...and no. Your father has a good plan, but his standards have been too high, and only a few have reached them. Now, what was the last part of Jesse's letter that got you so upset?"

Laura was beginning to feel the fever pull her down again. This could be it--she had to finish helping Cissie before the fever swallowed her up. If she remembered right, Jesse's letter would almost do it for her.

Cecily found the place in the letter and began again.

We have just received 756 recaptives freed from the slave ship Pons and we are all trying to help them recover. Theire was 900 slaves being taken to Brazil, but many died--young boys and girls--in the miserable bowels of the ship where the racks they were chained to was only 16 inches high! The U.S. African Squadron caught it, and brought it to Monrovia as fast as it could so no more would die. We are all helping in our homes, schools, churches, and the missions. They are so sick and it will take a long time to bring them back to health.

*But our community is doing its best. We are saving these
boys and girls from a miserable life of slavery.'*

"Mama Laura, those boys and girls on my plantation--I don't
want them to grow up to be slaves! But if I must train them for
freedom like Papa ..."

Laura's heart was almost bursting with love for Cissie.

"You can do it, Cissie. Your husband doesn't own them, like
mine--you do! Train them quickly, and send them to their freedom
on the Society's ship. Jesse is waiting for ..."

Her voice trailed off, and Cecily leaned forward.

"Mama Laura, are you all right? I'll do it! Can you hear?
I'll do it right away! Mama Laura?"

Cecily saw her step-mother's eyelids settle as the last glint
of intelligence faded, but from the smile on her lips Cecily knew she
had heard and was dying happy in her heart. Cecily thought of her
promise--there would be problems, but she would find a way to
prepare her youngest slaves for their freedom in Africa.

Monrovia, Liberia
July, 1847

Elijah's wife adjusted his string tie and picked a piece of
white lint from his black frock coat. He leaned over and kissed her.

"My handsome husband, going off to make the
Constitution," Sarah said, smiling in her teasing way.

Elijah sighed. "This is the third day and we haven't really
got started yet. See--it's empty."

He picked up his leopard-skin satchel, which Sarah had
gotten for him when he was elected as a delegate to the
Constitutional Convention, and turned it upside down.

"Not even one scrap of paper?" Sarah whooped. "I knew
it--all you men do is sit around and talk!"

"No, Benedict appointed five working committees, but
there's too much argument from the Bassa County delegates, and
we can't get to our work. They keep coming up with resolutions,
trying to stall the whole process."

Sarah stopped teasing, and a frown creased her forehead.

"Ahhh. Maybe I know why. At the market this morning
they were saying Bassa County is sending a boat load of men up to
persuade people on the streets to stop the convention. They'll go all

over town, get in all our meeting places, and raise a ruckus if we won't listen."

"I wouldn't be surprised," Elijah said, walking to the front door. "They're threatening secession from the Commonwealth if we go ahead with plans for independence. They claim we're not ready for it, and we need the Society's help for quite a while yet. But they elected and sent their four delegates to the convention, so Governor Roberts is going ahead."

He opened the door, but turned back to her.

"Did you hear from your market friends what time the boat from Bassa would arrive?"

"This evening--somebody said John Hansen's boat left from here early this morning to go down and pick them up."

Elijah called goodbye and strode out his front gate. Swinging through, he headed up Ashmun street in a hurry, hoping to see Roberts before the day's session began. Those hotheads from Bassa could make the whole constitutional process look ridiculous, he thought. Just when the Society is watching so closely. For almost two years they had been negotiating with the Society to make this move. This is no time to mess up!

"Oops! Sorry!" He'd bumped into someone in his hurry. "John! It's you."

John Bannon grinned. "My regular time to go open the store. I don't usually see you out this time of the morning, Elijah."

Elijah stopped, embarrassed that he'd been so distracted.

"I--I'm in a hurry. Those hotheads from Bassa are coming up with a mob to talk the town out of independence! The fools!"

"Careful now, that's no way to be a politician, Elijah."

"I'm not a politician! Independence is too important to play around with John! Bassa County is still angry because they lost in the party politics fight when Buchanan was here. But this is the wrong time to get back at their opponents. We need to keep this constitution-making clean and fair, to show people we can govern ourselves!"

John Bannon's grin faded, replaced by a knowing gleam in his eyes.

"I agree, Elijah. But it will take a little persuasion. Why don't I meet the boat this evening and invite them to my store? It's a good place for politicking like that."

"You?" Elijah was startled. But Carrie had said John spent a lot of after-hours politicking.

351

"Well, somebody needs to change their minds," Elijah admitted, "and I sure wouldn't know how to do it. Let the Governor know how you come out tomorrow, will you John? I'll tell him you're meeting them tonight."

####

Elijah sat with the other delegates in the large room of the new court house, listening to Colin Teague read the final draft of the Declaration of Independence. Governor Roberts had told Elijah that once the declaration was finished and signed by all the delegates, they would move on to the constitution itself. If the Bassa delegates signed the declaration, it would be too late for them to turn back. Roberts hoped that John Bannon could keep the Bassa men from the boat occupied until the declaration was pushed through. That way there would be no pressure from crowds in the street to disrupt the convention.

"Keep working on the declaration as fast as you can," Roberts had urged Elijah.

So now Teague was on the final reading, Elijah having used all his persuasion and good reputation to get the delegates to compromise their differences on nearly every paragraph. If all went well on this final reading, it would be signed and committed to within the hour. Elijah felt the sweat soaking his shirt under the frock coat--could John Bannon keep the Bassa boys occupied long enough?

Teague's voice soared:

" ... do hereby, in the name and on behalf of the
people of this Commonwealth, publish and declare
the said Commonwealth a FREE, SOVEREIGN
AND INDEPENDENT STATE, by the name and
title of the REPUBLIC OF LIBERIA. While
announcing to the nations ..."

In spite of the delegate's nitpicking, they had not destroyed the majesty of Teague's phrases, and Elijah was proud of this manifesto that explained to the world the causes of their struggle. He listened raptly.

"We were originally the inhabitants of the United
States of North America. In some parts of that
country, we were debarred by law from all rights

and privileges of men--in other parts, public sentiment
more powerful than law, frowned us down. We were
everywhere shut out from all civic office; excluded from
all participation in ...”

Elijah's eyes misted as the wrongs and injustices rolled out in
Teague's doleful recounting. He nodded at each one and in his mind
he murmured "True!" It was as if he were reliving them again.
The litany went on:

"All hope of a favorable change in our country was
thus wholly extinguished in our bosoms, and we looked
with anxiety abroad for some asylum from the deep
degradation. The Western coast of Africa was the place
selected...Under the auspices of the American Colonization
Society, we established ourselves here, on land acquired
from the lords of the soil ...”

When Teague finished they made no move, but sat and let
the memory of his words echo in their minds. It was good! They all
signed off on it and then Samuel Benedict directed them to their
committee assignments: Bill of Rights, the Executive, the
Legislative, the Judicial, and lastly the Miscellaneous Provisions.
That was Elijah's committee--the Miscellaneous. But he would do
his best. He wasn't really worried--they had a fine model for the
constitution. The Society had offered its services in providing one,
and when the Council accepted, the Society had asked Professor
Simon Greenleaf of Harvard to draft one.

It had looked alright to Elijah, but Beverly Wilson, the
Montserrado County delegate, had raised a rumpus, declaring it
insulting to have a white man doing it when they were capable of
writing one themselves. They had given him permission to write
one of his own, and when he brought it back to convention it was
amazingly similar to Greenleaf's. But they'd smiled behind their
hands and accepted Wilson's draft as their working document.
Elijah knew they would spend days or even weeks in arguing every
point, whichever draft they started with.

Walking home for lunch, Elijah looked for evidence of the
Bassa crowd, but everything seemed normal on the streets. On
sitting down to Sarah's usual noonday fare of rice and greens, he
was about to ask what she'd heard from the market, but she offered
it first.

"Somebody said they saw a bunch of rum-soaked Bassa men
stagger on to John Hanson's boat about eleven o'clock this morning,

singing and laughing. Where do you s'pose they've been all this time?" she asked.

"Have they left the harbor? Are you sure they're gone?" Elijah pressed.

"I told you--they left at eleven." Sarah looked at Elijah suspiciously. "Do you know something about it?"

"Well, they came up here to politick, so I suppose that's what they've been doing."

Elijah realized he'd just learned another disappointing thing about John Bannon. The politicking going on at night in John's store was a way for him to ply unwitting men with rum, so they'd do his bidding--or forget what they intended to do. John was one of the few merchants who could afford the new $500 license fee to sell rum, and his desire to be a backroom political power was probably taking a lot of his stock.

Elijah worried about what this was doing to Carrie. He knew she liked the fine style John's wealth made it possible for her to set in Monrovia's high society. She and John, and all five of their children, were as light-skinned as any in the mulatto elite. Yes, the Bannon family was rising fast (except maybe for Junior). John's drive for commercial success to gain hidden political power was not too far different from Carrie's social climbing so she could have her own base to speak out for better relations between settlers and Africans. But Elijah liked Carrie's goal better.

"Pass the greens, Sarah. You sure know how to make them tasty," he said.

Sarah smiled, reaching for the crockery bowl of dark collard greens.

"It just took some of those strong red peppers and a little onion in the palm oil, like the Bassa cook said at the mission. I'm so glad you're eating African foods now, Elijah."

So am I, thought Elijah. It was the only way they could get by anymore. It had come naturally, living on the mission, traveling in the bush to village churches. There was no talk of imported foods or pressure to live by Monrovia's fancy standards. And Sarah worked hard to make every African food delicious so he and the children could adjust to it. He smiled at Sarah, grateful for her down-to-earth ways.

She never complained about his meagre income now that he'd left government service and become a minister. Of course, they still had this house in Monrovia. But it was cheaper to live on the mission station at White Plains. And their children were getting a good education there. Except for these interruptions like the Constitutional Convention or an occasional request from Governor Roberts, Elijah was finding a deep peace living upriver and preaching to the Africans.

There were some things more important than riches and high society--Sarah knew that, too. They were both getting old, and needed to get out of the way of the younger ones coming up in the new government. If he could live long enough to see the colony become a nation, and see his second family get a good start ...

White Plains, Liberia
March 23, 1849

"Time for some more broth, Elijah honey."

Sarah poured the big spoonful down his throat and kissed him. He tried to return the kiss but she was gone. The house was full and she was busy. They had all gathered, all his children--and Carrie and John and their children. He knew it was because they thought he was about to die, but he wasn't ready yet, and he'd told them so. Doctor Henry Roberts, J.J. Robert's brother who'd studied medicine in the States, agreed with Elijah and gave orders for them to leave him alone. But Elijah could hear them around the house and in the yard, waiting for when he would call them in. He'd said he wanted to tell them something after he'd gone over it in his mind, so he'd better get down to it. His mind faded and he dozed, but it came back and he was staring at the mango plum trees outside the window.

Let's see--the Inauguration of the President was--no, before that, after they'd completed the Constitution, Governor Roberts had proclaimed July 26, 1847, as the day for the Declaration of Independence celebration. It was grand; the military marched the Governor and members of the Constitutional Convention around the town and back to Government Square. Elijah sat on the platform with the other signers of the Declaration, receiving the honors from a great crowd, and the cannons of Fort Norris and Fort Hill boomed while J. M. Prout read the Declaration and the Constitution. And Governor Roberts told the people how hard the convention members had worked, and how their names would be inscribed in the nation's future Hall of Fame and...his mind faded...

He woke again and his mind moved on to the Inauguration, January 3, 1848, remembering Sarah's sewing madly to make herself a dress for it. After the parade and cannons they sat on the platform in front of the State House on Ashmun Street, Elijah in his dress uniform as General, right next to President Roberts and Vice President Brander and their wives. Roberts gave the longest speech they'd ever heard, and told them all that there would be 'sore difficulties' yet to contend with in the nation's progress to maturity, and that maybe God had helped to establish Liberia so that it might be the means of introducing civilization and religion among the barbarous nations of Africa...Elijah dozed again, but was awakened by shouts from the children playing on the mission grounds. He had to get on--his time was running out. Where was he?

Oh yes, after the Inauguration Roberts called on Elijah to come down to Monrovia and asked him about getting recognition of Liberia as a sovereign state. Elijah and others urged Roberts to go to Europe first, and the Legislature voted permission for it. On December 8, 1848, while Roberts was in England, the Legislature voted that Elijah become acting President of the Senate because the Vice President was acting as President of the nation. Roberts went on to France, and returned home having won recognition from both countries, with Belgium, Prussia, and the Netherlands to follow. Elijah's service in the Senate was brief, but it was a high honor...

There was something more--his last trip to Monrovia. Called on again by President Roberts, just last week. It was the same old story, a Spanish slaver at New Cess. Elijah advised Roberts to get up a strong militia force and ask for U.S. Navy ships--but Roberts had just formed warm relations with Britain and France so he said he would ask their ships to help.

Elijah knew now he would never see or hear about that battle--he would be dead by the time it was over. He had come back up the river from Monrovia in a violent rain storm, soaked to the skin, anxious to get back to the mission and prepare for his Sunday preaching circuit of the village churches. Shivering uncontrollably, he had walked from the river dock to the mission house and collapsed on his bed. Sarah had piled on blankets and stuffed him with hot broth, and sent down to Monrovia for the doctor. But it was too much for his old body...

Awake again, Elijah saw that they had all assembled around his bed, waiting silently. He concentrated hard. Now what should he say from all he had seen and done here in Africa?...why had he come?...what should they do? He was going...got to say it quick.

He got it out slowly in short rasping whispers that Sarah repeated to them. "He says...we came back...to our homeland...to build it up again...for all of us...don't forget."

Carrie smiled through her tears as Elijah breathed his last. She knew what he meant by 'all of us'--he included the Africans. And her first born son, too--John, Jr., who would soon graduate from the White Plains mission school. Nobody knew but herself and Elijah that Togba was Junior's real father, that her first child was the first real mixture of American colonist and African blood. He might grow up to be a leader who could unite both sides! But John, Sr., would be outraged if he knew Junior was not his child. Someday maybe she could reveal it, but not now. Her secret had died with Elijah's lips still sealed. Elijah was an honorable man.

She looked at her four other children, comparing them with Elijah and Sarah's. John wanted the best for their children; the best clothes, the best school in Monrovia, the best social crowd--and she had seen to it. But now she was noticing their superior airs and disdain for the crude simplicity of the mission and the unsophisticated children of Elijah and Sarah. She had seen it at the noon meal when Sarah had fed them all from the mission's simple African fare. Carrie's children had barely concealed their distaste, smirking at the others who ate what was served them without question.

For the first time Carrie realized what wealth and privilege in Monrovia were doing to her children. It shook her. She'd secretly determined to gain influence and power to speak out and work toward more equality between Americans and Africans, and wasn't sure yet how she could really do this best. But had she chosen the wisest way? Elijah hadn't chosen a position of power--instead he'd served on a rural mission station and had succeeded in bridging the widening gap between Americans and Africans, becoming poorer to do it. Even in his death Elijah is teaching us something, Carrie thought. How could they build up Liberia--for all its people--like Elijah asked? She would try to find a way.

August, 1849 Dispatch to African Repository and Colonial Journal, Washington, D.C., from Hilary Teague: Obituary of Elijah Johnson, as first published in the Liberia Herald

"Rev. Elijah Johnson departed this life at White Plains, a station of the M.E. Mission, on Friday, 23d March... He was one of the pioneers in the enterprise of Americo-African Colonization. He came out in 1820 in the ship Elizabeth--the Mayflower of Liberia-- and was among the ill-fated ones who were thrown out upon the deadly swamps of Sherbro...and perhaps it was to his sagacity and constancy more than to any other man, that a vestige of the colony remained, when in 1821 the Nautilus arrived at Sierra Leone...

Mr. Johnson removed to Cape Mesurado with the shattered remains of the two expeditions. The agents of the Society...were not long in discovering his worth, and he was soon appointed to offices of responsibility in the colony...His services in the conflicts in which the colony has been engaged...in most of which he bore a conspicuous part, were invaluable...when the enemy presented himself, Johnson met him with sure discomfiture.

Mr. Johnson was at one time entrusted with the administration of the affairs of the colony during the temporary absence of the Society's agent. His conduct in that affair evinced his fidelity as an agent, and his firmness and impartiality as a presiding officer...He was also at different times charged with commissions, to treat with chiefs of the country...In every instance he so discharged his trust as not only to prove his qualification for the business...but at the same time he impressed the natives with a deep sense of his impartiality and justice.

Mr. Johnson...was always on the side of government. Not that he was blind to errors, or to peccancies in men or measures; but he deemed that the government had never been so distinctly marked by either, as to demand that he should put himself in hostile array against it. The colony was his nursling, and he preferred to trust to the modifying hand of time before a resort to violent correctives...he has left an example which many would do well to ponder...

Mr. Johnson attached himself to the M.E. Church, and soon asked and obtained permission from the church to preach...from that time until his death he remained an active, indefatigable minister...he was with the church in her destitution, in the infancy of the colony, when there were but few to help."

(Source: African Repository and Colonial Journal, Vol. XXV, 1849)

The Freedom Ships

The ships referred to in this novel were only a few of the ships, brigs, schooners, barques and packets that steadily brought freed slaves to Liberia.   Listed below are the three ships mentioned and what states the emigrants came from:

1. Ship *Elizabeth*, sailed in 1820 with 86 emigrants: 40 from N.Y., 33 from Penn., 2 from Md., 2 from D.C., 9 from Va.
2. Brig *Nautilus,* sailed in 1821 with 33 emigrants: 8 from Md., 25 from Va.
3. Brig *Strong,* sailed in 1822 with 37 emigrants: 12 from Penn., 25 from Md.

By 1849, when this novel ends, 75 ships had carried approximately 5,500 freedmen and their families to Liberia. See the names of those ships and what states the emigrants came from on the next page. See a passenger list of emigrants on the last one of those 75 ships, the *Liberia Packet*, on the following page.

The American Colonization Society continued to finance shiploads of emigrants up through the year 1892 when the last group of 50 sailed from New York on the bark *Liberia* and were settled near Johnsonville, Liberia. This brought the total number of emigrants to 16,413. Adding the 5,722 recaptured Africans which the U.S. Navy landed, it made a grand total of 22,135 persons whom the Society had assisted in finding homes in Liberia up to that time. Thereafter, a small stream of individual emigrants or families continued to go to Liberia at their own expense--as they still do.

African-Americans who think some of their relatives might have gone to Liberia may find help in the soon-to-be-published *Af-Am Links Genealogical Guide and Handbook*. If you or someone you know is interested, write to us or visit the Af-Am Links Press web site at *www.Af-AmLinksPress.com* for more details. The Af-Am Links Press only publishes books about the Africa-America connection--on such topics as African art, African food and recipes, African wisdom, and African-American genealogy. Also: visit our web site for free news from Africa today and interesting information about Africa's contribution to the Americas.

Ships and Emigrants That Sailed to Liberia through the Auspices of the American Colonization Society and its Auxiliaries from 1820 to 1849 when Elijah Johnson died

No.	Names of vessels	Date of sailing	Mass.	R.I.	Conn.	N.Y.	N.J.	Penn.	Del.	Md.	Dist. Col.	Va.	N.C.	S.C.	Geo.	Ala.	Miss.	La.	Tenn.	Ky.	Ohio.	Ind.	Ill.	Mo.	Mich.	Iowa.	Total num'r.
1	Ship Elizabeth	Feb. '20				40	33			2	2	9															86
2	Brig Nautilus	Feb. '21								8		25															33
3	Brig Strong	June '22					12	25																			37
4	Brig Oswego	Mar. '23					19			24		17															60
5	Sch. Fidelity	June '23						1		4																	5
6	Ship Cyrus	Jan. '24										103															103
7	Brig Hunter	Jan. '25								2		62	2														66
8	Brig Vine	Jan. '26	32																								32
9	S'p Indian Chief	Feb. '26								12		12	26														50
10	Brig Doris	Feb. '27								12		8	72														92
11	Brig Doris	Nov. '27				14				2		65	22														103
12	Sch. Randolph	Dec. '27													27												27
13	Brig Nautilus	Jan. '28										12	8	143													163
14	Ship Harriet	Jan. '29										17	2	125	1				2								147
15	Brig Liberia	Dec. '29						2				42							13					1			58
16	B'g Montgomery	April '30								7		31	1		30		1										70
17	Sch. Carolinian	Nov. '30			1							9	80			9	8										107
18	Brig Valador	Dec. '30										41	40				1										82
19	Sch. Reaper	Jan. '31								6																	6
20	Brig Criterion	July '31								6		1	21							18							46
21	Sch. Orion	Oct. '31								31																	31
22	S'p Jas. Perkins	Dec. '31										291	47														338
23	Sch. Crawford	Jan. '32																		22							22
24	Ship Jupiter	May '32				4						68	22	34	39	2											169
25	Brig American	July '32									13	26	87														126
26	Ship Jupiter	Nov. '32								1		37															38
27	Ship Hercules	Dec. '32													146	22											168
28	Ship Lafayette	Dec. '32						1		144		1															146
29	Ship Roanoke	Dec. '32										98	20		2				1								127
30	Brig American	Mar. '33				6																					6
31	Brig Ajax	May '33																	2	5	99	41				1	148
32	S'r Marg. Mercer	'33			3							1	2														6
33	Ship Jupiter	Nov. '33										50		2													52
34	Brig Argus	Dec. '33				2						12	37	7													58
35	Ship Ninus	Oct. '34										16	110			1											127
36	Brig Rover	Mar. '35								1			1					69									71
37	Ship Louisiana	Mar. '35																9									9
38	Ship Indiana	June '35				1											61										62
39	Brig Independence	Dec. '35					4																				4
40	Brig Luna	Mar. '36										80	2														82
41	Schr Swift	April '36													42												42
42	Brig Luna	July '38				2						69				14											85
43	Brig Roundout	Dec. '36								1		10	23														34
44	Schr Oriental	May '37					4										34										38
45	Ship Emperor	Dec. '37										95													1		96
46	Schr Charlotte Harper	Dec. '38					4																				4
47	Barque Marine	Jan. '38											72														72
48	Brig Mail	May '38															37										37
49	Ship Saluda	Feb. '39				2						13				2											17
50	Do.	Aug. '39										10	20														30
51	Do.	Feb. '40										60	30			3				12	5						110
52	Barque Hobart	Sep. '40										1	4														5
53	B'g Rulolph Groning	Feb. '41										30								10							40
54	Barque Union	May '41																		20	20						40
55	Ship Saluda	Oct. '41			1							4															5
56	Ship Mariposa	June '42										16	10	14	5	81	84							2	14	3	223
57	Barque Globe	Dec. '42					1					18															19
58	Barque Renown	June '43														3	77										80
59	Barque Latrobe	Nov. '43										5															5
60	Brig Lime Rock	Mar. '44															91										91
61	Ship Virginia	June '44										7	33												18		58
62	Brig Chipola	Nov. '44																		21							21
63	Ship Roanoke	Nov. '45				7						166	13	1													187
64	Barq. Rothchild	Jan. '46																		25	34	2					61
65	Barque Chatham	May '46			1																	1					2
66	Sch Mary Wilkes	Jan. '47														4		1		3					3		11
67	Liberia Packet	Dec. '46										25	1														26
68	Do.	Sep. '47				2						13	24	1													40
69	Barq. Nehemiah Rich	Jan. '48															23	33	37	28				6			129
70	Brig Amazon	Feb. '48				1		8				28	1		6												44
71	Liberia Packet	April '48										134	4														138
72	Brig Col. Howard	May '48													45	54											99
73	Liberia Packet	Sep. '48				4		1		15		8			2										1		31
74	Barque Laura	Jan. '49														9	142										151
75	Liberia Packet	Feb. '49				3		3				1	46	2													55
76	Clintonia Wright	April '49														2				19							21
77	Barque Hunn	May '49													50	131											181
78	Liberia Packet	Aug. '49										1	2			11											14
79	Do.	Jan. '49										69	65	1													135
80	Barque Chieftain	Feb. '50													13	154											167
81	Schr D. C. Foster	Mar. '50																	7	35	19		17				78
82	Liberia Packet	July '50				2		1				37	1			14							1				56
83	Barque Edgar	Oct. '50		1		9		8				12												1			31
84	Liberia Packet	Dec. '50				2	3			6	3	9											15				38

Source: The African Repository and Colonial Journal, Vol. XXVII
(Washington: American Colonization Society, 1851)

List of Emigrants by the *Liberia Packet,* which sailed from
Baltimore, February 24, 1849. It was the last ship to
arrive before Elijah Johnson died and this novel closes.

No.	Names.	Age	Profession.	Where from.	Remarks.
1	Joe Adams, -	35	Farmer, -	Rockbridge, Va.	Freed by Capt. Hugh Adams.
2	James More, -	19	Blacksmith,	Staunton, -	
3	Oscar Swingler,	18	Barber, -	do	
4	Edloe Baker, -	50	Cup.&Leech.	Richmond, -	
5	Fanny Baker, -	50	—	do	His wife.
6	Sally Carter Baker, -	11	—	do	} His children.
7	Mary Baker, -	2	—	do	
8	Nisa Davis, -	30	—	Lynchburg, -	
9	Brista Davis, -	4	—	do	Liberated by will of Mrs. Teass.
10	Washington Davis, -	7	—	do	
11	Lucy Davis, -	2	—	do	
12	John B. Phillips, -	21	Lawyer, -	do	
13	Thornton W. Scott, -	21	Farmer, -	Hanover, C. H.	
14	Harry Williams, -	19			
15	Billy Helms, -	41	Millwright,	Lynchburg, Va.	Freed by W. Helms.
16	Esther Helms, -	45	—	do	His wife.
17	Octavia Helms, -	6	—	do	His children.
18	Caroline, -	4	—	do	
19	Cary Jordon, -	70	Farmer, -	Shepherdstown	
20	Moses Jorden, -	35	—	do	Freed by will of Jacob Heiss.
21	Kitty Jorden, -	30	—	do	
22	Henry Jorden, -	7	—	do	
23	John Burns, -	18	—	do	
24	Benjamin Thompson, -	30	—	do	Freed by Jacob Rheinhart.
25	Clary Thompson, -	20	—	do	
26	Milly Thompson, -	28	—	do	
27	George Anderson, -	8	—	do	Milly's son.
28	Mary Anderson, -	8	—	do	do daughter.
29	John Henry Corns, -	1	—	do	do son.
30	Wm. M. Butler, -	22	Shoemaker,	Geo'town, D.C.	
31	Charles Starks, -	41	Wheelwrig't,	Blakely, Va.	Freed by Mrs. Jane C. Washington.
32	Joanna D. Starks, -	—	—	do	His wife.
33	Eugehia Starks, -	21	—	do	
34	Wilson Mills Starks, -	19	—	do	
35	Catherine Starks, -	16	—	do	
36	George Starks, -	13	—	do	
37	Eliza Starks, -	11	—	do	} His children.
38	Sally Starks, -	6	—	do	
39	Thomas Starks, -	4	—	do	
40	Charles Starks, -	2	—	do	
41	Infant, (a few mos. old,)	—	—	do	
42	Lewis Wiggins, -	24	Shoemaker,	do	
43	Rev. Geo. J. Hargrave,	29	Carpenter, -	Petersburgh, -	
44	Betsey Hargrave, -	30	—	do	His wife.
45	Marcia Hooper, -	40	Clerk, -	Fayetteville, N. C.	
46	Rachael Hooper, -	45	—	N. C.	His wife.
47	George Gantt, -	21	Carpenter, -	Philadelphia.	
48	Caroline Gantt, -	18	—	do	
49	J. P. Burton, -	19	Farmer, -	do	
50	Amelia Cooper, -	34	—	New York. -	
51	Elias Edward Cooper, -	4	—	do	
52	Jesse De Gress, -	18	Farmer, -	do	
53	Wm. R. Ballandine, -	42	Barber, -	Richmond, Va.	
54	Venus Clarke, -	60	—	do	
55	Sally Ann Jackson, -	13	—		

Source: The African Repository and Colonial Journal, Vol. XXV
(Washington: American Colonization Society, 1849)